At 350,000 feet, the stars were brilliant, but have time to notice.

Grant eased his sub-orbital XSO-5 into a wide circle, cruising at a speed of Mach 5.25. He could see Dmitri on his left wing, but knew he was only minutes behind. Rotating the safety collar on the toggle switch, he armed his number one Hellwinder missile and clicked in on his commo frequency TAC-3.

"Dmitri, I'm going to active radar in zero-three."

"Ready," the Soviet pilot acknowledged.

Counting seconds, Grant went active. Suddenly, the green screen was crawling with targets, the sweep painting the two enemy sub-orbitals at 270,000 feet. His heading locked, he shut down his radar and rolled hard to the right to 160 degrees.

A low-level chirp started to sound in his ear as the letters on his screen blinked, then went solid: LOCK ON.

Suddenly his threat receiver screamed an emergency signal. The enemy had launched a heat-seeking missile aimed directly at his engines. Grant fingered the commit button and the computer decided it was time to launch. He saw the white hot trail of the Hellwinder leap ahead of him.

He cut his engines and floated in a black, silent oblivion as the seconds passed slowly.

Then the fireball exploded . . .

THE FINEST IN SUSPENSE!

THE URSA ULTIMATUM   (2310, $3.95)
by Terry Baxter
In the dead of night, twelve nuclear warheads are smuggled north across the Mexican border to be detonated simultaneously in major cities throughout the U.S. And only a small-town desert lawman stands between a face-less Russian superspy and World War Three!

THE LAST ASSASSIN   (1989, $3.95)
by Daniel Easterman
From New York City to the Middle East, the devastating flames of revolution and terrorism sweep across a world gone mad . . . as the most terrifying conspiracy in the history of mankind is born!

FLOWERS FROM BERLIN   (2060, $4.50)
by Noel Hynd
With the Earth on the brink of World War Two, the Third Reich's deadliest professional killer is dispatched on the most heinous assignment of his murderous career: the assassination of Franklin Delano Roosevelt!

THE BIG NEEDLE   (2776, $3.50)
by Ken Follett
All across Europe, innocent people are being terrorized, homes are destroyed, and dead bodies have become an unnervingly common sight. And the horrors will continue until the most powerful organization on Earth finds Chadwell Carstairs—and kills him!

Available wherever paperbacks are sold, or order direct from the Publisher. Send cover price plus 50¢ per copy for mailing and handling to Zebra Books, Dept. 3236, 475 Park Avenue South, New York, N.Y. 10016. Residents of New York, New Jersey and Pennsylvania must include sales tax. DO NOT SEND CASH.

BLACK SKY

WILLIAM H. LOVEJOY

ZEBRA BOOKS
KENSINGTON PUBLISHING CORP.

ZEBRA BOOKS

are published by

Kensington Publishing Corp.
475 Park Avenue South
New York, NY 10016

First printing: December, 1990

Printed in the United States of America

DEDICATION

A book should frequently be dedicated to its readers, for they are very much appreciated. This book is so dedicated.

Among them are superfans Martha and Carl T.; Pamela B.; Carol and Brian D.; Chuck, Doris, Brian, Brad, and Randy H.; and Joyce K.

And the relentless Marcia.

ATMOSPHERIC CHART

KM	Miles	Feet	Atmospheric Levels		Objects/Phenomena
			Heterosphere	Exosphere	Satellites
500	311	1642080		Thermosphere	
= =	= =	= = =	= = = =	= = = =	X-15 = = = =
100	62	327360			
90	56	295680	Ionosphere		
80	50	264000			Meteors burn up
70	43	227040	Homosphere	Mesosphere	Meteorological Rockets
60	37	195360			
50	31	163680			Ozone layer
40	25	132000		Stratosphere	
30	19	100320			Weather Balloons
20	12	63360			Sub-Orbitals
10	6	31680		Troposphere	
8	5	26400			Clouds
6	4	21120			
4	2	10560			Weather
2	1	5280			
Sea Level					

One

"Three . . . two . . . one. . . ."

Static on the air.

"We have ignition. We have lift-off! The bird's away!"

There was a quiet exuberance in the mission controller's voice. It was like a sub-carrier wave in Grant's headphones. The man was proud of his accomplishment.

From his vantage point at 120,000 feet and thirty miles south of Vandenberg Air Base, Dallas Grant had an unobstructed view of the launch. He was a private audience. With a synchronized movement of his ailerons, which did not have much effect at that altitude, and a spurt of thrust from the roll thrusters, he banked to the right, then added a touch of elevator and down thrust to put himself into a long and shallow right turn. This detour was not on his test schedule, but he thought he would tag along with the Titan IV for as long as he could. Grant had never felt entirely bound by other people's schedules, anyway.

There was a haze spread over the entire West Coast, so he did not see the rocket until it achieved a few thousand feet of altitude. In fact, he could barely make out the milky-white cylinder of the Titan itself. What he saw was a quarter-mile-long trail of white-hot gases which quickly turned to white vapor and then dissipated in the Pacific winds. The rocket accelerated rapidly, climbing toward the ether and moving westward, away from him.

He advanced the throttles until the panel readout gave him Mach 4.2.

"Six miles down-range . . . velocity five-point-six . . . altitude four-four thousand. . . ." reported one of the technicians manning a telemetry console.

On the numeric keypad recessed into his left armrest, just behind the throttle cluster, Grant punched in a computer order. The radar display on the CRT centered in his instrument panel dissolved to be replaced by a true visual display, relayed by the video camera lens in the lower nose of the craft. He cut in his video recorder, then tapped in the code for a magnification of three, and the stratocumulus clouds way below on the Pacific horizon jumped at him. After a quick search, he found the Titan in the bottom right corner of the screen.

Grant nudged the self-centering control stick and leveled out, keeping his eyes on the rocket as it climbed to the center of his screen.

"We've got fifteen miles down-range . . . velocity seven-point-two . . . altitude seven-six thousand feet."

He would never catch it, of course, but the view was magnificent. Pulling up his nose a trifle, he anticipated the rocket's climb.

"Twenty-two miles down-range."

8

Grant kicked the magnification to six, and the Titan grew to four inches long on his screen. The image was fuzzy, but he could almost make out the USAF insignia. Of course, he knew what he was looking for.

"Thirty-seven miles down-range . . . altitude nine-one thousand."

He was falling way behind, though his altimeter now read over 150,000 feet while his speed had climbed to Mach 4.5. The image on his screen rose quickly to his level, but diminished as it headed west.

And then disappeared.

In a bright orange fireball.

"Malfunction . . . malfunction!"

"No readings!" screamed a telemetry officer.

"Vandenberg Control, this is Piper Two." From earlier transmissions on which he had eavesdropped, Grant knew that the Piper Two codename was that of a naval frigate acting as down-range observer.

"Vandenberg. Go ahead Piper Two."

"We've got a fireball, Vandenberg. Looks like complete destruction."

"Confirmed, Piper Two. We have complete destruction." The restrained excitement had gone out of the controller's voice, replaced by a resignation that sounded habitual.

All Grant saw on the screen now was a miniscule pale gray vaporous cloud.

Grant stayed out of the radio conversations. Identifying himself meant trying to explain who he was, and where he was, and why he was not showing up on Vandenberg's radar screens. It could get very complex very quickly.

He had video tape of the event, but it would be up to General Billings whether or not it was to be sent over to

9

the analysts in the ICBM program.

The zest had gone out of his day, and having already completed his scheduled test sequence, Grant decided on an early return. He rolled the sub-orbital into another slow right turn and retarded the throttles. The descending circular flight path would bring him back over the coast north of San Francisco and get him closer to the ground in northern Nevada.

Automatically, his eyes scanned the red digital readouts for fuel levels, exhaust pressures and temperatures on the rocket engines, and the status of the turbojet. Though it was the newest vehicle in the world's skies, the sub-orbital was already becoming second nature to him.

The prototype had been nicknamed *Lake Havasu City* in flowing orange letters across its matte black nose because it looked so much like a twin-sponsoned hydroplane racing boat, and Lake Havasu on the Colorado River in Arizona hosted many of the major hydroplane races.

The prototype had disintegrated in less than thirty seconds at 48,000 feet of altitude, its carbon fiber-impregnated skin peeling away at Mach 3.5 and spilling Major Harold Peters into the almost non-existent atmosphere at three times the speed of sound. Major Peters disintegrated, also.

The XSO-4 was the fourth design in the series, and Dallas Grant was relatively pleased with its performance. He had only taken it to 200,000 feet this morning, to run a test sequence on the directional thrusters, and he would rate the execution almost flawless in his post-flight briefing. Grant thought that yaw control was a trifle sensitive, but he wanted a snappier response in roll. That was because he was an

10

ex-fighter pilot with Vietnam experience, and he was just as happy upside-down as right-side up. Crossing the coast, he cut in the modified Identify Friend or Foe transmitter, which generated his blip on radar screens and identified it with the code used by the program and which had become familiar by now to local air controllers.

He noted his recommendations for the de-briefing on the notepad velcroed to his right thigh. On the stack of pushbuttons to the right of the panel, he found the one marked "GEN PORT," and punched it. A green light told him that the panel flush with the skin on the lower fuselage had retracted and the port was now scooping air to spin the turbine blades of the auxiliary generator. The activation was confirmed by the readout of the digital ammeter.

He retarded the twin rocket throttles until they reached their back stops.

At 35,000 feet and Mach 2.4, he picked out Lake Mead some eighty miles off his left wing, to the east. Las Vegas was a smudge that flashed sun glints at him. Checking his electrical power levels and finding the battery pack in good shape, Grant initiated his turbojet ignition checklist, opening the intake door, working through the toggles, then lifting the red flap and depressing the start button. The RPM indicator told him the turbine was turning, and at 16% RPM's, he switched the ignition on. He did not hear the whine of the turbine, but the readout indicated that he had a slowly growing thrust on the engine, and after a minute, he advanced the throttle to 100%. When the numbers showed him 25,000 pounds of thrust, he went through the next checklist and shut down the rocket engines. With that loss of power, the sub-orbital immediately began to slow. Lightly loaded with fuel, the craft could barely maintain Mach 1.3 on the single turbojet. At full load on takeoff, the supersonic numbers were out of reach for the jet engine.

Thumbing the transmit button on the stick for his Tac-1 channel, Grant activated his throat mike. "Nellis Air Control, SOL-zero-four."

"Nellis. Go ahead, zero-four."

"Zero-four. I'm leaving your area."

"Bye-bye zero-four. Keep the sunny side up. Nellis Air Control over and out."

"Zero-four over and out."

The air controller did not know it, nor did anyone at Nellis Air Force Base, but XSO-4 did not have a shiny side. Much of the Blackbird and Stealth technology had found its way into the Sub-orbiters. The matte black nose and leading edges faded into flat dark gray along the fuselage and curved surfaces of the delta wing. The paint used was pioneered on the Lockheed U-2 spy plane and contained "iron balls" which gave the surface the dark gray appearance at optical wavelengths. The electrically conducting paint, however, leveled surface voltages and gave the craft a smaller RCS, radar cross-section, at D through J radar band wavelengths. It was especially not shiny on radar, a fact that air controllers in test areas had complained about. On all test flights over populated areas, or in heavy air traffic, the pilots were supposed to keep their special IFF transmitters operating.

The SOL radio codename for the experimental sub-orbiter (XSO) program had evolved on its own after *Lake Havasu City* was destroyed. Major Dennis Blake, one of the three pilots—including himself—in Dallas Grant's test squadron, had come up with it: "Shitoutta-luck."

Grant banked slightly to the right and turned to a compass heading of 190 degrees. The Avawatz Mountains spread across his windscreen, Fort Irwin hidden on the other side of them.

The three throttle handles, two of them vertical and the closest one bent out at a 45-degree angle were located alongside his left hand. He was still slowing rapidly, but he went ahead and retarded his turbojet throttle another notch.

On the left center of the instrument panel, the digital read-out of the velocity indicator gauge decreased steadily. 1.05 . . . 1.03 . . . 1.00.

At Mach .97, he felt a tiny shudder in the control stick.

The aircraft shivered.

The vibration immediately ceased, but Grant made a notation on his thigh pad.

At Mach .95, the velocity indicator automatically converted itself and provided readings in miles per hour. He had slowed the craft to 700 miles per hour and lowered his altitude to 12,000 feet by the time Barstow showed up on his left. Heat waves shimmered over the city. Beyond, the San Gabriel Mountains disguised Los Angeles, but the pale brown atmosphere domed over the city gave away its location. Farther to the north, the mid-morning sun had burned off most of the morning's ground fog.

Grant punched in a new frequency on his Nav-Com radios, gave his SOL call-sign, and checked in with Edwards Air Control. The controller cleared him for the area, and he tapped the keyboard again to switch the radios to the independent control tower for the XSO program.

Lieutenant General Lane Billings, who headed the American side of the development program, was famous for a variety of endeavors, not the least of which was getting his own way. He had secured a private corner of Edwards for the program. When he was running a partially secret project, Billings liked to be a long way from politicians, media superstars, and interfering military brass. He had succeeded here. The compound was called Rosie, in reference to the city of Rosamond, ten miles to the southwest. There was one twelve-thousand-foot runway with a shack someone had had the guts to call a control tower. Set well back from the runway were six hangars, a mess hall, a building converted to offices, and eight barracks buildings. The Air Force liked to call them residence halls, but Grant called them what they were. All of the structures were of 1950s vintage.

Grant crossed the Edwards outer boundaries almost on the deck. While they were not a top secret project, they did try to keep a low profile. Many of the test flights were conducted at night. Daytime flights stayed clear of population centers and tried to avoid being spotted as much as possible. The program had been in existence for three years and flight-operational for fifteen months. In the last year, UFO sightings by concerned citizens had increased tenfold.

The controller at Rosie gave him a straight-in clearance, and Grant turned onto a heading of 270 degrees and bled off power. The sub-orbital aircraft did not have flaps and could not increase its lift at low speeds. The landing speed was 245 miles per hour. It had taken Grant a while to become accustomed to it.

On either side of him, the tan landscape melted into infinity. Ahead, the blue-gray asphalt came up fast. He

14

dropped his landing gear and got three reassuring green LED's on the panel.

The outer marker flashed below.

Grant brought the throttle back to detent and leveled the stub wings with a twitch of the stick.

The nose tried to lift on him.

He touched the throttle and brought it back down in line.

Airspeed 290.

Then 265.

Then 250.

The main gear touched down with a shriek of rubber he could hear through the insulated cockpit walls. Seconds later, the nose gear squeaked as the tire found the yellow center line. At a speed of 190 miles per hour, Grant brought the throttle back past the detent and began to introduce reverse thrust.

The buildings of Rosie shot past him on the right, gray blurry blots. They moved pretty good for forty-year-olds, he thought to himself.

He was just about out of runway before the indicator showed him thirty miles an hour. Grant braked a bit harder and used the nosewheel steering stud on the stick to veer off the runway onto a taxiway. Seven minutes later, he brought it to a stop in front of Hangar One and depressurized the cockpits. The forward and the aft cockpit were separate environments. He touched the button that elevated the front canopy.

As the soft rubber seals popped, the hot desert air of May rushed inside and ruined his environment.

Tech Sergeant Henry Gloom waved at him as he tractored toward the sub-orbiter. Gloom drove the tractor as if it were a dune buggy. He whipped a 180-degree turn in front of the nose, then backed up at ten miles per hour, lowering the boom that attached to the nose wheel.

As Grant disconnected communications cables and oxygen fittings, unsnapped his oxygen mask and lifted his helmet off, and unbuckled his harness, Gloom towed the craft toward the refueling station. After a flight, the aircraft were fueled with JP-4 for the turbojet, and the liquid hydrogen and liquid oxygen fuels for the rocket engines were suctioned out of the tanks. They were not pumped aboard until just before takeoff, and then only after the fuel cells were purged with gaseous helium to remove air impurities and dry the tanks. After the combination fueling and de-fueling, the craft were parked in a hangar, ready for the technicians and engineers to make any corrections noted as necessary in the test flight report.

Grant stood up in the cockpit and hooked his helmet over the windscreen. The front cockpit was almost six feet wide, but it was so crammed with electronics and control consoles that it made a six-foot, wide-shouldered man feel cramped. Under his pressure suit and flight suit, his skin felt clammy, the moisture of perspiration trapped.

Gloom towed the sub-orbiter to a parking place in front of the fueling station, and two airmen dressed in protective asbestos suits and hoods scampered out of an air-conditioned hut and went to work connecting hoses to the receptacles on the aircraft. Grant read the remaining fuel poundage from the digital readouts, called the numbers down to them, then shut off power to the instrument panel.

The tech sergeant got off his tractor, removed a ladder hung on the side of the hood, and brought it back to fasten into the fuselage.

Grant levered his left leg out of the cockpit first, sat on the coaming, and then worked his right leg outside. Getting out of the damned thing required talent usually reserved for circuses. Below the canopy, the fuselage swooped outward, into a lateral fin that gave the machine a pancake-ish front end. The lateral fins spread out as they went back, eventually molding into the stubby delta wing.

He retrieved his helmet, then slid down the fuselage slope and got a toe-hold on the ladder, rolled over, and backed his way down to the tarmac.

"How'd it go, Colonel?" Gloom asked.

"Smooth as maple syrup, Sarge."

"Goddamned good."

"With maybe a lump or two in it."

Gloom fit his name. Smiles came hard, but he managed a lopsided grin. "We'll find 'em for you, sir."

"I'm counting on it."

Grant was about to head for the dressing room and a shower, then to the operations hut and a de-briefing with General Billings when he saw Vidorov walking toward him. Colonel Dmitri Vidorov had to stretch to achieve five-ten, but he was a fit and muscled man, thirty years of flight experience crammed into his head and reflexes. He headed the three-member group of Soviet pilots. He wore an olive drab pressure suit that sported only his name over the right breast pocket and his insignia on his shoulder. His helmet hung from his left hand.

Grant's name was on his own flight suit, and his lieutenant colonel's silver oak leaves were embroidered on the top of his shoulders, but Grant and his two pilots wore the specifically developed unit patch on their left shoulders—a silver circle enclosing a black field. There

17

was no unit number. They were simply the Black Sky Squadron.

"Well, Colonel Grant?"

"Eventually," Grant grinned at him, "you'll get around to calling me Dallas like everyone else."

"Socially, perhaps. My discipline is well-ingrained, Colonel."

And his socializing was practically nonexistent.

"I listened to your test description over the radio. You are only concerned about the degree of directional thrust available?"

"It may be a personal peccadillo," Grant admitted.

"And there was nothing else of consequence?"

"Not in the test sequence." Grant told him about the Mach .97 vibration. He did not mention the Titan IV failure.

Vidorov nodded, his dark eyes pondering. "I will look for it."

"Tomorrow. This baby's going to bed now, until we talk about the flight results."

"I am taking it now," the Red Air Force pilot said, turned away from Grant, and scampered up the ladder.

There was not a figurative word available in Dmitri Vidorov's English, Grant thought. Everything he said was literal.

Sergeant Gloom looked at him, and Grant shrugged his shoulders. "Let him have it, Gloomy. After you change out the video cassette packs."

Two

Alain Moncreiux arrived at the complex at three-thirty in the morning, passing through the tight security gate on his special credential and receiving a lapel badge with his picture on it. A sophisticated image, he thought, with the limpid brown eyes over high cheekbones, the knowing smile.

He drove down the well-lit boulevard, turned right at the indicated sign, drove five more kilometers, and went through another security check. After another six kilometer drive, he found an automobile lot and parked his Peugeot in the space marked for visitors.

There was a light ground fog present, and the car park was bathed in light from a dozen high-placed sodium vapor lamps. More of the lamps blazed a trail toward a large building along a white sidewalk surrounded by gray-yellow grass. Every window in the building was lit, the lights creating halos in the haze. Though it was late in May, it felt damp and chilly. He judged that there were some one hundred cars in the lot, many of them carrying diplomatic and military

19

license plates. His was the only car in the visitor section.

Moncreiux got out of the car, leaned against it, and lit an English Benson and Hedges with a gold Ronson lighter. His movements were fluid. He would have liked a cup of coffee. Turkish, perhaps, very hot and strong enough to stand on its own.

He had international and expensive tastes, developed as a result of his job. Moncreiux traveled a great deal, selling the services of his government.

Twelve minutes elapsed before an American Oldsmobile sedan pulled into the car park, its headlights searching. When the lights passed over him, the car accelerated, shot down the lane, and whipped into the slot next to him. Americans were so impatient.

Henry Parker got out of the car and locked it. The representative from Radio Corporation of America was a young forty, very energetic, and from Moncreiux's viewpoint, very agitated this morning.

He tossed his cigarette out toward the grass. "Good morning, Henri." He gave the name the French pronunciation since Parker seemed to like it.

"Mornin', Al. We have shit for weather."

"Yes. I suspect there will be a delay. Do not fear, however. It will burn away before long."

Together, the two of them crossed the lot and followed the sidewalk toward the big building, the headquarters of France's aerospace command. They did not go inside, but skirted the structure to where six golf cart-like vehicles waited outside the side door. Each was manned by a French airman. Leading Parker to the first cart in line, the two of them crawled under the surrey top and settled on the fake leather seats.

20

With an electric *whish,* the driver urged the cart away. The single headlamp followed the concrete path, and the speed created droplets of moisture that pelted Moncreiux's face.

"Damn this weather," Parker said.

"Henri, you are simply looking for a culprit—on which to blame imponderables."

"Goddamn right."

"Our program, over the past three years, has had a ninety-six percent launch effectiveness. Correct orbit has been achieved in eighty-nine percent of the successful launches. And of those machines that did not insert into the correct orbit, every one was subsequently adjusted to the desired coordinates through post-launch maneuvering." Alain Moncreiux did not know all of the details, but he knew all of the statistics because his job was to sell space on launch vehicles to companies like the one Parker represented. Launch capability was fast becoming a commercial enterprise, and as far as Moncreiux was concerned, France was leading the world.

"You've lost two in the past two months, Alain. That doesn't make me sleep any easier."

"Those were machines belonging to ESA, Henri."

While France was part of the European Space Agency—composed of Belgium, Denmark, France, Germany, Ireland, Italy, Netherlands, Spain, Switzerland, and the United Kingdom—which launched mutually agreed payloads aboard the *Ariane* rocket, the French Defense Ministry had determined to use its newest rocket independently in meeting the increased demand of private enterprise, as well as its own needs.

"And this is a new rocket, you told me."

21

"Yes, this is true. This will be the fourth flight, however, Henri, and the previous three launches were fully successful."

"I got six hundred-goddamn-million riding in the nose of that thing."

Insured, of course, though not for the cost of time lost in building a new satellite, nor for the delays involved in expanding RCA's satellite communications network. A breakdown in that schedule meant lost revenues for the company, less satellite time sold.

"And I'm paying you guys sixteen million to put it up there."

Americans always made their companies their own. "It" became "I." But sixteen million U.S. dollars certainly defrayed the costs of France's military aerospace development as well as the cost of other endeavors. Mr. Henry Parker did not know that the cargo compartment housing his precious satellite also contained a smaller, but more expensive, satellite belonging to French military intelligence. It was getting a free ride, so to speak.

"Maybe we should have gone with NASA. We'd have saved a couple, three mil."

"Perhaps, Henri. But was there not a Titan IV failure last week?"

"That was the Air Force's, not NASA's."

"Of course."

The cart came smoothly to a stop in front of the bunker. Beyond the bunker to the east, faint pink streamers of dawn were barely visible, the light diffused by the overcast skies. Also beyond the bunker, the skeletal and ghoulish figures of eight gantries were emerging from the dark. They were spread in a zigzag

22

pattern over a ten kilometers square area, with at least a half-kilometer between each of them.

Moncreiux led his client into the bunker, descending the outdoor steps and entering through a steel door. Once again, security policemen double-checked their badges and their credentials.

They were not allowed into the control room, of course. Instead, they passed through a door to the left and entered a long and narrow reception room and lounge. Along the non-windowed west wall was a full-length upholstered bench. At the north end was a table laden with two large coffee urns, stacks of coffee mugs, and several platters heaped with croissants. Chafing dishes held scrambled eggs and sausages. An air force steward tended the table.

The east wall contained two rows of windows. The upper row was composed of bronzed safety glass and looked across the roof of the eastern side of the bunker. As dawn brightened, the view would be of the launch gantries. The lower row of windows looked in upon the launch control center. It was constructed like a theater, the room descending toward the front where a huge screen would display the flight in televised visual modes, in radar modes, or in graphic modes. Three rows of consoles were stepped up from the front wall. Some fifty white-coated technicians and supervisors either sat at the consoles or moved around the center, most of them with their backs to the viewers in the lounge. To supplement the big screen, a number of monitors were placed throughout the center and suspended from the ceiling in the viewers' lounge.

The lounge had been constructed some years after the main body of the bunker, primarily to accom-

23

modate visitors like Parker. Still, in addition to Moncreiux's client, a dozen politicians, some with wives or girlfriends, and a few military people mixed with each other, having breakfast, and enjoying a holiday.

An advisory in French was issued from speakers set in the ceilings.

"What's he saying?" Parker asked.

"The launch director has delayed the launch."

"I knew it!"

"We are at T-minus-thirty-one and holding. They say it may be an hour."

Moncreiux led Parker to the north end tables. He filled a mug with the coffee he had been thinking about for over an hour, and then added two teaspoons of sugar. The steward filled a cup for Parker, who did not add anything.

"Try the croissants, Henri. They are very good."

"I'm not hungry." Parker kept glancing up at the monitors, which were blank.

"What's your title, again?"

"Defense Ministry Liaison to Commercial Enterprise. Eloquent, is it not?" He winked at Parker. "What it means is that I am a salesman of high-tech concepts."

"Sales, I understand. That other crap, no. You on commission?"

"A small stipend, and a large commission."

"Commissions, I understand, too. Jesus, I wish some of the guys around here would just *do* something."

As if to alleviate Parker's nervousness, the monitors suddenly burst into life, showing, first, a dimly lit rocket pad, then a center-stage view of the vehicle as flood lights were turned on.

24

Moncreiux tapped Parker's shoulder and indicated the upper window. "It's on Pad Five."

The launch pad was some four kilometers distant, and through the mist, the rocket looked like a miniature, a child's toy. On the monitor, the *Rapier* was much more elegant, its sleek lines flowing downward from the blunt nose cone through the three stages. The first and second stages had fins, though they were quite small on the second stage. The third stage, which would operate outside of the atmosphere, had no fins. A jungle of hoses and umbilical cords draped from the rocket to the spider-like gantry. As they watched, figures moved about, tending to the machine, going up and down in the elevators.

Moncreiux, whose job was not to know rocketry, but to be able to explain its function in broader, layman's terms, pointed out the various stages to Parker, and finished with a description of the cargo module.

Then for forty-five minutes, he moved the two of them about the room and introduced the man to ministers, assistant ministers, bureaucrats, and military people. General Jacques Desmoine, whose air force command included the aerospace division, was able to entertain Parker for some time, though the American kept glancing at the monitors and demanded interpretations every time an announcement was made over the public address system.

It was a two-hour wait before Moncreiux was able to say, "The launch director has released the hold."

"Okay! 'Bout damned time."

Though the horizons were puffy with mist, the launch complex had cleared completely. Overhead clouds had finally moved eastward, and the sun shown brightly from a brassy blue sky.

At eight-thirty-two in the morning, with the gantry crane moved way back and the umbilical cords dropped, vapor and flame belched from the base of the *Rapier*. She rose a foot, hesitated, and then shot away. In seconds, the machine was out of visual range, and all eyes in the lounge moved toward the monitors. Ground-based telescopic cameras followed the rocket, and then were replaced by cameras aimed by Mirage jet chase planes. When the aircraft could no longer track the *Rapier*, previously prepared graphics appeared on the screen.

Moncreiux and Parker moved to the bench and sat down, and Moncreiux provided the translations almost as soon as they came over the speaker.

"The launch director has handed off to the flight control director . . . speed is now 23,000 kilometers per hour . . . the altitude of 50 kilometers has been achieved—that is about 160,000 of your feet, Henri . . . third stage ignition has taken place. . . ."

The technicians in the control room went rigid, a frozen tableau.

". . . and the machine has exploded, Henri."

Nesei Aerospace Industries had located its brand new launch complex on the northern coast of Hokkaido Island, in a somewhat desolate area. The nearby coastal town of Omu had benefited tremendously from first, the influx of construction workers, then the importation of scientists and technicians with large amounts of disposable income.

26

Though the NAI employees enjoyed quarters and recreation facilities provided on the company living compound, many spent leisure time in the coastal village, which had grown enough to be called a town. Many of Omu's fishermen and farmers had transformed themselves overnight into entrepreneurs. A Burger King, a McDonald's, a Pizza Hut, and a Colonel Sander's Kentucky Fried Chicken shared main street space with a Bennigans, a Red Lobster, a bowling alley called Melody Lanes, and at least ten more traditional Japanese establishments. There was even a large department store. In the summer months, a revitalized marina offered rental boats and scuba and water skiing instructions. A nine-hole golf course was in the planning stages.

Taking a newly black-topped two-lane highway some ten kilometers inland, visitors ran into a brick wall, or rather, an eight-foot-high and electrified fence enclosing some thirty thousand very expensive acres. Few visitors were allowed beyond the guard shacks to view the NAI development, and anyway, most important visitors arrived via helicopter or private jet on the single runway near the center of the acreage.

Nesei Aerospace Industries was guided by the firm hand of Maki Kyoto, its president and chief executive officer. He reported to a nine-member board of directors, all of whom also served on the boards of Japan's leading conglomerates. It was Kyoto who had named the complex "Sun Land."

Kyoto had arrived at Sun Land seven days before and his routine had been firmly entrenched in his on-site office and in living quarters located in line with the cabanas reserved for visiting dignitaries. He rose at five o'clock each morning, completed his exercises, bathed, dressed in whatever his valet had set out for him, then breakfasted on the veranda. At six-thirty, he left the residential row and walked the half-mile path that meandered through the broad lawn to the administration building.

All of the structures at Sun Land followed the same architectural scheme. They were strongly built of concrete and steel, though the concrete was skinned in aluminum anodized in pale blue. Flat-roofed, most of the structures were single-storied.

East of the administration building were the dormitories, apartment buildings, and recreation buildings for the employees of NAI.

Out of sight of the administration and residential buildings, over the crest of a low hill to the west, was the airfield. Parallel to the runway were numerous structures, including five assembly plants which received most of their components from the main island factories via air freight. On the coast to the north, a newly built concrete pier some twelve kilometers from Omu received the oversized components and the propellant chemicals, transferring them inland on rail lines. There were only three launch pads located seven kilometers to the north of the airfield, but the rotation time between pads was very efficient since the *Emperor* was based on solid propellants; there was no need to handle liquid oxygen and hydrogen fuels. Steel rails set in flat concrete guided the electrically powered trams and dollies that transported rocket segments from assembly plants to the final assembly building to any one of the three launch pads.

Within the administration area, the landscaping

28

between the buildings was serene, meant to induce security and contemplation. There were ponds stocked with goldfish, narrow streams, waterfalls, rock gardens, sculptured trees and hedges. Gravel paths meandered among the gardens. Western culture could be found in interior furnishings and in the tennis courts located near the dormitories.

When Maki Kyoto entered his Sun Land office, he was met by two secretaries and three aides. While they waited, he sped-read the night's Telex and cable traffic, then spent half an hour issuing orders. By the time he was finished, there was one secretary left, to whom he dictated his morning's correspondence.

At fifteen minutes after ten o'clock, his first appointment arrived. Meoshi Yakamata was a colonel in the Japanese Air Defense Forces. He was a pilot and, as head of the flight test command, had been a central figure in the joint Japanese-American development of the FSX fighter aircraft. That airplane was, Kyoto thought, a sort of Taiwanese copy of a real fighter aircraft.

Yakamata was tall for a Japanese, though his height was characteristic of his Off-Islander heritage. He was five-feet, eleven-inches tall. His black hair was militarily short, and his brown eyes had the penetrating steadiness of a pilot. His uniforms were tailored to his compact and healthy figure, but never exhibited the many ribbons for heroism and duty that Kyoto knew he had earned. The CEO had thoroughly researched his man, and he knew the reports of the pilot's competence, as well as those of his ruthlessness.

Kyoto only employed the best.

Colonel Yakamata always made Kyoto feel his

squatness. He was five-two and weighed 160 pounds, all of it the result of the rich food he had come to love, but which his morning regimen could not overcome. His smooth face, balding head, and expensive tailoring kept him from appearing like anything except the wealthy man he was, but in the presence of the pilot, he frequently felt dowdy.

"Please, Colonel Yakamata, do sit down."

The colonel looked at his watch. "Mr. Kyoto, should we not go to the launch site? It is about time."

"As the Air Defense observer, Colonel, can you not observe from here?" Kyoto waved toward his large window. He detested having to concern himself with details, even the details of the maiden flight of *Emperor,* the single rocket design around which he had built his company's entire aerospace effort. There were a great many more global issues upon which his time was better spent.

"But Mr. Kyoto, if it fails . . ."

"It will not."

"But, certainly . . ."

Dull thunder rolled across the ground, making the windows shudder in their frames. An instant later, the day grew brighter.

Colonel Yakamata raced to the window.

Maki Kyoto leafed through the files in his desk drawer, looking for the correspondence from James Lee.

"It is an inspiring sight," Yakamata said.

"Yes. Now, can we go on to another subject?" the industrialist asked.

"Of course." Yakamata reluctantly left the window and sat in a chair opposite Kyoto.

Kyoto shifted topics easily and rapidly. Among the many they discussed, Kyoto was most optimistic about the electronic gyro-stabilizer system being used on *Emperor* for the first time. "Every flight of our rocket is to be considered, not only in its return on investment for the payload carried, but also as a test bed for experimentation with new systems. The GS-106 stabilizer will be snapped up by the Americans. I feel it."

"I trust that it will work well," Yakamata said.

"Of course it will. Japanese electronics are the best in the world because they are the product of superior and disciplined minds."

"Yes. That is true."

Forty-seven minutes later, the telephone rang, and Kyoto answered it, listened, then ordered a copy of the GS-106 telemetry readings delivered to his office. When he hung up, he said, "Nesei Aerospace has its first communications satellite in orbit. It is functioning at one hundred percent."

"Congratulations."

"It will assist us in all endeavors, Colonel Yakamata."

General Grigori Malenovich Brezhenki was Deputy Commander in Chief of the Soviet Air Forces and also Commander of the Soviet Strategic Rocket Forces. He was not only responsible for the massive collection of intercontinental ballistic missiles resting in silos and aboard mobile launchers throughout the Soviet Union, but also for the space program. His command ranged from earth-level to space. However, after a successful launch, other commands or agencies assumed control of the satellites he had placed in orbit for them. His command launched about one hundred satellites a year, seventy percent of which served exclusively military goals. The remainder generally had dual roles for both civilian and military purposes.

As evidence of his stature within the Military Council of Command and Staff, General Brezhenki reported directly to the First Deputy Commander in Chief. He had not obtained his three stars by being complacent, and he did not allow complacency to develop anywhere within the broad reaches of his command. Brezhenki, a professional soldier of the old line, viewed with caution many of the new directions being taken in the motherland's domestic policies. He was relieved that, as yet, no sweeping changes had taken place in foreign policy positions, though the experimental cooperative subspace project with the United States might be cast as an omen of future disturbances in military relationships. He studied the reports of General Pyotr Mikhailovich Nemorovsky, who belonged to Brezhenki's space command, with as much concentration upon the unspoken thoughts between words as he did upon the words themselves.

Though the general most often located himself near Moscow, he frequently toured the outposts of his command. His visits were often unannounced, thereby inducing local commanders to remain alert. Grigori Brezhenki had been known to make abrupt changes in the ranks of his more inept commanders and their subordinates, not generally for the better.

The Soviet Space Command complex at Tyuratam had fifteen minutes warning before the landing gear of Brezhenki's Ilyushin Il-76 command plane touched down on the runway. The aircraft, called *Candid* by

NATO and similar in appearance to the American C-141, was powered by four large turbofan engines and was equipped with the latest in sophisticated computer electronics, communications, and radar. It was his office in the sky.

Fifteen minutes was sufficient time for the base commander, General Karl Antonovko. His black staff Zil automobile was warmed and waiting at the base of the portable stairway when General Brezhenki descended, trailed by a retinue of seven assistants.

Antonovko got out of the car, saluted, then grasped his superior in a hug.

"Karl Yurievich, it is good to see you."

"And you, Comrade General."

Both of the generals were broad men, though Brezhenki was the taller. Both were true Russians, having been born in White Russia S.S.R., although Brezhenki was the urbanite from Minsk and Antonovko's ancestors had been farmers outside of Polotsk. The base commander ushered his superior into the back of the Zil and motioned all of the assistants and aides-de-camp toward the trailing line of Volgas.

"You know why I have come, Karl Yurievich?"

"I expected you. I have arranged a briefing regarding the A2e failure, followed by luncheon, followed by an inspection of the vehicle assembly building."

The A2 and A2e launch vehicles were the workhorses of the Space Command's manned and unmanned programs. Veterans of better than a thousand missions, the failures were sparse and had occurred primarily in the early years.

"The Chairman of the *Komitet Gosudarstvennoy*

Bezopasnosti specifically asked me to look into it," Brezhenki explained. "The satellite destroyed was, of course, theirs."

"Yes, a Cosmos 758. It was to be placed in geostationary orbit over France. I do wish the KGB would move on to something better, Comrade General."

The Cosmos 758, a photographic reconnaissance satellite, was highly maneuverable once in orbit, but had a lifespan of only two months. The American satellites, like the digital imaging KH-11, remained useful for years, which explained why the USSR was required to inject some 35 satellites per year into space, compared with the United States's normal three. The lag in technology not only concerned the intelligence community, but also the CCCP—the Central Committee of the Communist Party—because of its high cost.

"So, tell me."

"The lift-off and first stage separation was as normal. The problem occurred at second stage ignition, when, we now think, the upper sections lost stability and began to tumble. Unbalanced, the vehicle went into gyrating loops and the flight control officer was compelled to push the destruct button. The briefing will include all of the photographic evidence we have gathered."

"How about physical evidence?"

"Recovery teams are out, now, Comrade General, but I do not expect that there will be much for them to gather."

The Zil pulled into the circular drive in front of the headquarters building, but the generals remained in the car as their underlings took to the sidewalks.

"So, Karl Yurievich, you believe our disaster may be

attributed to technical faults?"

"That is why I have scheduled a tour of the vehicle assembly building, General. Your presence will, I am quite certain, instill renewed vigor and attention to quality control in the technicians who work there."

"It could not have been sabotage?"

"I think not," Antonovko said.

Brezhenki looked at the driver on the other side of the glass partition, then said, "I would hate to admit to Chairman Cherevako that his loss is a result of ineptitude within my command."

The political light brightened for Antonovko. "Yes. I understand your concern. It is my concern, also."

"It would be far better should we discover that a lapse in KGB vigilance allowed Western, or perhaps some other, agents to somehow interfere with the launch vehicle. The A2e does, after all, have an enviable record of achievement. It does not fail as a matter of course. Yes, Karl Yurievich, it would be much easier to place such a report at the chairman's feet."

And perhaps affect future allocations of budgetary rubles, thought Antonovko, rubles that kept his command operating. "It is quite possible that, once we have reviewed all of the available evidence, Comrade General, new possibilities will emerge."

"I am quite certain of it," Brezhenki replied.

Three

Billy Shepard was a bantam-weight pilot. At five-seven and 140 pounds, with dark brown hair leveled into a flat-top and striking green eyes, he had barely made the Air Force's requirements. What had convinced the screening officers just before Shepard's graduation from the University of Oklahoma ROTC program, however, was his determination and ability. At age twenty-two, Shepard had, on his own, obtained his pilot's license, his instrument rating, and his dual engine rating. He was certified in nine types of civilian aircraft.

By the time Dallas Grant recruited him for the Black Sky Squadron, Shepard had flown every aircraft type available in the U.S. Air Force, including the B-1 and B-2 bombers. It was the same list Grant could put on a resume.

It may have been either his size or his accomplishments that made Shepard a trifle cocky. Grant did not care for the man's arrogance, but he did not care about it, either, as long as he performed.

Shepard loved his job, but was destined to be continually frustrated by it. He hated malfunctions in equipment, but in any test program, there were bound to be equipment failures and setbacks. That was, after all, what the test program was all about.

"Goddamn-son-of-a-bitch-bastard-motherfucker!" came over the Tactical Two frequency, the frequency Grant had specified for intersub-orbital communications.

Grant checked his right wing. Beyond it, he could see Shepard in XSO-3, his mouth going a mile a nanosecond. They were still at 15,000 feet, and Shepard had not fastened his oxygen mask in place.

"Let's have that oxygen mask, Billy."

Reluctantly, Shepard complied.

Fifty yards off Grant's left wing and fifteen feet above him, Vidorov was flying XSO-2. He too was studying the rooster pilot through the sub-orbital's bronzed canopy.

Grant touched the stud on the stick that activated his microphone on Tac-2. "Billy . . ."

"Son-of-a-bitching-mother-loving . . ."

"Billy."

"Goddamn it! What!"

"You want to explain the problem to me?"

"Bastard rocket engines won't light!"

"You have greens?"

"All the way. Every damn light."

"Kill it all, and let's go back through it."

Shepard reversed the checklist and shut down all of the switches, then Grant called up his own checklist on his screen and went through the procedures with him.

"Current nozzle temperatures?"

"Number one, four-five degrees. Number two, four-nine degrees."

Normal for cold engines at that altitude. "Fuel loads. Oxygen tanks?"

"Showing nine-eight percent, sir."

"Hydrogen?"

"Nine-six percent."

There was a little more leakage in the hydrogen tanks than normal, Grant thought, unless the loss could be attributed to the start procedure. He made a note on his thigh pad, captioning it, "XSO-3."

"Pressures?"

"One-six-two PSI on oxy, and I've got one-five-five pounds on hydrogen."

Well within parameters. In addition to the refrigeration necessary to keep the fuels in a liquid state, the fuel cells were pressurized in order to help force the liquids into the circulation system.

"Coolant system?"

"Full charge. Green."

"Coolant pumps?"

"Go, babies . . . on line, one . . . now two. Backup pumps show on standby, Colonel."

"Turbopumps?"

"Coming on line, now. Greens."

"Nozzles?"

"Sensors show clear. I've got green on both nozzles. Goddamn it! Everything's green."

"Combustion chambers?"

"Both clear."

"Pre-burners?"

"I've got one . . . now two. Now three and . . . four. All four showing good."

The hydrogen fuel and oxidizer were mixed and injected into pre-burners that converted them to gaseous form (at a temperature of 1400 degrees) which drove the turbopumps. The hot gases were then used more efficiently when injected into the main combustion chamber.

Grant made an automatic scan of his horizons. They were still climbing, going through 18,000. The Soviet pilot was hanging in place, being complacently patient. To the southwest, a dark squall was pouring rain on an empty Pacific. Other than that, the skies were clear and light blue. A thin dark blue line on the horizon separated the sky from the sea. A passenger airliner coming in from Hawaii or the Orient was passing far to his north.

"Enable the rocket throttles."

"Enabled. Green."

"Throttle position?"

"Full back."

"Kill buttons?" Grant looked down at his own kill switches, red buttons on each of the throttle handles, to shut down the rockets in an emergency.

"Got live buttons."

"Ignition system."

"Live system on both engines."

"Igniters?"

"One, two, three, four, five, six. Test sequence, six green, Colonel."

The spark igniters in the pre-burners and combustion chambers provided the initial combustion, then automatically shut off when the engines were running.

"Open oxygen valve."

"I'm showing good oxygen flow, point-zero-four

39

PPM on both engines."

"Open hydrogen."

"Open. Point-zero-zero-six on Number one. Point-zero-zero-seven on Number two."

"Adjust mixtures."

A short pause. "Adjusted. I've got a six-one ratio on each engine and four goddamn greens."

The fuel mixture used for combustion was six parts oxidizer to one part hydrogen.

"Arm igniters."

"Number one engine armed. Number two engine armed."

"Fire one."

"Fired. Negative reaction. No temp, no pressure."

"Try two."

"Fired. No temp, no pressure, no fucking engine. And I've got power on the electrodes, according to the goddamned Buck Rogers shit on the panel."

"Shut it all down again, Billy."

A longer pause. "Finis."

"Go to Tac-one and tell Rosie you're coming home."

"Ah, shit!"

"Now, Billy."

"Aye-aye, commodore."

XSO-3 angrily peeled away to the right, diving hard in frustration.

Grant touched the mike button again. "How about you, Colonel?"

"I have green lights."

So did Grant. "Let's torch 'em off."

He opened the fuel lines, checked the pressures and flow, then armed and fired the igniters. Immediately, he felt the lurch and the increase in thrust and tugged he turbo jet throttle back two notches. He set the rocket throttles at 45%. The operating range of the throttles was from 45% to 105%.

The airspeed readout was climbing rapidly. The sub-orbital passed through Mach 1 and continued to accelerate.

The rocket nozzle pressures both rose to about 2200 pounds per square inch, and the temperatures came up quickly to 5500 degrees Fahrenheit.

"I have ignition, Colonel," Vidorov radioed.

"So do I. Temperatures?"

"Five thousand on one, approaching five thousand on two."

"Shut down your turbo."

Mach 2.1.

Grant went through his own checklist, closing off fuel flow and power to the turbojet. He watched as the RPM's wound down to zero, then closed the intake doors for the jet and the auxiliary generator. When the right lights moved into the red indication, he said, "Let's go flying, Colonel."

He eased back on the stick as he pushed the throttles to their forward stops. Side by side, the sub-orbitals leaped toward the ionosphere. The air speed indicator displayed Mach numbers that advanced rapidly. Mach 2.8 . . . 3.2 . . . 3.6.

Grant felt the satisfying pressure of gravity forcing him back in his contoured seat. The flesh around his mouth and eyes sagged. The pressure suit filled with compressed air, attempting to keep his skin and organs in their normal positions. The G-force readout increased to 4.1.

The sub-orbitals utilized pressurized cockpits,

avoiding the need for cumbersome space suits, and Grant was appreciative of the design. The sub-orbiter altitudes were not high enough for extravehicular activity requiring a space suit, and he had no desire to leave any cockpit at an altitude of sixty miles or six hundred miles, anyway.

Rolling his eyes, then his head, to the left, he saw that Vidorov was right with him, but had moved out by another fifty yards. No telling what might happen in close formation if they hit unexpected turbulence.

The G-forces dropped off as his body caught up with the momentum of the sub-orbital. At Mach 4.3, the indication was .3 G's.

When the craft reached 200,000 feet, thirty-eight miles above the earth, Grant eased off the throttles and lowered the nose, beginning to level out. Vidorov leveled out at the same time, without directions from Grant. He had read the same test sequence plan.

At 225,000 feet, they were both in level flight at Mach 3.5. The Hawaiian Islands were emeralds on Grant's right, so far below that they would have blended into the blue seas if not for the white beaches and silver surf that surrounded them.

Grant checked his fuel loads and throttle settings. To date, they did not really know the top speed on the sub-orbiter, though it was calculated to be far less than necessary to break the final bonds of earth. Mach 4.5 was the arbitrarily set speed limit because the scientists were not yet certain of the stresses imposed on the carbon-impregnated skin, the structural girders, or especially, the key joints of the craft, even though they were designed to expand and contract with the changes in temperature. The Concorde SST, for instance, changed its length by nearly twelve inches during a flight.

Not quite trusting the honor system among risk-taking, hotshot test pilots, the software engineers had programmed the maximum speed into the sub-orbiters' computers. Once Mach 4.5 was reached, the throttles would not respond to requests for increased power.

At altitudes where the slowing friction of the atmosphere was reduced to almost nil, lower throttle settings could maintain the Mach 3.5 cruising speed. The theorists estimated that XSO-4 could probably stay aloft on rocket engines for about three-and-a-half hours at Mach 3.5, and perhaps much longer if the engines were shut down for long coasting periods. Down in the thick atmosphere, the fuel load was consumed in less than two hours. The turbojet used for takeoff and landing had a fifty-minute fuel supply.

"Let's go to Tac-three, Colonel Vidorov."

"I am switching over now."

Once they were both on the frequency which the engineeres and designers would monitor, Grant spoke for the audio recorders on board the craft with him and on the ground. "XSO test sequence seven-two-one-A and seven-two-one-B. Colonel Dmitri Vidorov is pilot of XSO-2, and Lieutenant Colonel Dallas Grant is pilot of XSO-4. Test sequence seven-two-one-C, craft XSO-3, has been aborted. Probable cause, rocket engine ignition malfunction."

Grant looked over at XSO-2. Against the sky, which had turned to a deep velvet purple, the sub-orbiter was difficult to see, even at one hundred yards' distance. Faint pinpricks of light, which were stars, sprinkled the background. At higher altitude, the stars were much sharper. Below, the earth's curvature was pronounced, the land masses were green and brown, and the sea was a slate blue. The definition between the Pacific Ocean and the western coast of the North American continent was blurred by spotty cloud buildups which were 185,000 feet below them. The ocean curved away into the western distance. Grant felt as if he should be able to see the Asian continent, but of course, he could not.

"The first sequence will be performed by XSO-2. Colonel, could I have some lights?"

Vidorov turned on his red and green wingtip lights, his belly-mounted blue anti-collision strobe, and his leading edge landing lights. The illumination would help Grant perform his role as observer of the maneuvers. He switched on his own lights, except for the landing lights, so that Vidorov could keep track of where he was. Keying the computer for video display, Grant started the camera and video recorder. He slowed his speed momentarily, then drifted over behind the Soviet and centered the camera on the sub-orbital. With the arrow keys on his keypad, he could oscillate the camera lens, though only through an arc of forty-five degrees. Unlike turreted cameras hung below a fuselage, this one was mounted behind an acrylic window formed into the curvature of the sub-orbital's lower nose panel.

"Colonel Vidorov, you have the floor."

The Soviet did not understand a lot of American idioms, but did understand that he was to begin his test. "One. Performing right three-six-zero degree roll."

With spurts of flame from the roll thrusters creating neon dashes in the dark, XSO-2 did a full roll. What

44

was more, Vidorov did it in eight points, with the craft hesitating momentarily at 45, 90, 135, 180, 225, 270, and 315 degrees. Grant watched the maneuver on his video screen and knew perfection when he saw it. It was difficult enough to accomplish in the dense air of the lower level Troposphere, but up here, in what was labeled the Mesosphere—part of the Ionosphere, a pilot could not rely on centering his ailerons to stop the roll. The hesitations were accomplished with reverse thrusters countering the momentum of the initial thrust, and the reference points of earth and sea were illusory. Vidorov had to have depended entirely on his roll indicator.

"And now exercise two. Performing left three-six-zero degree roll."

The Soviet pilot did it the same way he had done the first roll, and just as perfectly. Grant grinned to himself. The man was not very demonstrative on the ground, but at the controls, he was a bit of a show-off.

For the next forty minutes, Grant trailed XSO-2, video-taping displacements along lateral and longitudinal axes, executed at varying rates of acceleration. They tested sudden decreases and increases in power while the craft was in different attitudes of flight. The engineers were also collecting the live data from transmitted telemetry.

Then they climbed to sixty miles of altitude, into the Thermosphere, and almost to the altitudes at which Yeager had flown the X-15. Grant and Vidorov switched positions during a 180-degree turn back toward the east and home base. The sun was getting low in the southwest now, and twilight would have already fallen on the West Coast. The black line of night crossed the continent a few hundred miles inland. The coastline was a barely discernible blemish ahead of him, almost four thousand miles away, but the sun behind him showed a smudge on the sea that he took to be either Kingman Reef or Palmyra Atoll. Grant thought how easy it would be to take a little deserved holiday in Pago Pago or Papeete. Grant frequently thought about his well-earned vacations. He could be approaching either place in little more than an hour. Without, of course, a place to land.

With Vidarov filming, Grant started the same testing sequence. He made one exception. He executed his first two maneuvers as twelve-point rolls.

"That was very good, Colonel Grant. Excellent," Vidorov told him.

"I'll tell you this, Dmitri. I've never done that before in an airplane. It was a hell of a lot easier than I expected it to be."

"What the hell's going on up there?" The bull voice belonged to Major General Lane Billings.

"Three," Grant keyed his mike as if Billings had not intervened, "fifteen-degree left turn."

"You'd better damn well have whatever it was on tape," Billings warned, but did not press either of them for an immediate answer.

They were about seventeen hundred miles off the coast when Grant completed his test series. Switching off the video cameras and recorders, the two of them signed off Tac-3 and went to Tac-2.

Almost before he realized what was happening, XSO-2 had completed a half-roll and sideslip, flopping upside down just above Grant. He looked up to see

46

Vidorov's cockpit less than ten feet away, the Soviet pilot looking down at him. Or looking up, from Vidorov's point of view.

Grant flipped him a finger, shoved his nose down, and went into a tight outside loop which, because of his speed, covered a twenty-mile-long area. The blood rushed to his head as he lifted toward the canopy—held in place by his harness, the pressure suit gagged a few times. He came out on the top of his loop at 207,000 feet to find Vidorov diving down behind him, just emerging from an inside loop.

Rolling hard left, he watched his rear view in the small video screen to the left of the main screen. Vidorov was right on him. He rolled right, then hard left again, pulled the throttles, and dumped the speed brakes. The brakes had very little effect at that altitude.

But the abrupt changes were enough.

Vidorov shot by on the right, and Grant slammed the throttles forward and retracted the brakes as he turned in on XSO-2's tail.

"Hell, I should be getting this on tape," he mused. "Both Billings and Nemorosky would crap yellow for a week."

The Soviet floorboarded it, going into a shallow dive. By all rights, in a dive, the sub-orbital should exceed the maximum Mach 4.5, but the damned software people and their infernal computers had anticipated that. The computer's sensors could taste a nose-down attitude, in combination with throttle settings and velocity—which was determined by a communications link with inertial navigation satellites, and if the computer did not like what it saw, it intervened and decreased fuel flow to the motors or invoked the speed brakes or accomplished both actions.

Vidorov could not outrun him, though he tried. Grant watched his own speed rise as he stayed on the twin-ruddered tail of the sub-orbiter. He knew they had maxed it out when he saw the speed brake slats rise on Vidorov's craft. Computer taking command.

The Soviet rolled right, and Grant followed him, anticipating a tight right turn. Instead, Vidorov kicked in down thrusters and zipped away to the left, in an inverted, outside turn.

Son of a bitch. That was good.

He rolled on over and tried to pursue, but Vidorov had again reversed elevator thrust and was now in a normal right turn.

Grant whisked by him, a little close on the whisk. His belly could not have missed XSO-2's rudders by more than five feet.

He was going to attempt a modified Immelmann in order to get back behind the Soviet when Billings's boom interrupted his Tac-2 channel. "You two want to settle down up there, or maybe explain what it is you're doing?"

Grant touched his mike button, "We're making for home, General."

"Not according to the telemetry."

In the aft cockpit was about two hundred pounds of supplementary radio equipment which provided the engineers on the ground with remote readings of the major sensors on board the sub-orbiter. Grant figured the ink pens which traced lines on moving paper had been jumping all over the scale.

"Just testing some reaction times, sir."

"Bullshit."

Vidorov settled in beside him, and the two grinned at each other across two hundred feet of near-vacuum. Grant still felt good when they crossed the darkened coast of Northern California thirty minutes later.

At Mach 3 and 6,000 feet, they did a scheduled low-level run over the salt flats at Bonneville, holding the speed and altitude for sixty seconds to get fuel consumption readings. They made the same run at Mach 2.5 for more readings, then climbed back to 11,000 feet and circled north of Nellis Air Base, preparing to go back on turbojets. Grant opened his generator air intake. Battery power available was a bit lower than usual. He touched another button, and the light told him that his turbojet air intake had opened. It was totally dark now, and Grant could see the colorful beacon of Las Vegas. He squawked his IFF signal as the radar blip and identifier for the two of them.

What the hell?

He had heard more than felt the collision. Checking to his left, he saw Vidorov's face in the red glow of his instrument panel. He scanned his own panel. Hydrogen fuel flow to the number two rocket engine was almost nonexistent. Combustion chamber pressure had gone almost to zero. But he still showed thirty-one percent fuel in the fuel cell. All he had in the number two nozzle was oxygen-fed flames. He tapped the button on the throttle handle and killed the engine.

XSO-2 drifted on ahead of him as the power loss slowed Grant down.

Running quickly through his checklist, he cranked the turbojet, looking for a quick rise in RPM's.

Nothing.

He tried it again. The readouts did not even show a drain on the batteries.

Once more he tried to start it, with the same results.

Vidorov had noticed his absence and slowed down to accommodate him. The Soviet was still on rocket engines, but now had his own turbojet operating. He shut down one of the rockets in order to slow his speed.

Punching in Rosie's frequency on Tac-1, Grant said, "Rosie, this is SOL-zero-four."

"Rosie. Go ahead zero-four."

Grant gave his coordinates and altitude. "I'm reporting a collision of some kind. Most likely a bird in the generator port since I'm not getting generator readings. I've lost Number two rocket engine for lack of hydrogen flow, and the turbo's not responding."

"Any other damage, zero-four?"

"Not that I can tell. I'm holding my own at indicated air speed one-point six."

"Hold one, zero-four."

As he waited, Vidorov side-slipped below him, then up the right side, then over the top, looking for damage.

On Tac-2, he asked, "What do you see, Dmitri?"

"Not very much in the dark, Dallas. I believe there is a large indentation in the fuselage forward of the generator air port."

It was the first time the Soviet pilot had used his first name.

Tac-1 came alive. "Dallas, you all right?"

"Sure, General." He reported Vidorov's observation.

"Okay. Put her down at Nellis."

"Won't be necessary, General. I'm sure I can limp

50

it home."

"You know how much those damned things cost?" the general asked.

"Sure."

"You know how much is left in my budget?"

"No, sir."

"If you bend that bird, you walk for the rest of this fiscal year and part of the next."

"Rosie, SOL-zero-four requests permission for emergency landing at Nellis Air Force Base."

"Permission granted, zero-four. Rosie out."

Grant keyed in the memorized frequency for Nellis Air Control on his Tac-1, explained his circumstances, and requested landing instructions.

"SOL-zero-four, in two minutes, you will have clearance for Runway one-eight. I am alerting the emergency crews now."

"Thank you, Nellis. It should be pretty clean, however, I am requesting an out-of-the-way hangar for the aircraft. It's slightly classified."

"How do you slightly classify, zero-four? Never mind, my supervisor has some general on the line. Do you need a pilot's assistance?"

Grant doubted that there was a pilot at Nellis Air Force Base who had even seen the sub-orbital, much less one who could help talk him down.

Vidorov came on the air. "Nellis Air Control, this is SOL-zero-two."

"Nellis. Go ahead, zero-two. I didn't know you were there."

"Zero-two. I will be the escort. I am turning on my IFF now."

"I think I've got you, zero-two. You guys are awfully

close together."

On Tac-2, Vidorov asked, "Have you landed on rocket engines before, Dallas?"

"No. I don't know if it's possible to get the speed down far enough."

"Try the air brakes."

Grant dumped the speed brakes and watched as his velocity slowed to under Mach 1. The readout switched to miles-per-hour. Looking quickly to the left, he saw that Vidorov had shut off his second rocket engine.

"There's a first time for everything, I guess, Dmitri. If it happens to you, remember there's a hell of a pull to the right. I'm fighting yaw all the way."

The Soviet stayed right beside him all the way, fifty feet off his left wing tip. Within ten minutes, he spotted the beacon, then the runway lights of Nellis.

Grant tried to create drag by closing the turbojet intake. He was still doing 450 miles-per-hour.

"Nellis, this is zero-four."

"Nellis. Go ahead, zero-four."

"I'm going to do this VFR."

"We confirm Visual Flight Rules, zero-four."

Grant could see the flashing blue strobes of the emergency vehicles, set to pick up on him about halfway down the strip. He figured he was about fifteen miles out, and with the speed brakes in their full-raised position, he did not have to force as much rudder. Still, he had slowed about as much as he could.

At ten miles, he was down to 425 miles per hour and four thousand feet.

"Lower your landing gear," Vidorov said. "That will help, Dallas."

Grant dropped the landing gear and got three lights,

but Vidorov dipped below him to check anyway. As he pulled back up into view, he said, "They look to be locked."

"Thank you."

Air speed 390.

As the landing lights became two welcoming white lines, he said, "You haven't corrected me yet, Dmitri."

"You would think me arrogant."

At five miles out, Vidorov said, "I have just had a thought."

"Share it, please."

"I have been thinking about the combination of oxygen, hydrogen, a hot combustion chamber, and a possible *blini* landing."

"Blini?"

"Pancake, I think. Flat, anyway."

One single white flash, then oblivion.

"It's not a good thought, Dmitri." Four miles.

"No, Dallas, it is not."

"I wonder why we never considered parachutes? I'm going to kill it now." Grant reached down with his forefinger and pressed the kill button on the throttle handle.

The combusion chamber pressure went to zero, as did the fuel flows. He clogged the toggles on the ignition system.

The sub-orbital sagged, her tail going down, and he corrected with the forward stick. The loss of the engine made her yaw left, and he eased in the rudder and got her straightened out.

With his left hand, he opened the emergency tank valves on the hydrogen fuel cells, then pressurized the tanks. It was quiet enough that he could hear the whistle of the escaping gas.

When he cut off the compressed air, the hydrogen tank gauges showed empty. He opened up and blew the oxygen cells, then killed the refrigeration. The oxygen took longer to evacuate.

Two miles.

One.

The outer markers winked at him as he shot over them.

He kept his eyes on the center line.

"Air speed two-seven-zero," Vidorov said quietly.

He seemed to be floating above the concrete. It was awfully quiet.

"Air speed two-five-zero."

She did not want to settle down. The blue strobes of the emergency vehicles were coming up.

"Two-four-five, Dallas. You may land the aircraft."

XSO-2 was almost stalling beside him. Vidorov accelerated away, climbing.

The tires screamed as they touched down. The craft did not even bounce. It stayed down, but it was rolling free since he did not have reverse thrust available. He used the brakes sparingly, not wanting to burn them out.

He shot past the emergency vehicles, which were already running with him.

"Damn." To himself. "The end of the runway is closer than it was the last time I was here."

The sub-orbital coasted to a stop a hundred feet short of the end of the runway. The trucks swarmed in around him, but he waved them off. While he waited for a tractor, Grant depressurized and raised his

54

canopy, then the rear canopy. There was a pneumatic hiss as the seals were broken. He could smell the hot brakes.

The fuselage widened to seven feet behind the front cockpit, and the rear cockpit had room in which to cram six seats for six passengers, or to store cargo that did not exceed 1400 pounds in total weight. Right then, some of the area was taken up with the flight test instrumentation and radios which were bolted to the floor.

And a small AWOL bag in air force blue, bungee-strapped to an electrical conduit.

As a pilot, Dallas Grant knew there would be times when he landed where he had not planned to land. Even as a teenager and as a college student at UCLA, Grant had always kept a change of clothes in the trunk of his car.

He levered himself out of the front cockpit, around the raised canopy, and into the rear compartment. It took him seven minutes to peel his way out of the helmet, pressure, suit, flight suit, long underwear, and flight boots. He stood naked under the angled-up canopy and let the warm desert air dry him off, then opened the bag. Digging past the spare uniform, he found gray slacks, a darker gray sport coat, a blue knit sport shirt, and polished black loafers. He was dressed, digging his wallet out of the flight suit leg pocket, by the time his tow arrived. He stepped out onto the delta wing and sat down, hanging his legs over the leading edge.

The tractor driver gaped first at the strange aircraft, then at the civilian sitting on its wing.

"Hi," Grant said.

"Uh, hi. Sir?"

"Could we get under way? There's a show starting at the Riviera at ten, and I don't want to miss it."

After landing and turning XSO-2 over to Sergeant Drandorov and his ground crew, Dmitri Vidorov slipped out of his pressure suit and went directly to the operations building to see his superior, General Pyotr Nemorosky.

General Billings was apparently over at the labs, and Nemorosky sat alone in his office, the twin to that of Billings's office, next to it. The Americans had gone out of their way to ensure that equal ranks received equal treatment and facilities.

Nemorosky was, Vidorov thought, a smart man, in addition to the connections he had in the Red Air Force hierarchy. He had achieved his first star the year before, at the age of forty-three. His face was lean, the cheeks almost cadaverous, and made more so by the heavy whiskers which required that he shave twice a day. He had a prominent Adam's apple and slightly protruding, brooding gray eyes. His eyebrows and hair were thickly black, the eyebrows almost coming together over a blunt nose. It was a peasant appearance, but one which hid a formidable intellect.

Vidorov himself was more fair, with darkly shaded blond hair, hazel eyes, and pale skin. He prided himself on his physique. At one time, Vidorov had competed with the Soviet Olympic boxing team, and he had never given up the regimen of exercise. As with everything about him, it was a quiet pride. Dmitri Vidorov did not like braggarts. One demonstrated his abilities; he did not talk about them.

"Come in, come in, Dmitri Vasilivich," Nemorosky commanded. "You appear tired."

He did not feel tired. "I am quite all right, Comrade General."

"Good. A drink?"

"Please."

The general retrieved a bottle of pepper vodka from his desk drawer and poured two glasses almost to the brim. There was no ice.

"To the project," Nemorosky said.

Hoisting his glass, Vidorov agreed. "To the project."

He took a large gulp, and the warmth coursed through him, revitalizing. Unzipping the upper part of his flight suit a few millimeters, he let the cool air produced by the building's refrigeration unit get closer to his skin.

Pulling a note pad close and clicking a ballpoint pen, the general said, "Let us begin."

While the general wrote his cryptic notes, Vidorov provided a chronological narrative of the flight, including the sham dogfight at 200,000 feet. Relating the story took him half an hour.

"And Colonel Grant has landed safely at Nellis Air Force Base?"

"Yes, General. He will be making arrangements to repair the sub-orbiter and return it to Edwards."

"General Billings flew to Nevada with a ground crew," Nemorosky informed him. "You are not certain of the damage, however?"

"No. It will take closer investigation."

"I see. Now, about the combat simulation. Do you

believe Grant was suspicious of your motives?"

"I do not think so. He seemed to think of the exercise as playful."

"That is well. And your impressions?"

"With the power unleashed, the machine would make a fine combat ship. However, a pilot's training would have to be intensive, General."

"Why is that?" Nemorosky asked.

"The dimensions are quite vast at those speeds. In the five minutes of our simulation, we covered almost one hundred and seventy kilometers in linear geography. A simple loop can use up twenty-five kilometers. It requires a new set of mind, as well as a mind able to accept the spatial concepts."

General Nemorosky jotted the information down without comment. He was not a pilot, and he would not understand, Vidorov knew. The man had come up through the ranks as an administrator. But he was quite competent at relaying information.

"This Colonel Grant is what the Americans call an ace, from his time in Vietnam. I have read his record, and it tells me that he shot down seven MiG airplanes," the general said. "Does he live up to his reputation?"

"Quite well."

"You were pitted against an expert, then?"

"Yes, I believe so."

"And how did you fare?"

"I could have shot him down twice."

"Excellent, Dmitri Vasilivich."

Four

Grant was asleep when the phone rang.

It rang three or four times before he decided he was going to have to answer it. He sat up in the bed, leaned against the headboard, and checked his watch: 3:30. Pretty damned early for a business call, he thought.

Gloria rolled over onto her back and moved next to him, her skin warm where it touched his. There was a lot of Gloria. At six-one, she was one inch taller than Grant. They had introduced themselves to the desk clerk as twins the night before. Both were fair-haired, though Gloria's was platinum blond where Grant's hair was more sun-bleached. His hair was trimmed a hell of a lot shorter than hers, too, an expectation of the military. She sported a full, thick mane that begged to have hands running through it. His face was sun-and-wind-weathered next to her flawless cream complexion, but they were both blue-eyed, hers animated and happy and his piercing and decisive. He had a pilot's squint that had placed early crow's feet at the corner of each eye. From there on down, the differences were strikingly distinctive.

He slid his right arm under Gloria's head and around her smooth shoulder. Then he picked up the phone with his left hand.

"Colonel Grant?"

"Good morning to you, Gloomy. I trust that this is a pleasure call?"

"Uh, hold on, sir, for General Billings."

It was a two-minute wait before the bullhorn came on the line. "It took Sergeant Gloom twenty-seven calls to locate you, Lieutenant."

Gloria stirred, sliding the sheet down and arching her back.

"It's not really lieutenant, is it, General?"

"It will be about an hour from now, when I don't see you standing in front of me. What in the hell are you doing, Grant?"

"Studying pneumatics, sir?" Grant prodded Gloria's right breast lightly with his forefinger.

"Uh-huh. While you've been out on the town carousing, losing your paycheck . . ."

"Only three hundred twenty-two dollars and forty cents," Grant protested.

"I've had a crew out here working all night on the ship you bent."

"How bad was it, sir?"

"You didn't look?" the general asked.

"Well, you know, superficially."

Gloria rolled over again, her breasts pressed against him, and moved her hand lightly over his stomach.

"They think it was a vulture you hit."

"The vulture hit me."

"Whatever. Appropriate bird, though. Hit the

60

fuselage above the generator air intake, then went into the impeller. Nine impeller blades broke loose, punched through the aluminum wall, and severed a hydrogen feed line and the umbilical cord to the turbojet."

Gloria got a grip on him and began to stroke. Grant did not think an hour was going to be enough time.

"Maybe we need some kind of grid in the air intake?" Grant suggested lamely.

"Maybe we need your ass out here. I want you off the ground before full light."

Grant had his hands full and was not concentrating very well on Billings.

"You hear me?"

"Yes, sir."

"You hit the deck running. I'm on my way to Washington."

"I'm moving now, sir."

He replaced the receiver in its cradle and turned to Gloria.

"Who was that?"

"My boss."

"Odd hours," she said.

"He's a slave driver. With cab time, I've only got forty-five minutes to play, shower, and have breakfast."

"You don't need me for all of that," she said.

As it turned out, he took a two-minute shower and skipped breakfast.

Lane Walker Billings intimidated most of the people who met him, except for a few congressional representatives who thought they were beyond intimidation.

He was six-feet eight-inches tall and constructed along the same lines as a fifty-five-gallon oil drum. He weighed 285 pounds, but observers would not have been able to spot an unnecessary pound. In his late fifties, Billings had had a silvered head of hair for twenty years, and his dark eyes had stabbed many a subordinate, as well as a number of superiors.

The general had started military life as a marine grunt bellying through frozen mud and flying shrapnel on Korean hills that were important to someone. After he was a civilian again, he parlayed two Purple Hearts, a Bronze Star, three Silver Stars, and a Distinguished Service Medal into an appointment to West Point. Upon graduation from the Point, before there was an Air Force Academy in Colorado Springs, he took his commission in the Air Force. They were looking for a few good engineers at the time. Beyond being a good engineer, Billings had, over time, achieved a pilot's license, polished his skills as a tactical officer, a strategic planning officer, a procurement officer, and a politician. In recent years, the last skill had become more important to military people.

The Experimental Sub-Orbital Program's assigned Cessna Citation put down at Andrews Air Force Base outside of Washington, D.C. a few minutes before noon on Tuesday. Billings was feeling pretty good. He had slept for three hours on the plane and then donned a fresh uniform and highly polished dress shoes. General Nemorosky, who had boarded the plane at Rosie, and then stopped at Nellis to pick up Billings, was also dolled up. Though none of them involved heroic action, the six rows of ribbons on his chest were almost as impressive as the nine rows worn by Billings.

The two of them deplaned to find a staff car waiting for them, and were immediately driven across the Potomac to the Pentagon. Washington in late June was as hot as ever, and a hell of a lot more humid than usual. Billings was coming to like the dry heat of the desert, and he was not looking forward to a reassignment to Washington. Their driver let them out at the River Entrance, below the office windows of the Secretary of Defense. He thought that the Soviet general, though he tried not to show it, was impressed by the sheer size of the building. This was Nemorosky's first time for a meeting within the Pentagon.

"We've got some twenty-five thousand people working here, Pyotr. Both military and civilian," Billings said as they entered and walked through the concourse of E-ring, the outermost of the five rings of the building.

"That makes it a small city, then?"

"Exactly like that," agreed Billings. "Though I'd have to qualify my statement a bit. Not all of them work. Some of them just draw a paycheck."

Nemorosky smiled. "It is the same in any bureaucracy, Lane."

"You'd understand that, wouldn't you? The U.S.S.R. has a large military component."

"But more dispersed. We do not put them all in one building."

Billings found the stairway he wanted, protected by a Marine gunnery sergeant with suspicious eyes. The marine was a trifle incredulous about letting a Soviet general onto the SecDef's floor, but found Nemorosky's on the approved list. He gave each of them badges to clip on their breast pockets, pointing out that

63

Nemorosky's was restricted to an escorted trek to Room 2116.

"I'll keep a close eye on him, Sergeant."

"Sir."

The conference room was a short walk down the second floor corridor, and Billings found Lieutenant General Mark Hansen waiting for them. Hansen was the director of Air Force Research and Development Programs, and he was not allowing the Soviet visitor into his section of the Pentagon. He had a Ph.D. in aeronautical engineering and a second masters degree in administration.

He also had a platter stacked with roast beef and ham sandwiches.

"I didn't think you'd get a chance to eat, Lane."

"You're a hell of an administrator, Mark," Billings said, moving four sandwiches to a paper plate and drawing a mug of coffee from the urn.

"How are you, Pyotr?" Hansen asked.

"Quite well. It is good to see you, Mark."

Nemorosky and Hansen loaded plates, and the three generals sat at the small conference table. In the three years of the program, the three of them had become comfortable with their odd situation. Comfortable, but not entirely at ease. Billings did not think there would ever be full trust placed in the Soviet side of the program, nor, from their viewpoint, would the Soviets show complete trust in the Americans.

Hansen passed them each a thin sheaf of papers stapled together, and Billings scanned through them quickly. Extracted from the R&D portion of the Air Force budget request, the five sheets simplified what they were doing at Edwards into nine paragraphs and

64

two sheets of numbers.

"Hell, that's exactly the same budget for me as last year, Mark."

"Yes. We're all having to tighten our belts, Lane."

"I don't even get inflation?"

"I'm afraid not."

"Shit. I've got two new ships sitting in the hangar, complete with jet and rocket engines, but without any avionics. This will mean that, if I complete those two, I only get to build one new one next year. Hell, we're regressing here," Billings complained. "This puts us another two years behind our schedule."

"All of this also hinges on the Soviet contribution to the program, too, Lane."

Nemorosky ran his finger down the revenue column. "You are expecting the U.S.S.R. to contribute twenty-five million U.S. dollars?"

"That's five less than we're putting into it," Hansen said, "and some of it is in-kind contributions, too— you, your pilots, your engineeres, and your ground crews. But it still comes out around twenty million in hard cash."

And it was hard cash, Billings knew. The Soviet ruble did not buy anything, and Moscow was expected to come up with hard currency—pounds, francs, dollars.

"Very well. I will be seeing the ambassador this evening, and I will have him forward this to the Kremlin. I cannot guarantee anything, of course."

Both Hansen and Billings were convinced that the Soviets would come up with whatever was necessary. They did not want to be expelled from the program at this late date for several reasons. One, at the end of

65

testing phase, they were to gain ownership of half of the craft. Two, they would have copies of the sophisticated electronics and avionics that went into the ships. And three, between them, Billings and Hansen figured the Soviets would eventually convert the aircraft to military configurations.

"We'll keep our fingers crossed," Hansen said. "Now, in an hour, we're going up to the Hill to meet with the Armed Services committee. . . ."

"Senate or House?" Billings asked.

"House."

"Damn."

"They'll want a progress report, and I want you to give them a progress report, Lane. They'll want some performance guarantees about next year's activities, and you'll give them that, too."

"And that's all?"

"Damn it, I've known you for thirty years, Lane, and I know who your political friends are. You're not to go beyond the numbers on those sheets. There's no gravy in your . . ."

"I don't ask for gravy."

". . . appropriation, and you're not to start padding it now."

"I've never padded a billing yet. Every buck I get goes into the program."

"You don't ask anyone on that committee for extra bucks. Not even to get back on schedule."

"What if the committee decides to recommend to the appropriations committee extra dollars for my program, anyway? You going to take it away from me?"

"And finally, Lane. The President told me to specifically tell you that you were not to lobby committee members on your own, or their own, time."

"Shit."

"You come to town, you make your report, and you go back to California."

"Shit, again." Lane Billings narrowed his eyes into daggers.

Hansen had learned to ignore them. "But, before you go back, I'm having a little barbecue tonight. I'd like to have you both there. Janet hasn't seen you in two years, Lane."

"I'll be there. I may take Janet with me when I go, though, just to get back at you."

"And don't go recruiting her into your lobbying effort, either."

"She's a good friend of Polly Enburton, isn't she? Went to school together, I think."

"Lane."

So that was that. They spent forty-five minutes rehearsing potential responses to questions posed by the committee, then took a staff car into the District. The three generals were accompanied by a captain and a lieutenant carrying four big briefcases full of files. Expenditure detail was available, just in case a sticky question came up.

The hearing room was bright with the floodlights mounted on standards for the television cameras. This hearing was not expected to involve classified material, and the media had been allowed access. Five minutes before the scheduled banging of the gavel, the crowd milled about the room in confusion, everybody talking to everybody else. Billings estimated that there were two dozen reporters present, maybe five civilian spectators—probably anti-military activists, and eight

67

of the nine committee members. There were also a dozen committee staffers.

The XSO Program was the only item on the agenda, so Hansen, Billings, and Nemorosky moved right to the witness table, sat down, and squared away their notes. Billings thought that Nemorosky appeared much more comfortable this year, in his third appearance before the committee.

Behind them, the junior officers drew up chairs and opened their briefcases.

Billings knew all of the committee members personally, and even liked a couple of them. The chairman, John Hammond, was a Texas Republican and a friend of the Department of Defense. There were four more Republicans on the committee, two of them staunch supporters, and two of them so-so supporters. Polly Enburton of Iowa was a so-so supporter. She frequently relied on data, rather than patriotism, to bolster her decisions. He respected her for it. Of the four Democrats, Donald Sunwallow of New Hampshire was the most strident, the most derisive of military traditions and objectives, and the most likely to unthinkingly dribble classified information from his oversized mouth in front of God and the Capitol Hill press corps.

By far the worst aspect of his XSO Program, as far as Billings was concerned, was the fact that the politics, and the politicians, were reversed on him.

His conservative acquaintances on the committee were highly suspicious of Soviet motives and inclined to devote the least amount of resources as possible to the project, even though it had been proposed by a Republican president.

The more liberal members of the committee, though usually out-voted, were enthusiastic about the new spirit of Sovict-Amcrican cooperation. They saw the XSO Program as but the first step in an ever-growing set of cooperative programs that would tear down old rivalries and bring increased trust and reduced tension.

The hell of it was, Billings thought, after three years, he still agreed with both sides. His political challenges were sensitive, to say the least.

Chairman Hammond sat down in his center seat behind the long table on the dais and winked at Billings. The general grinned back at him, and the chairman brought the meeting to order exactly as the clock's second hand ticked the twelve. "General Nemorosky, General Hansen, and General Billings, I welcome you."

Hammond was not stupid, giving precedence to the visiting Soviet officer.

They spent almost an hour providing oral support to the budget numbers and responding to questions directly related to the budget.

That out of the way, the chairman opened the discussion to broader issues.

Representative Sunwallow brought up old business. "General Billings, I want to ask if you remember the question I put to you last year?"

"Yes, Congressman, I do. And I provided you with a written response shortly after the hearing."

"Would you please explain the response for the entire panel?"

Billings had anticipated. He beckoned to a page, gave him eight photocopies of a diagram, and waited until the page had passed them out to the committee members. "The question posed to me was: could the sub-orbital be modified to serve as a photo-reconnaissance platform, in addition to its other mission objectives?"

"That is correct," Sunwallow said. "I have always had some reservations about the stated objectives. Not that all of the high-altitude scientific and astro-navigational experimentation isn't important, mind you, but that the cost-benefit ratio was very high."

Billings waited patiently.

"And yes, I know the high-speed cargo and passenger transit aspect is important to the Air Force.

"Just very damned expensive. But now, I think we're really on to something. Go on, General."

"The diagram I just passed out to you shows both a top view and a left side elevation view of the rear compartment of the sub-orbital," Billings explained. "The cutaway side view offers the clearest detail. As you can see, the floor of the compartment rests on top of three main wing root beams. Below the roots is a shallow compartment currently housing gyroscopic equipment and other electronics. And below that, midway back in relation to the compartment, is the intake scoop of the turbojet engine. Still, at the front of the compartment, we have about four longitudinal feet to work with. Our engineers have determined that, without overly affecting the center of gravity, they can shift the gyroscopic package backward and move electronic packs to either side. There are electrical conduits and hydraulic lines that would have to be moved. A rigid substructure between the first and second wing roots would have to be modified. That modification is shown in the top view. Still, we can find

70

the tunnel space we need to mount a camera in the forward part of the compartment, with an aperture port on the bottom side of the fuselage."

"And the camera, General?" Sunwallow asked.

"Its design is classified, Congressman. It is a high-resolution, multi-spectrum camera."

Sunwallow looked at the Soviet general, who was paying close attention to the design modifications, then nodded his understanding. It was, in fact, not a new design. Billings and his aeronautical engineers had had it in the vault from almost the beginning. There were a few tricks like this hidden away, that Billings had not previously intended sharing with the Soviets.

Until the son of a bitch Sunwallow forced him to disclose the design.

Sunwallow went on. "And the capability, then?"

"The sub-orbital would be capable of providing over-flight verification of conventional and nuclear weapons reduction treaties. From both sides," Billings added, "since the Soviet Air Force would have the same craft available."

"And thereby, your sub-orbitals become a factor in reducing military tensions in the world?"

"Only one factor, Congressman."

"But a large one. And well worth the cost."

Billings saw Polly Enburton's chief aide, a woman he thought was named Jamieson, move up and whisper in the congresswoman's ear.

Enburton asked, "How much would it cost to modify the craft, General Billings?"

"If you'll give me a moment, I'll check on that," Billings said, motioning to the captain behind him.

The captain pulled a file from the briefcase and

71

moved to squat behind Billings and Hansen.

Under his breath, Hansen said, "You son of a bitch."

"I didn't start it, Mark."

"Here we go, sir." The captain had opened a thick book to the right page.

Hansen asked, "What's the bottom line?"

"Forty-five thousand, three hundred apiece," Billings said.

"Goddamn."

"Expensive cameras. And I ought to have some contingency, since you're not giving me inflation coverage."

"How much?"

"Hundred grand each."

"Fuck that."

"Seventy-five."

"Okay. I doubt you're going to get it, though."

They all straightened up, and Billings said, "With the three operational ships, the two in final assembly, and the one requested for next year, the total modification cost comes to four hundred and fifty thousand dollars, Congresswoman Enburton."

"All to take some pictures?"

"Yes, ma'am."

"Damned important pictures, in my opinion," Sunwallow said. "I'll make the recommendation to add that to the budget as a line item."

"We'll take it up at the next committee meeting," Chairman Hammond told him. "Any other questions?"

They fielded some more questions, including one about a rumor that one sub-orbital had crashed the day before. Washington was a magnet for rumors. Billings told them about the deceased vulture and the capabilities of the pilot named Grant.

All the while, he was thinking about how Nemorosky was going to have to come up with another $450,000 in matching fund money. The additional bucks would give him some breathing room and let him make a modification he wanted to make anyway.

He would use some old CIA cast-offs for cameras, though. The SR-71 Blackbirds were being phased out, and Billings thought he could latch onto the SCT-134 TIMBAL cameras. He was not about to let Nemorosky's people see anything newer than that.

All he had to do was get the money. For that, he had to line up the votes.

As they left the building, walking down the broad steps, Billings mentally rehearsed the speech he would make to Janet Hansen tonight. Janet would get to Polly Enburton, and that could be the deciding vote. As insurance, however, he thought he also ought to have a private chat with Senator Brock Canfield.

Canfield was a retired Air Force colonel, but he was also having an affair with the other so-so Republican on the House Armed Services Committee, Scott Penrose.

"Stop grinning like that," Hansen said.

"You do appear quite pleased with yourself," Nemorosky told him.

"Hey, I didn't get what I wanted."

"But you may get more than you're entitled to," the director of R&D told him.

"All I want is to have my steak rare."

"And about twice as thick, and twice as big as anyone else's, Lane."

"That goes without saying, Mark."

Five

The engineers wanted to talk about fuel tanks on Thursday morning after XSO-2 and XSO-3 took off for their morning test sequences.

And after Grant had a long telephone conversation with General Lane Billings relative to the degree of Grant's maturity.

The majority of Grant's dialogue began and ended with, "But, General . . ."

"You're a hell of a pilot, Grant, but you're also an officer in this goddamned unit, and you don't walk away from a thirty million dollar aircraft when you've left it in strange country, got me?"

"Yes, but . . ."

"I don't know why you think you've got to screw everything within a hundred mile radius . . ."

Grant had tried it the other way. He had been a relatively serious student majoring in business at UCLA, enrolled in Air Force ROTC because his father, a career military officer, thought it was good for him. He dated the same girl for four years. He and

Marisa Walker were nearly inseparable, and their marriage after graduation and Grant's commissioning was all but foreordained from the beginning. It was a military wedding, tunnel of raised sabers and all. His father came home from Vietnam to attend.

And then Dallas Grant discovered airplanes. He had never had much interest until his aptitude tests put him into flight training, but once there, he was hooked. The marriage lasted three-and-a-half years, until he came home from his second tour in Vietnam and discovered that Marisa was living with his best friend from the university. Grant swore off permanent and involved relationships.

". . . but you'd be in a hell of a lot better shape if you'd settle down with one good woman."

"But, General . . ."

"Because I think that would help you get a grip on your responsibilities—to yourself, to me, and to the unit. Goddamn it, you're the exec officer, and you're setting a terrible example. Shit, Grant, I shouldn't have to have Sergeant Gloom calling all over hell, looking for you."

"Yes, sir."

"And to top it off, I've got to write your damned efficiency report. What the hell do you want me to say? You're at the top of the full colonel's list, and sure as hell at this point, I can't write anything that's going to get you those eagles."

"No, sir."

Billings's voice actually softened a tad. "You're not always going to be a sky-jockey, Dallas. You've got to get a handle on the desk end of it. That's administration, and that's the damned politics. I know you don't

75

give a shit, but as long as you continue to work for me, you're going to start pulling your weight on the ground."

"Yes, sir. I'll give it a shot."

"You'll do more than give it a shot. I want world class, Grant. That's what you're going to give me."

All the fun was going out of his life, Grant thought, after he hung up. He acknowledged the general's concerns, and he even made a minor resolution to get his personal flight plan filed and followed.

Unless something really super came along, of course.

After Dallas Grant watched Major Dennis Blake—a lanky, drawling Texan—and Senior Lieutenant Anatoly Smertevo lift off with the sub-orbiters on the video monitors located in Hangar One's control center, he walked over to where Vidorov was sitting at one of the telemetry boards. There were twenty technicians in the room, working with the telemetry and communications systems. There were, Grant thought, more people involved than necessary, but the Soviets insisted upon having just as many experts involved as did the United States.

Vidorov looked up. "Are you ready, Colonel?"

"Let's get it out of the way, Dmitri."

"You talked to General Billings?"

"General Billings talked to me."

"Anything important?" Vidorov asked.

"Nah."

The two of them walked out into the bright sunshine and around to the side of the hangar where Grant had parked his car. It was a 1967 silver-blue Pontiac Firebird convertible, and there were a few parking lot dings in it, but it ran well from Point A to Point B and did not make many stops for repairs to emissions, computer, or fuel injection equipment because it did not have any. Most of its 350 cubic inches were still connected to the ground, instead of to smog pumps and air conditioning compressors Grant considered unnecessary. They got in and Grant lowered the top first, then cranked the engine. It caught on the first revolution, and the free-flow exhaust rumbled like a diesel locomotive behind them.

Vidorov grinned at him, then waved a thumb at the long rows of Nissans, Buicks, Fords, and Dodges in the lot. Most of them were fifteen or twenty years newer than his convertible. "Why is it, Dallas, that you do not own a new automobile, like everyone else?"

"I'm not into planned obsolescence, Dmitri."

"You are an enigma. You want the best, and the latest, of aircraft, but not automobiles?"

"Maybe it's because I don't have to pay for the airplanes?" Grant suggested.

When the Soviet team, most of whom had never been outside Mother Russia before, had arrived in-country three years earlier, two of their amazements had been the inexhaustible availability of cars and the never-ending supply of paved roads. In the Soviet Union, very few highways were paved beyond the city limits. The Soviet scientists and pilots haunted the used car lots on Figueroa and Vermont in L.A., pooled their resources, and bought several used vehicles. In the last three years, they had steadily traded upward. Whenever they had a long weekend, they piled four or five men in a car and explored the wine country of Northern California, the glitter areas of Nevada, and frequently, the friendly neighbor to the south, Tijuana.

77

Grant drove one-and-a-quarter miles down to Hangar Five and parked in the rear. "By the way, Dmitri, I haven't thanked you for sticking with me last Monday night."

"Appreciation is not required, Dallas. It is simply the job of people in the same squadron, is it not?"

It was kind of a startling thought for Grant. "Anyway, I didn't expect it, and I'm thanking you."

Vidorov smiled, and they got out of the Firebird. They entered the hangar through the small door cut into the back wall.

The large building had been gutted and refinished with drywall painted white. Even the concrete floor had been acid-washed, then coated with a gray oil-and-grease resistant paint. It was laboratory clean. Under the banks of bright fluorescent lights, the racks of digitalized electronic equipment, tools, mobile scaffolds, and white-coated workers looked very efficient. XSO-4 was parked, nose in, at the front of the hangar with the forward fairing of its turbojet already removed. XSO-5 and XSO-6 were at the back, facing the doors, their noses raised so that the technicians could install the Hughes APG-63 radar antennas. The radar was the same as that fitted to the F-15 Eagle and would make these craft slightly different from their predecessors. Most of the differences between the sub-orbitals could be found on the inside, rather than the outside.

Both of the sub-orbiters were in approximately the same state of completion. Topside, except for the absence of access doors, they appeared finished. The XSO numbers were painted on the vertical fins and on the top right side of the delta wing. On the top left was a

USAF insignia, overlaid to the right with a red Soviet star. Below the combination insignia were foot-high letters: "USAF/CCCP." From a view directly above, the shape of the delta wing was strikingly similar to that of the Space Shuttle Orbiter. Unlike the Orbiter, the leading edges of the wing were slightly concave, curved inward, so as not to provide a sharp reflecting line for radar.

The sub-orbitals were completely hand built, which was a major factor in their high cost. The exotic materials used, such as the heat resistant carbon-fiber skin was another necessary luxury. Hangar Six held the massive presses and forming machines for the primary airframe components. In fact, XSO-7 and XSO-8 were located in Hangar Six, if one looked long enough. They were simply stacks of wing ribs, wing spars, and fuselage bulkheads, although a few parts had been borrowed from the stacks at one time or another.

The technicians wandering purposefully about came from a variety of sources. On the American side, Martin Marietta was the prime contractor, but representatives of the five subcontractors—Lockheed, Boeing, Hughes, GE, and McDonnell-Douglas—were also present. On the Soviet side, the design office (OKB) of Mikoyan and Guryevich was the appointed participant. Grant did not think that competitive bidding had taken place in order to determine the OKB which would be involved with the project. Though the pioneer designers Mikoyan and Guryevich, responsible for numerous early versions of MiG aircraft were no longer alive, the OKB had retained their names. In some ways, Soviet and American mentalities ran the same course. Who in the United States would give up a successful brand name, like Boeing?

As Grant and Vidorov came into the hangar, they were met by the chief engineer/designers. Jeremy Restwick of Martin Marietta was a darkly handsome man behind quarter-inch-thick, horn-rimmed glasses. He smiled often, took most problems in stride, and administered his team with a minimum amount of resentment from the managees. His only regret about the program, he had once told Grant, was that he had had to move his family into Rosamond for the duration, renting out his comfortable mountain home in Evergreen, Colorado.

The MiG OKB boss was a swarthy, tall man with a pinched face named Alexandre Murychenko. He had extremely thick eyebrows which shaded his almost-black eyes. Though he appeared somewhat cadaverous and inflexible, Grant had learned that it was easy to get along with the man. He had taken to his job with enthusiasm and with a head full of intelligent and innovative ideas. He seemed to like what he was doing, and he was able to divide himself between the job and the exploration of Southern California life styles. Some of the hard science people Grant had worked with in the past got so wrapped up in their work that they developed tunnel vision, too stubborn to look beyond their own desires. On a Friday night, Grant would see him waving extravagantly at his co-workers from a two-year-old bright red Nissan sports car as he headed for the city glitz.

Grant was an expert in the field of leisure time usage. When he was not in the cockpit, or working with the engineers, he was looking for new friends like Gloria

Whatever-Her-Last-Name-Was. Or lately, spending some time in Santa Monica with Patricia Price. He truly shed his job when he was not in it, probably a trait that Billings would not approve.

"Come on over and look at this, Dallas," Jeremy Restwick said.

The group moved over to XSO-5 and ducked slightly to walk under the wing. The underside of the craft carried all of the propulsion. The turbojet was centered in the fuselage, its intake fairing extending down from the main fuselage, somewhat like that of an F-16 Fighting Falcon. The two rocket engines were contained in long, not-quite-flat, rectangular pods that were mounted to the underside of the wings, about five feet out from either side of the fuselage. They looked like the sponsons under a hydroplane boat. The front ends of the nacelles curved steeply up into the lower surface of the wing, with no openings since the rocket engines did not require an air source.

Currently, the lower side of the craft was exposed, the wing skin and the nacelle skins not yet bonded into place. Finely machined wing ribs, tanks, auxiliary direction thruster nozzles, solenoids, actuators, main landing gear, and incomprehensible bundles of hydraulic tubing and wiring conduits were exposed.

The rocket engines themselves did not take up much space, and were placed at the far back end of the nacelles. Where the Space Shuttle's three main engines each produced 375,000 pounds of thrust at lift off, consuming the External Tank's 143,000 gallons of liquid oxygen and 383,000 gallons of liquid hydrogen in eight-and-a-half minutes, the sub-orbital's engines were considerably smaller. The engines each produced

30,000 pounds of thrust and were substantially less thirsty than the Space Shuttle's engines.

Still, the amount of fuel required was staggering, and the mechanics of storing it aboard the sub-orbital complex. The mix ratio was six parts oxidizer to one part hydrogen, but the storage tank configuration did not follow the same ratio. The volume of the hydrogen tanks was two-and-a-half times that of the oxygen tanks, but only weighed one-third as much when full, because liquid oxygen weighed sixteen times more than liquid hydrogen.

Fuel tanks for the turbojet were placed in the interior leading edges of the wings. The fuselage behind the cockpits and the nacelles ahead of the rocket engines contained hydrogen tanks. The interior of almost the entire wing structure was the liquid oxygen tank, the wing ribs serving as baffles and containing the refrigerant tubing. The coolant system for the combustion chamber linings was another maze of tubing which carried a quarter of the supercooled hydrogen fuel through the combustion chamber linings.

Grant stood underneath the wing, looking up. He was happy as hell that he was not an engineer. "Okay, Jerry, what's a fuel tank?"

"The whole damned thing."

"Believe me we are aware of that when we're riding it. But beyond that?"

"Alex and I have been going through the last six months' worth of flight reports. It struck us that, in almost every landing description, nearly all of the pilots complained about the aft fuselage-heavy landing configuration."

Grant was barely aware by now that when landing he

always gave the craft a spurt of power or a tap of down-elevator to compensate for the dragging rear end. Some aircraft had negative traits of one kind or another that even became quirky, endearing qualities. The heavy wing-loading of a P-51 Mustang made it dicey on takeoff and landing, but did not matter a whit at speed. If anything, P-51 pilots were proud of their ability to handle it.

"It's not too bad, Jerry. Hell, you're one of the guys who put the center of gravity where you did."

Murychenko, who was picking up American idiom quickly, said, "The CG is optimum for takeoff, Dallas, but after we burn off the fuel load, it slides back on us."

"And you have a solution?"

Restwick said, "Alex suggested we extend the front end of the rocket nacelles."

Vidorov looked up at the exposed pod. "How much, Comrade Murychenko?"

"We have 882 millimeters to work with."

"Into which we could install additional hydrogen tanks, one on each side," Restwick said. He moved backward and pointed up. "Then, here, ahead of Number Six spar, we can slip in corresponding oxy tanks."

"They would act as reserve tanks, then?" Vidorov asked.

"You could look at it that way," Restwick said. "At full load on takeoff, the CG is a bit over three inches farther forward. It'll be slightly nose-heavy."

"But at landing with empty tanks," Murychenko said, "we'll have a CG that is twelve millimeters farther forward, or with reserve fuel aboard, twenty-two millimeters ahead of the present location."

"Could you two talk in the same measurement system?" Grant asked.

"In pilot talk," Restwick said, "it's less ass-heavy."

"Gotcha. What's the increased time?"

"Maybe fifteen minutes at cruise."

"And what does it do to payload, Jerry?"

"Reduces it from 1400 to 1200 pounds."

"What do you think, Dmitri?" Grant asked.

The Soviet pilot mulled over. "It is worth the attempt, I suspect."

"Hell, let's do it then."

"We'll have to clear it with the generals. We'd like your support," Restwick said.

"You've got mine."

"And mine," Vidorov said.

"Anything else, Jerry? Alex?"

"Yes," Murychenko said. "One of your reports mentioned a need for increased roll response on thrusters?"

"Yeah, I put that in there. I don't know how Dmitri feels about it."

"It could be helpful," Vidorov said.

"Okay, we're going to give you another fifty pounds on each thruster to start with," Restwick said. "Then, let's go back here."

The American engineer led the way to the back of the sub-orbital and picked up a yardstick with which to point to modifications. "On these birds, we've changed the rocket engine nozzle configuration."

He tapped around, pointing out curvature, aperture, venturi, and other changes that Grant could understand, but would not have been able to see under any circumstance, much less at the end of a

84

wooden yardstick.

"And what does that do, Mr. Restwick?" Vidorov asked.

"Without affecting fuel consumption, we should get a few more pounds of thrust. Overall, I'd expect an increase in cruise speed and top end speed."

"We'll never know it, if you keep us reined in," Grant said.

"We're going to change the software to allow you Mach four-point-seven-five."

"How about Mach five?"

"One step at a time, Dallas."

Grant looked at the nozzle, then toward the front of the hangar where XSO-4 sat, a team of four working on its belly. "You have more of these nozzles, Jerry?"

"We have a spare set."

"The way the money's flowing, it may be a while before we get the new ships off the ground. Why don't you install the new nozzles on XSO-4? Let's find out how they work."

Restwick worked his lips with his tongue as he thought about it. "Well . . ."

"You've already got it in here."

"Hell, why not?"

"And re-program the computer, while you're at it?"

"Goddamned hot-rodder."

One of the benefits of his job was the view, Alain Moncrieux thought. His office was tiny and somewhat shabby, as much an afterthought as was the position of Liaison to Commercial Enterprise, tacked on at the last minute. However small, the office in the *Ministere de la*

Defense had a single tall window that overlooked the *Rue de l'Universite*.

To his left was the magnificent architecture of the National Assembly, and between it and the Commerce Ministry, he had a view of the Seine and the Concorde Bridge. On the last day of May, the trees along the narrow streets and wide boulevards were fully leafed out. Splashes of yellow, violet and red were planted in the flower gardens and window boxes. The view was nice, though at this time of year, anyone with sense and extra francs was already thinking about leaving the city for the south of France.

It was hot.

Only poor students and cheap-fare tourists wandered the streets three stories below him.

"Monsieur Moncreiux?"

He spun his chair away from the window and back to his desk. "Yes, Yvonne?"

Yvonne was his entire staff, but like the view outside, well worth the concentration on quality, rather than quantity. Voluptuously petite, she had been the focus of more than one of his fantasies, but Moncrieux would never think of upsetting delicate office balance. Yvonne was polite, loyal, competent, and very intelligent. Employees like her were quite rare.

She called from her even smaller outer office. "Your overseas call has gone through."

"Merci," he said, picking up the receiver. "Good morning, Henri."

"Hey, how you doing?" Henry Parker said.

"Quite well. And you?"

"It's goddamned hot here in New York. I'm melting the pounds off like I was an ice cream cone."

"The reason I called, Henri, is to find out about your schedule. I am going to be in New York next week."

"Oh, hell. It's not going to work out, buddy."

"Oh?"

"I'm going to be in Tokyo."

Moncrieux felt a pang of regret. There went the New York trip. No matter the heat, he did like to travel to the United States. "Perhaps later in the summer, then? I'd like to discuss our current launch schedule, in relation to the completion date for your next communications satellite."

He could hear Parker's sigh over the line, and there was an overly long pause. "Well, yeah, Alain. We could do that, but you see, I'm stuck right in the middle of talks with Nesei Aerospace about that."

"I see."

"You know they've had three successful launches in the past three weeks?"

"I was aware of that, yes, Henri."

"Well, hell, you know we have to look out for our best interests, right?"

Moncrieux wondered if Nesei Aerospace supplied geishas and saki with as much abandon as his office supplied high-priced Parisian ladies and vintage champagne. "I quite understand, Henri. However, once you have talked with them, could we also talk? Before you make a commitment? We would certainly be willing to make a competitive offer."

"Hell, yes. I don't mind seeing a price war."

The Frenchman flinched at that. The Defense Minister was a rigid man. When a price was set by the economists, he did not like to move off of it. However, he might be forced to give a little since the disaster with *Rapier*.

Moncrieux forced a cheerful laugh. "I do not know about a war, Henri."

"Well, you're going to have to get down in the trenches, buddy. This guy Kyoto is talking twelve mil."

"That is interesting," he said.

"But you're right, Alain. We'll talk again 'cause I like to get to Paris pretty regular."

Perhaps it would be a short discussion, Moncrieux thought, the inflexible face of his defense minister centered in his mind.

Colonel ,Meoshi Yakamata of the Japanese Air Defense Forces orbited his FSX fighter off the northern coast of Hokkaido Island until the controller at Sun Land gave him clearance for landing. The airplane was agile enough, and he enjoyed flying it, but it was a compromise. He thought it barely met its mission objective for close-in fighter defenses. Personally, he would have much preferred a joint Japanese-American effort in producing the F-15 Eagle or, better, the F-14 Tomcat. Those were real airplanes. They were, however, astronomically expensive.

His landing was flawless, as always, and he parked the FSX in line with two Cessna Citation business jets, a French Embraer Xingu twin-engined business plane, and two Bell JetRanger helicopters. All of the aircraft carried the Nesei Aerospace Industries logo.

A Toyota Camry sedan with a driver was waiting for him, and after shedding his pressure suit and helmet, Yakamata donned his uniform cap and got in the backseat. The driver knew where he was going.

Juggling three jobs had become something of a hassle. Yakamata was squadron commander of a test flight squadron based at Hakodate Air Base, on the southern end of Hokkaido Island. His group had been given responsibility for test-flying the FSX fighter during its development trials. Additionally, because of his aeronautical engineering degree and his expertise in aerodynamics, Yakamata had been assigned at NAI's request four years before as the Air Defense observer for Nesei Aerospace's rocket program.

That association had been a career-bender for Yakamata. Within a year, Maki Kyoto had offered him an interesting proposition and he had accepted immediately and without reservation. Yakamata was a consultant and recruiter for NAI, though his name did not appear on any employment contract or payroll record. Instead, his numbered account in the *Banque Geneve* increased monthly, as if by financial magic. By the time he retired after twenty-five years of military service, after the FSX program was finished, and went to work full time for Nesei, he would have over a million U.S. dollars accumulated in his secret account.

For that stipend, Yakamata provided aviation expertise and assisted NAI in its other programs. It was a satisfying arrangement, but not, of course, one that his superiors would condone. His superiors, however, being ardent nationalists, had not complained about the increasing time requirements of his position as JADF observer at Nesei Aerospace. They fully supported a Japanese entry into the space race.

Yakamata got out of the car in front of the administration building, crossed the wide, red-lacquered bridge over a small trout stream, and pushed through the glass doors. He nodded to the pretty girl tending the reception desk, then turned down the corridor leading to the executive offices. One day, he would have his own office in this wing.

Kyoto was waiting with a man Yakamata had not seen before.

"Colonel Yakamata, may I present James Lee?"

They bowed formally toward each other.

"James Lee is from Hong Kong," Kyoto explained.

And therefore Chinese. Was Kyoto going to move into Chinese interests? Probably. His tentacles were all over the globe.

"Mr. Lee was educated at Harvard University and the Wharton School of Business, and is our representative in the United States."

As they sat down in comfortable chairs around a conference table, Yakamata said, "I was unaware of an American branch of the company, Mr. Kyoto."

"It is but a humble beginning."

"Our offices," Lee said, "are located in the Century City complex in Los Angeles."

"Mr. Lee has made an interesting contact with the Radio Corporation of America."

"I understand," Yakamata said, and did.

"On the afternoon of next Wednesday, the three of us are to meet with a Mr. Henry Parker at our offices in Tokyo. He will want to have full knowledge of our program, which Mr. Lee will provide. He will want a tour of the facilities, which you will provide. You may use one of the Cessna Citations."

"Of course, Mr. Kyoto."

"I am certain he will feel reassured if he knows that the Japanese military is supportive of our program.

90

You will wear your uniform."

"Very well."

"He may desire other diversions."

"If so, I shall see to it," the colonel said.

"Very well." Kyoto looked at his watch. "For the next hour, we will devise our presentation to Mr. Henry Parker. Are there any questions before we begin?"

"Do we know anything about Mr. Parker's background?" Yakamata asked.

James Lee smiled. "I will give you a very full file, Colonel. It should help you in designing an entertaining diversion program."

Six

"Four out of five admirals surveyed recommend Trident to their subs who chew missiles."

Jay Leno's one-liner kept repeating itself in Captain Barry Trebarton's mind. The humor had, however, gone out of it long before.

Trebarton and CPO Cattersall were the last two men on the conning tower of the *Ohio*. He took one last look around. There was nothing visible on the horizons, except darkly ominous cumulus clouds in the southwest and one P-3 Orion which was going to photograph them. Though he could not see them, he knew that a couple of Tomcats from the *Kennedy* were at 40,000 feet and fifteen miles down-range. The sea was choppy, with two- to three-foot seas running, and the action caused the submarine to roll in a five-degree arc.

"Okay, Chief, let's close her up."

"Aye-aye, sir." Cattersall went through the hatch and down the access trunk of the sail, and Trebarton followed him, stopping on the ladder to pull the hatch closed and dog it tight.

As he stepped off the ladder, the PA was already blaring, "Secure all hatches! Secure all hatches! Prepare for sub-surface running."

They had gone to General Quarters fifteen minutes before, the lighting was already set at red, and the men were at battle stations. Trebarton looked around, satisfied that everyone was in position. The executive officer, Dansen, was bent over the plotting table.

Lieutenant Mike Belson, standing by at the periscope stack, surveyed the indicator panel and said, "All external and bulkhead hatches show sealed, sir."

Trebarton nodded to him. "Commander Dansen?"

"Nine hundred yards and seven minutes from launch point, sir."

Traberton took three steps to the bulkhead and depressed the intercom button. "Sonar, conn. What have we got for contacts?"

"Conn, sonar. I'm still showing a return on the *Typhoon.*"

The Soviet submarine's propeller signature had been identified by the computers almost as soon as it had started dogging their trail yesterday afternoon. Like the Orion, it was there to observe, also.

"What's the range, sonar?"

"Still two-thousand two-hundred, sir. He's staying well back."

The captain released the intercom. "XO, go to launch depth."

As the order was repeated to controllers, diving planes altered, and ballast taken on, Captain Trebarton called, "Weapons Officer."

"Aye-aye, sir!"

"Do you still want Number Three Tube?"

"Aye, sir!"

"Prepare to launch from Number Three," Trebarton ordered.

And then mentally crossed his fingers.

The mid-June sun was almost directly overhead when Grant reached his planned altitude of 200,000 feet. The bronzed acrylic canopy filtered out the harsher rays generated by the sun and tinted his view of the Pacific. The seas to the south were rougher today, providing plenty of radar noise when he had been on radar earlier. Below to the southwest, wide banks of cloud cover stretched for over a thousand miles. From his point of view, they were white, but Grant suspected that those on the surface were seeing a darker side.

A map of the Pacific Ocean was displayed on his screen, the map selected from computer data storage by the inertial navigation system, which had, on its own whim, checked in with the Navstar Global Positioning System. The GPS was a group of eighteen satellites orbiting at 640 miles above the earth. Constantly transmitting coordinate and time data, the GPS satellites provided ship and aircraft on-board computers with the information necessary to plot very accurate positions. The time was not very damned far away, Grant often reflected, when he and his kind would be unnecessary to the mundane task of flying.

The computer plotted his position on the map as a small green blip. He was 812 miles south of Hawaii and 3127 miles southwest of the North American continent, give or take a hundred yards.

"Y'all are on station," Dennis Blake drawled over the intercom.

"Close enough for Air Force work anyway, Denny."

Blake was in the rear compartment of XSO-3, strapped into a second contoured pilot's seat that had been bolted to the floor ahead of the telemetry transmitters. He was manning the radar console jury-rigged into the compartment. The mission today was to test the Hughes APG-67 radar for the fourth time. It was a modification of the APG-63, altered when they had run into problems with the original configuration. If it went well, the radar would be finally fitted to XSO-5 and XSO-6, and the earlier sub-orbitals would be scheduled for retrofit to the new electronics, integrating the radar system into the pilot's control.

"You have our target picked out, Denny?"

"Nope. She done went down with the fishies. But I marked her last position 'fore she dove."

"What else have we got around?"

"I show three F-14s down around forty thousand and sixteen miles south of us. P-3's orbitin' a mile north of where the *Ohio* went down. Out west, there's seven big boats on the Honolulu track. Several UFO's—probably airliners—to the west, also. Couple of 'em got their noses on Aussie-land."

Grant used his stick to activate thrusters and put the sub-orbiter into a circular track.

"Radar recording deck running?"

"Running."

"You are active, aren't you, Denny?"

"I'm an active man, Colonel."

Radar was all but blind unless it was actively sending out signals to bounce off objects. When it was active,

95

however, the radar, and its carrier, became very clear targets for hostile fire. They were not overtly at war with anyone that Grant was aware of, but old habits died hard. Grant had flown F-5A Freedom Fighters out of the 4503rd Tactical Fighter Wing at Bien Hoa Air Base a couple decades before and had downed his first MiG in the aircraft. But on a night run on Hanoi, flying cover for a bombing flight of Navy Intruders, he had gone to active radar, and fifteen seconds later, a Fan Song radar locked onto him. The threat alarm chirped in his ears as an SA-2 surface-to-air missile zipped right up his tailpipe. It blew out the side of the fuselage and vaporized his starboard engine. Shrapnel from the warhead and the engine cut off most of his weapons, instrumentation, and control systems. The right wing looked like a cheese grater. He made it sixty miles to the east before the aircraft totally disintegrated on him, ejected over the South China Sea, and was picked up by a Navy Sea Stallion Search and Rescue chopper. Still today, an echo of a threat warning receiver sounded silently in his mind whenever he had an active radar.

He checked the chronometer on the instrument panel. "I show three minutes to launch."

"If the Navy is at all like the Air Force, Colonel, I figure we got ten, fifteen minutes to go."

The Lockheed Trident missile that was being tested today had a history of calamities. It was an advanced, three-stage Submarine Launched Ballistic Missile developed by Lockheed, Thiokol, and Hercules to provide a more powerful successor to Poseidon. The early confidence in it had resulted in a Navy program to build thirty submarines large enough to carry it. At the moment, however, the Trident was about ten years behind in its development schedule, and the sub building program was just about as far behind. Sub-surface launch testing had had about a forty percent success rate. As Grant understood it, the major problem was sea current turbulence encountered as soon as the missile left its launch tube.

Lane Billings had briefed them that morning, Nemorosky having been recalled to Moscow, and suggested the Trident test as the exercise for their own radar test. General Billings's suggestions were law.

"Here we go!"

"Got it?"

"Lock on, Colonel."

Grant put the orbiter into a slight bank so he could see the ocean below him and began to scan the area. He found a moving dot that was probably the Orion. Ten seconds later, he found the Trident. It had cleared the ocean surface and its first-stage booster trail of flame was a tiny glare against the sea.

"Two thousand feet, Colonel."

"This one's a go, Denny. The bad ones always blow just above the surface."

As he watched, the missile leaned toward the south, heading down-range.

"Seven thousand."

"Twelve thousand."

He saw the first stage separation a moment before Blake announced, "I'm paintin' two targets."

Grant leveled his wings and came out of his orbit at a compass reading of 185 degrees and trailed after the missile at Mach 4.

Second-stage separation went perfectly as the missile

passed through 45,000 feet.

"This baby's haulin' ass," Blake told him. "Still climbin', still acceleratin'. Sixty thousand."

With a little forward stick, Grant put the nose down and found the target visually. It was now about ten miles ahead of them. He found the chase planes. The Tomcats were hot on the trail, but losing ground.

"What the hell!" Blake shouted.

The Trident disintegrated.

Grant could not be certain, but he thought the missile tumbled first, then blew apart. He had not been tracking on the screen, but the video camera had been running, and they would probably have pictures.

"What'd you see, Denny?"

"Hell, I don't know. There was something funny. I'm rewinding, now."

Switching his radar screen to replay, Blake ran the tape again in slow motion. "At first, I thought it was background flicker off the sea, Colonel. Pretty dim. But in the sweep, it's beginnin' to look like a target. Yup. Comes in from the top and merges with the Trident. Then, I got pieces all over hell."

"Run it in reverse, Denny."

"Wilco."

Grant wished he could see the screen. He pulled the nose up and tapped the throttles all of the way forward. The velocity indicator soon read 4.5.

"What's happening?"

"Hang on, Colonel. This thing's damned hard to read. I've got it backtracked to a hundred thousand feet, but it fades out on me. Shit. Here we go. Hundred and twenty thousand. Lost it."

Grant punched his key pad to switch the screen to

visual and fed in a magnification of twelve. With the remote control, he panned the nose camera through its arc of twenty degrees, scanning the skies above him.

"There we go! Got it again. Hundred and sixty-five thousand."

Grant could not find a thing on his screen.

"She's gone again."

On impulse, he switched his screen to replay and rewound the video tape.

"Shit, Colonel, I can't find it again."

"Okay, Denny. Do this: rerun it again and plot the bearing. Get me a trajectory."

"Wilco."

Grant finally found a picture of the Trident. He had not been tracking the camera, and the image was in the lower left hand corner of the screen. He had also not been tracking in one of the magnification modes, so the missile appeared on the screen as approximately the size of a thin, white eraser. Enhancing the video image would have to wait until they returned to Edwards.

He advanced the tape to the point of explosion, stopped it, and rewound a couple of inches. Leaning forward, he pushed his face near the surface of the screen.

It was almost there.

A shadow.

Against the blue of the sea, just a shadow.

Backing up the tape some more, he stopped it and looked again.

He saw it against a patch of clouds.

Compared to the eraser size of the Trident, it was half of a toothpick.

"There's definitely something on visual, Denny."

99

"I don't doubt it. I've got a trajectory for you, Colonel. Go to one-seven-two degrees."

"Go back to full scan on your radar, Denny. Let's have full range."

"Gone to two-two-zero." The modifications to the APG-63, to fit it into the sub-orbital, gave them a radar range of 220 miles.

Grant increased his rate of climb, and then leveled out at 300,000 feet. Almost sixty miles above the surface of the Pacific.

"Radar don't show shit."

"I wish to hell we had an ignition point to home on," Grant told him.

"It could have come from anywhere, Colonel. Maybe even a satellite."

Putting the sub-orbiter into a wide circle, he searched the black skies with the magnified video camera.

Nothing. Pinpricks of stars, but none of them moving.

At this altitude, relative motion seemed suspended. There was no sensation of their speed over 3000 miles per hour.

"You want me to radio this back to Edwards?" Blake asked him.

"No. Let's keep it to ourselves for now, and off the airwaves." Grant did not want unfriendly ears copying a radio transmission.

He came out of his turn on a heading of forty degrees and began to lose altitude as he aimed for home.

That threat warning receiver was going off in his mind.

There was something up here with them.

Hell, everything was impossible, he told himself, until someone proved it was not impossible.

"Denny, go passive."

"What, Colonel?"

"Shut down the damned radar!"

General Pyotr Nemorosky was suffering the pangs of jet-lag. There were eleven time zones between Los Angeles, California, and Moscow. His mind felt fuzzy, and his eyelids drooped uncontrollably.

It was nine o'clock in the morning, and the general was still thinking that he had missed dinner. No food had been served on the last leg of his trip, an Aeroflot flight from London to Moscow. He was hungry.

General Brezhenki and General Antonovko were obviously not hungry, so he did not bring up his own needs.

His immediate superior, Antonovko, did order a steward to bring them tea, and that was welcome. While it was being poured, he looked around the conference room. It was stark, one large table surrounded by a dozen chairs. There were no windows in this interior room of Stavka, the headquarters of the general staff. Rolled maps were hung at the tops of the walls, none of them pulled down, and one wall held a gigantic screen, now blank.

The steward left quietly, securely closing the door behind him.

"Well, Pyotr Mikailovich," Brezhenki said, "you appear fit and tanned with California sun."

It sounded like a condemnation. "I am well, Comrade General, but the tan comes from California desert, I am afraid. A hot desert."

Nemorosky asked about the families of both generals, and a few minutes were devoted to inconsequentials.

Antonovko produced a small stack of papers and placed them on the table in front of him. "Pyotr Mikailovich, I believe our first order of business is this budgetary request for the sub-orbital program."

He had sent it two weeks before, and they were just getting to it? Bloody bureaucracies. "Yes, General. I recall that the total comes to twenty million, six hundred and forty-five thousand U.S dollars."

"Plus the cost of salaries and expenses for your project team," Antonovko said.

The Americans were providing food and shelter, but he did not argue the point. "Yes, of course."

"It is over a million dollars more than last year's requirement."

"That is true, General, though we must remember that in the first two years, during prototype construction, our contribution amounted to over one hundred million dollars each year. We are now in maintenance stages."

Nemorosky kept his eyes on his superior, but he was intensely aware of General Brezhenki sitting silent at the head of the table.

"So far, the Motherland has devoted almost three hundred million dollars worth of hard resources to this escapade. The costs escalate enormously, yet the program only intends to produce one more craft in the next year."

"That is true also, General. Inflation, cost overruns, re-design costs . . ."

"You begin to sound like an American bureaucrat, Pyotr Mikailovich."

"Perhaps, General. But I have attended each of the budget preparation meetings, and even testified once again before their congressional committees. The request was initially much higher, but was cut by the Department of Defense. Also, it is well to remember that the Americans have paid for the larger portion of the costs."

"Americans always seem to think they should pay for more than their partners in cooperative efforts," General Brezhenki interjected. "I believe they think it gives them substantially more control."

"How much longer is this program to go on?" Antonovko asked.

"The completion date is targeted for two-and-a-half years from now."

"And how many sub-orbitals will have been produced?"

The plan still called for a total of ten craft, so that was the figure Nemorosky provided. "And five of them will become the property of the U.S.S.R."

"Along with spare parts and support systems?"

"Yes, General."

"And, in your opinion, General Nemorosky, the expenditure is worth the result?"

"Absolutely, Comrade General. Alexandre Murychenko and Colonel Vidorov both agree on that. We will have expended perhaps four hundred million dollars on the program, but had we conducted it on our own, it would have cost three times as much."

Brezhenki said, "That is a plus, of course, but only if we find that the craft meet our needs."

103

Nemorosky told him about the new mission of supporting the nuclear reduction treaties.

"Yes. If the treaties proceed to completion."

Though the sentiment had never been voiced aloud to him, Nemorosky well knew that Brezhenki and Antonovko were not fully supportive of the General Secretary's domestic policies.

The commanding general went on, "Karl Yurievich and I have both read your reports, naturally. Colonel Vidorov is certain that the sub-orbital can be converted to a combat role?"

"Yes," agreed Nemorosky, appealing to their military instincts, "and it is a craft that is not covered by the weapons limitation treaties. With a concentrated devotion of resources, the Motherland could have a force of fifty sub-orbital weapons platforms in the skies within eight to ten years. By the time the West became aware of them, we could immediately agree to a non-expansion treaty, locking our own force in place while the Americans do not have even one armed sub-orbital."

Brezhenki mulled that while Antonovko asked, "And what of the other systems we have discussed in the past, Pyotr Mikailovich? What progress have you had?"

"We will have access to their latest surveillance cameras if the reconnaissance mission is approved by Congress. Murychenko says the new Hughes radar system surpasses much of what we are currently using in the Red Air Force. The flight-control computers and the sophisticated software programs alone are probably worth the entire cost of the program development.

There are nothing but benefits for us, General Antonovko:"

"Weapons systems?"

"There are, of course, many tests of new weapons systems and aircraft taking place at Edwards Air Base. However, our access is extremely restricted. I am certain that General Billings selected the particular site primarily to keep us isolated."

"Well, you must keep trying, Pyotr Mikailovich," Brezhenki said.

"I will, Comrade General."

"Very well. That will be all for the present. You may go back to California now."

Dismissed, Nemorosky left the room in relief. He would not be told of the decision made by the two generals. The result of his report would only come as a *fait accompli,* an order directed to him after the Politburo assembled in its Kremlin chamber had made its collective decision.

Lowly, new junior generals were like children to the men who had worn stars for many years. Nemorosky would not worry about it. Instead, he would seek relief for his ravenous appetite. He was indeed happy to satisfy a craving for a good Russian meal. Despite his time in America, Nemorosky had not become accustomed to fast food, and his mouth watered for borscht.

Seven

The mess hall at Rosie served fairly decent food to those living on the base—mostly military people, and the lead item that night was a thick hot roast beef sandwich with brown country gravy. Grant had two of them, along with coffee, but skipped the strawberry shortcake.

The dining room was packed, and the conversation level was as high as morale seemed to be.

Lane Billings, across the table from him, asked, "You have plans tonight, Dallas?"

"Tricia wanted me to come down to L.A. for awhile." Grant had been dating Patricia Price on-and-off for a couple months. She was five years younger than he, no longer had illusions about an acting career that included superstardom, but did work as the chief administrative assistant to a film producer, and did get a small part in a movie now and then. He had bought the video tape of *Million To One* because he liked the scene in which Tricia, playing an on-the-rise woman executive, reads off her superior in very clear-cut terms. In the part, Tricia was both sensual and logical. Much like her role in real life, Grant had learned.

Billings said, "Restwick, Blake, and I are getting up a bridge game."

"What the hell. I'll see her tomorrow anyway."

Dmitri Vidorov, sitting between Grant and another Soviet pilot, said, "One of these days, you will have to teach me to play bridge."

"We play like barracuda," the general told him. "Two cents a point."

Vidorov shook his head. "I will not ever understand the American mentality. You place wagers on the most trivial of events."

"Hey, the Rams against the Forty-Niners is not a trivial event," Blake told him.

By seven-thirty, most of the diners had drifted out of the dining room, headed for their rooms in the barracks buildings or for the recreation room next door. When the last of the Soviets had left, Billings nodded, and he, Grant, Restwick, and Blake rose from the table and took their trays over to the kitchen window.

The four of them left the mess hall and walked in silence across a grass square where a dozen people were playing volleyball, then on across the street to Hangar One. Billings unlocked it.

The hangar had been divided into a control room, a communications room, a computer room, and several laboratories. Billings picked the lab-office where Restwick normally resided, and flicked a thumb at it. The chief engineer unlocked his door and turned on his overhead lights.

"Jesus, I thought our friends from the East were

107

never goin' home," Blake said.

"You have to have patience, Major," Billings said.

"Pretty soon now," Restwick said, "I suspect you're going to break down and tell me what's going on. Or is that too much to pray for?"

"Hang on, Jerry." Billings opened his briefcase and withdrew the video and radar cassette packs from XSO-3's flight. "You tell him, Dallas."

Grant took ten minutes to capsulize the story.

"Right now," Billings said, "it's between the four of us. Let's keep it that way. I don't want anyone on the Soviet team to know about it."

"Because . . ." Restwick probed.

"Because . . . we don't know anything yet. Okay, Jerry, you're the expert. Let's see what we've got here."

"You haven't seen it yet?"

"I know as much as Dallas told you."

Restwick took the video cassette from Billings and moved to the back of the room. Behind his desk, from wall to wall, was a long counter that supported a personal computer, a printer, a terminal connected to the main-frame computer, two video playback machines, and some more exotic instruments that Grant did not care to know about.

"Lock that door for us, will you, Blake?" Billings said.

Blake flipped the button on the door handle.

Restwick sat down in his swivel, castered chair, inserted the cassette, and spent a few minutes finding the right spot on the tape as Grant directed his search. When the toothpick against the white cloud showed up on the screen, Restwick leaned in close to the monitor's screen to examine it. "I'll be damned."

108

The general took one quick look and said, "Let's blow it up."

Restwick cranked up his main-frame terminal and invoked some program that copied the image from the video machine. It now appeared on the computer's monitor. Another set of deft finger movements and a large ring appeared on top of the image. The engineer used the arrow keys to move the circle down the screen and to the left, capturing the toothpick and the eraser within its boundaries. He typed another command into the keyboard.

The eraser blossomed into the third stage and payload module of the Trident. The toothpick grew into a larger toothpick.

Despite the high resolution of the monitor, the image was fuzzy with a coarse grain in it.

Restwick pulled a Hewlett-Packard calculator close to him and tapped away. "If what I remember of the Trident's specifications is correct, in terms of comparison, what we've got here is a cylinder about six inches in diameter and about seven feet long. I can't really see it, but my mind tells me there are three or four small fins near the back. Maybe not if it's meant to operate strictly in the ionosphere."

"A missile?" Grant asked.

"Well, yes. Anything tossed through air or space is a missile, Dallas." Restwick leaned into the screen. "I can't tell if there are any segments to it. The front end is shaped like an elongated cone. There is no obvious propellant trail. At the point when this picture was taken, I suspect the propellant had already been exhausted."

"Explosive warhead?" Billings asked.

"We'll find out." Restwick typed in a command and the printer started to chatter. "How many copies of this picture do you want, General?"

Billings thought for a moment. "You going to store this in computer memory?"

"I can do that."

"Under some kind of security?"

"I can do that, too."

"I don't want any of this getting out. Let me have six copies for now."

While they waited for the printer to complete its chore, Restwick said, "I'm not set up to run the radar tape. What did it look like, Dallas?"

"Denny was on that end of it."

"It looked like it wasn't there, Jer. At first, I thought it was background noise. Dim as hell, and it kept fadin' out on me."

"Could be we have a body composed of some kind of plastic or carbon-fiber. I'd guess the propellant is solid, and the body would have to be able to take the heat of the burn. Your radar image would come off of a metallic nose cone or maybe internal components."

"What about guidance?" Billings asked him.

"Radio emissions. Has to be. It was in the wrong position to be homing on heat or infrared, and the Trident wasn't emitting a radar signal."

"Telemetry, then?" Grant asked.

"Yes. Once Defense has a proven missile, they don't worry much about telemetry readings beamed back to earth. But in testing programs, those rockets are sending continuous telemetry signals to the ground so the ground controllers can monitor them. In this case, the aggressor missile can home in on the signal if it knows the frequency. There would be some scanning operation aboard either the launch platform or the missile itself in order to determine the frequency."

Grant thought about the continuous telemetry signals generated by the sub-orbital. An active radar should not have been his worry.

Blake apparently thought about the same thing. He offered Grant a sickly grin.

Grant ripped the printed images from the printer, separated them, and gave them to Billings. Restwick advanced the video tape, copied the new image into the computer, and enhanced the picture on the screen.

The photo showed the moment of impact, or perhaps a millisecond after impact.

"Non-explosive warhead," the engineer said. "It wouldn't have to be, up at those altitudes. You blow out a bulkhead, puncture a fuel tank, or just cause the rocket to go unstable, and it will tumble, destroying itself."

"Hard metal?" Grant asked.

"I'd guess it's something like the depleted uranium penetrator used in armor-piercing artillery shells. It just doesn't have the high explosive content."

"Son of a bitch!" the general said.

Grant went over and sat on the desktop. "Whatever it is, it's lethal to U.S. rockets. Or, for that matter, sub-orbitals. I'd hate to have one of those things go through one of my hydrogen tanks at 200,000 feet. They'd be picking up pieces of me from Alaska to New Caledonia."

"Nah, Dallas. I don't think there'd be any pieces left to pick up," Blake said.

"This is a bit unreal," Restwick said. "Wouldn't you

consider this an attack on the United States, General?"

"I would, yes. But at the moment, we have two more problems."

"Where is it coming from, and who does it belong to?" Grant said.

"Those are the two problems I'm thinking about. Anybody have an idea?"

"From the bearings I ran, it's comin' from angel-land," Dennis Blake said.

"Which," Grant added, "gives us the possibilities of alien invaders, one of a few hundred satellites in orbit, or just as remotely, another sub-orbiter."

"You don't suppose," Restwick asked, "that the Soviets are secretly building their own sub-orbitals concurrent with this program?"

"Is that possible or likely?" Billings asked.

"Both, I imagine. We're doing all of the engineering here, and they have copies of all the paperwork, blueprints, and schematics. They could be matching us, design for design, at Tyuratam."

"That's expensive when they don't know what the final design is goin' to look like," Blake pointed out. "Unless maybe they have some design twists they're not tellin' us about. Wouldn't put it past 'em."

"That scenario is contrary to what CIA and DIA think they know about the state of their military finances. The Red Air Force is under as much restriction as we are." General Billings moved across the room and sat in a visitor chair, drumming his fingers on its arm.

Restwick started printing off a set of pictures from the latest photo on the screen.

112

Grant said, "We've got some hard evidence. But what do we do with it?"

"I've an idea," Billings said, "but I'd guess you have one, too."

"I'd see if I couldn't get hold of any video or radar tapes from other failed launches, give them to Jerry, and see what he can find. Maybe this isn't an isolated case and we can build up our battery of evidence. With luck, we might find an ignition point, or a weapons platform."

"Just one or two minutes here," Restwick said. "I have a different job, remember? I'm not an intelligence analyst, unless Martin-Marietta tells me I am. You're talking hundreds of man-hours, and I'm one man."

Billings was a pilot and accustomed to quick decisions. Apparently, he had made his. He picked up his chair by the arms and scooted it next to the desk, scooping the telephone out of its cradle.

Grant watched his forefinger punch in the number of the control shack. There would be one duty officer sleeping on a desk over there.

"This is General Billings, Lieutenant. I want you to dig up a ground crew and get the Citation ready to go."

As he hung up, Grant said, "You forgot to have him call in the pilots."

Billings was dialing a long-distance number. "You and Blake are flying it."

"Oh."

"You're both the witnesses. Plus, you're the goddamned exec officer, and you're about to start acting like it."

The next number rang for awhile before it was

answered. "Glad I caught you at home, Mark . . . Yes, I know what time it is there. Twelve-thirty, right? . . . what?"

Billings covered the mouthpiece with his big hand. "House Armed Services Subcommittee is still meeting tonight on Defense budget recommendations."

He listened for a moment, then said, "Hell, Mark, we've got it aced . . . look, I've got something more important . . . damned right . . . I need to have you get on the phone yet tonight and make some friendly calls to people you know."

The general waited through a long reponse. Grant only heard babble.

"This has to be as tight as we can make it, Mark. We need someone from CIA, preferably at deputy director level. Try for the Deputy Director for Intelligence. We need his counterparts from DIA and the National Security Agency. You'd better get someone from the Joint Chiefs, like that assistant to the Air Force Chief of Staff. What's his name, Galdorf? Then, I think it'd be nice to have the CNO, Admiral Zeiman, there. Yeah, this affects him most right now. See if you can set it up for nine in the morning."

Billings cocked his head to one side and held the receiver high, and Grant could hear the stream of blue invective being generated in Washington.

"I didn't know General Hansen knew words like that," Grant siad. "That's Navy talk."

After Hansen wound down, Billings said, "We'll be leaving here within the hour . . . no, I'm not going to tell you over an unsecured line. Besides, you'll want to see the pictures. No, Mark, I didn't take them in Tijuana."

114

When he hung up, he said, "Jerry, I want you to keep one copy of each of those pictures in your safe. I'll take the rest of them, and the cassettes, with me. In the morning, you switch the flight duty roster and put Billy Shepard in Grant's place in XSO-2. Grant, you and Blake get over to your quarters and change uniforms."

Grant looked down at his rumpled flight suit. "What's wrong with this?"

"I'm not a desk jockey," Blake added.

"You're both going to look like Air Force officers for this meeting. Just for a change."

"What if someone here asks us where we're going?" Grant asked.

"You just tell them the Armed Services Committee is meeting. That's true enough."

The Nissan Z-car growled nicely as it climbed the canyon road. The red paint on the hood glistened every time it passed under a street lamp. When he reached the sharp right turn identified as Stone Canyon Road, Murychenko slowed, dropped down a gear, then shot into it, turning some more as the road snaked back in a horseshoe.

He drove up the steeply sloped road for almost another mile in third gear before slowing again, then easing off the road and down a slight incline into the driveway. Pressing the button of the transmitter, he watched as the garage door rose and the light came on.

He never ceased to marvel at the toys available to America's general public. Someday, he intended to buy most of them—stereo systems, CD players, videotape recorders. A home computer. That was something he would never be allowed in the Soviet Union.

Murychenko pulled into the garage and shut off the engine. Getting out of the low-slung car, he closed the garage door and entered the house. Without turning on the lights, he walked through the small kitchen, the small dining room, and into the small living room. The whole eastern wall was composed of glass windows, overlooking a narrow deck built of redwood planks. The lights of neighboring houses shone through the shrubbery and vines down the steep hill below him. The city lights beyond were a carpet of winking diamonds. It was beautiful. Moscow seemed so dark in comparison, and in fact, was dark.

Then he turned on two table lamps, keeping them on their low settings.

The house belonged to Gerhard Strichmann, and it was worth over a million U.S. dollars. Not the house, actually, for it was simply a small bungalow built sometime in the early fifties. The land, however, was quite valuable. Rich Americans bought such properties, demolished the houses, and built new mansionlike structures on the land. Often, Murychenko would drive through Beverly Hills and Westwood and Brentwood and watch as the carpenters and masons constructed more giant residential fantasies.

The concept was unheard of in his homeland. So were the dollars involved. Alexandre Murychenko did not see the value in destroying a house such as the one he was in. It was already so much more comfortable than any apartment he had been inside in Moscow.

Murychenko had managed to get Friday off, and he had a full three-day weekend ahead of him. He was looking forward to it with a great deal of pleasure.

Throwing his suitcoat on the couch and tossing his tie on top of it, he went back into the kitchen and turned on the overhead light. The kitchen was a mess, dirty dishes stacked on the counter and in the sink, a forgotten carton of milk souring on the stove top. Gerhard Strichmann should get himself a maid, Murychenko thought.

From one of the cabinets—made of walnut rather than the painted metal to which he was accustomed—he extracted a new bottle of Stolichnaya vodka, spun the top off, and poured the liquid into one of the few remaining clean glasses. He did not add ice.

He carried his drink out onto the balcony and sat in a black wrought-iron chair with sun-faded blue cushions. Murychenko was so contented, reveling in his loneliness and the view, that he passed two hours without bothering to refill his glass.

At midnight, he pulled on his jacket, got back in his Nissan, pressed the buttons that lowered the windows, and went back down Stone Canyon Road. The breeze, though warm, felt good on his face. He wound his way through the hills at a slow speed. It was good to not be in a hurry.

He took Coldwater Canyon Avenue north, crossed Mulholland Drive, and joined increasing nighttime traffic as he neared Studio City.

More magic. The fantasy of motion pictures.

When he reached Ventura Boulevard, he turned left and drove on until he found the small shopping center on the right. Almost all of the stores were closed, but there were lights on over the parking lot, on the signs, and in many of the display windows. He parked in a slot in front of the private post office. Imagine. Private

117

persons competed with their own government.

He went inside, the only visitor. A steel window had been drawn down over the counter, but the banks of mail boxes were accessible. Murychenko found 3677, spun in his combination, and pulled the door open. There was a single manila envelope, and he pulled it out and slit the seal with his thumbnail.

It took him a while to count it since it was all in twenties and fifties. He missed a bill or two, but when he was done, he thought the amount was right.

Fifty thousand U.S. dollars.

The House Armed Services Subcommittee had started its meeting at two o'clock in the afternoon, and the chairman was determined to go until they were done. Their recommendations had to be finalized and placed before the Appropriations Committee, which was also running behind schedule. October first was coming up fast.

The doors were closed on the nine members and the twelve staffers because classified information was discussed from time to time. The dinner meal brought in by staff had been cold bacon, lettuce, and tomato sandwiches, warm French fries, and cherry pie.

Polly Enburton still felt relatively fresh by two in the morning, when they got to the last segment of the budget. Some of the fights had been horrendous, with members yelling at each other. There had even been accusations of collusion with the enemy or, conversely, war-mongering. Staffers had stayed out of the arguments, but still pressed their own opinions. Polly Enburton did not care for most of the professional staff. Certainly, they had more knowledge of detail than did the policy-makers, but sometimes, they thought they were the final decision-makers. Staff had way too much power as far as she was concerned.

Her own senior administrative assistant, Roberta Jamieson, had learned to not go too far in a debate with Enburton unless she had the data to back up her position. Jamieson was young yet, but coming along. She was perhaps too pretty, with her heart-shaped face, sensuous dark gray eyes, and busty figure. She was a romantic target for other staffers and, Enburton suspected, some wayward elected officials.

The chairman, John Hammond, said, "Finally. R&D."

They did the Navy first, then the Army, and cut nearly one billion dollars out of the request. Enburton argued for some of it, and against some of it.

Overall, the Department of Defense had requested a six percent increase over the previous year.

Enburton turned to the senior administrative aide to Hammond, "Mr. Delkinney, where are we now, in terms of the overall percentage?"

Delkinney had everything in his laptop computer. He scrolled to the bottom, then said, "The increase percentage is four-point-three percent, Congresswoman Enburton."

"We promised ourselves a four percent cap," Enburton reminded everyone.

"Okay, Air Force R&D," Hammond said.

Donald Sunwallow said, "That bomber crap has got to go. I don't know about the rest of you, but they haven't shown me any progress whatsoever."

"So it's delayed," Enburton said. "It's still necessary,

and if we don't move ahead, we'll never have an adequately equipped strategic force in place."

"This is a high-tech age, Polly. We've got thousands of goddamned missiles. What do we need bombers for? And that makes me think of that damned new aircraft carrier we approved. We need to . . ."

"Navy's already decided, Don. Let's not go opening old issues, or we'll never get done." Hammond looked as if he was ready for bed.

With input from some of the others, including a normally pensive Scott Penrose, they finally reached a compromise that kept the bomber research program in place, but reduced it by half. The White House would come unglued at that. The lobbying war would get under way in earnest.

"Now," Sunwallow said, "on that sub-orbital program. We've got to put in some bucks for the treaty verification mission. How much was that, Delkinney?"

The staffer leafed through one of the many volumes of budget documents. "Four hundred and fifty thousand dollars."

"That amount doesn't even register as a hundredth of a percentage point in a budget this size," Sunwallow said. "Put it in."

Polly Enburton was sixty-two years old. She remembered wars, hot and cold, and she was privy to thousands of secrets through her position on the Intelligence Oversight Committee. She did not trust the Soviets one damned bit, and she had resisted this joint program from the start. No matter what anyone else said, and no matter the public image of the Soviet President, she was certain that there were hard-liners among the generals hanging around Stavka

120

who were using this program to steal American technology and ideas.

"In fact, Mr. Sunwallow," she said, "we should not only *not* add to the budget, we should cut it in half, and start phasing the program out. I don't see any valuable military or civilian result coming out of it."

"Oh, for Christ's sake, Polly! We finally get the generals and admirals doing something worthwhile, and you're going to veto it?"

"Unless things have changed dramatically, we all have a vote," Enburton told him.

Scott Penrose spoke up. "I don't know, Polly. It seems a small enough request, and there's a chance it might just serve a beneficial end."

That was a surprise, coming from Penrose. He was pretty much of a middle-of-the-roader and rarely took a leadership position on anything. He had not said a hundred words all night.

Enburton had to think this over. She looked over to Hammond. "Let's take a break, John. I've got to go to the bathroom."

"Fifteen minutes, everyone. Hey, Doris, could you run us down some more coffee?"

Enburton got back from the bathroom in six minutes. The members were scattered around the room, stretching their legs and filling their coffee cups. Sunwallow and his Democratic kin were gathered in one corner.

Jamieson approached her. "Polly, did you know that Penrose has a thing going with Brock Canfield?"

"Roberta, you don't mean it?"

"Yes."

"Are you certain?"

121

"Very certain, Polly. I got it from the senator's assistant, when I went out with him last Saturday."

"A closet faggot?"

"Definitely."

Enburton checked her watch. She still had a couple of minutes, and she looked around the room. The one she wanted to talk to was standing on the Republican fringe. A literal and figurative position for him.

She walked over, grabbed Penrose by the arm, and led him a few feet away. "Who got to you, Scott? General Hansen? Maybe General Billings?"

"Polly, I don't know what in the hell you're talking about."

"They went to someone else, then, to put the pressure on you. How strong are they, Scott? Strong enough to put your name in the paper?"

"Damn it, Polly. . . ."

"Plan on coming out of the closet, Scott. Just as soon as I find a reporter in the morning." She turned away and went back to her chair.

When they took a final vote on the Sub-Orbital Program, the expansion money for reconnaissance modifications was not included in the appropriation recommendation.

In fact, the program was cut by one-third, the first step in phasing it out of existence.

Eight

Dennis Blake took the first tour at the controls, while Grant napped on the floor of the center aisle. Billings sat up the whole trip, studying papers from his briefcase under the ceiling light. But then, Dallas Grant could not remember a time when General Lane Billings had put sleep high on his priority list.

Grant set the Citation down smoothly at Andrews Air Force Base a little before eight in the morning, Washington time. He parked where he was told to park and shut the engines down. Levering himself out of the seat, he stuck his head through the partition into the passenger cabin.

Billings was gathering his papers together. "That shirt looks like you slept in it, Grant."

"I did."

But he got the hint, unzipped his AWOL bag, and changed shirts. He knotted the hated tie, slipped into his uniform jacket, dusted the bill on his cap, whisked the tips of his shoes with his handkerchief, and deplaned. An air force sergeant with a waiting staff

123

car took them directly across the Potomac River and to the Pentagon.

General Hansen was waiting in his office for them, and he looked as sleepy as Grant felt. He offered his hand to all three of them. "Hello, Lane. Nice to see you again, Colonel Grant, Major Blake."

"Good to see you, sir."

"Coffee's over there, and then have a seat. We've got a few minutes yet."

Grant filled a cup and sat down. He looked around the office, which was plush enough, and wondered if he could live with something similar. It had a nice view of D-ring. One could look out the window at people looking back at you from their windows. There were people everywhere, underfoot and overhead. Grant's name was moving too damned close to the top of the promotion list for full colonel, and he was afraid that, if he ever made it, they would take him off flying duty and stick him in a godawful place like this. The thought was stifling, and the loss of air time would devastate him.

Maybe he could get a job flying crop dusters out of Norman, Oklahoma, or somewhere else just as charming. He did put almost half his paycheck into a savings program—CD's, money markets, and a few blue chips. He might have enough on hand to buy a mangled amphibian, and start a ferry service around the Hawaiian Islands. Now that Magnum and T.C. and his helicopter were off television, they probably needed a new ferry service.

Billings rifled in his briefcase as Hansen told them, "Bad news."

They all looked up.

"I've been worried about my B-2 program, so I've

124

stayed close to a committee staffer on the House Armed Services named Dilkenny. I talked to him at seven this morning, and the committee recommendation is to halve my budget."

"Shit," said Billings.

"And Lane, they cut thirty percent out of your program."

Billings sat down. Grant recalled few times when the general's face had displayed as much shock.

"There's no new sub-orbital, Lane. What's left are the dollars to complete your fifth and sixth birds, then begin to phase out the program. It officially ends a year from September 30th."

The federal government's fiscal year ran from October 1st to September 30th. Grant's job suddenly had a fourteen-month limitation on it, and he was saddened. He enjoyed the sub-orbitals. If, by some chance, they made them operational with one of the Air Force commands, maybe he could hang on somehow.

"Let's not fret too much yet, though," Hansen said. "We've still got friends in the Senate, and Lane, I'll want you to stay over for a couple days so we can talk to a few of them. Then, too, the appropriations committee might just ignore some of these cuts."

"Not very likely, Mark. Goddamn. I thought I had it covered."

"I know you did. In violation of my direct . . . hint, too."

"Did Dilkenny break the votes down for you?" Billings asked.

"Same vote on the B-2 and the sub-orbital." Hansen listed the names, some of which Grant had heard before. He was afraid, if he were promoted into a similar job, he would have to go and learn the names of a bunch of politicians. There were enough politics rampant in the Air Force without running around looking for more.

"Enburton and Penrose went against me?"

"You knew they were iffy, Lane."

"Son of a bitch," Billings said. "And on top of that, we've got this."

He tossed the photos on Hansen's desk.

"What the hell is this?"

"That's hostile fire directed at yesterday's Trident launch, Mark. Grant and Blake got the video and radar tapes of it."

Hansen went to the next photo. "You've got to be shitting me."

"No, sir. This is an example of a reconnaissance mission we didn't know the sub-orbital had, but now the damned politicians are killing it."

"Where in hell did it come from?"

Billings told him the story succinctly.

"All right. Damn." Hansen checked his watch, and Grant checked his own.

It was nine-fifteen.

"Okay, let's go down the hall, gentlemen."

Grant and Blake walked behind the two generals, the giant Billings towering over the shorter, but still six-foot tall, Hansen. Billings's massive torso seemed to take up most of the corridor.

Blake whispered to him, "I was hoping to come out of this damned thing with my silver oak leaves. Bastards are ruining that."

"Maybe not yet, Denny." Grant had an idea.

126

After a two-hundred-yard walk, Hansen led them into a large conference room. There were some expensive three-piece suits and some flag rank uniforms standing around. Blake appeared uncomfortable, and Grant understood his discomfort. He himself did not much care for idle chit-chat or serious palaver with the big boys. He had opted to stay in the Air Force to fly, not to seek his stars.

There was one Army full bird present, eventually introduced as Galdorf, and he was the senior aide to the Chairman of the Joint Chiefs. The CIA's Deputy Director of Intelligence had sent his assistant, a moody man named Mayberry. The intelligence director for the Defense Intelligence Agency was a brigadier named Ben Quigley. Grant had met him before. The NSA rep was a retired admiral named Foreman. The Chief of Naval Operations had appeared in person. He was an imposing block of granite named Zeiman. Among the military present, he was the ranking officer.

And without inquiring about a preference from the civilians, the CNO took charge. "General Hansen, you asked for this meeting. You'd better go first."

The bigwigs took seats at the table, the civilians bunching together on the window side.

Grant tapped Blake on the arm, and the two of them found chairs at the side of the room.

Hansen was comfortable enough in that group, Grant thought. He remained standing and said, "Gentlemen, we have stumbled upon a rather startling development. One of our sub-orbitals, while on a test flight, has obtained solid evidence that the Trident missile launched yesterday was destroyed by hostile fire."

127

The CNO's head snapped up and fire lit his eyes. People quit fiddling with their pencils.

Hansen had their attention. "Lieutenant Colonel Dallas Grant was the sub-orbital commander on the flight, and he will now brief you."

Grant had not planned on briefing anyone, but he stood up and took them through the sequence. He answered questions as Billings passed the photographs around. He introduced Blake, and Blake explained the radar tracking.

Then he sat down and listened to the intelligence people spend an hour going through the same kinds of questions they had raised the previous night at Rosie.

General Ben Quigley of DIA said, "I can show you our inventory of every satellite and piece of junk in space, placed there by every nation with the ability to do it. And I can pretty much swear that there isn't one of them capable of launching this kind of missile."

"You think it's another sub-orbital, Ben?" the CIA man asked.

"It has to be. Lane, did you account for your other aircraft?"

"All on the ground, Ben."

"Who else has the capability?"

The men around the table came to last night's conclusion. The only real possibility was a concurrent building program by the Soviets.

"Are your Soviet counterparts aware of this?" Zeiman tapped his thick finger on the photographs.

"No, Admiral, they're not," Billings said. "I want evidence enough to definitely exclude them before I talk to General Nemorosky."

"Good," Zeiman said. "Lane, you've had more time

128

to think about this. Do you have a recommendation?"

Billings rose from his chair and walked around the room as he spoke. "Yes, Bart, I do. It seems to me that the mission of this unknown aggressor has two objectives. One, for every Air Force or Navy launch failure, the cost of our program is doubled. It uses up our resources, and we've lost some damned expensive satellites. And two, it discredits our programs immensely. We receive a hell of a lot of media coverage each time we blow a launch. When we're successful, of course, nobody cares."

The moody CIA man interrupted, "General, you don't mean you'd include *Challenger?*"

That stopped Billings's pacing. "Mr. Mayberry, I hadn't thought about it, to be truthful. But it's something more to look at."

He went back to circling the room. "What I'd like to suggest, Bart, is a full back-examination of every aborted launch. We want to keep it as quiet as possible for now, but I think we want to have Air Force, Navy, and NASA provide DIA with their video and radar tapes. Let's find out if we can one, locate a similar hostile missile on the tapes, and two, locate a launch platform."

Grant raised his hand high, feeling much like a third grader.

"Colonel?"

He stood up. "Admiral, I'd like to recommend an expansion of that investigation. The French have lost some rockets. I don't know about the Soviets or the Japanese. They may well be hiding their mistakes from the public. If one or two of them are also suffering casualties, it might help to define our aggressor."

"Good idea, Colonel," the CNO said. "However, I doubt that any of them are going to provide the tapes we need. What can we get out of NSA, DIA, or CIA?"

Foreman said, "NSA should have the audio tapes of radio communications during any launch. Perhaps we have some of the telemetry data also. Voice would have to be translated and telemetry decoded."

"We've been covering every launch in the world by KH-11 satellite, if the satellite happens to be in the right place," Mayberry told them. "I'll get on our people and see what we have."

"And DIA tries to get a look at any launch with military overtones," General Quigley added. "There may be some video and radar coverage obtained by ships at sea or by aircraft, if we could get them into the area."

"Good," Bart Zeiman said. "Let's cull those inventories and get the data over to DIA. Ben, you'll coordinate the analysis?"

"Yeah, I'll do it. How about our future moves, though? Lane?"

Billings said, "I'd like to get some full-time Keyhole coverage of Tyuratum and any other sites in the Soviet Union that could support a sub-orbiter operation. Let's find out if they've got 'em."

"Keyhole" was the nickname for the KH-11 spy satellites operated by the CIA. Their multi-spectral and infrared sensors, along with a digital imaging capability, gave them real time performance. The images captured by the spies were relayed through the Defense Satellite Communications System to ground receivers located at the National Photographic Interpretation Center.

Mayberry said, "We've also got Aquacade in geostationary orbit over the Indian Ocean. That's given us steady monitoring of the Tyuratam and Plesetsk launch complexes. In fact, I think I saw some report that Tyuratam aborted a launch several weeks ago."

"Good," Admiral Zeiman said. He was fond of the word, but Grant was not certain whether the Chief of Naval Operations thought the data availability or the Soviet launch abortion was good.

"Maybe not," Mayberry countered. "I'm going to have to have some dollars. My budget won't cover moving a bunch of KH-11's around. I can't call the JPL until I know I can pay for it."

The Jet Propulsion Laboratory in Pasadena was responsible for programming orbital changes.

Zeiman said, "Colonel Galdorf, you'll be responsible for briefing the full membership of the Joint Chiefs, the SecDef, and the service secretaries on this. I want an analysis of whether or not we should suspend future launch dates until we get to the bottom of this. I also want you to prepare a request for contingency funds."

Grant raised his hand again.

"Colonel Grant?"

"I'm not sure if it's my place, Admiral, but I have another suggestion."

"Shoot."

Both of his immediate superiors, Lane Billings and Mark Hansen, eyed him speculatively.

He pressed onward. "The sub-orbital program belongs to Air Force and Soviet research and development divisions until it is either canceled or converted to an operational mission. Yet, from what I've heard this morning, we seem to think the aggressor is most

131

likely operating from a sub-orbiter. If it exists, we haven't seen it, and that probably makes it immune to missile attack. The only counter-weapon the United States has available is the sub-orbital. But it is unarmed and not approved for operational missions."

The light dawned on Billings's face.

Hansen frowned.

Admiral Zeiman took some time studying the rows of ribbons over Grant's breast pocket. There were some Silver Stars there in addition to the Distinguished Flying Cross with the pips that indicated it had been awarded three times. He asked, "Colonel, are you telling me that the sub-orbital could take on a combat role? Are you that sure of yourself?"

"Yes, sir. I have almost six hundred hours in the craft, and my pilots have nearly the same amount of time. I don't have any qualms about taking it into combat."

"Lane?"

"I haven't flown it, Bart, but I'll back up anything Colonel Grant says. And I'll tell you what we need." He looked at Hansen.

"Go ahead," Hansen told him.

"First of all, I need legality. In addition to our status as a research and development unit, I'll have to have at least temporary approval as an operational unit."

"We can transfer the squadron to a Tactical Air Wing," Zeiman said.

"I'd prefer stand-alone, and I damned sure want to retain command."

"I don't know. The TAC commander will have something to say about that."

"Bart, TAC doesn't have the first idea about sub-orbital operations."

"We'll have to see what happens, Lane. And all of this will have to go to the President. That's where the final say will come from."

Scowling, Billings went on. "I need emergency funding to complete my next two orbiters."

"What's the schedule?"

"They're both ready, except for some of the avionics, which have been ordered and are available, but not yet delivered. That was scheduled for after October one, when I get my next appropriation."

"Just a loan, then? From the JCS contingency to your program? You'll pay it back?"

Grant could tell that Billings did not want to, but he agreed. "Yes, sir. Then I need to have some ordnance experts assigned to the program, along with the necessary funding. We'll have to crash-design an armament system. That, I can't pay back."

Grant was still standing.

Admiral Zeiman looked over at him again. "You have more, Colonel?"

"One more thing, sir. You mentioned awhile ago the possibility of suspending launches?"

"I told Colonel Galdorf to look into it."

"I think we should proceed with all of the launches, Admiral."

Zeiman pursed his lips. "Tell me why."

"Cancellations will only alert the aggressor that we're onto something. It would be better if I were up there at sixty miles altitude watching over a launch."

They all looked at him.

"Use the launch as bait?"

"Yes, sir."

"Shit," Admiral Zeiman said. "That's another thing. We're going to have to ask the President to specify rules of engagement."

"Sir," Grant jumped in, "please don't make it, 'fire if fired upon.' Up there, one shot may be all I or my people will have."

"I'll make note of it, Colonel. Okay, good. We have anything else?"

There were a few questions to clarify assignments, then the admiral broke up the party.

Going back down the hall toward Hansen's office, Billings said, "Damned good job, Dallas. There's hope for you yet."

"Remember that everything said by anyone this morning is classified, Lane," Hansen said. "Grant, you and Blake remember that, too."

"I'll wait until it's unclassified," Billings told him, "then I'll take it and shove it down Polly Enburton's goddamned throat."

Dmitri Vidorov was tired. He, Senior Lieutenant Valeri Zbibari, and Major Shepard had been up for over four hours in the afternoon. The test sequence involved shutting down the rocket engines at altitude and experimenting with glide ratios, deterioration of velocity, and re-ignition of the engines. The latter test could be nerve-wracking.

Especially nerve-wracking because the ebullient Billy Shepard kept the radio alive with inane chatter. "Ready for ignition . . . I've got my fingers crossed . . . I've got my legs crossed . . . pray for me, guys. Whoops. You guys don't pray, do you?"

After dinner, Vidorov went up to his single room in Residence Hall 120A. His room was above Dallas Grant's room, on the second floor, near the head of the stairs, and it was comfortable enough. Two rooms had been combined to give him a bedroom and a sitting/study room. The bathroom and shower facility was down the hall, but he did have a small refrigerator.

He took a cold bottle of vodka from the refrigerator and poured himself a small drink, turned the radio to a classical music station from Los Angeles, and then collapsed into the lone easy chair. It was Friday night. Most of the Soviet team had already left for Los Angeles or other weekend destinations. Vidorov had gone with them to Los Angeles several times, and once to San Francisco, but he was not particularly enthused about visiting topless bars. Vidorov's wife, Nadia, lived in their apartment in Moscow, and offered him more, he thought, than the visual sights of North Beach in the City by the Bay. He frequently missed her, despite her weekly letters and their monthly telephone calls.

Further, he thought it disgustingly ironic that a New Soviet Man who deplored the immorality and depravity of America should be among the first to push his way to the edge of the stage for the dubious pleasure of stuffing dollar bills in G-strings.

He had a nineteen-inch color television set in his room. Nadia would have liked that—their own set was black-and-white, but Vidorov had yet to find many programs of substance among the countless channels available. The situation comedies were constructed of air and sexual innuendos that were difficult to grasp, and the dramas were composed more of automobile pursuits than of drama. He did enjoy most of the

135

Sunday news shows, and if he was not flying, he usually watched *Nightline*. Vidorov was not entirely consumed by the Soviet way of life; he liked the openness with which American commentators and their guests discussed current politics and the goals of the military and the crises in everyday life. He would like to see TASS and *Pravda* and *Izvestia* allowed many of the same latitudes.

When his drink was finished, Vidorov got up to make just one more.

There was a rapping at his door.

He opened it on Nemorosky.

"General Nemorosky. When did you return?"

"About an hour ago, Dmitri Vasilivich."

"Come in, please. Would you care for vodka?"

"Very much."

The general looked entirely fatigued. There were gloomy dark bags under his gray eyes, and his shoulders slumped in apparent defeat.

Vidorov made the drinks, then sat in the desk chair in order to leave the single soft chair for his superior. Nemorosky sat in it, sighing. He took a long sip from his glass.

"I am not made for round-the-world flight, Dmitri Vasilivich. My wristwatch says 'California,' but my mind debates between Sweden and Greenland."

Vidorov nodded his understanding.

"Have you seen General Billings?"

"No. I believe he and Grant were told to return to Washington. It is something to do with their congressional committee, I think."

"I looked for him, but he was not in his office or in his room."

136

"How was your meeting?"

"As I expected it to be. I believe Brezhenki will recommend that the funding be approved. General Antonovko sends his regards."

Dmitri Vidorov had served with General Antonovko in Afghanistan.

"And your Nadia sends her love."

"You saw her?"

"No, but I called while waiting for my flight at Sheremetyevo."

"Thank you, General."

Nemorosky waved it off and sipped more of his vodka. "I believe we have been put on notice."

"Comrade?"

"Nothing was stated outright, naturally, but I left Stavka with the distinct impression that you and I, and all of us, could be doing more to acquire technical knowledge outside of that which we have already provided."

"Then, General, they should have sent KGB or GRU people as part of our team."

"They tried, do you know? But General Billings was allowed to screen the roster. For some reason, he permitted only those of us with scientific, administrative, or aviation backgrounds to join the team."

Vidorov smiled.

"We must do better, Dmitri Vasilivich."

Vidorov shrugged.

"Or I suspect that we will be recalled to assignments less pleasant than this one."

And Vidorov sighed. He very much wanted to return to his homeland, but not to some posting that would keep him from Nadia for another three years.

Nine

On the morning of the sixteenth of July, Alain Moncrieux had already ruined his first silk shirt of the day by the time he reached his office. He was drenched in perspiration, and he lamented the distressing fact that he was so far behind in his quota that it was unlikely he would get a holiday in cooler climates.

In reality, Moncrieux did not have a quota; he had an "expected performance." He was behind in his expected performance.

It was not his fault—he did not blow up the rocket machines, but his income was suffering dreadfully. In the past three years, his expenses had risen to meet his income, and when the income disappeared, the loss of expensive dinners, jaunts to Switzerland and Italy with beautiful companions, and monthly visits to his tailor had had to be curtailed. The monthly payments on his Lamborghini Countach now looked astronomical. And they were.

Yvonne had the coffee ready, and as she brought his first cup in, he marveled at her appearance. Fresh as a daisy in a pressed yellow sundress with a scoop neck that provided a glimpse of yet more freshness, she looked as if she had just left Switzerland.

"*Merci.*"

"Do not worry so much, Monsieur Moncrieux. It is not good for your health."

"Does it show?"

"I am afraid that it does. Let me have the list."

Moncrieux gave her the list of the telephone calls for the day, and she went back to her cramped office. He then opened his new copy of *Aviation Week*, which he had pored over the night before, and found the item he had marked with red ink in the margin.

Drinking his coffee, he re-read the article, with occasional glances out the window toward the serene river. A young couple stood near the middle of the Concorde Bridge throwing something in the water. Flower petals? How romantic. How simple.

Sometimes, Moncrieux wished he were back at the university, pursuing young ladies with more zeal than he had pursued his studies.

Yvonne announced his first call, and he picked up the telephone. "Sir Neil?"

"Hullo there, Alain."

Moncrieux had a good working relationship with Sir Neil Holmes, a man he had known for fifteen years. They took care of the innocuous small talk about the Londoner's family in five minutes.

"I have been reading, Sir Neil, about the intention of the British Broadcasting Corporation to deploy another television relay satellite."

"Yes, that's true, Alain, though the announcement is not formal as yet. These snoopy magazine reporters seem to have an inexhaustible supply of people who enjoy leaking important information."

"Do you have a timetable available as yet?" Moncrieux asked.

"There is nothing finalized, but perhaps in late August or early September."

"That soon? That is wonderful, Sir Neil."

"The success of the last satellite—the public response —compelled us to move ahead with our plans."

"And I am quite certain that you recall that it was our joint enterprise that resulted in the BBC's success," Moncrieux said.

"Of course."

"When would be a good time for us to get together, Sir Neil?"

"We can discuss the possibilities, naturally, Alain, but I should alert you to the fact that we are also examining the feasibility of using Nesei Aerospace Industries for this launch."

"I see."

"Your people did lose another Rapier the first of the month, did they not, Alain?"

"Yes. An unfortunate incident." When a payload did not achieve orbit, Moncrieux received but fifteen percent of his commission.

"Well, we can discuss it, anyway, I suppose. I have my calendar right here. How about on the twenty-second of this month?" Holmes suggested.

"That would be . . . let me see . . . yes, I can work that in, Sir Neil. I will hop over on the seven A.M. shuttle on the morning of that day." In fact, his calendar for July was all but blank.

When he hung up the telephone, Moncrieux was

happy to have the appointment, but still not entirely optimistic. He had lost Henry Parker to Nesei Aerospace. The defense minister would not even consider matching NAI's twelve-million-dollar fee. When Moncrieux had pointed out that twelve million was better than nothing, the minister had reminded him that a Frenchman was not a beggar.

Not yet, anyway.

He waited for Yvonne to tell him that his call to Schmidt in Bonn was ready, but a few minutes later, she appeared in the doorway.

"Monsieur Moncrieux, there is a gentleman to see you."

"Oh?"

"A man named Francois Duchatrcau."

He gave her a quizzical look.

She returned it.

"Please show him in, Yvonne."

The man who entered his office was small and dark, with sharp planes to his face and with flinty eyes. He would not be an interesting conversationalist.

Moncrieux stood up and extended his hand. "How may I help you, Monsieur Duchatreau?"

The man did not shake his hand, but did flip open a leather credential folder and held it up for Moncrieux to read. "I am with the *Service de Documentation Exterieure et Contre-Espionage.*"

SDECE. The French intelligence organization.

"I am going to go through all of your records," the little man told him.

Alain Moncrieux felt mildly ill.

*   *   *

141

Colonel Meoshi Yakamata functioned as the host for Mr. Henry Parker for the day preceding the launch. Maki Kyoto was supposedly unavailable due to the press of business, but in reality had simply removed himself to the Tokyo offices of Nesei Aerospace Industries. He did not like to waste time in a diplomatic role. He had once told Yakamata that there were too many ideas to refine and too many profits to be made to allow other people to dictate one's schedule. Discipline was required.

Frequently, Yakamata became irritated at Kyoto's little lectures. As a military officer, Yakamata was quite familiar with discipline and thought that his own was superior to that of Maki Kyoto. He also thought that the president's life had been much softer than his own. Yakamata had been required to fight for every grade in school, for the scholarship that took him through college, for the positions of trust in the Japanese Air Defense Forces. *His* father, a struggling merchant, had not been able to spread yen in his pathway.

And yet, Meoshi Yakamata, a man among military men, felt inadequate in the presence of the industrialist. The power of command was not equal to the power of wealth. And so he played the subservient role expected of him because one day it would lead to that greater power.

Yakamata thought Henry Parker somewhat crude in appearance and manner, but he also thought that the man was playing his own role of slightly inept American businessman. Underneath the veneer was a sharp mind, revealed occasionally in the man's calculating eyes. He seemed to bumble his way through negotiations, but he also seemed to come out of them with what he wanted.

Just then, in the comfortable executive dining room located in the administration building at Sun Land, the two of them worked on a light lunch of tea, salad, and sushi. Parker pointed at his plate with one of his chopsticks. "Now what's this here, Colonel?"

"That is squid, Mr. Parker."

A grimace. "Well, hell, I'll give it a try, I guess. Always something new to learn."

Yakamata did not think so. The man handled his chopsticks as if he had been doing so for twenty years. The colonel thought that the American presented himself as something of a country bumpkin while hiding his intelligent grasp of the script.

"You get paid by Nesei for squiring me around like this, Colonel?"

"I receive a free lunch," Yakamata said, smiling. Parker had been told, the first time they met in the Haito Building in Tokyo, that Yakamata was simply an observer for the Japanese Air Defense Forces.

They completed their lunch in twenty minutes, then moved outside to where a driver waited with a Toyota Camry. Settling into the back seat, they did not say much as the driver pulled away from the administration building and rolled down the curving drive.

Parker commented on the landscaping.

Yakamata explained some Japanese culture.

His experience was military, concerned with discipline and orders and airplanes. This diplomatic, salesman's role was new to him, and Yakamata was not yet comfortable with it. He frequently felt at a loss for words, and he relied chiefly on courtesy to get him through a day. Kyoto had told him, however, that that was the best tactic. People like Henry Parker spoke mainly to hear themselves speak. What they wanted most in life, or in business, was a good listener.

The Toyota climbed the low hill that hid the airfield from the administrative/residential complex, then started down the other side. Ahead of them were the laboratories and assembly buildings lined up in a row parallel to the single long runway. The runway ran northeast to southwest, with the structures on the southern side of it. At the foot of the hill, the driver turned right onto the road leading to the launch area. They drove alongside the assembly buildings, then the small terminal and parked aircraft on the northern end of the airfield, skirted the end of the runway, and continued to the north. The route kept them away from the south end and the hangars containing classified development work.

Twelve minutes later, after a six-kilometer trip through rolling hills, they passed the Final Assembly Building and went directly to Launch Pad Two. The Emperor rocket stood regally on its base, grasped tenderly by the clamping arms of the gantry. Two dozen people moved about, seemingly without purpose, preparing the missile for its flight in the morning. Five hundred meters away, at Launch Pad Three, another Emperor was being raised from its cradle on a flatbed railroad car into place on the pad by a monster crane.

When the Toyota stopped near the gantry crane, they got out.

Parker said, "I can't believe how clean you people keep this place."

"Mr. Kyoto might be considered somewhat fanatic on the subject, Mr. Parker. He believes that cleanliness represents good maintenance."

Parker swept his hand toward the base of the gantry, which was immaculate. After a launch, scrubbers with high-pressure steam hoses cleaned away the sooty residue. "I wish my house was that clean."

In fact, Parker did not have a house. He owned a large apartment on Park Avenue in New York. According to the thick file that James Lee had accumulated, Parker was not married and did not have a family. If he enjoyed himself with liquor and, as Yakamata had learned, multiple women, there was nothing in the way he took his pleasures with which to apply leverage. He merely accepted the gifts provided him as if they were an expected perquisite of his job.

They took the gantry elevator to the top level and stepped out on the fenced steel mesh deck. A light breeze was blowing. Parker did not, as many people did, show any sign of dizziness as a result of the height.

Parker had wanted one more look at his precious satellite before they sealed the cargo module. Yakamata introduced him to the senior launch supervisor, then stood aside. The supervisor led him across a steel-grate bridge and through an open hatchway. They disappeared inside.

Twenty minutes elapsed before they re-emerged into the sunlight. Parker had a happy look on his face, and that was important.

Yakamata smiled at him. "Everything is satisfactory, Mr. Parker?"

"Abso-damned-lutely, Colonel Yakamata. You people run a tight ship."

Yakamata wondered if the man actually understood anything that he had seen inside the module. It was a maze of structural girders, electronic black boxes, and pyrotechnic devices to explode retaining bolts and eject the communications satellite from the module once it was in space. However, Henry Parker's file said that he had an aerospace engineering degree, so Yakamata supposed that the puzzle of the module was clear to him.

They took the elevator down, made a sight-seeing circuit around the gantry and the rocket, then returned to the automobile.

As the driver pulled away, Parker looked back through the rear window. "I'm about as eager as a kid waiting for Christmas."

"It won't be long now," Yakamata said, as if he were the father.

"Damned tootin'."

"What would you like to see, now?"

"Ah, hell, I think I'll just go back to that little cottage you got me in, maybe take a bath and a nap. I'm sure you've got more important things you could be doing, Colonel."

Yakamata shrugged. "I'd be happy to show you through some of the assembly buildings."

"Naw. That little gal, Susie, she said she'd come over and keep me company this afternoon."

"As you like, Mr. Parker."

Coming down the low hill to the airfield, Yakamata looked ahead and swore under his breath.

The massive doors of Hangar C, one of three fenced into a separate complex on the south end of the field, were gaping wide open. Through the opening, under

146

the glaring fluorescent lights, could be seen the snouts of four matte black aircraft. Though they were a couple kilometers away, they were clearly visible and clearly exotic.

Yakamata tried to think of something to say, to divert his guest's attention.

Parker sat up in his seat. "What in hell's that?"

"Nesei Aerospace is conducting a development program for the JADF."

"Yeah. I'd like to see those."

"I am afraid that they are highly classified, Mr. Parker. And I do wish you would not mention what you have seen to anyone."

As if happy to play the part of a confidant, Parker said, "You betcha. I can keep my mouth shut."

"I, and Nesei Aerospace Industries, would very much appreciate it."

Kyoto was going to be an angry man, and Yakamata was going to severely chastise the man responsible for ignoring procedures.

"Now I understand why your government put you on the job over here, Colonel."

Yakamata shrugged, accepting the explanation.

Maki Kyoto was not merely staying away from Henry Parker. He was conducting a previously scheduled meeting of the board of directors of Nesei Aerospace Industries.

NAI's Tokyo offices were housed on one floor of the Haito Building a mile away from the Ginza. The interior appointments were Westernized, simple, and obviously expensive. The board room was large, with walls finished in delicately textured grass cloth. A long boat-shaped table painstakingly crafted of cherrywood dominated the room. Around it, ten soft tan leather chairs contained ten of Japan's most powerful men, if Kyoto included himself.

Each of the nine men waiting for his report represented nine of the nation's industrial and electronic giants. Those nine corporations had each invested 250 million U.S. dollars in Nesei Aerospace Industries. In effect, no real person owned NAI; the two-and-a-quarter-billion-dollar company was owned by other companies. In effect, nine other boards of directors had placed their unwavering trust in the abilities of Maki Kyoto, who had previously been employed by Saito and then by Mitsubishi as an executive vice president.

These men had one expectation, and that was that they expected him to perform at the levels he had so glowingly promised when he proposed the creation of NAI.

But he was behind schedule, and therefore working in a defensive environment.

After the trivia of accepting the minutes of the previous meeting and setting the agenda for today, Kyoto presented his report.

"Gentlemen, since the first launch of the Emperor rocket, the company has conducted nine successful launches. We are currently averaging about one launch per week, and we have served eight clients. As we continue to build our client base, we will eventually move to the expected schedule of two launches per week."

"Mr. Kyoto," said the steel man, "at this point in time, you were already to have been at two launches per

148

week. By March of next year, it was to have been three."

"Unfortunately, we have met with more reluctance than expected in terms of clients leaving their previous vendors," Kyoto explained.

"For what reason?"

"It is simply loyalty for most, with perhaps a touch of nationalism," the CEO explained. He was already losing control of his report. Now, the presentation would be reactive, and Kyoto did not like that. "We have developed the most efficient, lowest-cost, space transportation system in the world, yet the very people who popularly seek the lowest bid are hesitant to accept the facts."

"What is the current cost per launch?" the automobile man asked.

"Fourteen million, two hundred twenty-seven thousand American dollars."

"And revenues to date?" the banker asked.

"One hundred twelve million."

"We would have fared better simply by placing our money in an interest-bearing account in your bank," the electronics man told the banker.

No one laughed.

"Mr. Kyoto, please detail the revenues," the banker ordered.

Kyoto was prepared for the question. "For the two payloads of the Japanese government, we charged the exact costs. From the beginning, we set a policy of not profiting from national needs."

"That is true," the steel man said.

"For the others, we billed each twelve million."

"That is far below cost," the ship builder said. "Why is that?"

"To gain trust. To gain the client. Once we have the client in our fold, he will not leave, even as the price escalates." Kyoto played the hole card. "Our success ratio is one hundred percent. Other services in the world charge more and yet have the occasional failure. We have credibility, gentlemen, and that is valuable. As our launch schedule rises to the objective of forty per year, the cost per launch will drop to eleven-point-seven million, and the fee will rise to eighteen-point-five million. The profit margin will be almost seven million dollars per launch."

"That is two hundred eighty million dollars per annum," the banker said.

"Probably somewhat less," Kyoto admitted, "for some payloads will be those of the government."

"So the return of investment is now nine years away?" the automobile man asked.

"Perhaps ten. That is only two years more than projected, and still much better than an investment in any commodity or industry anywhere in the world. And keep in mind, gentlemen, that Nesei Aerospace is quite solvent. We have almost eight hundred million dollars in liquid investments; we have a physical plant that is advantageously financed, and we have a four-month inventory on hand."

The banker nodded, but said, "To achieve what you had promised, Mr. Kyoto, you might consider raising your objective to forty-five launches per year."

Kyoto sighed. "Certainly, I could consider it."

"Better," the steel man said, "the board should direct the President to set that goal."

And so they did.

*　　　*　　　*

The six pilots, American and Soviet, of the Experimental Sub-Orbital Program were required to keep their flying talents honed in conventional aircraft, and General Lane Billings had made arrangements with the resident air wing for the use of Cessna T-37 jet trainers belonging to a permanent squadron at Edwards Air Force Base.

Dmitri Vidorov normally scheduled himself for one two-hour flight per week. The airplane was very tame, and the flights relaxing. He flew to various parts of the American Southwest and familiarized himself with the scenery.

It was a beautiful country, he admitted to himself, with startling contrasts. The massive Grand Canyon split the earth just north of arid and hauntingly attractive desert regions. The Sierra Nevada range climbed to snowcaps even in summer. The lakes along the range were ice-blue cold and plentiful. And to the east were the Rocky Mountains, somewhat reminiscent of his own Aral Mountains.

After his first few flights, Vidorov had purchased a Nikon 35-millimeter camera and several lenses for himself. He was not a photographer, but he had taught himself from the enclosed directions, and he had shot hundreds of pictures that he mailed to Nadia, to help her understand the beauty of what he was seeing with his own eyes.

Today, he had flown the T-37 south along the Colorado River, clear to the Mexican border, and taken a full roll of thirty-six pictures. He reloaded the camera during his return to Edwards and laid it on the empty seat beside him.

Landing at the air base behind a flight of two F-15 Eagle fighters, he turned off onto a parallel taxiway and started back toward the section where the training aircraft were parked. Keeping one eye on the yellow line ahead of him, he quickly switched lenses on the camera, inserting the new 300-millimeter telephoto lens.

All along the route of the taxiway were the airparks for aircraft currently assigned to the base. Edwards was an Air Force Communications Base, but it also had some tactical squadrons, some national guard squadrons in training from time to time, and several experimental aviation and weapons system programs in progress.

He ignored the more mundane squadrons, but he quickly shot several pictures of F-15 Eagles that had been retrofitted with some new system. He did not know what it was, but the squadron marking on the tail indicated an airplane with an experimental mission.

There were two F-16 Falcons with strange bulges on the fuselage behind the canopy. He snapped the shutter, and the battery-operated film winder zipped the film to the next unexposed frame.

For an unknown reason, there was an Israeli IAI Lavi present at the base. He got it on film.

There was an F-111 swing-wing fighter bomber in desert pink and tan camouflage paint with no unit markings. It was intriguing and also captured on the Kodak film.

There was a Grumman A-6 Intruder with a radome mounted above the rear fuselage.

He knew that there were one or two Lockheed F-19 stealth fighters on the base, purely by rumor, but he did not see an aircraft that might have been one of them.

He passed a hangar with large "Access Restricted" signs on it, and with the doors partially open, and though he could not see much inside, took two pictures. Perhaps the low-light film would capture something.

He put the camera in its soft holding bag as a jeep with a yellow "Follow Me" sign came out to meet him, then lead him to his parking place.

He had opened the canopy and shut down the twin turbojets when he saw the pulsing blue strobe light coming at him. Underneath it was a blue Air Force jeep marked for the Air Police.

There was not much that frightened Dmitri Vidorov, but he was frightened now.

He cursed those in Moscow who wanted him to be more than he was. He was a very good pilot, not a spy.

In fact, he was certain he would prove to be a completely inept spy.

There was no real reason for the XSO program to need a secure line, so General Lane Billings had to go over to the massive communications building at Edwards proper to take his call. His driver drove him in the XSO program's only Chevy staff car. When he arrived, a tech sergeant showed him to a booth sheathed with an acoustics-deadening material, and he picked up the red telephone and dialed the number he had been given.

It was answered immediately. "Office of the Chief of Naval Operations."

"This is General Lane Billings."

"One moment, sir."

He waited two minutes, then Zeiman came on. "Hello, Lane."

"Bart."

"I've got Ben Quigley with me on this end."

"Hello, Ben."

Zeiman said, "Ben'll summarize it for you."

The Deputy Director for Intelligence for the DIA was an organized man. "We've been able to gather visual, radar, infrared, or audio records on the following launches: U.S., thirty-nine; French, twenty-eight; Japanese, nine; Soviet Union, sixty-eight. We didn't get all of them, but we have one hundred and forty-four launches over a two-year period, except for the Japanese. Their program has only been operational for a couple months.

"Here's an interesting aspect, Lane: Until fourteen months ago, the average rate of failure ran around eight percent. In the last fourteen months, the rate of failure has risen to thirty-seven percent."

"There's got to be a helping hand in there somewhere," Billings said.

"Damned right. Now, I've got some people analyzing the payloads, wherever we can find out what they were. I'm trying to determine whether or not the type, or the cost, of the payload may have influenced the statistics."

"Good point," Billings agreed.

"Of the failures," Quigley continued, "and with the material we have to work with, we can positively say that six Soviet, three French, and twelve U.S. rockets were shot down on purpose."

"No shit?"

"No shit. There were probably more overall, and probably more foreign casualties, but cameras and radar were operating at the wrong angles or at too great a distance. We had a bit of a fiasco in France."

"What was that?"

154

"One of CIA's assets tried too hard to get data for us, and was picked up by SDECE. I don't know what's going to come out of that."

"How about the weapons configuration on what you've got?" Billings asked.

"Where we got a clear shot, it appeared to be the same as the one your boys captured on tape."

"Launch platform?"

"Negative. Nothing seen, nothing recorded. Our experts think the firing point is way in the hell out of the picture. From the scope of the most distant visual shots, they're giving the aggressor missile a range of at least nineteen, twenty miles."

"I'll pass that data to my ordnance people."

"Do that."

"Now, you say the Soviets are having the same problem we are?" Billings said.

"Correct."

"What about our surveillance of the Soviet space complexes?"

"Neither the KH-11's nor Aquacade have provided any evidence that the Soviets have an operational sub-orbital capability, Lane. A survey of our human agents within Soviet borders also came up with nothing."

"Goddamn it."

"We've got to look elsewhere, or start examining the possibility that some of those Soviet satellites have been armed. In fact, Lane, the President has already authorized us to do both."

"All right, Ben. Good work," Billings said. "Where do we go from here?"

Bart Zeiman said, "Let's start with you, Lane. What's your progress?"

"Five and six will be ready for maiden flights in

ten days."

"Good. How about the ordnance people we gave you? What's shaking there?"

"We've got them working in a restricted area at Edwards with Dallas Grant. We couldn't very well move them into Rosie and still keep it from the Soviet side of this party."

"I trust that you're staying theoretical at this point?" Zeiman asked.

"I haven't been given a go-ahead to actually build deadly missiles," Billings reminded him.

"You've got it, now. You'll have it in writing by the end of the day."

That was good, especially because Grant had told him that he and his armorers had gone ahead and constructed some prototypes without authorization.

"This next part you're going to like, Lane."

"I hope so."

"The President figured he had to bring in the National Security Council. And he brought them in without any of their staffers present."

"Ah, shit." Secrecy control was going to become unmanageable.

"He made each member of the NSC sign a statement."

"What the hell?"

"If this thing leaks to the press, and we determine the source of the leak, the cabinet member, the agency head, or the joint chief in line of authority will resign."

"I'm impressed," Billings said, and was.

"They're going to have to take it to the intelligence oversight committees, though. The President and the DCI both have to protect themselves."

"There goes our confidentiality," Billings said.

"Maybe."

"Well, I'll keep my rabbit foot handy."

"Good. Okay, next. Lane, you're still a part of the Air Force R&D command. But you are hereby authorized to create a temporary operational component which will report through Headquarters, Aerospace Defense Command. You will report directly to Lieutenant General Alan Messerman. You retain command locally."

"Thanks, Bart."

"You owe me a beer. Strategy and tactics are yours to develop. You're the commander on the scene."

"How about rules of engagement?"

Zeiman sighed. "You are not to engage any unidentified craft with hostile fire at present."

"Son of a bitch."

"But you are to be prepared for that to change at any moment."

"I'll be ready. What do I do about Nemorosky and his buddies?"

"We'll go with your judgment," Zeiman said.

"There is no evidence that the Soviets are conspiring against us," Quigley added. "From apparent evidence, they've been victimized too."

"Unless that's a ruse to keep us off the track," Billings said.

"The thought crossed my mind," Quigley told him, "though it would be a damned expensive ruse."

"Still," the CNO said, "the decision is yours. I will say that the President intends to talk to the Soviet President. How much the President tells him will depend upon the President's mood."

"What does that mean, Bart?"

"It means he's going to play it by ear. He wants to see

how much the General Secretary seems to know about everything that's going on. I'll get back to you with the results of the conversation."

"What about the French?"

"As cooperative as they've been lately, I think the President will let them figure it out for themselves. I don't honestly know at this point, Lane. Maybe he'll call, maybe he won't."

"The Japanese?"

"They haven't had a failure yet."

"But they've only been in business for a few months," Ben Quigley put in.

"I suspect that what will happen is that the President will provide an 'Eyes Only' report to the intelligence heads of any nation that is launching space vehicles. We'll have to wait and see on that."

Billings evaluated the pros and cons of involving Nemorosky and his group as he left the building and went back out to his staff car. Sergeant McEvoy was leaning against the fender, waiting for him.

"Let's go, Mac."

McEvoy handed him a slip of paper with a telephone number on it. "Lieutenant Colonel Grant called the car phone, General. He's got some sort of emergency back at Rosie, and he said it's the kind of thing that fits your pay grade much better than it fits his."

Ten

Polly Enburton left the secure room under the Capitol dome where the House Intelligence Oversight Committee held its meetings. The committee had just been briefed by the CIA's Deputy Director for Intelligence.

He had shown them an Executive Finding signed by the President which was almost preposterous in its content. Preposterous or not, the finding was required when the intelligence community was going to spend some large sums of money on clandestine activities or engage in such activities without first obtaining the approval of the oversight committees of Congress. The spending and the covert activity had already begun under that authority.

She went directly to the office of the Chairman of the Armed Services Committee and waited ten minutes while Hammond finished with another appointment. When the door finally opened, Hammond accompanied a visiting constituent into the outer office, spotted her and nodded, then shook the visitor's hand vigorously. "I'm sure glad we got this chance to talk about this particular issue, Mr. Aggemon. Next time you're in town, let's get together again."

The man thanked him profusely and left.

Hammond turned to her and said, "Polly, you got your dander up?"

"I'm weighing the possibility of it, John."

"What can I do for you?"

"I need your authorization for a CODEL airplane." The 89th Military Airlift Wing at Andrews Air Force Base provided global transport for congressional delegations, and only certain Senate or House chairmen were designated to approve flights. With hawk-eyed media people watching constantly, frivolous junkets were a thing of the past.

Hammond led her into his office, where he picked up a pipe from his ashtray and started striking wooden kitchen matches against the sole of his shoe in the effort to get it restarted. The pipe and matches were a Hammond trademark. When he finally had his head wreathed in blue smoke, he asked, "This a committee topic?"

"Indirectly, John. The subject affects some decisions we make, or have already made, but it comes out of the House Intelligence Committee. I don't think I should talk about it yet."

"You going outside the Continental U.S.?"

"No. California."

"If it's Palm Springs, I'll go with you."

She smiled at him. John Hammond and Gerald Ford played a lot of golf together. "I'm afraid it's more military than Palm Springs offers."

"You should get it from the chairman of Intelligence,

160

you know."

"John."

"Yeah, I know."

The Intelligence committee chairman was a Democrat from Arkansas whose mission in life was to set out obstacles for intelligence professionals as well as his own staff and his colleagues.

"Please."

"Damn." He called to the outer office, "Hey, Ginnie, fix up a CODEL authorization for me."

"Thank you, John."

Dallas Grant met the staff car outside Residence Hall 120A. Billings got out, a scowl on his face, but no discernible emotion in his voice.

"Tell me about it, Dallas."

"The Air Police detained Dmitri at Edwards for about an hour while they developed the film. Then they called over here, got the duty officer, and he referred them to me since I was already on the main base, and neither of us knew where you were. I went over to the AP station, talked to Vidorov, and looked at the pictures."

"You talk to him alone?"

"No."

"What's he told them?"

"That he was just taking pictures for his wife. That he's been doing it for months."

"What's your impression?"

"I don't think his wife is interested in an F-16 that's testing tank-killer radar or in an F-19."

"Goddamn. He shot the stealth fighter?"

"Not so's you'd really notice," Grant told him. "It's more like a silhouette through barely opened hangar doors. The aviation magazines have gotten better pictures."

"What do you think, Dallas?"

Grant thought about Vidorov's aviation expertise and his behavior over the past three years, the way the man had begun to open up a little in the last few months. He recalled the way the Soviet pilot had stuck with him during the emergency landing at Nellis.

Still.

"It's espionage activity, General. Pretty damned badly done, however."

"And your recommendation?"

"I don't think we want any trial publicity. I don't think we even want to expel him from the research program. He's got abilities we can use."

Billings leaned against the car door and mused. "If we determined that the Russkis weren't the aggressor in the attacks on missile launches, how would you feel about having Vidorov involved in operational missions?"

Grant did not have to think about it. "I'd want him on my wing, or vice versa."

"Okay. Where are they?"

"Up in his room. I talked them into coming over here and looking at the other photos he's taken."

"Let's go."

Grant followed Billings into the hall and up the stairs. There was an air policeman leaning against the wall outside Vidorov's room, and he came to swift attention when he saw Billings.

Billings returned the airman's salute and bulled his

162

way past the guard and into the room.

Another air policeman, with captain's bars, and a criminal investigator in civilian clothes stood over the bed, rifling through snapshots and holding strips of negatives up to the light. The closet doors were opened, Vidorov's luggage rested open and empty on the floor, and every drawer in the place had been ransacked. Vidorov sat in his chair, looking as pale as Grant had ever seen him. He stood up and assumed a rigid stance as they entered.

The captain looked up, snapped to attention, and said, "Ten-*hutt!*"

The man in the suit came to half a parade rest. He was not afraid of generals. Grant thought it was going to turn out to be a poor attitude.

"Who's in charge?" Billings demanded. His bull voice had taken on deeper, more threatening tones.

"I'm Major Potter," the investigator said, losing what semblance of a parade rest he had had.

"Have you arrested Colonel Vidorov?"

"No, sir. Not yet."

"And what have you found?"

The major waved a hand lazily at the photos on the bed. "Nothing here."

"And what else?"

"Anything else I have accumulated is restricted by my investigation."

"Goddamn it, Major! I want to see it, and I want to see it now."

Billings's voice seemed to vibrate the walls of the room. The investigator reached into his pocket and withdrew a small manila envelope.

Billings whipped it out of his hand, opened it, and

flipped through the photos. Grant watched over the general's shoulder as Billings tossed the innocuous river photographs on the bed. He kept the negatives and the shots of aircraft and then stuffed the envelope in his own pocket.

"That will be all, Major. There's nothing for you people here."

"Now just a minute, General. You can't interfere in my investigation."

Grant noticed that the AP captain had slowly retreated to the wall. He could not retreat any farther.

Billings turned to Vidorov. "Colonel, what's your explanation?"

Vidorov was still standing at attention. "My explanation is stupidity, General Billings. I did not think. Simply, I was taking pictures with a new lens and not considering my subject at all."

"When did you buy the lens?"

"Two days ago, sir. I have the receipt from the base exchange."

"Good enough for me. Take off, Major."

His face red with indignation, the major said, "I am going to have to write a fully detailed report of this incident, General."

"You do that, Major, and you provide a copy to me and a copy to General Hansen at the Pentagon. Be sure to keep a personal copy for your hearing."

"Hearing?" The major nearly choked.

"We're going to start with insubordination. You're not showing due respect to a superior officer, Major Potter. I think you've been waltzing around in civvies too long. You've gotten used to freedoms you can't handle. The captain will bear me out on that, won't

164

you, Captain?"

The air policeman gulped. "Yes, sir."

"I don't care how anything else comes out, Major, but you're going to re-learn military discipline in a uniform on the DMZ in Korea."

The major's face got redder, but he came to attention, saluted, and eased out of the room. His air police colleagues disappeared with him.

Grant shut the door behind them.

Billings turned to Vidorov. "At ease, Colonel."

"I cannot thank you enough, General."

"I don't believe your story for a goddamned minute, Dmitri. What you tell Nemorosky is up to you, but from here on out, you walk a very fine line. Don't ever get yourself in a position where anyone can mistake your intentions. Don't make me regret the decision I've made."

Grant thought Vidorov's color was coming back, though slowly. "I will not, General Billings. It is a promise I freely make to you."

"And shit-can that camera. You've taken more than enough pictures."

"Yes, I will."

Grant almost winked at Vidorov, but then thought better of it. He did not want to be a major again, or worse, flying out of a cold spot like Kimpo Air Base.

"Come on, Grant. It's still the middle of the day, and we've got work to do."

Grant followed in the general's wake as they went down the stairs and out to where Sergeant McEvoy waited with the staff car.

"Leave your car here, Dallas, and come with me."

Grant went around the back of the Chevy and

165

crawled into the back seat.

Billings got in and slammed the door. "We're going back to Edwards, Mac, but stop by Hangar Five first and run in and get Jeremy Restwick."

McEvoy drove down to the hangar, and while he went in to find the chief engineer, Grant asked, "Do you think Potter will file a report, General?"

"No. The man thought he was doing his duty, but he's gotten sloppy at it, and he can't take a hint. Still I don't leave my threats hanging, or I'll lose credibility. I'll call Diangelo at Personnel and see that Potter gets a regular duty assignment."

Grant and Billings went back a long way together, and Grant thought their relationship had a special quality to it. Still, Grant sometimes skated close to the edge of the general's tolerance. Incidents like this made him resolve to be kinder to the general in the future. He was not very good at resolutions, however. They slipped away in the heat of new moments.

McEvoy came out of the hangar with Restwick in tow, and the two of them got into the front seat. The sergeant started the car and headed for Edwards.

Restwick turned sideways in the seat and raised an eyebrow in question.

"We're going to look at what Grant's been up to," Billings said.

"Ah. I thought as much, and I brought along some of the sketches I've been working on." Restwick tapped his breast pocket.

Billings had commandeered an old Quonset hut on the back edge of Edwards for his weapons development team. McEvoy parked in front of the door, and Grant, Billings, and Restwick presented credentials to the

166

airman guarding the entrance, then went inside.

The team was composed of five men in addition to Grant, three of them military experts, and two of them from civilian defense contractors. There were blackboards on easels around the perimeter of the room, crammed with formulae and drawings. There were seven computer terminals. There were large workbenches in the center of the concrete floor, with disassembled rocket parts scattered over their surfaces. Backed into one corner was a small crane used to lift and move the heavier missiles that had been delivered to their front door by canvas-covered pickups. A large sign near the door read, "Flammables Present. No Goddamned Smoking!"

Everyone had been introduced to each other before, so Grant went right to the closest work table, turned around, and leaned against it. "I'll recap the premises we've been working under. One, Jerry doesn't want anything hung underneath the sub-orbital, so we're not developing a system requiring a hard-point mount."

"Why not?" Billings asked.

"There are several factors to consider," Restwick said. "The sub-orbital fully loaded at takeoff is so heavy that we don't want anything at all to increase drag. We've only got twenty-five thousand pounds of turbojet thrust to work with, after all. With capacity payload on the jet engine, we have a top end of Mach point-eight-nine. On the rocket engines, we have a throttle range of forty-five to one-hundred-five percent. If the top speed is around Mach five-point-three, as we're estimating, the kick-in speed at low throttle is Mach two-point-three. Hell, we already know that. The transition from jet engine to rocket engines is a real jump now. We don't want to make it worse."

"I'll verify that," Grant said. "When we switch to rockets, we go into immediate high-G's. I wouldn't want to make it any worse. And given those factors, we have two locations to work with. The front end of the rocket nacelles—where we've been planning to install more fuel tanks—was one, but it was discarded as soon as I thought about a hung-up rocket burning through the bulkhead into a hydrogen tank. That left the fuselage underside, ahead of the turbojet and generator intakes. Jerry figures we can devise a retractable pod five-and-a-half feet wide and ten feet long. It's situated under the front cockpit and the forward half of the rear compartment."

"It is, if we shift some electronics boxes and the gyroscopic stabilizers to new locations." Restwick dug his sketches out of his breast pocket, unfolded them, and spread them out on the table.

Billings leaned over to look and pointed to the aft fuselage. "We were going to put reconnaissance camera lens there."

"I've got some space in the wing leading edges, General. I'll take a look at that."

"What about ECM?"

"Yes, sir," Restwick answered. "We're changing the long fairing that attaches under the turbojet housing to give us a little more volume. It'll give us enough room for the Electronic Counter-Measures. We'll get threat warning receivers, flare and chaff ejection, and infrared and radar jammers into it."

"We figured there was no sense in getting armed to go bear hunting, without preparing for the possibility that the bear is armed, too," Grant said.

168

"Good." The general slid his finger forward on the drawing, from the ECM installation to the weapons rack. "When the pod is in the down position, the turbojet intakes are blocked. You can't use the jet engine, right?"

"Well, we can't have everything we'd like to have in this life," Grant said. "These birds were just not envisioned as combat craft."

"What if you have a malfunction and can't retract the damned pod?"

"I've practiced one dead-stick landing. It wasn't too bad," Grant told him.

"You don't always get a handy runway, Grant."

"Maybe it'll float?"

"The likelihood of a malfunction is remote, General," Restwick said. "The retract mechanics are already designed and available. They've been around since the F-86 Saber jet was operating in Korea. All we have to do is cut the fuselage skin to the configuration we want, rearrange some structural members, and build a platform that will match the curvature of the bottom panel and will support the ignition thrust of the ordnance we select."

"You damned engineers always make it sound so simple. Then you want four years to develop it, produce it, and test it," Billings said.

Restwick grinned at him. "That's only to assure that we have ample steady income from the Defense Department until we get our next simple idea."

"I believe you."

"I sent Billy Shepard and a crew down to the graveyard at Davis-Monthan in Arizona," Grant said. "They're stripping the mechanical and hydraulic parts

169

we need from mothballed aircraft."

"Okay. Go on."

"We wanted a solid-propellant rocket for reliability's sake, and we wanted to be able to arm ourselves with at least four missiles. We set our maximum total weight at one thousand pounds, to give us some leeway in addition to the retract mechanics and the ECM. That's also allowing for fuel tank modifications that are under way.

"With those specifications in mind for the missile body, we've looked at some fifteen missiles, but Rockwell Hellfire, Hughes TOW, Hughes Falcon, and Ford/Raytheon Sidewinder came closest to meeting our needs." Grant swept his hand back, indicating all of the parts lying on the tables.

"I already see some possible limitations in those," Billings said.

"True. We threw out the Hellfire, for example, because it was sub-sonic. We're already launching at Mach four or better, and we're in thin air that will allow these babies to really fly, but we wanted a lot more punch," Grant said.

"Some of those have got a hell of a wing span across the fins," Billings pointed out.

Restwick held up his hand. "We'll chop off the fins, General. We don't need them up there. But we do have to devise directional thrusters, or better, a gimbal mounted nozzle, to give us directional control."

Grant reached out and rolled a rocket body toward him until it was centered on the table. "The Sidewinder is going to be our propulsion package. It gives us Mach three at forty thousand feet, and probably twice that at three hundred thousand. Its normal range is eleven

170

miles, but we're calculating about twenty miles as we cut the weight and friction and boost the speed."

"That's good," Billings said. "The DIA analysts figure our aggressor has about the same range."

Three of the engineers quickly jotted memos in their pocket notebooks.

One of the ordnance engineers handed him a nose cone, and Grant laid it on the table twelve inches in front of the missile body.

"We're dumping the twenty-five-pound warhead and substituting a penetrator of our own design. Actually, Tim Forrester's design." Grant always tried to provide earned credit when it was due.

The engineer nodded in acknowledgement.

"It doesn't fit," Billings said.

"We asked Tim to design it for the Falcon, before we changed our minds. It'll fit when we're done."

"Okay. Control?"

Another of the engineers rolled a module into place between the nose cone and the missile body.

"Kerry Rand is responsible for that, General. The electronics come out of the Hellfire, mostly. It's dual-mode, with infra-red seeking on one side, and laser designator on the other. For the sub-orbital, we're adapting the Target Acquisition and Designation System, that's TADS, as currently used on the AH-64 Apache helicopter. Jerry's got a couple of people modifying the interface software."

"That's a big bastard."

"Jerry says that once we take it out of the external case used on the chopper, most of the black box will mount behind the radar antenna."

"That's after we move the antenna forward,"

171

Restwick clarified.

"We come out at one hundred and seventy-two pounds each on the missiles, and four of them fit in the space that Jerry has given us."

"What the hell you calling it?" Billings asked.

"What else? The Hellwinder."

"What's your production ability? This will have to be done by hand."

"We don't know yet, but we'll damned well have a full load for each sub-orbital, as Jerry brings it on-line with the fuel nacelle, electronics, and weapons pod modifications."

"And that brings up another point," Restwick said. "The minute I start cutting into a fuselage, the Soviets are going to ask me why. What do I tell them?"

"I haven't decided yet," Billings said.

That was highly unusual for the general, Grant thought. Normally, his decisions in regard to solutions came right behind his problems.

"Nesei Aerospace Industries will one day, and very soon, be the predominant supplier of transportation to orbits in space for very many nations."

Yakamata agreed with his superior, as he should. "I am certain of it, Mr. Kyoto."

"I envision a time when even the United States's program cannot keep up with commercial or military demands and their defense department comes to us for assistance."

"I can see how that would be true," Yakamata said. Kyoto had been going on and on about the bright future of the company. Yakamata assumed that Kyoto had been getting some pressure from others. In Japan's

172

corporate economy, it seemed as if everyone was pressured by someone else.

"Pakistan and India have both made overtures to us," Kyoto said. "In fact, they have asked about our providing them with the communications satellites, as well as placing them in orbit."

Indeed, the future did appear rosy to Yakamata, and he was eager to complete his military service and join the company as a full-time, and recognized, executive. What was the point in having all of that money in his Swiss account, when he could not use it?

The driver stopped at the gate, and the guard came out of the hut to examine their credentials. Security was so tight that even Kyoto underwent the ritual every time he entered the compound.

The gate was opened for them, and the Toyota moved across the asphalted lot and parked in front of Hangar C. Yakamata got out and followed Kyoto into the small office situated in one corner of the building. Two of Yakamata's pilots sat on a low divan, drinking coffee and thumbing through ragged copies of *Playboy*. They leaped to their feet when they saw the visitors.

"At ease," Yakamata ordered.

So far, Yakamata had recruited seven pilots for this project. They were all extremely competent, and for the right money, they had been induced to leave their military service for flying positions in private enterprise when their terms of service ended.

Kyoto waved them back to their leisure and passed through the office and into the hangar proper.

Yakamata closed the door behind him, and joined his employer in perusing the craft.

There were seven of them facing toward the other

173

end of the hangar—where the aircraft doors were. They were strangely dark under the bright fluorescent lights. Their flat black surfaces appeared to absorb the light. The continual soft curves did not provide an angle which reflected light, much less a radar image. Internally, the honeycomb structural design was also derived from angles calculated to not directly reflect the signals generated by a seeking radar transmitter. In Hangar B, two more of the craft were under construction. Yakamata thought them evil-looking machines, but he loved to fly them. There was nothing in the world, or in the atmosphere, like it.

Under cover of the name, "NAI Futures Program, Under Contract to Dissonex International," the project was funded out of banking accounts located in Switzerland and the Bahamas. Yakamata assumed that, after several changes in banks, the funds actually derived from Nesei Aerospace Industries investments. He did not know for certain, but he thought it a safe assumption.

Kyoto's eyes had a soft look. "And when the time is right, when the joint American-Soviet program has run its course, we will show the world what a properly designed sub-orbital craft looks like."

"We will do that," Yakamata said. For, even, more than Kyoto, he felt the sub-orbitals resting before them were his very own. He was going to break world records with them and shine his name around the globe.

Like Lindbergh, or Yeager, or Neil Armstrong, Meoshi Yakamata would leave his mark.

*　　　*　　　*

Grant was working weekends now, but on Friday night, he thought he was due some rest and recuperation. He drove the Firebird into Los Angeles, cutting west at Palmdale to cross the San Gabriel Mountains. The top was down, and though the air had a nip in it, it was refreshing and pretty much smog-free. There were a couple hours of sunlight left, all of it directly in his eyes. He wore his dark glasses and kept the windshield visor down.

For most of the way, he found that he was following Alexandre Murychenko in his bright red Nissan sports car. Grant was in no hurry, and without thinking about it, stayed a quarter mile behind the Russian as they both joined Interstate 5, then shortly after, veered off onto the San Diego Freeway.

The traffic was heavier leaving Los Angeles and its environs on a Friday night, but the inbound automobiles were still numerous and Grant concentrated on watching for idiots. There were enough of them, switching lanes unannounced, hopping on the brakes, then the accelerator pedal, and even passing on the right shoulder when they felt that the world was blocking their rightful ways.

He knew that Murychenko spent a lot of time in the city, but he did not think much about it until he saw Murychenko's right turn-signal begin to blink. Looking up at the overhead sign, Grant saw they were coming up on the exit for Sepulveda Boulevard and Mulholland Drive.

Grant could understand the Soviets spending a lot of time around Hollywood, or in downtown Los Angeles, or even farther south in San Diego and Tijuana, but Beverly Hills?

175

Grant's curiosity and impetuosity crashed together, and he signaled, then slipped into the right lane. He let three cars in ahead of him.

Coming off the exit ramp, Murychenko turned back north and followed Sepulveda to the intersection with Mulholland Drive, where he turned right and crossed back under the San Diego Freeway into Beverly Hills.

Grant drifted a few more cars back as the traffic thinned out, just keeping the top of the red car in sight. Winding through the hills, the sun was cut off from time to time, and the Firebird rolled in and out of deep shadow. The steep slopes were heavy with foliage and vines. The Pontiac's dual exhaust rumbled among the hills. It was cooler than on the freeways.

Yet, as they drove along the roads curving through the hills, Grant thought that the Russian drove with confidence, as if he knew where he was going, and as if he had been there before. The sports car did not hesitate indecisively at intersections.

Stone Canyon Road.

By the time Grant reached the corner, made the turn, and started to climb back along the steep road, Murychenko and his Nissan had disappeared.

He searched the randomly spaced driveways on both sides as the Pontiac picked up speed.

There!

A garage door on the right was just closing behind the Nissan.

Grant could not imagine the lanky and pinched Murychenko in liaison with some golden-skinned, honey-haired, Southern California nymphet. But Grant had been known to be wrong a few times before in his life.

He found a driveway, pulled in, and got himself turned around. He drove back down the hill, made his way out of the hills south through the exotic town of Beverly Hills, and turned toward the coast on Santa Monica Boulevard. Crossing under the San Diego Freeway, he drove into Santa Monica. Fifteen minutes later, he parked the Firebird in front of the fifties-style apartment house that looked across Highway One toward the Pacific Ocean.

Patricia Price's apartment was on the fourth floor, and Grant took the elevator up, walked down the thickly carpeted hall, and rang the doorbell.

He waited.

He rang the doorbell again after a two-minute wait.

Finally, the door opened.

Tricia was in a kimono that was oversized, even for her. She was five-feet, ten-inches tall, but her slim build and small-boned face made her seem smaller on screen. The planes of her face had Grace Kelly and Ava Gardner overtones, Grant thought. She had penetrating green eyes and cream-and-gold hair cut at medium length.

"Hi, love."

"You son of a bitch."

"Me?"

"Alexander Graham Bell invented all those telephones for a purpose. To call ahead."

"I'm stealing time from the U. S. and AF. All for you, my dear."

"Go away."

"I sure do love you all wet." The moisture from her

177

damp flesh was invading the silk of her robe in several suggestive places.

She softened a tad. "You're the most discourteous bastard I've ever known."

"Your eyes are like emeralds in the twilight."

"Get the hell out of here." She jerked her robe tighter, both of her hands pulling at the lapels. Which served to emphasize her nipples.

She was warming to him.

Grant reached forward and put his hands on her hips. "I was thinking of dinner, some place quiet and expensive. Dark. Candles. A nice Chardonnay. Dancing later."

"You didn't ask me about your plans. You never do. I'm supposed to be here, waiting eagerly for the hero. Include me out."

She was coming around. Grant pulled her an inch closer, and she moved her right foot forward to resist.

"You're an asshole, too."

"The night is young. We can kick off our shoes and walk on the beach and get sand between our toes." Grant tugged her an inch closer.

"I don't like you," she said, and threw her arms around his neck.

Grant kissed her with easy pressure, felt the soft heat of her lips.

Tricia pulled away. There was fire and ice in her green eyes. "I don't want you coming here again."

"No?"

"Not unless you call first."

He leaned forward to kiss her again.

She dodged his lips. "You have to promise."

The hell of it was, she knew he kept promises, if he

made them. "Hon, I don't always know when . . ."

"Promise, damn it!"

"Okay. Promised."

She pulled her kimono open and pressed her damp body against him, and Grant returned to his kiss. He could feel the demand increasing.

And the phone rang.

"Don't answer it," he suggested.

"It's probably Dan," she sighed. "We're trying to acquire a hot script."

Dan Moretti was the producer for whom she worked. Tricia disengaged from him, turned, and went across the living room to pick up the phone.

Grant closed the door and checked on the sun setting against the Pacific. There were nice orange/red combinations tonight. Her apartment had a window wall on the ocean side, with a balcony supporting two chaise longues and a couple small tables. The living room was furnished in shades of gray and blue, with deep blue carpet.

"It's for you."

"Damn. How do they find me?"

It had to be Billings, who knew about and had met Tricia a couple of times, and it was. "Got a schedule change for you, Dallas."

"Yes, sir."

"The Titan four launch at Canaveral has been moved up to August sixth."

Grant thought for a moment. "That's the same date as the French launch."

"You got it."

"All right. What's more important to you, General?"

"Our own."

179

"Vidorov and I will cover it. We'll send Dennis to watch the other." The date of the launches was before they would have any of the sub-orbitals armed, but they were not going to delay launches and possibly create suspicion.

"You're including Vidorov?" Billings asked.

"I don't see that we have any choice, and I want to keep an eye on him."

"You're right about the choices available. I'm going to break the news to Nemorosky in the morning."

"Good decision, General," Grant said. "I'll see you on Monday."

"I appreciate your support, Grant," Billings said with sarcasm evident in his tone. "And I'll see you at seven in the morning."

He hung up.

Grant dropped the receiver in its cradle.

"What was that all about?" Tricia asked.

"I don't know what your boss tells you, but my boss told me that I have to get up at five in the morning."

"I'm glad I'm not in the Air Force." Tricia slipped out of her robe, draped it over her arm, and then turned toward the bedroom.

Grant started after her. "Where are you going?"

"To get dressed for the romantic dinner you offered me."

"Oh."

She stopped and spun toward him. "Unless you want to eat later?"

"I do."

Eleven

On the fourth of August, Dallas Grant, in his dreaded paper-pushing role as executive officer of the XSO Program, and dressed in Class A uniform, waited outside the operations building at Edwards Air Force Base at ten-fifteen in the morning. The C-137C was right on time. A military VIP version of the Boeing 707, the transport landed smoothly and taxied up to a parking place near where Grant stood.

He waited until the portable stairway had been ushered into place, then walked across the hot tarmac and waited at its base. The door opened, and Polly Enburton emerged, accompanied by a young lady with fluffed raven hair which framed a pixie face. Enburton blinked her eyes against the bright sunlight, then descended the stairway.

Grant took off his sunglasses and slid them into his pocket. "Congresswoman Enburton, I am Lieutenant Colonel Dallas Grant."

She offered her hand, and Grant shook it. "I expected General Billings, Colonel."

"I'm afraid he'll be getting back from Seattle late. He's attending a funeral."

"Oh? Whose?"

"His former wife," Grant told her, irritated at the question.

"I didn't know he'd ever been married."

"Yes." Billings had never spoken much about his personal life to Grant. He knew only that there had been a wife and two children who did not get along with the general, or more likely, with the Air Force. It had come apart in the late sixties, and the woman had remarried. It did not mean that Billings did not care.

"Well, we'll make do without him. I heard from some source that you are a pilot, Colonel. What else do you do?"

"I serve as commander of the test squadron and as executive officer of the program."

"So you'll be able to answer our questions?"

"I hope so, ma'am."

"I do, too. Oh, this is Miss Jamieson, my administrative assistant."

"How do you do?" Grant offered his hand and Jamieson shook it, trying to make her tiny hand produce a firm grasp. She had dark, serious eyes in a smoothly tanned face, a tan not expected in people who haunted the caverns of Congress. She was petite, but sufficiently voluptuous in a tailored white linen dress to draw second and third glances. Grant seriously reconsidered his long-standing attraction to tall women.

"Colonel," she said in a syrupy voice.

"Right this way, ladies. Sergeant Gloom, will you see to the luggage, please? Take it over to Residence Hall

121A at Rosie."

"Yessir." Gloom, extremely glum in a Class A uniform and with uncharacteristically clean fingernails, offered a halfhearted salute, and climbed the stairway.

Grant walked the visitors to his Firebird and opened the passenger door. With the general gone, he could have had McEvoy and the unit's staff car, but Grant was not inclined toward pretentious behavior.

Jamieson pulled the seat-back forward and got into the back seat, and Enburton settled into the passenger-side bucket seat. He closed the door, walked around the back of the Pontiac, and got in behind the wheel. "I'd be happy to put up the top, if you like."

"No. This is rather nice," Enburton said.

Jamieson, who would get the brunt of the wind, did not agree, Grant's glance at her face in the rearview mirror told him, but she also did not complain.

He drove back to Rosie twenty miles an hour slower than his normal pace, keeping an anxious eye on Jamieson's blowing hair. It was flying all over hell, and he supposed he was not making a good first impression on the congressional aide.

"You're the one who first spotted this . . . this hostile missile," Enburton said.

Billings had briefed him on Enburton's status on the intelligence and armed committees. She had security classifications higher than his own, and Jamieson supposedly had the same clearances. "Yes, ma'am. Along with Major Blake, of course."

"I'd like to hear about it from you."

He told the story again, in the same way. He was getting tired of telling it.

Jamieson moved forward to sit on the front edge of her seat and listen as he narrated the tale. Whatever perfume she was wearing, it had sensual overtones.

"And you have no idea where it came from?" Jamieson asked.

"No. We're still looking."

"And you feel you need to look with the sub-orbital?"

"Our radar, ground surveillance, and satellite surveillance have not been able to pin it down, Miss Jamieson. That leaves the sub-orbital, don't you think?"

"I think it may have been a fortunate occurrence."

"I don't know what you mean," Grant said, but thought that he did.

"I mean that, just as soon as the committee decides to phase out your sub-orbital program, you all of a sudden find a new role for the aircraft."

Enburton watched his face closely as she waited for his response.

"Miss Jamieson, our video and radar recording decks automatically place the date and time on the tapes. I think you'll find that the tapes were recorded prior to the committee's decision."

"Those can be faked."

With some degree of discipline, Grant was able to just shrug his shoulders.

"Let's not jump to conclusions just yet, Roberta," Enburton told her.

Roberta. She probably went by some asinine nickname, like Bobbi.

Grant took them first to the operations building and the converted Hangar 1 and toured them through the labs and offices. He introduced them to Jeremy Restwick, Alexandre Murychenko, and General Nemorosky. Though she had an occasional query, Jamieson took notes and was mostly silent as Enburton delivered batteries of questions which she must have stayed up all night composing. Almost all of them had to do with scheduling, design changes, personnel assignments, and cost overruns. The XSO Program had been good about staying within budget. Though there were a few overruns in the three years of the program, the total was less than three hundred thousand dollars. Better, General Billings had absorbed the costs from other areas of his budget, and had not gone back to Congress to make up the difference.

Grant thought Enburton was impressed by that, but he was guessing. The lady's face did not give away much, though he thought he saw some reticence when she spoke to General Nemorosky.

On the other hand, Grant was impressed by Enburton's grasp of the details involving the program. She knew what she was talking about. He did not know exactly where she stood, but he began to like her.

Just before noon, he took them over to the mess hall. There was a small VIP dining room located off the main dining room, but as with the staff car, Grant had not thought it worth using for just a couple of big shots from Washington. He ushered them through the cafeteria line and loaded his plate with meat loaf and mashed potatoes. He poured gravy over everything. Polly Enburton matched him, ounce for ounce, while Roberta Jamieson had the tossed salad and a bran muffin. They sat at a table near the middle of the room.

No one around them paid much attention to them, and the conversation level was high, some of it conducted in Russian.

"Strange to hear that in an air force facility," the representative said.

"You get used to it," Grant said. "But you're right. It took me a long time to become accustomed."

"You trust them?" Jamieson asked.

"Within reason."

"What are your personal standards, then?" Enburton asked.

"This program and nothing more."

"Uh-huh."

"They have free run of the base?" the aide asked.

Grant thought about the fiasco with Vidorov, but said, "The Soviets are allowed complete access at Rosie, and of course, they spend their weekends in Los Angeles and elsewhere. But most of Edwards is off-limits to them."

"You're sure?" Jamieson pressed.

"Now, Robbi," Enburton cautioned.

Robbi. He might have known.

"I'm sure."

Jamieson finished her salad, replenished her coffee from the insulated pot on the table, and leaned back in her chair. Grant thought her bustline was about one cup-size too large for her frame. To counter those thoughts, he concentrated on the congresswoman and answered more questions.

After lunch, he walked them over to Hangar 5 and displayed a little of his pride as he explained the modifications made to XSO-5 and XSO-6. The suborbitals were all but complete, and the technicians were

186

running final systems checks. The lower wing skins had been bonded in place, and the longer rocket engine nacelles made them look even more like hydroplane boats.

The rocket pod on XSO-5 was in its down position, but was not particularly lethal. The four rocket tubes were empty.

Enburton stopped and looked at it. "General Billings showed the Armed Service Committee some drawings relative to modifications for installing surveillance cameras. They didn't look like this, Colonel."

"No, ma'am."

She turned toward him. "That's not an erudite response."

"As a member of the intelligence committee, you're aware of the presidential order allowing us to arm the sub-orbitals?"

"Yes. That's what I'm here to see."

"That's it, Congresswoman."

Enburton turned back and peered into the tubes. "I thought you'd just kind of hang them under the wing."

Grant took five minutes to give a layman's version of wing loading, speed, drag, and lift requirements.

"And now you have a combat aircraft," Jamieson said.

"More or less. More armament, less air. There's not much to breathe up where we operate," he grinned.

"One that was never requested, and that never went through a comprehensive needs assessment," she said.

"We didn't need it until this month, Miss Jamieson. But fortunately, we have it available."

"And because of that, you think you deserve to have the program re-funded?"

He did, but said, "We still have to test it, Miss Jamieson. We'll know soon enough."

"What missiles are you using?" Enburton asked.

"I don't have an example here, Congresswoman, but I can describe it for you." Grant told her about the changes that had produced the Hellwinder.

"Do you have any more questions?" he asked after an hour of questions.

"I'd like to see the other sub-orbitals," she told him.

For a gray-haired and somewhat aristocratic lady, she was indefatigable, Grant thought. He led them out of the hanger and toward the structure next door.

"There is one thing that amazes me," Enburton said.

"What's that?"

"The progress you've made in two weeks. You've converted the sub-orbital into an armed craft in a damned short time."

Grant smiled. "You know us Americans, Congresswoman. When pressed, etcetera, etcetera."

In Hangar 4, XSO-2, XSO-3, and XSO-4 were being prepared for the morning's flight. All of the pilots were present, except for Blake, who was doing his trainer time in a T-37. The pilots and ground crews were intently examining all of the sub-orbiters' sub-systems. Grant introduced them to the visitors.

Enburton did not demonstrate her knowledge in front of the Soviet pilots or technicians.

"These haven't been converted?" Robbie Jamieson asked.

"Not yet, no. The modified nacelles, fuel tanks, missile pods, and avionics black boxes are being prepared in advance, so that the conversions can be made quickly. We don't want any of them to have too much downtime."

"Can we see inside?" Enburton asked.

"Sure." Grant commandeered a couple of airmen and had them scoot a castered scaffolding into place next to XSO-4. Enburton and Jamieson preceded him up the ladder, Grant waiting a modest six feet away from the ladder until the skirted women completed their climbs. Robbi Jamieson had nicely turned calves.

He scampered up the ladder to join them and leaned over the windscreen to point out the various controls and indicators in the cockpit.

"It's very much like *Star Wars,* isn't it?"

"I suppose it is, Congresswoman Enburton, though I haven't seen the movie."

Her eyes went a bit fuzzy as she fantasized something. "From the video tapes I've seen, it must be fascinating up there."

"Yes, ma'am, it is," Grant admitted. And then on an impulse for which Billings would eventually have him executed, he said, "Would you like to go up?"

Enburton straightened up from where she had been leaning over the cockpit and looked him in the eyes. "Yes, Colonel, I would. However, I'm sixty-two years old."

"Age hasn't slowed down General Yeager much. From what I've seen today, it hasn't slowed you, either."

"That's kind of you, Colonel. But I'm going to hang onto whatever common sense I still have."

"I'll go," Robbie Jamieson said.

There was a moment's silence on the platform. Grant looked to Enburton, and she said, "It wouldn't hurt for the committee to have a viewpoint that's not entirely air force."

Before there was a chance for second thoughts, Grant called down, "Gloomy!"

"Yo, Colonel!"

"I need a passenger seat in this bird, then tow it out and give me a half-load of fuel."

"Gotcha, sir!"

Grant's ground crew went into motion as he helped the women down from the scaffolding. Most of the men stood around with half-amused looks on their faces. He picked the one most amused. "Billy, get me your helmet and pressure suit."

Shepard said, "Ah shit, Colonel."

"Major."

Shepard went ahead of them toward the lounge and dressing room built into one corner of the hangar. In the lounge, Grant got a Coke from the machine for Enburton, and she took it to one of the beat up sofas.

"Right this way, Miss Jamieson." He took her into the dressing room, accepted a fortunately clean pair of long underwear and the pressure suit from a disgruntled Shepard, and held the suit up against Jamieson's shoulders. The size was about right, though there was going to be some flattened anatomy. "This'll do, I think."

Grant collected his own flight gear from his locker. "We only have one dressing room, and I'll leave it to you, Miss Jamieson. You need any help?"

"I'll manage, thank you." The smile she gave him was not very confident. All of the paraphernalia was beginning to create those famous second thoughts.

Grant went into the bathroom to change, then waited outside the dressing room door. When it finally

190

opened a few inches, Jamieson peeked out at him.

"All set?"

"I feel ridiculous," she said.

"We all do."

She opened the door the rest of the way, and Grant stepped inside. She did look a little squashed in the pressure suit, but he tried not to show special interest. He went to his locker and hung up his uniform.

As they went through the lounge on the way out to the apron, Enburton said, "Robbi, I don't think you're built for an air force career."

"I won't plan on it, Polly."

They had to wait forty-five minutes for the fueling operation, and Grant went through his ground inspection with Gloom in attendance. Finally, he helped Jamieson up the ladder and into the rear cockpit. She settled into the seat, and he showed her how to strap in.

"This isn't very comfortable."

"See," he smiled, "you thought we enjoyed it."

She gave him a pout.

Grant settled Shepard's helmet on her head. With all of that fluffy hair, it was a tight fit. Then he crawled into his own seat while Gloom hooked up her pressure suit and communications and showed her how to use the intercom.

Powering up the instrument panel and radios, Grant filed a brief flight plan over the air with Rosie Control. Twenty minutes later, XSO-4 was passing through 20,000 feet, leaving the West Coast behind.

Jamieson did not say anything throughout the takeoff and climb-out, and he could not see her face because of the bulkhead behind him. When he ignited the rocket engines, and the sub-orbital leaped forward, throwing them into high-G's, she finally used the intercom.

"What's wrong?" Her teeth chattered.

"Not a thing, Miss Jamieson. We just went over to rocket engines." He began to shut down the turbo jet.

"Oh."

"Are you cold? On the panel in front of you, to the lower right side, is the temperature control. See it?"

"I don't . . . yes."

"Turn it clockwise if you want more heat."

By the time he had completed his jet shut-down checklist, she came back on the intercom. "That's much better."

"Good."

Grant pulled the nose up, slammed the rocket throttles forward, and watched the readout rise to Mach 4.

Silence from the rear. He wished he could watch the reaction on her face or, failing that, have the intercom locked open so he could hear her.

"How you doing?"

"I'm scared, you shit."

"Sorry. There's nothing to worry about, though. This is my six hundred and twenty-second hour in the bird. Just watch the scenery."

"I am watching it. How high are we?"

"Just going through one hundred and eight-five thousand feet. That's about thirty-five miles above the sea. I'll be leveling out at two hundred thousand." Grant felt like a damned airliner captain.

After he leveled the sub-orbital, Grant turned to

follow the coast of Mexico south. He was not going to subject her to any radical stunting, and he thought that keeping a continent in sight would be helpful, too.

It was a good day. They were at a level where the stars were becoming apparent against deep blue skies. The curvature of the earth was prominent, a dark blue, purplish line against the horizons. Most of the land mass on his left was clear, browns and beiges and thin blue-green rivers. Cloud cover was prominent along the west coast, with brighter, higher clouds moving inland.

"Getting used to it?" he asked over the intercom.

There was a long pause, then, "Yes. It *is* beautiful."

"I like it."

"You don't suppose . . ."

"Suppose what?"

"That they're up here somewhere?"

Christ! He had not even thought about it.

"I wouldn't think so, Miss Jamieson. There aren't any launches scheduled."

But he began to scan the skies more closely, and he switched his screen display to the APG-67 radar now permanently fitted to the sub-orbiter.

After twenty minutes, Grant made a slow turn back toward the north.

"This is all you do up here? Ride back and forth?"

"We shut off the engines now and then, and see how far we can glide."

"Oh don't do that!"

"I won't. And then we also work on other maneuvers, to see how the craft responds to different stresses. Don't be alarmed, now."

Grant went into a slow roll, then stopped the sub-orbital upside down. The earth was directly above them.

"My God!"

"You like that?"

"I don't feel like I'm falling."

"You're not."

He rolled on out, then began to lose altitude as he headed back toward the continental United States. Crossing the coast over Mexico, Grant pointed out a few features like the Grant Canyon and the Rockies as he circled toward home base. He felt as if he were flying a cargo of eggs.

It was a completely uneventful flight.

The real action took place on the ground after Grant parked the sub-orbital and Gloomy hooked up his tractor.

General Billings had returned.

His face was livid.

Grant was certain Billings must be close to a heart attack, and was holding off only because Representative Enburton was standing next to him.

He slipped out of the cockpit, then helped Jamieson get unhooked and unstrapped. Descending the ladder first, he helped her down.

As the sub-orbital was towed away, Grant shed his helmet, helped Jamieson out of hers, and then carried both of them during the long walk to where Billings and Enburton waited.

"Well, Robbi?" the congresswoman asked.

"I was scared to death," Jamieson said.

Billings's face got bluer.

"Hi, General," Grant said, trying for exuberance.

194

Billings stepped off several paces to the side, and Grant had no choice but to follow him.

Leaning close, Billings whispered, "You're grounded."

"Now, sir . . ."

Billings turned away abruptly and signaled for McEvoy, who brought the staff car up.

And worse, after dinner, when Grant called the guest room in 121A that was assigned to Jamieson, she told him that she very definitely was not interested in having a drink with him.

Many years had passed since General Grigori Brezhenki had been scolded so severely. He had not liked it then, and he did not like it now.

Some aide had gathered all, or at least many, of Brezhenki's reports to the General Staff and marked them for the President. Brezhenki had been required to sit stiffly on a wooden chair in front of the President's desk as the leader of the Communist Party went through each report, pointing out errors, omissions, and inadequacies.

A smirking Chairman Cherevako of the KGB sat in a soft leather chair at one side of the room during the process, full of silence and condemnation. Here was a man who sought KGB domination over the military.

"And here!" the President exclaimed. "Here! In May, you claimed that an A2e was self-destructed as a result of sabotage by an unknown infiltrator at Tyuratam. Very craftily, General, you place the fault on Chairman Cherevako's desk."

"It is the responsibility of the Committee for State Security to ferret out saboteurs before they penetrate our borders," Brezhenki insisted.

"Yes. When they come from expected and traditional sources." The President picked up a large photograph by a corner and sailed it across the desk at him.

Brezhenki, surprised by the action, threw up his hand and knocked the photograph to the floor. He bent over and picked it up. He looked at it carefully, rotating it. He did not know what it was.

"That photograph," the President said, "comes from an American satellite, the one they call Aquacade. The American President, though somewhat condescending, was kind enough to provide it to me."

"I do not know what this represents, Comrade President."

"That is your May launch of the A2e."

"It is?"

"It is. You will note that it is in the process of being destroyed by an unknown missile."

Brezhenki reluctantly took his reading glasses from an inside pocket of his uniform jacket and put them on. Turning the photo over once again, he peered closely at the image.

No. It could not be.

"How is it, General Brezhenki, that your own command goes merrily onward, unaware that it is being attacked by some foreign entity? What kind of self-protection do you have in place? Do you merely throw things into space without knowing what else is there ahead of you?"

It was not the time to appear either simple or cowardly. "Comrade President, are we in declared war

196

with another nation?"

"Of course not, General."

"Then do you fully expect me to be prepared for hostile action? Has the *Protivo-vozdushnaya Oborono* with their thousands of early-warning radars told you something they have not told me?"

The President backed off a little. "They have not."

Brezhenki retrieved a dash of his credibility without admitting he had falsified a report. "Certainly, I knew the A2e had been sabotaged. Without evidence such as this, however," he waved the photograph, "I could only request that the Committee for State Security look into it."

Cherevako started to speak, but the President warded him off with a raised hand. "Seeing that picture, General, who would you nominate as the offender?"

"The Americans have the capability."

"But the Americans are the ones who have brought it to our attention, humiliating as it is. They too have lost missiles in similar fashion."

Brezhenki was facing a new idea without the time for decent consideration. "Comrade President, before I make a rash decision, I must have time to consult with my experts. We will go over this, and any other evidence we can find, and report back to you."

The President pushed a manila folder across the desk toward him. It rasped on the desk top, causing an icy thrill to charge up Brezhenki's spine. "There is more, in here. And General, you are to make certain that your report is factual and accurate."

"Of course, Secretary."

"Then, there is one more matter."

Brezhenki waited, impatient to call Antonovko and begin turning the wheels of investigation. Though he was a friend, Antonovko might well face demotion or reassignment.

"I have agreed with the American President to an escalation of the joint sub-orbital program. Toward that end, I have released twenty million dollars' worth of hard currencies to meet the next year's funding. The amount is charged to your budget."

"Of course, President."

"Additionally, I have released another four million dollars' worth of hard currencies to assist the sub-orbital program with unexpected development. That amount has been subtracted from the submarine program of the Northern Fleet."

Which will make a large number of selfish admirals very difficult to get along with, Brezhenki thought. "What are these unexpected developments, Comrade President?"

"The sub-orbital craft are to be armed."

There went the advantage. Now the Americans would have armed craft at the end of the program, as well. Antonovko was going to be as depressed as Brezhenki already felt.

Alain Moncrieux had been called into six meetings by the weasel-like Inspector Francois Duchatreau. He was becoming thoroughly disenchanted with the machinations of the *Service de Documentation Exterieure et Contre-Espionage.*

He had endured their hours of questioning about people like Henry Parker and Sir Neil Holmes and

Baron Boris von Untermeier and Delbert Jenkins and a dozen others Moncrieux had served the last couple of years. He had watched silently when his, or rather, Yvonne's, meticulous files were spilled all over the office as a team of SDECE investigators went through them, typed line by typed line. All that was lacking, he thought, was a large magnifying glass and they would appear to be real detectives.

On the fifth of August, another in an unending string of sultry, burning days, one of Duchatreau's flunkies called again and ordered him to report to their office at five o'clock.

"No."

"What!"

"Let me talk to Duchatreau."

The inspector came on the line a minute later and growled, "We expect you to come in, as any good citizen, Monsieur Moncreiux."

"Incorrect, Inspector. Tomorrow, we have another launch of the *Rapier*, and I must be there." It was not a big thing. The European Space Agency had fallen behind, and the *Rapier* was to lift a Belgian satellite into orbit. The revenues were insignificant; it was a trade-out, and Moncreiux received no commission.

"Perhaps you will be there," Duchatreau said. "Who can tell about these things?"

"I'm not doing another damned thing until you tell what this is all about."

There was a long hesitation. "Very well. We have learned from an excellent source that the failures of the *Rapier* rocket are the result of sabotage. It is our job to locate the perpetrator."

Incredible! "And you think that this . . . this culprit

is one of the companies paying us sixteen million dollars for the privilege of blowing up a missile? A company that would waste a multi-million-dollar satellite in order to make the French space program look silly? Is it you, or your superior, who is insane?"

Duchatreau ignored the insult. "This is but one of the lines of inquiry, Monsieur. We will expect you at five o'clock."

Moncreiux was suddenly tired of his job. Clients deserting him, income evaporating, and silly bureaucrats accusing him. "Not me. I am tired of participating in your fantasy. If you think me guilty of such stupidity, arrest me. Otherwise, leave me alone."

"Very well, Monsieur, we will arrest you."

Major Conrad Farrell was an Army officer assigned to Northeast Asia analysis in the Defense Intelligence Agency, and the telephone call was bucked around the building and finally upstairs to him.

"Major Farrell. May I help you?"

"My name is Henry Parker, Major, and I'm mad as hell."

"Sir?"

"Let's start this on an even keel," Parker told him. "This isn't an anonymous call. My name is Henry Parker. I'm a vice president with RCA, and I'm in charge of negotiations between RCA and vendors of space transportation."

"Yes, sir. I've got that." Farrell pulled a memo pad close and jotted quickly.

"We've just recently launched a communications satellite into space, and we used Nesei Aerospace

Industries to do it. They're located on the northern end of Hokkaido Island."

"Yes, sir." Farrell knew that.

"Now then, Major, while I was there for the launch, I saw something that disturbed me."

"What's that, Mr. Parker?"

"Down at their airfield, they've got some secret hangars I wasn't allowed to get close to. But I did see some strange-looking airplanes."

"What did they look like, sir?" Farrell was ready to doodle a sketch.

"That's just it. We weren't very close, and I didn't get a good look, but they weren't anything like I've ever seen before, and I've seen a hell of a lot of airplanes, where I go."

"Of course, sir. But what did you see?"

"Well, first, they're all black. I didn't see any kind of marking on them. Looks like they've got two jet engines on top of the wings, like the B-2, and . . ."

"What was the shape of the wings, Mr. Parker?"

"I wasn't close enough to tell. But from where I was, the planes looked very smooth. I mean, there weren't any sharp angles, like you see on a Hornet or a Falcon or an Eagle."

"Did it look like anything you've seen before, sir? Perhaps a Blackbird?"

"I've never seen a Blackbird, except in a picture. No, it looked like . . . well, maybe like a boat. Some kind of racing boat."

"I see. And how many did you see, Mr. Parker?"

"Four of them, I think, but there may have been more in the back of the hangar."

Farrell drew a picture of a Cigarette boat, hydroplaning the sea, hauling cocaine. "What is it about these airplanes that has made you angry, Mr. Parker?"

"It's not the airplanes. It's the goddamned American bureaucracy. Since I got back from Japan, I've been calling the Air Force, the CIA, the FBI, even the goddamned Navy. Everyone listens to the story, then says they'll get back to me—they don't."

Farrell sighed. "Mr. Parker, I'll look into this and call you back in a few days, but it's going to take a while. May I have your phone number?"

Parker gave it to him, then hung up.

Major Farrell looked at his picture. He was not too worried about a Cigarette boat. And if the Air Force and CIA were not pursuing Parker's story, he saw no reason why he should waste his own time.

Ripping the page from his memo pad, he dropped it in the shredder beside his desk.

Twelve

"With these babies, you don't just pull into the first Texaco that comes along," Dallas Grant had quipped.

Based on that philosophy, and requirement, Dmitri Vidorov, Grant, and Blake had taken off from Edwards Air Force Base in the three operational suborbitals at three o'clock in the afternoon on August fifth. They would spend the night at the Kennedy Space Center at Cape Canaveral in the state of Florida, which had the facilities available for producing their liquid hydrogen and oxygen fuels. Vidorov and Grant could have based themselves out of California, but with the distances involved, Major Dennis Blake's mission to France was impossible from the American West Coast.

In effect, the combined squadron—the Black Sky Squadron and Vidorov's 1st Sub-space Squadron—had been mobilized. Each of the pilots took with him two members of his ground crew and several large chests of tools and critical small replacement parts. The rear compartments had been stripped of the telemetry gear, and two seats and the tool cases were bolted in place.

It was the first time aloft in the sub-orbitals for the four American and two Soviet crewmen.

They were ecstatic, to say the least, Vidorov thought, though they flew the flight plan at only 100,000 feet. The intercom and the intercraft frequencies remained alive with happy and obscene transmissions for the one-and-a-half hours duration of the flight.

Except for the commercial flight which had brought Vidorov and his colleagues to California, and from whose windows he had seen little, it was Vidorov's first experience with geography east of Arizona. All of the testing for a year-and-a-half had taken place primarily over the Pacific Ocean.

Though he had the U.S. map in his head and on the screen in front of him, the territory was strange. Dallas Grant pointed out Phoenix, El Paso, and the major airport of Dallas-Fort Worth. "You need inertial navigation to get from one terminal to another."

The Texas city of Dallas was apparently the inspiration for Grant's first name. Though the three sub-orbiters flew over very many obvious military installations, Grant did not specify them.

The Mississippi River was impossibly large, a great dividing line.

Colonel Dmitri Vidorov was suffering from his own dividing line. He was still uncertain of his status. Several days before, after General Billings had approached Nemorosky with the startling evidence of foreign sabotage in both the U.S. and Soviet space programs, Vidorov and Nemorosky had had their own long conversation.

"There is no mutual nonaggression treaty between

204

the United States and the Union of Soviet Socialist Republics," Nemorosky had said. "And therefore, there is no rationale for either you or me to participate in any of these operations, Dmitri Vasilivich."

"We are certain that the same attacks have been made against the *rodina,* General?"

"Yes. I have spoken at length with General Antonovko. Between you and me, Dmitri Vasilivich, the Soviet Rocket Forces seem frantic. Launch schedules have been suspended. There are, if I read between the lines correctly, many investigations taking place. Antonovko says they have discovered sabotaged flights both at Tyuratam and Plesetsk."

"This is hardly believable, Comrade General."

"I agree. But apparently true."

"And what do we do? General Billings has requested that I accompany Grant on this overflight of Cape Canaveral as part of our cooperative venture."

"I know. I am inclined, Dmitri Vasilivich, to put into my mind an assumed, and temporary, mutual nonaggression treaty. But you and your men are the ones who must fly the missions. Tell me what you feel."

Vidorov had been honest with his superior and with himself. "I have a debt to General Billings."

Nemorosky sighed. "I know. The bloody, botched picture-taking."

"I am not trained for this work."

"Nor I," Nemorosky concurred.

"But I do not wish to ally myself with an American cause simply because an Air Force general has kept me out of prison. I do not want to appear traitor to my country, no matter the circumstances."

Nemorosky sighed again. "You make a good argument, Dmitri Vasilivich."

"And yet, beyond what I owe to General Billings, I do not want to run from the threat, especially if it is a threat also against my country. And if what the Americans are telling us is true, then my expertise with the sub-orbital craft may be beneficial in eliminating the threat."

"You are talking yourself into participation, Comrade Colonel."

"Yes. I suppose I am. Still, I would prefer to have a written order from you."

"You will have it, Dmitri Vasilivich."

So, while he had the order, Vidorov also knew that it was based on flimsy rationales. And in addition to the wavery legality, there were other bothersome flies in his ointment. He had been raised, and then trained in the military, to completely distrust the Americans. They were the enemy, declared or not. Every training exercise he had ever taken part in, when learning to fly fighter aircraft and later advanced interceptors, had assumed an enemy with the stars and bars displayed on his wing.

And now, out there on his own wing, was the stars and bars insignia overlaid with the Soviet star. It did not seem right, but it also appeared as if he were, as the Americans said, "stuck with it."

Grant's voice came over the Tac-2 frequency. "Take a look at your left horizon, Dmitri. Just about ten o'clock. That's Nashville."

"In Tennessee, am I right?"

"You're absolutely right. That's where a lot of my music comes from."

"Your music?"

"I like all kinds, but much of it is produced there. Put on records and tapes."

"I understand. The country music. I am afraid that I have more classical tastes, Dallas."

Dennis Blake cut into the conversation. "Hey, Dmitri. Y'all take a close look at Dolly Parton or Winona Judd, your tastes are goin' to change overnight."

"Damn sure," Sergeant Gloom added from the rear compartment of Grant's craft.

Grant switched frequencies and contacted an air controller. Shortly afterward, they began to lose altitude and decrease speed from the Mach 3.5 they had been holding. The three sub-orbitals were flying in echelon, Grant in the lead and Vidorov, then Blake, behind and off his right wing.

After crossing a portion of the Gulf of Mexico and then the west coast of Florida, all three went back onto turbojets without incident.

The Kennedy Space Center launch complex was huge, much larger than its counterpart the Baikonur Cosmodrome at Tyuratam, Vidorov thought. They landed on the long concrete runway that also returned the Space Shuttles to Canaveral, piggy-backed on top of Boeing 747 transports.

They were met by a jeep vehicle which led them, in single file, over a few kilometers of taxiways and roads to a launch pad which would serve as their fueling station. One by one, the sub-orbitals were lined up in a row, then shut down.

They had brought along only one ladder, stowed in the back of XSO-4, and Grant's crew chief worked it out of the rear compartment, deplaned XSO-4, then brought it over to XSO-3, which Vidorov was flying. Finally, Sergeant Gloom helped Blake and his two crewmen down to ground level.

The nine of them gathered around XSO-4 and were joined by some fueling specialists from the space center. The outsiders appeared awed by the suborbitals.

"Gloomy," Grant said, "I understand that you have to put some adaptors on the fueling hoses?"

"That's right, Colonel."

"Okay. You show everybody what has to be done, then suction off the volatile fuels. Sometime soon, there's supposed to be a tanker of JP-4 showing up here, and you can refuel the turbojet tanks. Then let's have a thorough check of all the systems. We don't want any foul-ups at the last minute."

"Gotcha, Colonel. When's takeoff?"

"Major Blake departs at five-thirty. Colonel Vidorov and I will go at six-thirty. When you're done this afternoon, Gloomy, you grab some taxis and go into the Travelodge. You've got reservations there."

The three pilots, with their overnight bags, caught a ride aboard a jeep to the security station, then switched to a taxi cab. The driver chatted aimlessly at them as he took them into the town of Titusville. The town was a tribute to space flight. Everywhere he looked, Vidorov saw souvenirs and banners in support of the NASA and Air Force efforts at the Kennedy Space Center. Cape Canaveral was an industry in its own right. Businesses and motels and cafes were named after Apollo and Mercury and Titan and the Space Shuttle. Obviously, the populace thrived on a tourist trade generated by the space complex, but just as obviously,

:hey celebrated their nation's policies.

Vidorov would have been amazed to see the citizens of the Soviet Socialist Republic of Kazakh engaged in the same celebration and adoration of the Soviet complex at Tyuratam. The activities there were rarely publicized. How was it that the USSR did not involve its citizens so completely in its space policies as did the United States? Perhaps because so many Soviet launches involved secrecy. The Motherland did not want its people to know what it was placing in orbit.

There were three motel rooms reserved for them, and they split up to change into (as Grant suggested) civilian clothes. Vidorov suspected that Dallas Grant did not want to have to explain to a Titusville questioner the presence of a Red Air Force uniform.

After he had changed out of his flight gear, Vidorov went back down the long hall to the central part of the motel. He found the dining room and also discovered that Grant and Blake were already at a table at the back. It was beside a window that overlooked the swimming pool, and the two Americans were flipping quarters.

Vidorov walked across the carpeted room and neared the table.

Grant stopped flipping his coin and looked up at him. "I ordered you a Mai Tai, Dmitri."

He sat down and looked at the concoction in front of him. "Is it safe?"

"You bet. You've just got to expand your taste beyond Stolichnaya."

Sipping from the glass, Vidorov swirled the liquid under his tongue, then said, "It is sweet."

"And misleadin'," Blake said. "Y'all got to watch

your intake on those things."

He pointed to the quarters resting on the linen table cloth. You are wagering, again?"

"Nah, not really," Blake said. "We're tryin' to determine who gets first shot at the redhead out there."

He aimed a thumb at the window. Around the swimming pool were many young ladies, most of them dressed in swimming suits that were almost not there. The one of interest, the redhead, was tall, and her hair almost flamed in the light of the sinking sun. Her suit was composed of two swooping patches of a green fabric that barely covered her pelvis and buttocks, and two smaller, triangular patches that did not fully contain her large breasts.

Vidorov thought of Nadia.

"And we done made the determination," Blake said.

"I lost," Grant admitted. "A rare occurrence."

They placed their orders for steaks and baked potatoes for dinner. One of the aspects that Vidorov did appreciate about America was the availability of great amounts of food, especially meat and bread. In almost any place, at almost any time of day, there was food to be purchased. Despite his exercise, he had put on twelve pounds since arriving in the country.

"Dallas," he said, "you had an argument with General Billings?"

"You heard that on the grapevine?"

"Nobody needed a grapevine," Blake said. "Y'all just had to be in the hall, or maybe within a hundred yards of the ops building."

Grant grinned at them, perhaps a trifle ruefully. "The general thinks very little of my diplomatic abilities as a commander in his absence. He was a bit stressed about my taking a civilian, much less a congressional staffer, up in the sub-orbital."

"Did not one of your senators accompany the crew on a Shuttle flight?" Vidorov asked.

"Jake Garn. Yeah, I pointed that out, but I don't think Billings cared much about my argument. He said Garn liked his flight, but Miss Jamieson hated hers. I've ruined the whole program."

"Y'all sure about that?"

"Well, he said he and Hansen had convinced the Senate Armed Services Committee to maintain it at present levels, and that's the way it is in the Senate's version of the appropriations bill. There's supposedly some compromise talks taking place between the Senate and House this week. Now, Billings thinks that Polly Enburton and Roberta Jamieson will undermine what they've done. Hell, he's probably right. I'm just lucky to be flying."

"Why is that, Dallas?" the Soviet asked.

"Oh, he grounded me for a couple hours, until I reminded him that I'd already prepared for tomorrow's mission. Currently, I'm on temporary flying status, the foundation of which is very fragile. His words."

"Your politics continue to confound me, Dallas."

"You're confused? I'm overwhelmed," Grant said.

Their food was delivered to the table, and Vidorov changed his concentration to the New York Strip Steak. They were almost finished when the rest of the crew appeared. After dinner, the nine of them moved to the lounge and listened to a female singer croon what the Americans called torch songs.

The crew members indulged themselves heavily in Budweiser, but the pilots nursed one drink apiece.

They were flying in the morning.

Vidorov found himself enjoying the camaraderie. His two crewmen, Sergeants Drandorov and Mezbecko, seemed to fit well with Sergeant Gloom and his friends. The talk was apolitical, involving everything from aircraft to the baseball team standings. Drandorov and Mezbecko, after three years in the United States, had memorized all of the teams and the names of many of the players. Apparently, there were wagers being placed.

At eleven o'clock, Grant broke up the party and stopped at the desk to leave wakeup calls for all of the rooms.

Vidorov went back to his pleasant room, stripped off his clothes, and sank into his soft mattress. He recalled that Dennis Blake had not attempted to engage the redhead.

Sometimes he thought that Americans were mostly composed of talk.

The morning air was chilled, and there was a low-lying mist covering the cape at five o'clock in the morning.

They had all arrived at Launch Pad Nine at four A.M., in time to fuel XSO-2. All six of the ground crewmen had performed the pre-flight checks on the sub-orbital.

Grant stood at the top of the ladder, exposed to a brisk, salty breeze off the Atlantic, as Blake hooked himself into the cockpit. "Okay, Denny, read it back to me."

"Ah'm off the ground at oh-five-thirty hours. It's

212

only five thousand, four hundred miles to my rendezvous, and if I hold her at Mach four, I'll be in place at oh-seven-fifteen hours, Florida time, thirteen-fifteen hours in mam'selle time. The launch is scheduled for thirteen-thirty hours."

"Altitude?"

"I'm goin' to hang in at two hundred thousand."

"Now, damn it, Denny, don't wait around for more than forty minutes. If they have a delayed launch, you abort and get your butt back here."

"I can coast it, if I need to, Dallas."

"I don't want you planning that. Give yourself enough lead time that you don't have to worry about reserves."

"I got it."

"Luck." Grant slipped down the ladder and Gloomy pulled it away.

The turbo jet started right away, and XSO-2 pulled away, following the guiding jeep.

While the crew began fueling the two remaining sub-orbiters, Grant and Vidorov crawled into their cockpits and monitored Blake's radio transmissions with ground control, then with air control. He was off the ground at five-twenty-five, and climbing through 150,000 feet twenty minutes later.

The Canaveral launch was scheduled for seven A.M. It was a Titan IV with a military package, a KH-11 satellite intended to replace a similar satellite that was, after thirty-one months, beginning to die. It was, Billings had said, a better target than the French *Rapier* launch, which was transporting a Belgian communications module, and Grant thought so, too.

When the fueling was complete, Grant looked over

to Vidorov and raised his thumb. He closed the canopies and pressurized the cabins. He went through the turbojet start procedure as if it were second nature, which it was by now, but not familiar enough to ignore using the checklist readout that was displayed on the rearview screen at the left of the instrument panel. As soon as the Soviet pilot signaled his readiness, Grant waved at Gloomy, came off the brakes, and used the stick's nosewheel control to turn in behind the jeep.

By six-forty-five, the two of them were at 200,000 feet, orbiting the Cape in a two-hundred-mile-diameter circle. They remained opposite each other, two hundred miles apart, so that if their intruder appeared, they would have two different angles on him. At least, Grant's best guess was that they remained opposite each other; he could not see Vidorov's blacked-out suborbital.

In previous strategy sessions, they had agreed that they would not use the radios, possibly providing the aggressor with a homing signal. The telemetry transmitting radios had been removed for the same reason. Neither of the XSOs was transmitting an IFF signal. To radar installations along the eastern coast, they would be invisible. Hopefully, that invisibility extended to the aggressor.

Grant's display screen was showing a map of the Florida east coast and the Cape, his blip placed on the map by the Navstar navigation system. Receiving those signals was a passive action. The APG-67 radar was warmed up and ready to go active as soon as he keyed the code into his lefthand keyboard.

He turned on the video camera and activated the video and radar recording decks.

And then Grant waited it out, circling the eastern coast of Florida at 2800 miles per hour. At his altitude, the sun was high in the sky, and despite the bronzed canopy, forced him to squint every time he turned into it.

Grant's Tac-1 frequency was dailed into the Kennedy Space Center's launch control, and he had Tac-3 standing by, already tuned to the frequency utilized by Houston's flight control.

He wondered about Dennis Blake. They had given him the expected frequencies for the French launch, but Denny did not speak, or "listen," French.

The ground mist had cleared, but there was a short delay for some unexplained reason. The chronometer on the panel read 0709 hours when he heard the launch controller announce, "The bird's off!"

He watched it from first ignition, the exhaust vapors perfectly visible against the blue-green of the offshore waters. Following their pre-planned strategy, as soon as the Titan launched, Grant rolled out of his circular orbit and aimed toward the southeast, following the flight path of the missile. He assumed that Vidorov had also made the course change and was still around two hundred miles away, on Grant's left.

"One-seven-zero feet, velocity eight-point-two," the controller let him know.

Grant went to video, magnified to six, rotated the lens downward, and caught the Titan in his screen.

"One-two-zero-zero feet."

It was coming up through 120,000 feet. Some controllers dropped the last two zeros in their broadcast. He still had it on the screen.

"Velocity twenty-three thousand miles per hour."

215

Grant began to climb, his throttles in full forward, as the Titan screamed ahead of him, achieving Grant's altitude. His readout indicated Mach 5, the software-controlled maximum recently changed after a long debate with Restwick and Murychenko.

As Grant went through 225,000 feet, he was surprised to see Vidorov closing in on him. XSO-3 had not been visible to him until it was within a couple hundred yards. The Soviet fell in alongside and the two of them continued after the rocket.

Grant punched in the code for radar, and the screen immediately converted, the radar sweep turning lazily on the display. He found both Vidorov's blip and the one representing the Titan. The missile was quickly out-pacing them.

The threat warning he thought he heard was only in his head.

There was nothing out there.

At 350,000 feet, they gave up the chase. It was as high as Grant or Vidorov had ever been in the sub-orbitals.

The launch controller was still in his headset. "We have an altitude of seven-five miles, third-stage burning, one-three seconds to burn-out. Houston, I'm handing off to you."

Houston said, "We've got it. Gentlemen, we're going to have a successful insertion."

Grant and Vidorov continued to search the immediate skies with active radar for thirty minutes, but found no one but themselves.

Grant finally broke radio silence, "Dmitri, let's go back and get ourselves a Mai Tai."

* * *

216

Dennis Blake enjoyed the hell out of his trip to Europe. He liked the solitude at 200,000 feet, the closeness of the stars, the serenity of the Atlantic. At the moment, the only thing he liked better was that redhead he had seen last night, but it turned out she had a friend. A big friend.

Closing on the coast of France, he made certain that all of his systems that could radiate a signal were inoperative. He did not know what the French would say about an overflight at this altitude, but they could be pretty damned picky. He remembered when they had denied overflight rights to the bombers flying out of England to harass the Khadaffi asshole.

He was high enough that the Spanish peninsula and the Mediterranean Sea, on his right oblique in the far distance, actually looked something like the maps. The Swiss Alps were white under the sun, a strong contrast to the summery browns and golds of the fields below. Green forests trailed after greenish-silver streams.

He achieved his coordinates, confirmed by Navstar, at 0713 hours. It seemed funny that he had gotten out of bed in the dark just three hours before, and below him, the Frenchies were just sopping up the ends of their lunches. The thought made him hungry.

Blake put XSO-2 into orbit above the launch complex as soon as he had picked it out of the countryside. There was a little village to the south. A bunch of tiny ant-cars zoomed along the lanes and highways, almost indiscernible. It was more like the road was undulating.

On his Tac-1 frequency, he keyed into the French launch controller, and assumed he had the right frequency. He could not understand the words, but

217

after a while, it began to sound right. The spacing, the subdued urgency, the numeric syllables had to be those of a controller. He picked out a *tres bien,* and that sounded okay.

Blake watched his chronometer, but 0730 passed without a corresponding launch. He also watched the skies, but was pretty sure that he was alone.

When the chronometer readout displayed 0751, he cussed to himself, and prepared to abort the mission. Grant had told him forty minutes, which meant 0755. He decided to extend it by five minutes. To him, 0800 had a better ring to it.

At 0753, the launch controller's voice picked up a couple octaves. Blake checked the ground and saw the *Rapier* immediately. It appeared to be climbing pretty damned fast.

By the time he rolled out of his orbit and picked up a heading of 145 degrees, the damned thing had closed the distance by half. He kicked in his camera and rotated the lens down until he had it centered in the screen.

Really motivating along at Mach 5, Blake steadily brought the camera lens, then the nose, up, to keep the image centered as the rocket rose to meet him. When it hit 200,000, it was far to the southeast of him.

Blake punched in his radar.

There was the *Rapier.* Eleven miles ahead of him.

Nothing else showing on the screen at that altitude.

He kept climbing.

A flicker in the scan.

Two flickers.

Three.

Abruptly looking up, through his windscreen, he

saw the *Rapier* erupt.

Back to the radar screen.

Something.

The screen painted a target.

Two hundred and seventy-five thousand feet and seventeen miles away! The bearing was 190 degrees.

Blake rolled into a slow right turn, still climbing, centering on his target. He pushed the throttles forward uselessly. He was maxxed out.

He was going to find this bastard.

He ignored the skies around him and kept his eyes on the radar screen.

Suddenly, there was a new blip on the screen.

Flat fucking moving!

Coming at him.

He knew what it was.

Blake rolled hard to the right, and inverted, dove for the surface of the earth.

The screen told him that he was not going to shake it.

He killed the radar.

Counted seconds.

Killed the rockets.

He was watching his right wing when it exploded.

The world went orange.

Then black.

Thirteen

Grant and Vidorov landed one after the other at Canaveral and taxied back to Launch Pad Nine. While the men began to de-fuel the sub-orbitals, Grant removed his helmet and unzipped his pressure suit, but stayed in the cockpit, fiddling with the radios. The helmet, with its earphones, was hung on the top of the windscreen, and he turned up the volume so he could hear what was coming over the air.

Vidorov brought their only ladder over, climbed it, and sat on the cockpit coaming beside him.

After a while, he found what he was looking for: A National Security Agency spy satellite was eavesdropping on the French launch.

"Shit. It's in French," he said.

Vidorov laughed. "What did you expect, Dallas? Be quiet a moment."

Vidorov dipped his head forward as he listened. Several minutes later, he said, "The *Rapier* program has suffered another fatality."

"Damn. Hey, you speak French?"

"A little."

"Oh, hell! Where's Denny? How long ago?"

"The missile exploded just a few minutes ago, Dallas."

Grant keyed in Blake's frequency on Tac-2, channeling it through the Defense Communications Satellite Network. "SOL-two, this is SOL-four."

Releasing the microphone stud, he heard static issuing from the helmet.

"SOL-two, this is SOL-four."

Again, no response. Grant was getting worried.

"He may have his radios shut down, or doesn't want to use them," Vidorov said.

"SOL-two, this is SOL-four."

Nothing.

"SOL-four, Rosie here." Billings was listening on the net, also.

"Go Rosie."

"You hang in there, I'm going to make some calls."

Radar specialist Kevin MacGruder had sounded the alarm.

"Radar, Bridge. Repeat that."

"Repeating, Bridge. I've painted, Jesus, thirty-plus targets. They came out of nowhere. They wink in and out on me. Bearing two-five-five, altitude two-zero-thousand. They're coming down fast, sir."

"Heading?" the exec asked from the bridge.

"Uh, Bridge, they're just coming straight down. No heading at all."

"Range?"

"Four-seven-zero-zero yards, sir."

"Give me your best guess, MacGruder."

"Got to be a blown-up airplane, Commander. It's

221

debris, but it's scattered over two miles wide."

He had visions of a 747 strewn all over the Mediterranean. Bodies everywhere.

"Bridge out."

MacGruder waited one minute, then felt the expected surge as the missile frigate *Bronstein* dug her heels in. The stern went down. Soon, they would be making at least twenty-seven knots.

But not in time to do much good, MacGruder thought.

Almost an hour passed before Billings got back to him. Grant had tried fruitlessly to contact Blake a dozen times. He had not moved out of his seat.

"SOL-four, Rosie."

"Go ahead, Rosie."

"We want scrambler mode three."

Grant entered the code that inserted the scrambler into the radio circuit. "SOL-four is ready, Rosie."

"Okay, Dallas," Billings said, "I've been in touch with the Pentagon. NSA didn't pick up anything except the missile detonation. DIA was monitoring through Commander, Sixth Fleet, although the fleet didn't know what they were looking at."

"Come on, General! Goddamn it!"

"He went down."

"Son of a bitch!"

"There's a task force on the scene now. They've found debris that mystifies them, but it's definitely XSO-2. There's not much left."

Grant felt as if he were sinking into his seat.

"Body?" he asked.

"No."

There would not be. No trace of Hal Peters, who went down with the prototype, had ever been found.

"Flight recorders?"

"Be reasonable, Dallas. The crash site covers over a couple square miles of the western Med. The water there is deep."

"Ask Zeiman to look. Please, sir."

"All right. I'll ask. You gather up your people and come home."

"Tell Restwick that Vidorov and I want XSO-5 and XSO-6 ready to go first thing in the morning."

"Rosie, out."

He did not know whether or not the crewmen on the ground had heard any of the conversation, but from their faces, Grant could tell they already knew Blake was not returning. They stood around the nose of XSO-4, heads hanging. Tech Sergeant Dick Olson, Blake's crew chief, had tears streaming down his face.

Sergeant Gloom turned toward the east and saluted. It was the best damned salute he had ever seen Gloom present.

Grant saluted, too, and the rest of them turned eastward and followed suit. Vidorov pushed himself erect on the top of the ladder and joined them.

Grant snapped his hand down. "Gloomy, let's get the seats back into the rear compartments, then fuel 'em up. Sergeant Olson, you ride with me, and Airman Evers can ride with Colonel Vidorov."

The flight back to California at 100,000 feet was completed in almost total silence. Grant reset his watch and the instrument panel chronometer back to local time just before he made his turn into the base leg of his landing approach. It was nine-thirty in the morning, and already battles had been lost. He felt as badly as he had felt on some return flights to Bien Hoa, when he had been short a wingman. He felt worse; he had known Denny for much longer than he had known many of the men who flew his wing in Vietnam.

When they parked the sub-orbitals near the fueling station, Billings and Nemorosky were waiting for them. The general had roused another crew to handle the post-flight de-fueling operations.

Grant slid down the ladder.

"We all feel the same way you do, Dallas," Billings told him.

"Yeah, sure. Restwick in Hangar five?"

"He might be. It doesn't matter." Billings used his open palm to indicate all the crew exiting the sub-orbiters. "All of you are taking the rest of the day off. Get off the base. Relax a little."

"We don't have time to relax, General. I want these two birds in the shop, undergoing their modifications."

"You want to take a week off, Grant?"

Grant stared hard at the general, but he was not going to stare the general down. He was already cruising in chancy waters with Billings.

"No, sir."

"Then get out of here." Billings turned to Vidorov and the others. "The rest of you scatter until reveille."

Grant accepted the AWOL bag Gloomy handed down to him, then walked slowly across the tarmac to the hangar. He changed into civilian clothes in the dressing room and went out to his car. He did not feel like putting the top down.

He did not feel like going back to his room.

Vidorov stopped next to him. "Would you like to get a drink, Dallas?"

"Thanks, Dmitri. No, not now."

He would go see Tricia. Getting into the front seat, Grant started the car and backed out of his slot.

He dropped the gearshift into drive and pulled out onto the street.

That turned out to be a bust, too. He did not call first, and she was not there when he got to Santa Monica.

Meoshi Yakamata spent most of the day with his test squadron pilots at Hakodate Air Base, compiling a collective report on the FSX performance, as of the end of the fifth month of flight testing.

The younger men in his group were impressed with the fighter's agility and maneuverability while the older men complained of its lack of power and the inadequacy of electronics systems. In this day of high technology aircraft, the older men felt it was a waste of money to build an airplane that did not match the capabilities of aircraft flown by countries just to the north and west of Japan.

Yakamata wrote both viewpoints into his rough draft, then dismissed the pilots. He spent an hour editing, then turned it over to his secretary for typing.

He left his office, which was tucked away on the second floor of the hangar housing the FSX fighters, and went down to the apron. The wind had come up, bringing with it a threat of cold and rainy weather. It was going to be an early winter, and a long one, he thought.

As was his custom when he was on the base, the colonel walked over to operations, chatted with the officers on duty, and reviewed the missions so far scheduled for the week. They were listed on a clipboard hanging on the wall behind the counter.

Afterwards, he went back out and found his car, a four-year-old Mazda sedan, and unlocked it. One day, and soon, he would drive what he could actually now afford, he told himself. He drove the four blocks to the base headquarters and, also customary, presented himself to his superior, the general presiding over special operations. Yakamata brought him up to date on the FSX program, promising the month-end report by tomorrow. He also informed him of progress with the Nesei Aerospace rocket program.

On his way out of the building, he stopped by the Air Wing intelligence office and talked to his friend, Arabella Shiuku. She was a captain, the daughter of a Japanese-British union. Many years before, they had had an affair. They were still close friends.

"Are we in imminent danger of invasion, Captain Shiuku?"

She got up from her desk and came to the counter. "The country is not. Perhaps I am?"

He smiled at her. Their repartee was often risqué, but he did not know whether or not she was serious about reinstating their previous relationship. As a senior executive with Nesei Aerospace, however, he thought that a good wife could be beneficial.

"Would you like to be?"

"When there is nothing better to do."

"I am free on Friday night," he said. "Would you be interested in dinner?"

She cocked her head to one side. "Certainly, Meoshi. But are we simply entertaining each other, or debating, or are we opening old closets?"

"Let us find the answer to that on Friday."

"I will prepare by bringing a sword and a flower," she said.

Yakamata laughed. "While we speak of swords, is there information yet on the French launch?"

Yakamata held high security clearances, and his work with the Nesei Aerospace program entitled him to both open and classified information about the other space programs taking place in the world.

"Yes," she said. "The *Rapier* did not achieve orbit."

"Well, I cannot say I am unhappy. Perhaps yet another country will see a need for Japanese assistance."

Yakamata returned to his car and drove to the bachelor officer quarters. As a field grade officer, his rooms were more spacious than others in the building and were quite comfortable. He was allowed furniture of his own selection from government stores, but he had purchased most of it himself. Both his bedroom and sitting room were finished in traditional Japanese fashion. He removed his shoes as he entered, set them to one side, and then settled to his knees before the low table placed on a woven bamboo mat.

He was tired, and he was considering a short nap before dinner when the telephone rang.

Pushing to his feet, he walked across the room to his desk and answered it.

"You must come to Sun Land at once."

Tired as he was, there should have been but one response—his immediate departure. However, Yakamata determined that the time had come for him to begin asserting some of the command presence for which he was known in the JADF. "Of course, Mr. Kyoto. I will be there first thing in the morning."

Fourteen

Colonel Meoshi Yakamata stood on the other side of the desk in Maki Kyoto's elegant office. He had often seen the chief executive officer of Nesei Aerospace Industries preoccupied or a trifle irate at unexplained delays, but never before so intensely angry.

Though he understood the gist of it, the story was disjointed by Kyoto's rage, and the man finished with, "You are the cause, Colonel!"

"But, Mr. Kyoto . . ." His intention of the night before to be more assertive had waned.

"Did you not hire the pilot, this man Matsushima?"

"Of course, but . . ."

"Were you not to retain pilots of some degree of wisdom and maturity?"

"Mr. Kyoto, the only criteria I was provided was that the pilots must be highly competent and adaptable. It appears that Mr. Matsushima adapted to unexpected circumstances."

"Get out! Get out and discover what went wrong. It must not happen again."

As Yakamata turned on his heel to leave, he heard Kyoto pick up the telephone and order one of his secretaries to "Place a transpacific call to Mr. Lee."

The president of Nesei Aerospace never dwelt for long on any particular detail.

Now enraged himself, and with his future at Nesei Aerospace Industries at stake, Yakamata left the administration building and reentered the Nissan Maxima that had picked him up at the airfield. He directed the driver to take him back to the secured hangars.

On the journey, he composed himself and brought his anger under control. A commander must not let emotional nuances color his decisions.

The pilots were waiting for him, and they all appeared fearful. Yakamata picked out one of them, crossed the room, and stood a meter in front of him. Yakamata's height made the former JADF captain seem much smaller and more vulnerable than he actually was.

"Tell me why, Mr. Matsushima."

"The other craft was coming after me, Colonel. I could do nothing else."

"You are so certain? You could not have slipped away, silent and unseen?"

"I was tracking on radar, active, and his radar had locked on. My threat warning receiver signaled me, Colonel Yakamata. By estimate, he was less than a minute away, and I do not know whether or not he had weapons available. I took the action necessary to protect myself and my craft, and to keep the mission secret."

Would Yakamata have done less? Or more? It was

the proper response, under the circumstances. But it did not bode well for the future. Could this have been an accidental meeting? Or had NAI's intrusions been discovered earlier? Would they now face Soviet-American sub-orbitals protecting other launches? And in France?

There were many questions to be discussed with Mr. Kyoto, when the man had calmed down.

"All of us will review the tapes. Now."

His pilots bowed their heads in acquiescence.

One of the things that Grant appreciated about Tricia was that she was an early riser. One of the things he was not too sure about, she was a nut for healthy breakfasts—there were no eggs anywhere in her apartment. He had searched it thoroughly one time.

They got up at five o'clock, and he drank his orange juice and decaffeinated coffee, and ate one piece of wheat toast. He passed on the oat bran, and watched her go through a big bowl of it, sitting on the opposite side of the dinette table. The filmy peignoir she wore attracted more of his attention than did the oat bran.

"Are you going to be all right today?" she asked.

"Sure." He had told her the whole story the night before, after sitting in the Golden Keg over Scotch-and-waters for two hours before his frequent phone calls caught her at home.

"Am I going to read this in the papers?"

"I hope not, hon. It'd blow some of our strategy. All of it, in fact."

"Have you been telling me things out of school?"

"Yup. That's because I don't think you're an

230

undercover agent."

She grinned at him. "Of course I am."

"Wrong covers."

Abruptly, she changed topics. "I'm leaving."

His mouthful of coffee almost went the wrong way. He swallowed and said, "You're leaving."

"For Hawaii. With Dan."

Grant attempted a degree of sophistication. "Permanent arrangement?"

"He got his script, and we're going to look at a couple of film locations."

"Hell, you can make the Malibu Hills look like anything from Korea to Afghanistan," he suggested with some logic. "Who needs Hawaii?"

"Dan does. This way, a few months in the islands comes out of the picture, instead of out of his pocket."

"Disagree with everything he likes," Grant said.

"You haven't grasped the importance of my position yet, have you? It's the other way around."

"How long are you going to be gone?"

"I don't know. A week or two."

"Is he taking his wife along?"

"You haven't heard?"

"Heard what? I don't chitty-chat with the industry people or read the trades."

"Jennifer Moretti found a new love. I think she's in Capri or somewhere like it."

Grant poured himself some more coffee.

Tricia leaned back in her chair, peering at him over the rim of her cup. "You jealous?"

"Of course not."

She smiled.

"A whole week?"

"Or two."

"Let's go back to bed."

He drove into Rosie at five minutes after eight, and went directly to Hangar 5. As he parked, Vidorov walked across the street, looking as cool, and as cold, as ever.

"You appear better this morning, Dallas."

"How about you, Dmitri? You get off the base?"

"No. But I called Nadia. It will cost a large portion of my paycheck, no doubt."

Which would not hurt too much, Grant thought. A colonel in the Red Air Force made substantially more than a doctor or scientist in the Soviet Union. Of course, Billings had said at one time or another that the Soviets were only getting about half their pay in U.S. dollars. The rest was in rubles, which stayed at home. For the enlisted men in the ground crews, it did not allow much carousing. They made about a quarter of what the Americans did.

They went into the hangar together and chased down the chief engineers. Restwick and Murychenko were overseeing the final buttoning-up of XSO-5. With all of the access hatches in place and the weapons pods retracted, the sub-orbitals finally looked airworthy. Or sub-space worthy.

Restwick looked up as they approached. "Finally, our test pilots are out of bed."

"They ready to go?"

"Maiden flights in," Restwick checked his watch, "about fifty minutes."

"Have you got our missiles aboard?"

232

"Not yet, Dallas. One step at a time. We'll make sure they fly, first."

"I want the missiles loaded," Grant said.

Restwick held his gaze. "The general . . ."

". . . isn't flying it," Grant finished for him.

Murychenko looked at Vidorov. "Colonel?"

"It is time, I think."

Restwick shrugged. "Well, shit. The skin comes off your ass, Dallas."

"It always does."

The SDECE did not arrest Alain Moncrieux.

No one from the weasel Francois Duchatreau's office showed up on his doorstep to claim him, nor did they call him at the office again.

After the disaster of the day before, however, Moncreiux decided that Duchatreau and his like in the intelligence and police services must have their hands full.

Moncreiux was satisfied in his own mind that the *Rapier* failure was not an accident. The odds were against it, and Moncreiux was a firm believer in statistical probability. He did not know the details, nor did he want to know them, but he was certain that outside influences were involved.

Still, he was a Frenchman, and the loss, not only to the space program, but to national pride, hurt him. He was so heartsick that he did not come into his office on the *Rue de l'Universite* until after noon.

Yvonne was waiting patiently at her desk. With no instructions for the day, she had taken it upon herself to begin reorganizing the filing system—a mess after its "dis-arrangement" by the investigators from SDECE. She was not the kind to file and polish her nails during slack periods.

"Monsieur Moncreiux, I am so sorry."

"It is out of our hands, Yvonne. I am certain the authorities will soon locate the cause."

"Still, I know how it affects you," she said.

Loss of confidence, loss of clients, loss of commission, loss of travel and other perquisites. Yes, she knew.

With a sweep of his left hand, Moncreiux indicated the file folders stacked on the floor, leaning against her desk. "I wonder if, in all of that, you might be able to locate my personal file?"

"Of course."

He went on into his own office, shed his topcoat and hung it on the hall tree, then slumped into his desk chair. He lit a Benson and Hedges. He was smoking too many of them.

Summer was beginning to depart his outside view. The trees were still green, but looked as if they were dying, heralding winter. Moncreiux did not like winter. It was a dead season.

Yvonne came in a few minutes later with his file and his cup of coffee. She had her steno pad, and she flipped it open as she sat down opposite him. She smiled at him, offering him her own confidence.

There was no list of phone numbers to give her this morning. Moncreiux had not felt like composing one after he arrived home last night.

He opened his personal file. It contained his private papers—deed of trust for his half-paid-for apartment, automobile title, passport, insurance policy, and the like. It also contained his bank statements and the passbooks to his two savings accounts.

He opened the passbooks and looked at the balances. "Yvonne, what is eight hundred and twenty-eight plus five thousand five hundred and seventy-three?"

"Six thousand four hundred and one, monsieur."

His accumulated francs were the equivalent of around thirteen hundred U.S. dollars. And in his checking account, he had another one hundred and seventy francs. If he had not been such a spendthrift on clothing, travel, and entertainment, the figure would have been quadruple what it was. His commission on a sixteen-million-dollar launch fee was twenty thousand dollars. In some years, he had earned as much as 250,000 dollars. Where did it all go?

"That is my life's savings, Yvonne. It is not much, is it?"

"It seems very much to me," she said.

"Enough to start my own business, do you suppose?"

"Oh, monsieur! You are not leaving?"

"I believe the future may be found in computers. Certainly, the future in space transportation appears to be waning for me. The Japanese will take it, and my livelihood, away from me."

"But, monsieur, if you have fortitude, surely . . ."

The telephone rang.

Yvonne put her pencil down and picked up the receiver. "Office of the Liaison to Commercial Enterprise," she said in French, then after listening several seconds, again in English. "One moment, please."

Moncreiux raised an eyebrow.

"Sir Neil Holmes."

He lifted the receiver from her tiny hand. "Good

afternoon, Sir Neil."

"Alain, I am with the managing director. Are you still prepared to match the Japanese?"

"At eighteen million six hundred thousand pounds, yes, Sir Neil." His debate with the defense minister two weeks before had lasted over two hours, but he had prevailed.

"The board of directors has instructed us to proceed with the lowest bid, Alain. In the event of a tie, we are to foster British-French relations."

"But that is wonderful, Sir Neil!" With the telephone clamped between his chin and his shoulder, Moncrieux returned his passbooks to the file and closed the file. "I must ask if you are aware of yesterday's unfortunate occurrence?"

"Yes, that we are. However, we will assume that the French space program has now taken care of its failure rate for the next two years or so."

"Excellent! I too am a student of statistics."

As he replaced the telephone in its cradle, Moncrieux wondered if Neil Holmes knew something he did not. Or perhaps did not know anything at all.

Yvonne's face beamed, and she took a deep, entrancing breath. "See, monsieur? Only patience is required."

He nodded his acknowledgement. With a sale imminent and a commission almost banked, Moncrieux should have been in a celebratory mood, but pessimism darkened it.

The SDECE had better move very quickly to capture this saboteur.

*   *   *

236

Grant and Vidorov learned that the Hellwinder worked pretty much as planned. At 250,000 feet, targeting on flares ejected from the Electronic Counter-Measures module installed under the turbojet, the missiles were extremely accurate in a twenty to twenty-two-mile range.

The computer calculated from the radar readings that the Hellwinder, when launched at Mach 4.5, achieved a speed of close to Mach 9. The missile covered twenty miles in thirty-nine seconds.

"Jesus Christ, Dmitri. No wonder Denny didn't have a chance."

"Even if he had been armed, Dallas, the probabilities are narrow that he would have survived. Reflexes will be important. We are going to have to develop a new set of combat tactics, also."

"I shouldn't have sent him to France without ECM, at least."

"You sent us to your Cape Canaveral," the Soviet pointed out.

They each saved one missile, and on the return trip, dropped flares on the desert forty miles from Bonneville and circled back to try a weapons run at near ground level. The missile's speed, range, and accuracy would be curtailed in the denser environment.

"I'll go at ten miles, Dmitri. You try it at five."

"Affirmative," the Soviet pilot told him on Tac-2.

Grant was nineteen miles from his target before the Hellwinder's infrared tracking system picked up the incandescent heat of the magnesium flares. He used his video camera and when the flares appeared on his screen, he jockeyed the sub-orbital a fraction to line up on the left flare. At fifteen miles out, he armed the missile and activated its infrared tracking mode. The missile did not give him a solid lock-on signal until just under eleven miles.

At ten miles, the signal was steady and high-pitched in his ears, and Grant touched the commit button on the stick's new and strange-feeling grip. A half-second later, the computer let the Hellwinder go.

The son of a bitch went all over the place. The gimbal-mounted exhaust nozzle that shifted position to provide directional control was sensitively set for the thin environment of the mesosphere and thermosphere. At near sea-level, with no stabilizing fins on the rocket body, the missile's computer was going nuts trying to provide sufficient correction in one direction, then over-reacting.

Grant lost visual contact with the missile within seconds and watched the final act on his screen. The rocket propellant burned out in four miles, and he jumped from video to radar to track it.

It missed the target by at least a mile.

Keying Tac-2, he said, "Very bad, Dmitri."

"I will try the LD."

Grant pulled up and reduced speed as quickly as he could, using twenty percent speed brakes to get down to Mach 1.6. He made a wide circle around the still burning flares, but he could not see the laser designator in operation.

"I have the target lit up. Six miles."

The sub-orbital streaking across the desert below him looked like a super-bat, its black shape chased by an equally fast shadow.

"Five miles. Fired."

Grant dove toward the target.

He saw the puff of sand as the non-explosive missile struck the earth—

—a quarter mile from the target.

"Dmitri, I think we'd better restrict our engagements to altitude."

"Perhaps we could install small folding fins on the missiles," Vidorov suggested.

"We'll talk it over with the ordnance honchos."

All of the brass—Billings, Nemorosky, Restwick, and Murychenko—were waiting for them when they landed. They had been able to listen to the radio conversations, but XSO-5 and XSO-6 did not have telemetry transmitting capability.

While Sergeants Gloom and Drandorov supervised the discharge of fuel, the group went over to the dressing room in Hangar 5. Grant and Vidorov stripped out of their flight gear, answered questions, and made their recommendations relative to the sub-orbitals and the missiles. Grant had two full sheets of notes, most of them related to trim or to the output of directional thrusters. Vidorov's comments were similar.

"Okay, that's good," Billings said. "Grant, get a uniform."

"Not again?"

"Again. We've got to be in Washington by six o'clock tonight."

"You know, General, if we set up a refueling station at Andrews, we could use the sub-orbiters. Hell, it'd only take about an hour."

"We'll never get to that stage if we get our funds cut off. And right now, I can't afford frills."

The reason for the hurried-up appearance of the program commander and his chief pilot was apparent

239

to Grant as soon as he was dressed and had crossed over to the operations office. The *Los Angeles Times* spread out on the counter had headlined the loss of XSO-2.

He picked it up and scanned through the article. There was no mention of a connection with the *Rapier* launch, and there were only guesses as to the cause of the accident. Though the Navy commanders on the scene were noncommittal, the local reporters had gathered quotations aplenty from fishermen and from freighter and tanker sailors in the western Mediterranean. One photo showed an oil tanker's first mate holding up a chunk of the APG-67 radar antenna which had crashed onto his deck. If the Soviets had not already had access to it through the sub-orbital program, they would have made the first mate a richer man.

Before he changed, he called the mess hall and asked one of the cooks to put together some box lunches. Billings could go without lunch or dinner, but Grant was hungry.

This trip, he did not have to fly the Cessna, and he spent a leisurely hour over a week-old *U.S. News and World Report* while devouring two thick ham sandwiches, a slab of apple pie, and two half-pint cartons of milk. Then he spent three hours going through the thick file Billings had accumulated.

General Mark Hansen met them at Andrews and brought them up-to-date on the political scene as they drove in to the Capitol. "The Senate Appropriations Committee has left the XSO program intact, Lane."

"Increases?"

"None. Not even enough to build XSO-7. But, damn it, man, be happy with what we've got."

"We're getting awfully damned close to October one, Mark. When does it go to the floor?"

"It was scheduled for tomorrow, but a couple of House members requested time before the committee. It will be granted, of course."

"Who?"

"Representative Sunwallow is going to testify about the sub-orbital's photo reconnaissance mission, and ask the Senate committee to instate your four hundred and fifty thousand bucks."

"Is he aware of what's going on up there?" Billings pointed his finger skyward.

"Not as far as I know," Hansen said.

"We must have a record going for unleaked classified data. Who else?"

"Enburton has requested time, but when I talked to her, she wouldn't tell me what she has in mind. The chairman of her committee, John Hammond, is going in with her, and they're both going to House appropriations, too."

"Okay, maybe something will go right. What are we doing now?" Billings asked.

"The chairman of the Senate intelligence oversight committee wants to know why we had a sub-orbital over the Med. And why we lost it."

"He hasn't been told yet?"

"No. To save time, we requested a joint meeting of the Senate and House committees. You get to tell them what happened."

"I don't know what happened," Billings said.

"But you have a good idea."

"Yes."

Security people were all over the place, and the hearing room was jammed. Grant recognized most of the politicians, but there were twenty others, probably staff, that he had never seen before. On appearances alone, if it were up to him, he would never have issued security classifications to six or seven of them.

He saw Robbi Jamieson.

She smiled a broad smile at him, and gave him a tiny wave of the hand.

A mystifying woman. He smiled back, but decided it would be prudent to stay away from her.

He joined the generals in seats at the witness table, sitting on the left end.

Hansen and Billings thought it would be best for the pilot to provide the initial briefing.

Grant did not agree with them, but when he counted, all of the stars outweighed his silver oak leaves.

Senator Malcolm Donohue, Chairman of the Senate Intelligence Oversight Committee, seemed to be in charge, and he banged the hearing into order.

"General Hansen?"

"Good evening, Senator. Lieutenant Colonel Grant, chief test pilot for the sub-orbital program, will brief."

"Go ahead, Colonel."

Billings had told him not to expect that any of the civilians knew, or if they did, remembered, anything that had been approved by the Presidential Finding. He went back over the original evidence of an aggressor craft and the strategy of using rocket launches as bait, to be covered by overflights of the sub-orbitals.

"On the morning of August six, XSO-three and XSO-four overflew the Canaveral launch, while XSO-two provided surveillance for the French launch . . ."

"Why two of you here?" chimed in some half-pint of a senator.

"Senator, we considered the American launch of a classified military satellite a higher priority than that of a Belgian communications satellite."

"You would."

Grant explained the mission tactics—the circling, the radio and radar silence, the stealth characteristics of the sub-orbitals and, apparently, also of the hostile craft.

Senator Donohue asked, "What evidence do we have that XSO-two was downed by hostile fire?"

"Sir, the aircraft carrier *Nimitz* had an Orion airborne to cover the French launch at the request of the Chief of Naval Operations. Backtracking the radar tapes, we have identified all but two radar targets. One of those, at three hundred thousand feet, first appeared when the *Rapier* achieved one hundred and ninety thousand feet. The second, at two hundred thousand feet, appeared a few seconds later. The second target was XSO-two."

"How can you be sure?" asked the half-pint.

"Because the pilot had been told to be at that altitude."

"Perhaps he didn't follow orders," Polly Enburton suggested.

"Congresswoman Enburton, Major Blake was not only my friend, he was a highly competent pilot and a disciplined Air Force officer. I told him what his coordinates and his altitude were to be, and that is exactly where he was." Grant could feel the heat rise in his face.

Billings tapped his leg under the table.

"Let's move on," Senator Donohue said.

Grant cleared his throat. "Shortly after that, the Rapier tumbled, then exploded. XSO-two appeared to take evasive action, then shut down its radar and disappeared from the Orion's screen. The UFO disappeared a second after that."

"There is no evidence of missiles being fired?" Enburton asked.

"No, ma'am. But from earlier tapes, we can make the assumption that . . ."

"Oh, I don't know about that," the half-pint put in. "We're always making half-baked assumptions."

For the next hour-and-a-half, the hearing degenerated: There were suggestions that XSO-2 had fallen prey to XSO-1's faults. Why was a Soviet pilot defending a U.S. military operation? If the Air Force and Navy were so certain about an armed aggressor, why had Dennis Blake been sent unarmed into possible combat?

That one was a question Grant had agonized about since the event.

Donohue broke up the hearing just before eight, with no consensus that Grant could see. A typical hearing, Billings told him.

"Who was the half-pint?" Grant asked.

"Chairman of the House Intelligence Oversight Committee," Hansen told him.

"Good Christ!"

"Exactly."

On his way out of the hearing room, Grant felt a tap on his arm and turned to find Jamieson. She looked particularly good in a modest cream-colored dress.

244

Chenile or something. Her dark hair was fluffed into a wide frame of her face. The last time he had seen it, it had been matted by Billy Shepard's flight helmet.

"Have you had dinner yet, Colonel?"

"I don't think the Air Force is allowing me dinner, Miss Jamieson." Grant turned to look at Billings.

Lane Billings very obviously thought that a Grant-Jamieson dinner date was the height of foolishness. His face darkened and his eyes stabbed a warning. He was about to come up with an excuse when General Hansen, who did not know the whole story, intervened. "You go on, Colonel. General Billings and I have another appointment."

"I've got my car somewhere near here," Jamieson said, and led him out of a side door of the Capitol.

Her car was a new Corvette convertible. Grant did not think it was the kind of car purchased on a staff salary and suspected there was family money, and perhaps family influence, supporting Robbi Jamieson.

She drove it with unconcerned abandon. Grant supposed she did not worry about dings and fender-benders. Somebody would fix it.

"Chinese, Italian, or French?"

"I'm not in a French mood," he said. "Italian?"

"Okay."

She gunned the car down Constitution, battling taxis for control of various lanes, whisked through a yellow light onto Pennsylvania, and hit fifty miles per hour before nearly locking up the brakes for a right turn onto Fourteenth Street. Following her lead, Grant had not hooked into his seat belt, and he began to regret the decision. A few minutes later, she had darted over to Eighteenth Street and skidded into a parking

245

place a block north of the front door of the Cantina d'Italia.

And the sub-orbital scared *her?* Grant thought it was safer at 200,000 feet.

"You'll like the veal, and the *cannoli* is superb."

"Is that what we're having?"

She gave him a look that suggested his questioning of her taste was unnecessary. He climbed up and out of the car, gained the sidewalk, and slammed the door shut.

She got out and slammed her own door.

"Aren't you going to lock it?"

"Oh. I guess so."

After she performed electronic magic on the doors, then armed an alarm system, she joined him on the sidewalk. Grant took the outside of the walk and offered his arm. He was halfway surprised when she took it, hanging her fingers lightly on his forearm.

"Miss Jamieson . . ."

"Let's make it Robbi, huh? How do you get a name like Dallas?"

"By having a mother raised in Texas, who was forced by my father to live in Germany, Kentucky, California, Colorado, and other sub-standard places."

"Your father is career military?"

"Was. He was an Army infantry commander. He was killed in Vietnam the year before I arrived in-country."

"Oh. Sorry."

"It happens." Soldiers knew that, even if the civilians did not.

"Is your mother living?"

"She and her widowed sister share a big, old house

246

in Houston."

"You married?"

"Once," he admitted. "My ex had more backbone than my mother. She wouldn't put up with the Air Force's rather rigid social structure." Over time, he had learned that the explanation was taken more easily than the accusation that she had been shacking up with his best friend.

"I can't say as I blame her," Jamieson said.

Grant could not quite figure out Jamieson. Working for Enburton, he would expect her to take conservative stances, possibly even be somewhat pro-DOD. In the short time he had known her, however, he had not heard her take a specific position.

Inside the restaurant, they were given a table near the back. Jamieson ordered the veal, and though he thought the veal sounded pretty good, Grant ordered ravioli. She was not going to boss him around. Jamieson wanted a bottle of some exotic wine, with an unpronounceable name; Grant ordered a carafe of the house burgundy, instead.

Over salad, which was fresh and crisp, Grant said, "You have a New England accent."

"New Hampshire. Daddy's an investment banker."

Probably invests heavily in the Republican Party, Grant thought.

"But I went to Chicago for my law degree," Jamieson said, and Grant detected a hint of defensiveness in the comment. But whether she was defending the University of Chicago or her decision to leave the Ivy League, he could not tell. Or maybe it was just a way to provide him with a clue as to her brilliance.

"You're not practicing, though?"

247

"I'm more interested in the political process."

"And how do you like it so far?"

"It's stimulating. Really exciting."

Well, there was one point of dissimilarity.

When the entree arrived, Grant said, "I need to apologize to you."

"For what?"

"For frightening you the other day."

"But you didn't. Not entirely."

"No?"

"I enjoyed the flight," she told him, "and I'd like to go up again, sometime."

"That's not the impression you left with either me or General Billings."

"It took me a little while to get my earth-legs back. I was scared for awhile, but I'd think that you would find that understandable."

"Well, sure. So, what do you think of the program?" Grant cut into his ravioli.

Jamieson took a moment to compose her answer. "I haven't decided yet. Mostly, I suppose I think it's unnecessary, an expensive toy for hot pilots."

Grant almost responded with a hot pilot comment, but fortunately remembered Billings and his dismayed look. "Even after what you heard today?"

"If there is some enemy up there, we can shoot them down with a missile."

He almost went into a lecture about the limitations of missile and electronic technology, not to mention the invisibility of the enemy, but decided she either would not understand it or would pooh-pooh it. He steered the conversation into other paths, and they finished dinner somewhat amiably, he thought, at

248

ten o'clock.

Walking back to her car, she said, "You know, I looked up your service record."

"Did you? What on earth for?"

"First, I wanted to find out what kind of a man I'd been flying with. Did you really kill seven Vietnamese pilots?"

"I shot down seven MiGs that were trying to blow me out of the sky."

Her grip on his arm got tighter, and he could feel her breast pressing against his bicep. The dark sidewalk was looking brighter.

"It said you had fifty-seven missions over North Vietnam. What kind of missions were they?"

Are we supposed to get into bombing villages and mothers? Where the hell was she coming from, Grant wondered.

"Standard stuff," he said, "but I've never been personally told that my targets have been de-classified."

"Strong, silent type, aren't you?"

"Not as silent as some generals have wanted me to be."

They found the car unmolested, and as Jamieson unlocked the alarm and the doors, she said, "It's early yet. Do you want to come over to my place? I've got a townhouse in Georgetown."

Grant had never turned down a similar invitation in his life. In his mind, he could already see all of that unleashed flesh. And just behind it, the eyes of Brigadier General Lane Billings. And behind Billings, a large granite boulder with his new resolution chiseled into its face.

"What the hell, why not? Just one, though."

Her house was small, but filled with expensive furniture and lots of gadgets. Grant left his hat on a credenza in the foyer. Jamieson slipped a disc into a CD player, and some symphonic orchestra moaned from six-foot-tall speakers. It was not Willie Nelson.

She found two brandy glasses in a sideboard in the dining room and got generous with some old Napoleon brandy. After handing him one of the balloon-like glasses, she disappeared down a hallway.

While she was gone, Grant began to regret his decision to follow her home. Like a stray dog.

Robbi Jamieson came back to her living room wearing some kind of hostess pantsuit of black velvet with a single red rose embroidered above the left breast.

"Do you mind? I've been trussed up all day long." She picked up her glass and sat on the couch next to him.

"Not at all." He was pretty sure she was un-trussed now, given the way her bodice shifted as she sat down. Grant looked her in the eyes, smiled, and considered that long, single zipper. He sipped sparingly from his glass.

"Good brandy."

"Christmas present from Daddy. I save it for special occasions."

"And this is special?"

Her eyes had lightened considerably, radiating sensuality. She leaned forward to place her glass on the table, and when she sat back, she was four inches closer to him.

"Sure. It's not often that a fighter pilot takes me to dinner."

"Bet it happens all the time," Grant said. He took a larger swig of his brandy. Lane Billings's eyes were floating in the liquid, and they were not kind eyes.

"Never." She leaned toward him.

Grant put his snifter down, then shifted his position to face her. He leaned forward, touched his lips to hers.

Hot. And surprisingly soft. She pressed her lips firmly to his. Her tongue darted experimentally.

Grant put his right hand on her waist and felt the weight of her breast on his wrist. Jamieson placed her left hand on top of his, moved her fingers lightly on the back of his hand.

That goddamned Billings stood there, just behind his eyelids.

Grant withdrew from the kiss, then kissed her one more time, lightly.

"Robbi, I hate like hell to say this, but I was telling the truth when I said I had time for only one short drink."

She smiled, but the ends of her lips were curved downward.

"I have to fly early tomorrow, and if I drink too much, or don't sleep enough, I might make mistakes which could be fatal."

"Surely not," she said.

"It's true. I take my job as seriously as you take yours." She could not fault him on that logic, he thought.

He kissed her again, felt much firmer lips, then released all grips and stood up. "But I would damned well like to see you again, the next time I'm in town. I'll plan a longer stay."

"Of course." She stood up, too, her flesh moving

251

under the clinging velvet, and Grant nearly lost his resolution.

"I'll drive you to wherever you're staying."

"That's okay, Robbi. I'll grab a cab."

He kissed her once again at the front door after retrieving his hat, and this time, her lips were more the consistency of hard rubber.

He had to walk ten blocks before he was able to flag a taxi, but he felt damned good about himself. He had resisted the temptation, and he had kept himself from becoming ensnared in an impossible relationship with a congressional aide.

Lane Billings was going to be proud of him.

At midnight (and six in the morning in Paris), Bart Zeiman and Lane Billings were finally connected with the man in charge of the French investigation into Rapier sabotage.

They were in Zeiman's office in the Pentagon, waiting while a Navy lieutenant commander making the call was shunted from one official to another.

Zeiman put it on the speaker.

"Admiral Zeiman, this is Inspector Francois Duchatreau."

"Good morning, Inspector. I'm sorry to be calling at this time of the morning."

"It is quite all right, Admiral. I have been up for some time."

Billings got up and refilled their coffee cups from a Thermos pitcher as he listened to the dialogue.

"What I'm calling about, Inspector, is to find out whether or not you've had a chance to review the radar and video tapes we forwarded to the Minister of Defense."

"Yes. I have looked at them."

"And what is your reaction?" the CNO asked.

"I have none. I do not know what these tapes are to tell me."

Zeiman frowned at Billings. "It seems to me that they suggest that a hostile force of some kind is responsible for several of your *Rapier* failures."

"Do you really think so, Admiral?"

"I do. And I'd like to suggest a cooperative arrangement in which both you and I can help each other."

"I don't think that will be necessary, Admiral. We already have several suspects in custody."

Billings said, "Shit they do."

Zeiman said, "That's wonderful, Inspector. I wonder if you would share the identities with us?"

"Not just yet, I think. Perhaps when our investigation is complete?"

"Of course. I understand," Zeiman said, aiming the middle finger of his right hand at the telephone.

Fifteen

For the first time, on August 16th, XSOs 3 through 6 flew together. Grant flew in the last position of the stepped echelon formation so that he could watch the other three sub-orbitals. Vidorov had the lead, followed by Billy Shepard and Valerie Zbibari.

The four of them had flown to Guam, switched to turbojets, and landed at Anderson Air Force Base. Before a large crowd of amazed spectators, and without shutting down the turbojets, they turned around, took off, climbed to twenty thousand feet, and kicked in the rocket engines once again.

No hitches.

XSO-5, which Grant was flying, had been tuned to his specifications. All of the controls, aerodynamic and thruster, felt good.

While the sub-orbital pilots still used the "SOL" call-sign in their test sequences, in their role as an operational squadron of Headquarters, Aerospace Defense Command, they now had another identification.

Grant hit the mike button. "Black Panther Flight, this is Panther one. Let's go to three-zero-zero."

As one, the noses came up, and the sub-orbitals climbed almost vertically toward the ionosphere. As the density of the atmosphere lessened, their velocity increased. At 200,000 feet, Grant's readout gave him Mach 4.7. Vidorov led the way, and Grant scanned the operating surfaces of the other craft. As the skies darkened around them, it became more difficult to spot deficiencies in the dark-skinned craft.

"Panther three, you have a vibration?"

"Hell, no," Shepard shot back. "I over-trimmed. Old four-baby is doing her stuff."

At 300,000 feet, they leveled out and went into their routine for gunnery practice. At that altitude, there could be no towed targets, no drones. Flares were the only option, and while the rest of the squadron slowed to Mach 4, Vidorov pulled away at Mach 5. When he was thirty miles ahead of them, Vidorov fired flares and chaff—the aluminized confetti gave everyone a radar image, and then climbed to 320,000 feet.

"Go Panthers three and four," Grant ordered.

Shepard and Zbibari advanced throttles and closed on the target. Grant followed along, dropping farther behind and below them. As he watched, the weapons pods slowly extended from the bellies of the two sub-orbiters. He reached out to the right-side panel and flicked the new switch, then waited until he had a green LED indicating his own pod was down. The instrument panels on each of the sub-orbitals had a jury-rigged feel to them now, with the addition of an armaments panel to control the pod, the arming of the missiles, and the selection of guidance systems.

At twenty-two miles from the target, and a half-mile ahead of Grant, Shepard and Zbibari each fired one missile, the Hellwinders guided by their infrared seekers.

Grant fired one of his own, with the infrared lock-on barely sounding in his earphones. He was able to track its path on the radar screen.

He counted to thirteen.

"Panther three, hit," Vidorov reported. "Panther four, hit. Panther one, missile veered off."

"I let go too early," Grant said. "Let's set up again."

They took turns as the monitor, and expended all of their missiles in twenty minutes. They fired two each on infrared tracking and two each on laser designation. The laser targeting device was more difficult to practice with because the targets were not clear enough to pin the laser targeting light on.

As they retracted the weapons pods and returned to formation for the flight home, Shepard said, "We use up Hellwinders faster than I used to use rolls of caps in my cap pistol."

"I'll bet you still have that cap pistol, Billy," Grant said.

"Somewhere, but I'd have to look for awhile."

"Our ordnance people are getting behind in their inventory," Vidorov said. "We may have to slow down the practice sessions."

Grant knew it. He was a firm believer in extensive practice, especially with completely new weapons systems, but they were taxing the output of the weapons shed at the back edge of Edwards.

The squadron stayed on Tac-2 for intercraft communications, and Grant keyed his Tac-1 frequency to ell Rosie they were enroute.

They were still in the stepped formation, on turbojets, and fifty miles out of Edwards when Shepard said, "Hey, big Panther, isn't it about time we had a fly-by for our buddies?"

"Why not?" Grant said.

He shifted his position to one off Vidorov's left wing, opposite Shepard. Without being told, Zbibari pulled over behind Vidorov, completing a diamond formation.

"All yours, Dmitri," Grant said.

"Thank you very much, Dallas. Better that General Nemorosky has my head than Billings yours."

"Damned right."

"Panther flight," Vidorov said, "On my lead. Air speed six-zero-zero. One-zero-zero feet above the runway. We will perform four-point to the left."

Grant kept an eye on Vidorov, keying to the leader, and retarding throttle. A quick glance at the velocity readout showed him 600.

"Final coming up. Turn now."

As a unit, they turned into the final approach leg. The pilot of the lead sub-orbital continued to lose altitude, and the three members of his team stayed right with him. Each of the craft was about forty feet from the next—not a precision formation, but it allowed for errors.

When they crossed the outer marker without losing more altitude or speed, or breaking up the formation, the flight controller at Rosie said, "Panther One, what's going on?"

"Rosie, Panther Two. You may want to get your camera."

People began spilling out of the buildings shortly after that as the word spread. Grant was surprised to not hear from Billings.

He kept his eyes on Vidorov.

"Now."

The four sub-orbitals went into a lefthand roll, hesitating at the four corners of the clock, inverted at one hundred feet above the runway as they shot by the main group of buildings.

"Very good," Vidorov said. "Forty-five-degree climb. Now."

The four sub-orbiters went into a climb passing over the end of the runway.

"Loop back, roll right . . . now."

Keeping his eye on Panther Two, Grant hauled the stick back, and once he was inverted, rolled upright to the right.

"Forty-five-degree dive. Now."

They shot past Rosie, this time seventy feet off the deck, and performed another four-point roll. A look to his left side gave Grant a fleeting snapshot of most of the personnel standing outside the buildings, waving.

"Left turn, in line, two, one, three, four. Now."

Vidorov went into a left turn, Grant fell in behind him, then was followed by Shepard and Zbibari, and they were in a single line, climbing slightly as they headed north.

The leader took them out over the desert for ten miles, at two hundred feet above the sand and sagebrush, then circled back into the landing approach. They landed one after another.

As they taxied toward the refueling station, the flight controller came back to them. "All personnel of

Panther Flight, you are to report to Generals Billings and Nemorosky as soon as you have changed."

"There goes my head, Dallas."

"Hell, Dmitri, all they can do is fire us. We can still fly crop dusters in Oklahoma."

"Perhaps for you and Billy."

And Grant had to consider for the first time that maybe second careers after mid-life crises were not available in the Soviet Union.

When they popped canopies, they got a round of applause from the ground crew. Other members of the XSO team shouted encouragement at them as they crossed the tarmac toward the dressing room in Hangar 5.

After changing, they walked down to Hangar 1 and presented themselves to the two commanders waiting in a conference room with Senior Lieutenant Anatoly Smertevo.

"Who was flying left point?" Billings asked.

"I was," Grant told him.

"Little sloppy there, in the half-loop. You were a fraction off the pace of the others."

Billy Shepard grinned at him.

"We'll practice some more, General," Grant said.

"Not too often. If we lose all four of those birds at once, we've lost it all. Still, it was a morale-builder, and we needed that."

"Please take a chair, gentlemen," Nemorosky said. "We are waiting for a telephone call."

"I do not want the Americans on my base," General Antonovko said, both heat and conviction in his voice.

259

It was five o'clock in the morning, and though he was alert enough, Antonovko felt slightly fatigued by yesterday's tour of the facilities with General Brezhenki.

Brezhenki used his fork to spear another pork sausage from the platter. "Nonsense, Karl Yurievich. You will be able to restrict their movements."

"It is unnecessary. We have our own sub-orbital pilots. Why can we not use them?"

The steward moved in and refilled his coffee cup. It was good Folger's coffee, processed in America.

"In point of fact, neither you nor I have a say in the matter. The order comes from the President, supported by the Politburo. We are part of a cooperative program, and we are to cooperate."

"Our national security is at stake, Comrade General," Antonovko pointed out, waving his arm about. "The base contains the most sensitive of our technology. Tell that to the President! They will steal us blind!"

"The Americans risk their secrets, with our people located at their Edwards Air Force Base, but has Nemorosky been able to obtain anything of substance?"

"He has not." Antonovko had not yet informed his superior of the close call with Vidorov, and this did not seem like the appropriate time to do so.

Brezhenki scooped another egg onto his plate.

Antonovko took one bite from a biscuit, then put it down. As he chewed, he asked, "Have you discussed the organizational matter with the general staff?"

Grigori Brezhenki laughed. "Do you mean the rather improbable development whereby a Soviet general and his unit have become an operational part of the American aerospace command?"

"I do. It is insulting."

"Perhaps. In any event, I thought it best not to nform the general staff just yet. This will be temporary, Karl Yurievich."

"I hope it is so," Antonovko said fervently. "These matters can only have negative influences on the morale of our men."

"You do not believe that Nemorosky allows his people to become . . . Westernized?"

Antonovko shrugged. "Everything is out of balance. A unit of my command has been armed and reports to the United States Pentagon. I am forced to allow the American military to make my base their own."

"There is another answer, of course," Brezhenki said. "There always is."

"And that is?"

"You may cancel the launch of A2e."

It was scheduled for August 18th, and it was to carry the replacement for the KGB's Cosmos 758 lost in May. "Chairman Cherevako would ask why, General. He has been most insistent since the Cosmos in orbit died. He says that he is blind in one eye. And that eye is on Germany."

"Tell him you are afraid of the consequences."

Antonovko gave up. "Very well, Comrade General. We will place the call to America."

Brezhenki pointed at the clock on the wall. "We have another few minutes. Eat your breakfast, Karl Yurievich."

"I am not hungry." Antonovko's stomach was tied in many knots.

* * *

261

Grant was getting hungry, and he walked down the corridor to a bank of vending machines and bought himself a Coke and a package of chocolate donuts.

"Jesus, Grant. Someday you're going to weigh three hundred pounds."

He thought that Billings probably already weighed that much, but thoughtfully refrained from saying so.

Billings shook the change in his hand, but did not find what he wanted. "You have a quarter?"

Grant found one, handed it over, and Billings got himself a cup of coffee. They sat down at one of the little tables clustered around the vending machines.

"You screw up my lobbying effort yet, Dallas?"

"I don't know what you mean, General. I stay as far away from that stuff as I can."

"I mean the Jamieson woman. She was fawning all over you, and you didn't have common sense enough to stay way in the hell away from her."

"You'd have been proud of me," Grant grinned. "I just said no."

"That'd be a first.'

"True, though."

"Which may be worse than saying yes," Billings said.

"What?"

They heard the telephone ring down the hall in the conference room.

"Come on." Billings led the way back, and Grant followed, gulping the last of his donut and chasing it with Coke. He closed the door behind him.

Nemorosky had answered the phone. He switched on the speaker so they could all hear the conversation, then introduced all of the participants on the California end.

The telephone speaker was squeaky and the man on the other end spoke in stilted English. "There is but General Brezhenki and myself here."

Billings lifted his eyebrows and turned to whisper to Grant, "The top man in the Strategic Rocket Forces."

"Yes, Comrade General Antonovko," Nemorosky said.

There had not been many "comrade" forms of address used around the Soviet team in California, and it sounded strange to Grant.

"Tell us again, General Nemorosky, of the plan that you have formed."

The Soviet commander explained the strategy.

"Perhaps we need to use only one sub-orbital," Antonovko said. "You could send Colonel Vidorov."

"General Antonovko, this is General Billings speaking. I personally have recommended the use of two sub-orbitals. We have already lost one man, and I don't want to lose another, yours or mine. As long as we do not know exactly what we are facing in terms of weaponry or the capabilities of the hostile craft, our only advantage may be in numbers."

After a long pause, the man at Tyuratam said, "I suppose you are right, General Billings. Which pilots do you recommend?"

Nemorosky responded. "We will send Colonel Vidorov and Lieutenant Colonel Grant, General."

"Colonel Vidorov will be in command." It was a statement.

Billings looked to Grant, who said, "Fine with me."

"And what else is required?" Antonovko asked.

"The cooperative team has devised a portable fueling

263

station, Comrade General, though we will need access to liquid oxygen and liquid hydrogen."

"We will make the arrangements," Antonovko said.

Nemorosky explained the makeup of the ground support crew. It was composed of ten men and four converted Air Force tanker trucks. "They will depart from this base at twenty-one hundred hours tonight. The transport will be a C-one-four-one Starlifter, Air Force two-four-seven-one-eight."

"Very well. I will inform Soviet air control."

Grant did not think that this Antonovko sounded very excited at the prospects. Grant himself was not thrilled at the idea of operating out of Tyuratam.

Antonovko said, "You attempted reconnaissance of the last French launch, did you not? When you lost the sub-orbital?"

"That is correct, Comrade General."

"What of their next launch? I believe it is scheduled for the nineteenth of August."

"Our participation has not been decided at this point," Billings said.

The contractor worked his way up the hill, bypassing a house with a yappy poodle. The grade was steep, but shrubs and vines gave him handholds, and he found himself at the base of the deck just before midnight. The balcony was high, fifteen feet above him.

He waited unmoving for ten minutes.

There were no noises from above, no last-minute flares of light from neighboring houses. The poodle had shut up. City lights twinkled in the distance.

He was dressed in black—windbreaker, turtle-neck,

264

chinos, and running shoes—and would have been difficult to see in the deep shadows at the back of the house, anyway.

When he was satisfied that he had raised no alarms, he used the cross-braces of the deck support to work his way upward. He felt blindly with his hands for a grip on a two-by-four, jerked upward, got a foot on the brace, then repeated himself until he had reached the third tier of braces and could peer over the edge of the flooring. There were no lights on in the house, and the drapes were pulled across the glass doors. He reached up, grabbed the lower rail of the protective redwood railing, pulled himself up, then slithered under the railing.

He had been told that there would be no alarm system, but he pulled on his thin suede gloves and spent a full five minutes verifying the fact, using a small penlight to trace the edges of the windows and sliding glass door.

The latch-lock was down on the door, but it was an old house, and the door was loose in its guiding channel. He pulled it back as far as the lock would let it travel, then tapped it forward a fraction, to take pressure off the latch. Using a thin flexible steel rod from the small pallet he carried in his windbreaker, he fitted it into the U-channel below the latch, rotated it with his fingers until it slipped around the door frame, then pushed upward against the latch. It took him three tries before he caught it right, and the lever flipped up. All in all, it took him less than one minute to open the door.

Inside the house, he locked on the penlight and began to search. There were two bedrooms, and he

265

went through both in less than five minutes. One was completely empty, and the other yielded nothing of interest. The single bathroom had dirty towels on the floor and masculine accessories in the medicine cabinet. Whatever he moved in cabinet or drawer, he was careful to return to its previous location.

The living room did not take long either. The drawers in end tables gave him telephone books, decks of playing cards, and a small chess set. The bookshelves and cabinets next to the fireplace held old *Reader's Digest* condensed books, a bunch of *National Geographic* magazines, and about a hundred record albums, mostly classical.

The breakfront in the dining room contained only tarnished silver and a partial set of china. The flowery design made it look like it was somebody's mother's hand-me-downs, the contractor thought.

The kitchen was a mess. The linoleum floor under his sneakers felt sticky. It had not been scrubbed in a long time. The sink and the counter next to it were stacked with dirty dishes.

He pulled back his sleeve and used the penlight to check his watch. It read 12:34. He was running out of time. Quickly, he went through the upper cabinets, but found only daily plates, glassware, canned goods, and liquor. The lower cabinets and drawers were a montage of old cooking utensils, beatup flatware, bowls, cleaning materials, and . . . six big boxes of cereal.

He pulled the boxes out, hefted them to test for weight, and selected three. The top lids were closed by the tab fitted into the opposing slot. Opening the first, he found corn flakes, but shoved his hand in, felt a plastic pouch, and pulled it out. He uncovered three pouches in the three boxes, then returned the boxes to the cabinet.

One of the transparent Zip-lock bags contained a variety of official-looking documents—deed, title, passport, birth certificate, naturalization papers. The other two bags contained cash, and the contractor's practiced eye estimated the count at around two hundred thousand.

It was a bonus, not expected by either the contractor or his client.

And the client need never know.

Despite the urgency of his expected timetable, he still had to wait twelve minutes before he heard the garage door. As soon as the motor growled, he moved over behind the kitchen door.

The car engine died, the garage door sounded again. The lock in the kitchen door scraped, then clicked. The door pushed open.

The man stepped up the single step from the garage floor, reached out, and flipped on the light.

He took two steps into the room, and the contractor glided in behind him, reached over his right shoulder, and jerked his arm tight around the man's throat.

"Hey!"

With the heel of his left hand, the contractor slammed the man in the back of the head. He heard the vertebrae snap.

The man went limp, hanging from the contractor's forearm, against his chest. There were a few gurgles, then nothing. He let the body slump to the floor and went through the pockets. He found a manila envelope with more cash. This was to be returned to the client, and he slipped the envelope into his windbreaker pocket.

As expected, he found two billfolds. He searched both for identification, kept one, and returned the other to the body's hip pocket. Locking the door to the garage, he turned off the overhead light, then lifted the corpse, bending to drape it over his shoulder.

In the living room, he turned on one table lamp at its lowest setting.

He left the sliding glass door open as he carried his burden out onto the deck. When he came up against the railing, he lowered the body until its feet touched the redwood planks, then levered it backward over the railing.

It tilted for a moment, then went on over. There was a heavy thump as it struck the hillside. He thought he heard it slide down the slope through the vines for a few feet, but he could not see the movement in the darkness.

Gerhard Strichmann had just had an unfortunate accident.

Sixteen

"The timing could not be better," Nemorosky said. "You will be landing at the Baikonur Cosmodrome at Tyuratam, and the film cassettes can be recovered by our people there. None of the Americans will be the wiser."

The SCT-134 TIMBAL cameras that Billings called the very latest in high resolution technology had been mounted in the left wing leading edges of XSO-5 and XSO-6, their relocation from initial designs required by the installation of the weapons pods in the lower fuselages.

"We are flying north, Comrade General," Vidorov pointed out. "I would take pictures only of ice floes."

The two of them were in Nemorosky's rooms in Residence Hall 120A, supposedly enjoying an after-dinner drink. Vidorov was not enjoying himself in the least.

"Ah, but after you take off, as you circle for altitude, you will pass over the Marine installation at Twenty-nine Palms, perhaps the Chocolate Mountain Gunnery

Range, and best, the San Diego Naval Base."

"If we take off to the east."

Nemorosky shrugged. "It would make no difference. In other directions, there is the China Lake Naval Weapons Center, Camp Roberts, Vandenberg Air Force Base, Hunter-Ligget Military Reservation. Perhaps the Army installation at Ford Ord. These would be photographs with clarity and detail never captured by our satellites."

"You very much want something, do you not, Comrade General? Anything will do."

"You must understand that I am under a great deal of pressure, Dmitri Vasilivich. We must produce something that will interest the analysts."

"I would prefer your order requiring me to attack the submarine docks at San Diego Naval Base, Comrade General. I am trained by the State to be a fighter pilot. That is what I do best."

"I know, Dmitri Vasilivich. Still?"

Vidorov sighed. "Yes, Comrade General. I will see what can be done."

He had already decided what could be done. He would personally locate and load the film cassettes into the camera. Vidorov would not be faulted by his superiors for not making the attempt, but he was determined to obey his promise to General Billings, also.

Polly Enburton, having had her testimony before the Senate Appropriations Committee delayed twice, was not too concerned. That was the way Washington worked.

Now, she was scheduled to appear in the morning, a Saturday, but that too was the way Washington worked. Congress was supposedly still recovering from its summer break, the constituencies believing that the members spent their time on junkets, glad-handing in the districts, or pursuing sixteen-year-olds, male and female. The committees and sub-committees of Congress were, however, hard at work. And this was an especially bad year since appropriations had not been settled due to all of the in-fighting for precious projects.

Enburton had painstakingly considered her own responsibilities as far as appropriations went. She was satisfied with her votes on all but the sub-orbital program. Though she was still highly concerned about the Soviet involvement in the program, the recent developments suggested the need for changes.

The Senate was in favor of keeping the program in a reduced form.

The President had already released contingency funds to arm the sub-orbitals and to keep them in operation for the short-term.

Pressure from senators and fellow representatives, along with calls from the White House and the Pentagon had been building steadily, but Enburton had always been able to resist such influences in the past. She was more concerned with her own conscience and with taking positions that she thought her constituency would approve, both as citizens and as taxpayers. A man, a pilot and a servant of the people, had died protecting their interests.

Roberta Jamieson, on the other side of the table in Enburton's den in Arlington Heights, looked up from the typewritten pages.

"What do you think, Roberta?"

Her aide frowned. "It's a complete reversal from your previous position, Polly."

"Yes, but stubbornness doesn't necessarily indicate wisdom, my dear."

"You don't want to appear wishy-washy."

"No. But we are dealing with new facts."

Jamieson frowned again. She tried so hard to be mature, Enburton thought, but it was going to take a few more years. She had hired the woman as a favor to Howard Jamieson, a longtime family friend. It was not simply patronage; Roberta had the necessary skills, and her frame of mind on most issues coincided with Enburton's. She was an excellent researcher, though like most staff people, she was becoming somewhat obsessed with increasing her power base. It was to be expected, of course.

Outside, a mist filled the night air, creating a yellow halo around the street lamp at the intersection. It reminded her of the wonderful two years in the embassy in London, before Jesse died. He had been a superb diplomat, and it was he who had introduced her to politics. She shook her head to erase the wandering of her mind.

"You don't agree with my recommendations, Roberta?"

"You'd not only give them funds for three more sub-orbitals and for weapons development, but also the money for the reconnaissance mission?"

"That's a sop for Don Sunwallow. I may need his vote."

"I have some strong reservations, Polly."

"What are they?"

"First, the sub-orbital is not a weapons platform. That was not part of the original design concept, and anything added now is only a Rube Goldberg contraption."

"I'm surprised you use the term, 'Rube Goldberg.'"

"At my tender age? Actually, it's one of Daddy's favorite terms. No, I think the integrity of the design is at stake. Then, too, I don't think a completely new weapons system is required to meet the challenge of this 'aggressor,' as the Pentagon is so fond of calling it."

"What would you use?"

"Certainly, Polly, we have the technology available to arm a satellite."

"Infringes a whole bunch of treaties, Roberta."

The frown again. "The SR-seventy-one . . ."

"Is also not an armed aircraft."

"If we're working so closely with the Soviets, we could perhaps get one of their Foxbats. They're armed, and they fly at eighty-some thousand feet."

Enburton could not understand Jamieson's resistance. Usually, they agreed on almost everything. "I don't want to beg from Moscow, Roberta. Do you? And I also suspect that the MiG-twenty-five isn't going to work, either. Like the Blackbird, the Foxbat cannot achieve the necessary altitude. The hostile craft operates some thirty-five miles above its ceiling, far out of missile range."

"They could modify an ICBM."

Something was really bothering Jamieson. "If possible, probably very expensive, Roberta."

"And mainly, Polly, I think your political image will suffer if you change your position."

"Fortunately, I don't worry a great deal about my

image, Roberta. No, I think we'll give Generals Hansen and Billings what they want, and a bit more."

And Jamieson frowned again.

Yakamata had not liked what he had seen on Matsushima's video and radar tapes. He had therefore revised the mission strategy and tactical plan for the eighteenth of August. He had typed it out himself on a single page, for that was the way that Mr. Kyoto liked it.

Kyoto read the report rapidly. "Under the rationale section, you say that the presence of the American sub-orbital over France was not by chance, Colonel."

"That is correct. It was lying in wait. The Americans are aware of us."

"That is alarming, to say the least," Kyoto said. "It was not to have happened."

"But it has happened."

"How?"

"I do not know, Mr. Kyoto. Perhaps one of our craft was sighted in some manner. No matter how it occurred, I am positive the Americans are aware."

"Of us, specifically?"

"That is unlikely," Yakamata said. "The craft are unmarked. The stealth characteristics would not allow return flights to be traced to Sun Land. They know only that their failures, and obviously, those of the French, have not been self-induced."

"You have heard this through Japanese intelligence sources?"

"No, sir. JADF intelligence has collected no such information."

Kyoto ruminated. "What do you suggest that we do, Colonel Yakamata?"

The colonel had already considered the options and suggested the most sane, but least desirable, alternative. "It may be best for us to terminate the strategy, Mr. Kyoto."

The strategy of shooting down foreign space vehicles had been intended simply to drive commercial enterprises with needs to place satellites into orbit away from their current vendors and into the arms of Nesei Aerospace Industries.

"That, we cannot do," Kyoto said. "If the Americans and the French regain credibility, we will not meet the launch objectives set for us."

"Then we must proceed with the plan as I have outlined it," Yakamata said.

"You will send two sub-orbitals this time?"

"That is correct. I will pilot one of them."

After a moment of reflection, the president said, "The mission is approved. You will take extreme care, Colonel Yakamata."

Which was to say, "Don't get caught."

At four o'clock on the morning of August seventeenth, Grant stumbled out of his bed, demolished the plastic alarm clock with one blow, and took a shower. He was a little groggy because Tricia had called him at two o'clock—midnight in Honolulu—to chat. They had talked for an hour because the studio was getting the telephone bill.

He packed an AWOL bag, then went out into the dark morning, raised the top on the Firebird, and locked the doors. Walking down to the mess hall, he found Nemorosky, Billings, and Vidorov gathered at one table with platters of pancakes and bacon. He sat down and poured coffee for himself.

Soviet and American enlisted men at another table were uncharacteristically quiet.

"What's with them?" Grant asked.

Vidorov grinned at him. "It is Saturday, Dallas. They have become accustomed to weekend freedoms."

"Plus," Billings said, "they think the job belongs to your crews."

Gloomy, Drandorov, and their subordinates had left the night before on the C-141.

"Well, hell. I had plans for the weekend, too." Grant picked up a piece of bacon and munched on it.

"In Hawaii?" Billings asked. Grant had told him about Price's trip.

"I'd thought about it."

"You'd better be careful there, Dallas. You're getting attached."

"The hell I am."

At four-thirty, the ground crews left the dining room to tow the sub-orbitals out of the hangar for fueling, and fifteen minutes later, Grant and Vidorov crossed over to the dressing room and climbed into their flight gear. Grant took his last leak for a while while Vidorov went out to the fueling station.

He zipped up, then walked outside. The dawn was coming in pink flares on the eastern horizon. It was struggling through a hazy overcast.

He toured XSO-5 with the crew chief, testing all of the movable surfaces, looking for oil and hydraulic fluid leaks. He could hear a barely audible hiss. There was always some loss of oxygen and hydrogen fuels.

XSO-6 was parked alongside. He crossed under the nose, looking for Vidorov, and found him standing on a short ladder under the left wing. The access door to the camera was open.

Grant walked to the ladder and looked up.

Vidorov snapped a film cassette in place, closed the camera cover, and looked down at him.

"We going sightseeing on this trip, Dmitri?"

"It is an empty cassette, Dallas."

Grant squinched his eyes, puzzled.

"Naturally, I believe it to be loaded with unexposed film."

"I don't get it, buddy."

"There are people in my service who believe I have two jobs, Dallas." Vidorov backed down the ladder after securing the access door.

Grant caught on. "Looked like a full cassette to me."

He went back to his sub-orbital and scampered up the ladder. While he was hooking in, the generals showed up, and Billings had portfolios containing their orders passed up to both Vidorov and Grant. He glanced inside, saw the listing of frequencies—a Defense Communications Satellite relay had been set up, the inventory of Hellwinder missiles, the agreement to work with the Soviet Strategic Rocket Forces.

And one more page. He took it out, scanned it, and leaned out to call down to Billings. "This right, General?"

"The President signed the order last night, Grant. After consultation with the Soviet President."

The authority to use the Hellwinders against an unknown enemy, without first being fired upon, had been granted to the flight commander. That was Vidorov on this trip.

"Makes me feel better," Grant said.

"Me, too," Billings told him.

He pulled his helmet on and activated Tac-2. "Let's go visit your folks, Dmitri."

A straight line being the shortest of many other kinds of lines, they went over the top of the world. Since they followed the earth's curvature, it was not actually straight, of course, but the distance from Edwards to Tyuratam was just about 7000 miles on the polar route and close to 9000 miles had they flown west on a latitudinal course. At Mach 4.5 and 150,000 feet, the flight time, including takeoff and landing, was just short of three hours.

Additionally, the flight gave them a chance to check out the navigational computers over the Arctic. Magnetic compasses were iffy at the altitudes in which the sub-orbitals worked anyway, and over either of the poles, a magnetic compass became a child's toy, spinning merrily and erratically. The reliance on the NavStar system was total. To further confuse the issue, the computer generated an artificial grid system for the compass, with numbers that did not correspond to magnetic lines. The North Pole was the equator. To pilots who regularly worked the Arctic or the Antarctic, it became second nature. To Grant, it gave him a headache.

He preferred the scenery. It was not totally white. Where the low sun struck the surface, the frozen landscape refracted light in glistening diamond shatters that hurt the eyes. Crevices and deep ice canyons were shadowed in the darkest ebony. Several storms of snow and clouds broiled the surface.

Grant was happy to know that if he had a problem, he could dump fuel and glide almost all the way to Greenland. He would not want to put down on the ice pack.

"I put us forty-eight kilometers off the North Pole, Dallas. Would you agree?"

"Jesus, Dmitri, I'm trying to convert to Arctic grid in my head, and you want me to convert to metric, too?" He had not been paying much attention. Calcualting quickly from the readout on the compass, he agreed. "Yeah, that's pretty close. If we get lost, I'll follow you."

Vidorov laughed on his open mike. "We are going to my country, my friend. When the air controller tells you four-five-zero, be aware that you are flying below the level of the desert."

On this trip, Vidorov served as the tour guide, pointing out the Kara and Barents Seas on their right as they neared the Asian land mass. Their southern route took them 1100 miles east of Moscow, but they were high enough for Vidorov to provide some geography. "We're over the Ural Mountains, Dallas. Our Rockies. That is the West Siberian Plain on the left."

"Pretty desolate," Grant said.

"It would be like taking a motor trip from Salt Lake City to Reno, only a much longer trip."

"That route has always bored me, Dmitri."

"Here, too. And the roads are not that good. On your right is Perm. It is a city of almost one million people. Soon we will pass over Sverdlovsky, with a population of one-and-a-quarter million. It is farming area, Dallas. Wheat and corn and oats. The people raise cattle also."

After a while, Grant began to sense what Vidorov must have felt as Grant identified Nashville and Dallas and Memphis. It did not mean much in the abstract.

It was still the height of summer, and greens turning to rust dominated the landscape. Higher in the Urals, winter was already inexorably moving in, creating toasty golds in some of the forests.

Farther to the south, in the Kazakh Soviet Socialist Republic, Vidorov contacted an air controller, and they began their descent. They were pretty much alone, Grant realized. To the west, he identified an Aeroflot airliner, but other air traffic was sparse. He wondered if the Soviets had cleared the skies on purpose, keeping military aircraft out of view of the American visitors.

The Baikonur Cosmodrome near the town of Tyuratam was a massive complex of launch pads, runways, roads, and buildings. They landed on an east-west runway, and Grant followed Vidorov along several taxiways to an isolated spot near the west end of the runway.

The C-141 was parked fifty yards off the taxiway. The blue air force semi-trucks with their tanker trailers were lined up a short distance away, backed up by six camouflage-painted tankers with red stars on their hoods. Several cars and utility vehicles were scattered about. It was an incongruous mix. Four modular buildings had been erected on, or moved to, the site. Grant had the distinct impression that he was an uninvited guest. The Americans were going to be kept away from the main base.

Vidorov was speaking in Russian to some ground controller. Grant could not understand the words, but he got the gist of the directions as he putted along behind XSO-6. The Soviet pilot turned off the taxiway and nosed up near the tankers, and Grant toed his brakes, used the nose wheel steering button on the stick grip to make the turn, and parked alongside. He started shutting down systems and depressurized the cockpits. As he raised his canopy, the ladder clamped in place, and Sergeant Gloom's face appeared at his side.

"Damn, sir, I sure am happy to see you."

"Not enjoying your stay, Gloomy?"

"These guys are kinda spooky, Colonel. They don't want us to leave the immediate area."

"The Soviet ground crew, too?"

"No. They stayed somewhere else last night. Just us Americans here."

Grant handed Gloom his helmet, then did his circus act getting out of the cockpit, retrieving his AWOL bag from the rear compartment, and sliding down the ladder to asphalt. He unzipped the bag and dug around in its contents until he found his overseas. He put it on.

Vidorov approached him, leading two generals. Stars everywhere. Both of them were Heroes of the Soviet Union, according to the medals. They were big guys, broad, and the four-star must have stood close to six-three.

Grant came to attention and offered a crisp salute. It was returned with Russian rigidity.

Vidorov said, "Lieutenant Colonel Grant, may I present General Brezhenki, Commander of the Soviet Strategic Rocket Forces, and General Antonovko, Commander of Tyuratam Space Command."

281

Grant was not taking any of those bear hugs, so he stuck out his hand, and it was shaken by each man in turn. "Happy to meet you, General. And you, sir."

Antonovko spoke, "I am most happy to welcome you to Tyuratam, Lieutenant Colonel. As you can see, we have provided you with quarters I am certain you will find comfortable."

"Very much appreciated, General."

The generals had not seen the sub-orbitals in the flesh, or the carbon-impregnated skin, before, so Vidorov and Grant were obliged to give them a close-up tour. Antonovko wanted to see the weapons pod, and Sergeant Drandorov scrambled up into XSO-6's cockpit to lower it. Both generals climbed the ladder to view the cockpit while Vidorov explained the system in Russian.

It took over an hour, and when they were done, Grant thought the honchos were suitably impressed, though they tried not to show it.

Grant smiled at Vidorov. "Well, Dmitri, are you going to show me your officers' club?"

Antonovko intervened, "Colonel Vidorov, I do have a surprise for you. We have flown your Nadia here from Moscow."

Grant liked the way Vidorov's eyes lit up.

Vidorov said, "Comrade General?"

"She waits for you."

The Soviet pilot turned to Grant. "Dallas, you will understand. . . ."

"Certainly, buddy. Take off."

Brezhenki's English was even more stilted than Antonovko's, with a definite British overtone in it. Perhaps that was why Antonovko did most of the speaking. Brezhenki swung a hand at the first prefab building and said, "Lieutenant Colonel, we have provided refreshment for you and your men. You will be comfortable."

With that sign-off, the Soviet brass pivoted and headed for a black limo.

Grant looked at Gloom and raised an eyebrow.

"The beer tastes like tiger piss," Gloom said.

"What the hell, Gloomy. It's just like camping out."

In the middle of a hell of a big country, in the middle of endless desert, all by themselves.

It was pretty lonely, Grant thought.

Seventeen

The Dissonex International sub-orbitals designed and built by Nesei Aerospace Industries resembled those of the Soviet-American program only super-ficially.

The delta-wing configuration was similar, though the trailing edge had more curve in it, and the forward angle was sharper. Like the original, the turbojet engine was mounted within the fuselage, but the dual rocket engine pods were on top of the wings, much like the intake nacelles of the B-2 Stealth bomber. The turbojet air intake was a twin set of closable scoops, one on either side of the fuselage, above the wing. Where the cross-section of the western fuselage was flattened, top to bottom, the oriental version was elongated, like a tall egg.

The tall fuselage resulted from designs that were, from the beginning, intended to house six specifically designed missiles, called *Samurai* by the president of the company. They were mounted in launch tubes located beneath the cockpit floors. To clear the missiles for ignition, a panel in the curved nose retracted, and a similar panel midway back on the fuselage bottom raised to a forty-five-degree angle, to deflect exhaust gases down and out of the craft. An unfortunate by-product of that design was that, with each firing of a missile, the momentary downward deflection of gas acted much like a directional thruster, causing a slight jump in the sub-orbital.

Colonel Meoshi Yakamata examined the missiles with as much attention as he gave to the preflight inspection of the sub-orbital. When he was satisfied, the crewman closed the missile access doors, and the sub-orbital was towed out of the hangar for fueling.

Yakamata joined his wingman, an ex-JADF lieutenant named Hirosiuta, and the two of them went to the lounge at the front of the hangar for a last cup of tea.

He had barely poured it before an agitated Kyoto burst through the doorway from the darkened parking lot. Yakamata looked up.

"Colonel Yakamata, I have just read the intelligence report you forwarded to me last night." He waved it uselessly in the air.

"Yes, Mr. Kyoto?"

"Your source is reliable?"

"Absolutely. It is Japan's own intelligence service."

"And two of the western sub-orbitals are missing from Edwards Air Force Base?"

"That is correct."

Kyoto rattled the paper again. "This does not tell me where they are."

"Because, Mr. Kyoto, we do not know."

The Nesei CEO sighed. "This is distressing."

"I do not know why. It will not concern us."

"But you yourself said that the French launch was under protection."

"That was my judgment, yes."

"Then do you not suppose that the Soviet launch is to receive similar protection? And this time, from two machines?"

"It is possible, Mr. Kyoto, even probable. However, given your objectives, I have mine, do I not? If they are there, then we will do what must be done."

Kyoto flopped on a divan. Yakamata had never seen him upset before. His hair was uncombed at five-thirty in the morning, though he had been shaved before reading his overnight correspondence. There were bags under his eyes.

"What you do not know, Colonel, is that Mr. Lee has forwarded a last . . . another message from our contact within the western sub-orbital program. All of the craft have been modified."

"In what way, Mr. Kyoto?"

"The Americans have armed the machines."

Ex-lieutenant Hirosiuta, who had been prudently examining a magazine on the far side of the room, snapped his head up.

This was, indeed, an interesting development. "Does the message provide technical data?"

Kyoto jerked another sheet of paper from his coat pocket and read from it. "There are . . . Electronic Counter Measures and . . . threat warning receivers and . . . laser targeting equipment . . . and infrared targeting and . . . four missiles per machine."

"Is there listed an effective range for the missiles? That is important," Yakamata said.

Kyoto searched. "It says somewhere here . . . about twenty-two miles."

Yakamata dipped his head while he converted to kilometers. If true, the western sub-orbitals had about a three-kilometer advantage with their missiles. It was not great, but it was there. As he pondered, however, he was certain the advantage could be countered. He and his pilots had superior skill combined with an extended training program.

"Well?" Kyoto demanded.

"We will take off as scheduled."

"You are not concerned?"

"My only concern is whether or not you wish to continue your program of destroying foreign rockets. Especially Soviet rockets."

"Initially, the Soviets were targeted, not because they sold their services to commercial interests, but because their losses would keep a pattern from emerging."

"Yes. I understand that."

Kyoto jutted his chin forward and looked him directly in the eyes. "Did you know that a diplomat from the Soviet embassy has approached us about the possibility of providing launch vehicles?"

"No. He was KGB, no doubt. JADF intelligence tells us that Cherevako is falling far behind in replacing his Cosmos spy satellites."

"Who cares, Colonel Yakamata, as long as he is willing to pay?"

Dollars and yen and sterling silver were more important than the fact that Cosmos satellites also spied on Japanese installations. "Then we will proceed as planned."

287

Hirosiuta looked across the room at him, many questions in his eyes. Yakamata knew what one of them was.

He told Kyoto, "We may have to begin paying a hostile fire stipend to our pilots."

"It is not in their contracts," the president insisted.

"Then you will amend the contracts."

Kyoto stared at him for only a moment before agreeing. "Very well, Colonel. As you say."

Signaling Hirosiuta, Yakamata left the lounge and crossed through the hangar, headed for the apron where the sub-orbitals were being fueled. He felt very good and very confident. He had just asserted himself, and he had won the battle.

He would win the next one, as well.

"Colonel Vidorov, the contents of your film cannisters were a disappointment."

"I do not understand, Comrade General Antonovko. I was able to pinpoint the China Lake facility, the Fort Irwin base, the Nellis . . ."

"The cannisters had no film, Vidorov."

The general's face was full of suppressed rage. Vidorov tried to keep his own expression neutral. He was very tired after his long and satisfying night with Nadia, and at this time of the morning, with the skies still utterly black, he did not need to face a winless confrontation.

"I was not aware of that, General. The Americans have been very secretive in regard to those cameras. It was purely by chance that I was able to obtain the cassettes for them, and since it was my first experience,

288

I did not know what to expect."

"Very secretive, you say?"

"About the cameras? Yes, General. I understand that they have the latest design in high resolution imaging. In addition to the cassettes, they may also transmit digital images to ground receivers for simultaneous viewing by ground personnel. It is something that the KGB would be interested in, I suspect."

"And we are to have the designs?"

"When the program is completed, yes. That is the plan, General Antonovko."

Vidorov did not know anything about the cameras installed in the sub-orbitals. He had heard a few technical terms uttered by General Billings and Jeremy Restwick, but the history and the development of the cameras were a mystery to him. His description, however, seemed to mollify the general for the moment, and that was his purpose.

"Very well, Colonel. You may proceed with your preparations."

Vidorov saluted and left the office, finding his way down a long corridor to the front doors of the administration building. It was raining, a light drizzle that would not alleviate the arid environs of Tyuratam, but which might interfere with the A2e launch. A bus loaded with his ground crew waited at the curb for him, its engine running and its headlights shining on a vacant, damp street.

He left the building, ran through the rain, and boarded the bus to take the seat immediately behind the driver. The bus lurched and pulled away.

Vidorov crossed his arms and closed his eyes. Antonovko's agitation with him had done much to erase his jubilation over being with Nadia again.

She was wonderful, a beauty who had once danced with the Moscow Ballet. They had been married for twelve years, but unfortunately, had been unable to have children. It was a disappointment, but it did not diminish their love for each other.

In her arms, Vidorov had felt his first contentment in many years. And in her arms, his desire to return to Moscow and their six-room apartment had resurfaced. Soon, he had told her with more hope in his voice than true expectation in his mind.

He expected, however, that the pressure from Antonovko and Nemorosky would not die away. They would continually push at him, demanding activity that he was not prepared to give them. The next time, he would not get away with a ruse similar to the empty film cassettes.

Supposedly fine general officers in the air force were forcing him toward a decision he did not want to make. Vidorov would be quite happy to be left alone and to serve his country in his aviation capacity. In the back of his mind, though, wisps of another idea were forming. If he were able to get Nadia free. . . .

No.

It would be an impossibility.

That was precisely why Antonovko had flown her to Tyuratam, to remind Vidorov of what he had at home. To subtly encourage him to perform as expected, or to plan on losing what he had at home.

The bus bounced over a rut and forced his eyes open. The American encampment, stuck out at the end of the runway, was fully lit. Tall poles with floodlights mounted on them had been placed at each corner of the housing area. Vidorov supposed that officers of the *Glavnoye Razvedyvatelnoye Upravleniye,* the military intelligence arm, had spent an uncomfortable night in the dark, keeping wary eyes on the unwanted visitors.

He was aware, of course, of the way the Americans had isolated the Soviet team at Rosie, but at least they had not been jailed. They were free to move about the State of California, except for restricted military or defense research areas.

Vidorov and his crew stepped down from the bus and ran across the muddy ground to the portable dining room. The rain was a little heavier, big droplets splashing against earth that had turned to mire.

As he climbed the short flight of steps, opened the door, and entered the room, a high level of conversation drained away into nothingness.

Grant got up and approached him. "How was your wife, Dmitri?"

"She was very fine, Dallas."

"Must have been. You look sleepy as hell."

The muted laughter caused some of the tension in the room to ebb.

"You sure you're ready to fly?" Grant asked him.

"If the rain keeps up, we may not have to fly."

"I think that you're conspiring with someone to bring about this rainstorm," Grant said. "You just want to go back to bed."

It was not a bad idea, Vidorov thought.

The runway at Baikonur was wide, and Dallas Grant and Vidorov waited at the end of it, the sub-orbitals standing side by side.

The flight commander, Vidorov, tested the new low-power radio tied into Tac-3. "Do you read me, Dallas?"

"Clear as a bell, Dmitri. Of course, at a hundred feet, I might expect that."

"We will test again at three hundred kilometers separation. I hope for the best."

The low-power radios, transmitting on VHF, were supposed to have a range of two hundred miles. It might give them a communications edge if they met an aggressor.

"We have a go-signal, then?" Vidorov was doing all the communicating with the controllers.

"Yes. The meteorologists say the rain will soon pass. Let us start the turbojets."

Grant signaled Gloom, standing beside the auxiliary power cart, went through his checklist, and XSO-5 came alive, the whine and vibration of the engine reassuring. XSO-6 started right away, too, and Vidorov went first, a cloud of spray and vapor trailing behind him.

The overcast was low, about three hundred feet off the ground, and the steady drizzle had lowered visibility to less than a mile. Grant came off the brakes, felt the sub-orbital begin to roll, then shoved his throttle to its stop.

Though there was a slight crown to it, the runway's concrete had not been poured exactly level. There were depressions which pooled water. Grant felt them tug at the nose wheel each time he hit one.

Then as his speed climbed to 200, the tire hydroplaned. Control felt sloppy. He tugged back lightly on the stick, taking some of the weight off the nose wheel.

Sheets of water rolled off the windscreen. Vidorov

had already disappeared.

Grant saw the runway end lights coming up as the speed reached 270. XSO-5 was fully loaded, nose heavy, and she did not seem eager to leave the ground for her true habitat this morning.

Finally, at 285, he was no longer fighting the nose. He rotated slightly, pulled in his gear less than ten feet off the concrete, and felt the surge of power. Half a mile later, the velocity indicator read 400. Grant increased his climb rate to one hundred feet per minute.

Rising into the clouds, he was blind, and Grant tapped his radar into active mode. He found Vidorov six miles ahead, in a right turn, at 8,000 feet.

He followed, and at 19,000 feet, burst out of the cloud cover into a brilliant morning. At 0645 hours, the sun was already far above the horizon. Grant shut down his radar. A few minutes later, he caught up with the Soviet pilot and fell into position off his right wing.

"We may go to rockets right away, Dallas. There are not many people here to be troubled by sonic booms."

"Let's go then, boss."

The ignition procedure went without fault, and five minutes later, the two of them were in a vertical climb at Mach 4, headed for 350,000 feet.

When they reached their altitude, they separated and went into an umbrella coverage similar to the one they had used over the Kennedy Space Center, a circle two hundred miles wide. They found out that the radios worked at that range, but the reception was weak, and the transmissions garbled. The best range was around 175 miles.

At that altitude, the skies were almost black, and the stars brilliant. Grant could not see Vidorov's sub-orbital, but was reassured by the fact that the man was less than three minutes away from him at Mach 5.25.

The features of the earth below were miniaturized. To the west, he could make out the Caspian Sea. About 1200 miles to the south and southwest he could see bluish smears that were the Arabian Sea and the Persian Gulf. The rugged mountains of Afghanistan and, far beyond, the white crests of the Himalayas were clearly visible. From his height, it was difficult to pick out the 29,000-foot peak of Mount Everest.

He keyed in his navigational computer and watched as the screen gave him a local map and a position. Setting the radar at its 220-mile maximum range, he left it on standby, ready to go. The Tac-1 frequency was dialed into launch control at Tyuratam, but the Russian voices did not tell him much. For total preparation, playing Boy Scout, Grant went ahead and deployed the weapons pod.

Vidorov's broken voice came in over Tac-3. ". . . controller . . . rain. . . ."

"Say again." The plains below were still overcast.

". . . as scheduled."

Grant guessed that the rain had let up, and despite the overcast, the Soviets were going ahead with the launch. With American observers present, God forbid that Mother Nature should cause them a delay.

The red numerals of the chronometer readout showed 0712 hours. Eighteen minutes away from launch.

He put the radio scanner on Tac-2 and coded it to scan frequencies in ranges used by military aircraft. It was not likely that the aggressor would be in radio contact with anyone, but he thought the effort might be worth it.

Within ten minutes, he decided the effort was going to drive him crazy. The scanner kept stopping on active channels, giving him unintelligible snatches of Russian, Indian, Pakistani, and Chinese dialogue between aircraft and air controllers. He shut it down.

". . . we go!"

The Soviets launched on schedule.

Grant scanned the cloud cover, but he was disoriented. The missile emerged from the clouds over two hundred miles from where he had been watching.

It was a big bastard. The Soviet space philosophy leaned toward rockets of bulk and massive thrust which would put heavy payloads into orbit.

Grant continued his circle, leaning into a left bank that gave him a better view of the missile. He switched his screen to radar, but left it passive. He rotated the safety collar on the toggle switch, then flipped the switch to arm his number one Hellwinder. With another switch, he set its target tracking system to infrared.

In one of their briefings with Restwick and Murychenko, Grant and Vidorov had decided that the hostile craft had another targeting system, in addition to the telemetry radiation tracking that hunted down launch vehicles. The downing of Denny Blake's suborbital had not come about by tracking telemetry transmissions. And Denny had shut down his radar, but had still been hit.

The aggressor would have either laser or infrared or both available. The laser designator would be limited to ranges at which the pilot could see his target, in order to place the red dot of the designator on it, so Grant was going to be alert for radar and infrared threats.

Visually, his best guess was that the A2e had closed the distance by half. It was slanting its climb toward the southwest now. About 180,000 feet.

Soon.

He poised his finger over the radar controls, waiting.

The missile hit 200,000 and Vidorov shouted, ". . . Now!"

He went active.

The screen crawled with targets, the sweep painting four of them. It took him a couple seconds to identify the A2e and XSO-6 by their altitude indications, indicated by boxed numbers next to the blips on the screen.

The two he wanted were nearly two hundred miles to the south and at 270,000 feet.

Two of the bastards!

He shut down the radar.

Grant rolled hard to the right, finding a heading of 160 degrees and diving. Velocity quickly rose to 5.25.

The next two minutes dragged. He felt blind.

Vidorov's voice was so clear that he must have closed on Grant by nearly a hundred miles. Their two vectors were aimed on the same point in the thermosphere.

"I will take the left, Dallas."

"You got it."

One more minute.

Grant was at 290,000 feet.

He hit the radar button.

His eyes were already focused and he immediately picked out the Soviet rocket, now at 245,000 feet, and Vidorov, ninety miles to his left.

The aggressors spotted them on radar immediately,

broke off their attack on the A2e, and spread out. They were about sixty miles apart, seventy-five miles away, and aiming directly at Grant.

They were also climbing through 305,000 feet.

Above him.

He hauled back on the stick, banking slightly to the right in order to pick up on the right blip.

Grant keyed the radar range, reducing it to a hundred miles, and clarifying his target.

Sixty miles.

One glance through the windscreen showed him only stars, and he refocused on the screen.

Fifty miles.

His neck muscles began to tense, waiting for the threat receiver to begin nagging at him.

Forty miles.

They had no idea as to the range of the hostile weapons, though they could expect something similar to their own. Maybe twenty to twenty-two miles.

Thirty miles. He was at 310,000 feet, still below his target. Vidorov, slightly behind him, looked to be over forty miles from his own target.

Twenty-five.

An intermittent, low-level chirp started to sound in his ears. In the upper right corner of the screen, letters blinked several times, then went solid. "LOCK-ON."

His radar had locked onto his target, but he did not have a radar-seeker missile. It was useless if the target shut down its radar.

He waited several seconds, then heard the Hell-winder's chirping grow stronger.

The second target, Vidorov's, veered toward him. *"Woop-woop-woop!"*

297

The threat receiver told him the enemy had launched its missile at him, a heat-seeker, and it was locked onto his heat signature.

He still could not see the son of a bitch.

Grant fingered the commit button and the computer decided it was time to launch. He saw the Hellwinder leap ahead of him, the bright white exhaust burning his vision.

He shut down the radar.

Reaching down the throttle handles with his forefinger, he killed both of his rocket engines, then laid the sub-orbital over into a hard, diving left turn.

He watched the exhaust trail of the Hellwinder until it winked out, its propellent gone.

He floated in a black, silent oblivion. The velocity readout moved steadily downward, 5.15 ... 4.98 ... 4.92.

Counting seconds.

The hostile missile must have missed Grant, though he never saw it. Having lost its heat source, it would attempt to locate another on the ground. Without power, however, it would be unable to maneuver.

Grant knew the hostile had missed when his target suddenly detonated in a bright orange-yellow burst that hurt his eyes. Out of the central fireball, several dozen plumes of flames and vapor erupted.

The explosion was off to his right oblique, and he gauged it at less than five miles away. They had closed on each other quickly.

Grant flashed his radar momentarily as he straightened out of his turn. Both Vidorov and the other aggressor were still there, but the blips were reversed. The aggressor was now behind them, now diving, headed north. Abruptly, he lost the hostile target as the pilot went off active radar. Half a second later, Vidorov's blip disappeared as he quit radiating radar emissions also.

He shut off his own radar again. "Dmitri?"

"I am restarting rocket engines. The target shut down his own engines, also, Dallas."

Grant reset his rocket engine switches and went through the checklist. He hurried, but two minutes slipped by until he was again under power.

He finished his turn as he built up speed and began to climb again. Going to active radar, he found Vidorov on a parallel course and banked right to close with him.

The target was nowhere to be seen on the screen. He realized that the radar was still set at one hundred miles, and quickly converted to the 220-mile range.

Still nothing.

"I'm afraid we've lost him, Dmitri."

"Yes. I think so. What of the other?"

"Let's go see."

They both turned back toward the scene of the battle and dove at full throttles.

"Did you see him, Dallas?"

"No. We still don't know what the bastards look like."

"You stay on radar, Dallas, and I will get a fix on our position."

At 100,000 feet, Grant's screen began to flicker with minute targets. Like the radar tapes recorded when Denny went down, and which he had reviewed a dozen times, the debris was scattered over a wide area. He judged that it was at least six miles wide in this case.

"I've got it, Dmitri. Debris at two-six thousand,

nine-one miles ahead."

"We will not catch up with it, Dallas, and we may not find it. It is going down in the Hindu Kush Mountains of Afghanistan."

They circled the crash area and confirmed the coordinates, then turned into a heading back to Tyuratam. Grant wondered if the Soviets would send a few helicopters into those rugged mountains, looking for the crash site. It would be nice to get some clues as to the sub-orbital's origins.

Before they got within a range where the people at the space center could overhear the low-power radios, Grant keyed his Tac-3 frequency. "Hey, Dmitri."

"Yes, Dallas."

"You sound a bit down."

"Perhaps I am just tired."

"Maybe. Look, nobody back on the ground could pick out who was who up where we were."

"That is true."

"You take the kill."

"What are you saying, Dallas?"

"Hell, we're in your country. I'd just as soon you got the brownie points with your people."

"I cannot do that."

"Sure you can. The deal is, though, I get the next one."

"To be truthful, General Antonovko is somewhat disenchanted with me at the moment."

"I can imagine that, after he opened those film cassettes."

"Do you understand my position, Dallas?"

"Yeah, I think I do. And I don't envy you. You go ahead and paint the first little sub-orbital under your canopy."

"There will be more, do you think?"

"Yeah, Dmitri, I do."

"I very much appreciate the offer, Dallas, but I cannot accept it."

Grant liked the man even better.

Eighteen

"That was a fifty-million-dollar machine, Colonel. Do you know how long it will take to recover the investment?"

Yakamata thought that the price tag was exaggerated. Nesei Aerospace had not invested a great deal in research and development for the sub-orbital. The Americans and the Soviets had done it for them.

He said nothing.

"And the Soviet diplomat has broken off discussions. We are no longer necessary to their program. The whole episode has been extremely costly."

Maki Kyoto had made it clear that he was not interested in the details of the mission, nor even the loss of a human life. He was concerned with results, and the results produced had not achieved his objectives. Or at least, had not met the objectives set for him by his board of directors.

Meoshi Yakamata *was* concerned about the details. He had been there, had seen Hirosiuta's sub-orbital disappear from his radar screen, then become a colorful Japanese flower. While Yakamata was more than competent as a pilot of tactical aircraft, he had never faced combat before. And in his first conflict, he had been forced to turn and run after firing but one of his six missiles. It was a humiliation he had kept to himself, but it still seared his soul.

"Mr. Kyoto, we may go over and over the past if you like. What is important, however, is the future. I assume we are talking about the profitable future of Nesei Aerospace Industries."

Kyoto's eyes refocused on the present and locked with the colonel's.

"The singular question is, do we proceed with our current strategy?"

"Fifty million dollars per mission is too expensive, Colonel."

"It could come to that, Mr. Kyoto. How important is it to you to be able to tell your directors that you have pocketed more contracts with foreign corporations?"

The question struck Kyoto where he lived. "Do you have the answer, Colonel Yakamata?"

The colonel let the planes of his face harden. He was on certain ground when it came to discussions of warfare. "That is what you pay me for, is it not? In California, there are but four sub-orbital craft, and the American Congress is preparing to terminate the program. We have six operational machines and two that are eighty percent complete. Simply with numbers, I can erase the threat of the Western sub-orbitals. It will probably be achieved within two missions."

"How?"

"You have never been concerned with details, Mr. Kyoto. Leave them to me."

"I want to know!" The timbre of Kyoto's demand vibrated in the air.

The colonel shrugged. "The tactics used against us were, and are, simple, but effective. The Western craft have, I believe, a slight advantage in the range of their weapons. They approach, fire their missiles, then turn off their radars and rocket engines, foiling our return fire. I used the same procedure to avoid becoming a casualty at Tyuratam."

"So?"

"The next scheduled launches are for the Americans at Vandenberg Air Force Base on September ninth and for the French on September eighth. Which would be your choice, Mr. Kyoto?"

The president of Nesei Aerospace turned to the computer terminal that was partially sunken into his desk top and fingered a few keys. After a moment, he had a listing on the screen.

"The French will attempt to place a spy satellite in orbit, and the Americans are launching a very expensive Cosmic Ray Observatory satellite. It must be the Americans."

"I believe, Mr. Kyoto, that two of the Western sub-orbitals will be sent to France to provide protection for their launch. That will leave two for the Vandenberg launch. I will lead a flight of four machines over California."

"And if they do not send two sub-orbitals to France?"

"Then I will take six of our machines."

"Our entire operational inventory!"

"Is Nesei Aerospace to succeed, Mr. Kyoto?"

The older man sighed deeply. "Go on, Colonel."

"Our source in the XSO program said that the maximum range of their radar is three hundred and fifty-five kilometers. I will send in two of our craft and hold the other two, or four, machines in reserve outside of their radar range. The Western sub-orbitals will attack our lead craft, then turn off their systems. Our lead machines will do the same, to protect themselves. As soon as the American and Soviet pilots shut down, we will launch an attack with the reserves. The Western sub-orbitals will re-ignite their rockets and activate their radar just in time to meet our Samurai missiles. We will also shoot down the Titan IV."

The CEO sat silently, his elbows on his desk, as he ruminated.

"In two, or perhaps in just one, operation, Mr. Kyoto, we can clear the skies of our opposition. Before a new threat can be mounted, Nesei Aerospace will have a long list of clients." Yakamata smiled briefly and said, "Perhaps the Americans and the Soviets might also come to our door to purchase sub-orbital craft."

"You are certain of yourself."

"And of my pilots. And while I think of them, I must ask that their, and my, salaries be doubled."

Kyoto nearly gagged.

"We did not contract with the company for high-risk combat missions."

"It is blackmail!"

"It is a chance to die, not only for Nesei Aerospace, but for Japan. Would you take that chance?"

After a long two minutes, Kyoto said, "You must not fail me, Colonel Yakamata."

"Failure for you is failure for me. I cannot abide

305

failure, Mr. Kyoto."

"Go. It is approved."

The Soviets had recovered less than four hundred pounds of scrap from the sub-orbital downed in the Hindu Kush Mountains, kept about half of it, and shipped the rest to the engineers at Rosie.

On the 26th of August, Billings called a meeting at 1500 hours to discuss the lab results.

Grant and Vidorov had spent the day monitoring test flights piloted by Shepard, Smertevo, and Zbibari. Grant was bored silly with sitting in a chair, listening to other people talk, and watching telemetry readouts. He was not looking forward to another meeting.

Before they left for Restwick's office, he tried Tricia's number again.

She answered.

"You're home!"

"Miss me, did you?"

"Of course not."

"Bye-bye."

"Well, just a little."

"I'm only back in town for a few days, Dallas. Dan's found his location and he's decided that he is going to proceed with the project."

"You going to be in it?"

"Just a walk-on."

"I'll buy a couple points," Grant said.

"Okay. Got a spare million or two?"

A million was about 940,000 dollars more in savings than Dallas Grant had managed to accumulate in his Air Force career. "Maybe a tenth of a point?"

306

"Sorry," she said. "We're looking for heavy hitters. Is there another reason for your call?"

"I'm calling because I'm supposed to call."

"Good. Tonight?"

"Yup, but I may be late."

After hanging up, Grant joined Vidorov, and the two of them headed down the corridor. Outside, he heard one of the sub-orbitals returning, the turbojet whining in reverse thrust as it raced down the runway.

Billings, Nemorosky, and Restwick were waiting for them, and Grant looked around the room, then went across the hallway to steal a couple more chairs.

"Okay, Jerry, kick it off," Billings said.

"I don't know what pieces Tyuratam hung onto," Restwick said, "but what we got were a few pieces of skin, some structural members, a chunk of the instrument panel, half a tire, forty-four feet of wiring cable, and a turbopump."

"Hell, those are more clues than Sherlock Holmes ever had," Grant told him.

Restwick was sitting on the counter that stretched across the back of his office, swinging his legs. "It was enough to tell me that Dmitri downed one of our own."

"What was that?" Billings asked, scowling.

"Well, it could have been. The turbopump is an exact copy of what we're using. The carbon-fibre skin matches our formula. The tire was manufactured by Goodyear, and the cross-section indicates that it will support the weight of our XSOs."

"What about the instrument panel?" Vidorov asked. "Surely, that is different."

"Slightly. If we'd gotten a digital readout, we might have powered it up and found out if it displayed in a

307

different language, in metric, or whatever. What we have though, is a set of switches, unmarked, and two integrated circuit boards. Most of the components were made in Japan, and a few of them in Taiwan."

"Japanese?" Billings asked.

"Don't read anything into that, General. Go behind our own instrument panels, and you'll find similar components, manufactured anywhere from Silicon Valley to Germany to Japan."

Grant pulled his chair forward and put his feet up on Restwick's desk. "What you're suggesting, Jer, is that the hostile sub-orbitals are rip-offs of our own."

"The suggestion is there, yes, Dallas."

"Who?"

"Who in the hell knows. This has not been a highly classified, high-security project. There's not much that's under lock and key."

"It has to be some country with the high-tech manufacturing capability," Billings said.

"And the bucks, General. But, shit, that still leaves a lot of candidates. Even in the Third World. An Iran or an Iraq could come up with the funding, if they didn't have to develop the technology."

"A goddamned terrorist operation?"

"It's only one scenario," Restwick said.

The general got up to pace the small office, his bulk a bit threatening as he weaved between the chairs. "Okay, Jerry, you did well. I'll turn the stuff over to DIA and see what they can come up with. How about the tapes?"

"Nothing. We have shadows on video, and enhancement doesn't help. We did get a brief shot of the one aggressor from the corner of Dmitri's video when it exploded, but it doesn't tell us anything. On radar, we have blips. Intermittent blips, because Dallas and Dmitri shut down and powered up a few times, as did the hostiles."

Billings spun on Grant. "You review the tapes?"

"A few dozen times. Dmitri and I were trying to figure out the tactics."

"And?"

"It's a whole new world, General. At those speeds, and with the weapons and visibility limitations, we've got to come up with something better than we used the last time."

"What's it going to be?"

"We don't know yet. Tomorrow, we're going to take up all four of the birds and try several possibilities. I'll let you know as soon as Dmitri and I have an answer."

Grant took a surreptitious glance at his watch. It was already after four, and he wanted to hit the road.

Billings saw him. "Okay. Anything else for now?"

Apparently not.

"Let's break it up, then."

As he got out of his chair, Grant asked, "Where's Alex?"

Wrong question.

Billings said, "AWOL."

"No shit?"

Nemorosky said, "He was supposed to have reported back to the base last Monday morning."

"We've been checking the state patrol, the hospitals, the Mexican border patrol. I've got police departments from San Diego to San Francisco looking for that red car of his." Billings was close to being irate.

Grant recalled the evening he had followed Murychenko into Los Angeles. "You check his girlfriend's place?"

"Girlfriend! What girlfriend?" Nemorosky asked. "Alexander has never mentioned a friend, male or female, to me."

"I assume he's got some cute chickadee stashed away in Beverly Hills," Grant said. He told them his story in about five minutes.

"Son of a bitch!" Billings said. "Who'd have thought . . . what's the address, Dallas?"

"Well, I don't know the number. It's on Stone Canyon Road. Get the cops to knock on doors."

"Not when you can find it for us," Billings said. "I want to keep the police out of it, if we can."

"Oh, hell!"

"Let's go." Billings was on his feet, impatient.

"I'm taking my own car," Grant said, "because I'm not coming back tonight."

Vidorov wanted to go along and rode with Grant. Billings and Nemorosky took the staff car, with Sergeant McEvoy at the wheel.

Like most Californians, Grant assumed the posted speed limits were only suggestions. He put the speedometer needle at eighty to see if McEvoy, in an official car, would stick with him.

He did.

When he reached the interstate, he slowed down to seventy, to keep the sergeant out of real trouble.

"Is this really something Alex would do, Dmitri?"

"I did not meet the man until this project, Dallas. He seems very intelligent, but also very private. I do not know what he would do."

There were still a couple hours of light left when

Grant took the Mulholland exit and threaded his way back into the hills. McEvoy stayed right on his bumper.

On Stone Canyon Road, he drove at twenty miles per hour and studied the houses on the right. He almost passed it, but remembered the way the driveway intersected the road at an oblique angle, then dipped down away from the road. Tapping the brakes, he jerked the wheel and pulled into the drive and stopped. He opened his door and levered himself out of the seat.

McEvoy parked behind him and got out of the Chevy with the two generals.

"This is it?" Billings asked.

"This is it."

"Looks vacant to me."

The windows on the front, and on the side they could see, had their drapes drawn, though it looked as if there was a light on inside. It was an older house, in need of paint. The dark brown trim paint had peeled in a number of places, leaving exposed wood. The lush vegetation—shrubs, vines, and trees—crowded up close to the building.

Billings crossed the drive to the front door and rang the doorbell.

He jabbed at the bell button five times, but got no response.

"You're sure about this, Dallas?"

"Hell, yes. I'll go around back."

Grant stepped off the driveway and slid his way down the steep slope, grabbing a succession of trailing vines and bougainvillea to slow his descent. At the bottom corner of the house, he looked around, then up to the deck. The sliding glass door was open.

He took that as an invitation and scaled the deck

supports, pulling himself up and over the railing. There were three pieces of wrought iron furniture on the deck.

He knocked on the wooden trim at the side of the door, and after getting no response, went on inside. One table lamp was turned on.

Quickly, he walked through the house. He checked the closet in the bedroom and thought he recognized some of the clothes hanging in it.

Moving back through the living room and dining room to the front door, he unlocked and opened it.

"Jesus Christ, Grant! That's breaking and entering."

"The back door was open, General. You might want to check the bedroom closet, General Nemorosky. I think those are Alex's clothes."

The five of them wandered through the house, then compared notes.

"Looks to me," Billings said, "as if only one person has been living here."

"And the clothes are definitely his," Vidorov said.

"These places sell for a million and more," Grant said. "He couldn't have afforded it."

"Maybe he rented it," Vidorov suggested.

"High rent."

"Maybe he just borrowed it, sir." McEvoy had delved into the box beside the front door which captured the mail shoved through a slot in the wall. "All of this is addressed to a Gerhard Strichmann."

Grant took the packet from McEvoy and leafed through it. Most of it was junk mail. There was an electric bill. There was an envelope with the return address of the California Department of Motor Vehicles. He had seen one like it several times before when he had been out of state at the Air Force's insistence and needed a renewal of his driver's license.

Grant ripped open the flap.

"That's a federal offense," Billings said.

He pulled out a renewal California driver's license, took one look at it, and passed it to Billings. "That's Gerhard Strichmann."

The picture was that of Alexander Murychenko.

"What the hell's going on?" Billings asked, passing the document to Nemorosky.

"I don't know about you, General, but I have a feeling that we've discovered the route taken by the XSO Program's blueprints."

"I cannot believe that," Nemorosky declared.

"Goddamn it! I'm going to have to bring in the CID, the DIA, and probably the damned FBI," Billings said.

While he debated his options and eyed the telephone, Grant walked out onto the deck and sat in one of the wrought iron chairs. Nice view, he thought.

Vidorov came out of the house and leaned against the outside railing, looking out at the city.

"This is difficult, Dallas."

"Yeah, it is." Grant did not find it so difficult to believe. He could understand a Soviet citizen wanting a better lifestyle.

"Bloody damn!"

Grant swung his head toward Vidorov and found him pointing a forefinger down the hill. He got out of his chair, crossed the deck, and followed Vidorov's aim.

A single leg projected upward from the vines fifteen feet down from the edge of the balcony.

"General," Grant called toward the house. "You'd better start with the FBI."

*   *   *

313

Polly Enburton took a break over the Memorial Day weekend and went home to Des Moines where the landscape was flat and familiar, and where the people were a trifle more naive, but a great deal more friendly.

Everything had gone just about as she had expected it to go. She had the backing of Senate and House intelligence committee members who were knowledgeable about the events at Tyuratam. John Hammond and Don Sunwallow helped her get her supplemental recommendation through the House armed services and appropriations committees, and with that support behind them, the supplement had sailed through the Senate committees. The White House had called every committee member with its appreciation.

The appropriations bills would go on the respective floors next week, and there would be more lobbying and more jockeying as amendments came from the floor, but she thought she would be able to control the movements that affected her.

Her job was not over, but she felt it was complete, and she was looking forward to a few days to herself.

Roberta Jamieson was unhappy. Until the last moments, she had thought that Polly's supplemental would meet defeat.

There had been very few times in her life when Jamieson had not gotten her way, so this had hit her pretty hard. She hated being a loser, and had never allowed herself to lose before.

Jamieson was not a liberal and not a reformer. She truly believed the sub-orbital program was entirely misdirected. The craft was not intended to be a

314

weapons platform, and the project's leadership was completely inadequate, if not incompetent.

She had always believed herself capable of making objective judgments. Many of her law professors had complimented her on that ability. In this instance, she knew she had fully divorced her emotions from her reasoning. She had pushed the rejection of that son of a bitch Grant clear out of the picture as she went through her decisioning process.

Her ability at swaying mock court juries had also impressed her law school professors, and Jamieson knew that all was not lost when the facts went against her case. One could always appeal to the jury.

Or to the public.

She flipped through her personal phone directory, found the number, and dialed it.

"AP. This is Murray."

"Mel Ordway, please."

"Comin' up. Hey, Mel!"

There were a couple of clicks on the line, then, "Ordway here."

"Mel, this is Robbi Jamieson."

"Hiya, babe. You going to finally give in to me?"

"I thought I'd let you take me to that expensive lunch you keep offering."

"Is there some way I'll be able to stiff the expense account for the tab?" he asked.

"You'll find a way, I'm sure. But only as background, Mel. Only as background."

"Deal. I'll meet you at Kelley's Beef in, oh, gimme half an hour."

"I had Il Giardino in mind."

"Jesus Christ, babe! This better be a two-hundred-dollar story."

"How much does the Pulitzer pay?"

An early snowfall crusted the roof of the National Assembly and covered the lawns of the parks. The sidewalks and streets had melted off by nine o'clock, but pedestrians were constantly in danger of slush attack by insensitive Parisians at the steering wheels of Peugeots and Citroens.

By eleven o'clock, Alain Moncrieux had read the story in *Le Monde* twice. He had read the longer article in the French edition of the *New York Times* three times.

The ineptitude of the SDECE was an insult to him, and he hoped, to the rest of France.

The call came as expected.

"Hello, Sir Neil."

"Alain, I'm afraid I have terrible news for you."

"I cannot imagine what that might be, Sir Neil."

"The board of directors has just met—in fact, they are still meeting, and are, quite naturally, concerned about the apparent . . . disruption in your program."

"Naturally."

"I'm quite saddened to have to tell you that the board has determined to cancel the French contract and reopen negotiations with the Japanese."

"I understand perfectly, Sir Neil. I wish you luck."

After hanging up, Moncrieux called to the other office. "Yvonne, will you place a telephone call to Inspector Duchatreau at SDECE. Then, please bring in my personal file."

Her response was subdued. "Of course, monsieur."

316

When the light blinked, he picked up the telephone. "Inspector Duchatreau here. How can I help you?"

"By admitting that you are an asshole." Moncrieux hung up, feeling immensely better.

Yvonne placed his personal file on his desk as he stood up and took his topcoat from the hall tree. Her face was pale.

"Yvonne, how would you like to begin calling me Alain?"

"Monsieur?"

"No. Alain."

"Alain."

"Would you like to go into the computer business with me, Yvonne?" He picked his file up from the desk.

Her eyes widened. "I would like that."

"Then let us do it now."

He lifted her coat from the tree, and held it for her. In the outer office, Yvonne retrieved her purse from the desk drawer. He held his arm out to her, and she gripped his forearm with her hand.

It felt good to him.

Nineteen

Lane Billings read the story in the *Los Angeles Times* while eating his breakfast in Rosie's mess hall. If anything, he was surprised it had not broken earlier. Too many people were privy to the information to have expected it to remain a secret for long. And perhaps it would have been better to control the release of the information, rather than to let it come out this way. Presidents and generals could not always be right.

The headline was the standard attention-grabber:

U.S. CONDUCTING SECRET WAR

The source was someone very close to the inside ring of classified knowledge because all the details were there, and they were accurate: The series of rocket failures, the loss of Dennis Blake and XSO-2, the President's approval for arming the sub-orbitals, and the executive order allowing the pilots to fire before being fired upon. The air battle over Tyuratam was exaggerated a bit.

The source and the reporter were just as stymied as

the American intelligence community, however, when it came to identifying the enemy. The speculation ranged from Middle East terrorists to Central American bandits to Colombian drug lords to duplicitous Soviets, which would not help cooperative attitudes. Billings assigned the speculation to the reporter, rather than the source, because the man, Melvin Ordway, seemed to have no appreciation for the enormous costs or the sophisticated technology involved. Worse, there was no hostility for an unknown enemy that had caused widespread damage in the space programs of three nations and had shot down an American aviator. The subtle accusation of the article was directed at an administration that operated in secrecy, or at least in secret meetings to which Melvin Ordway had not been invited.

The wrap-up was as expected: the Department of Defense and the President had no business engaging in hostilities without the concurrence of the American public, or at minimum, the United States Congress.

The hue and cry would begin shortly, and the strident voices would make the issues fuzzy and the vote-conscious politicians cautious—just as the appropriations bills went to the floors of both houses.

Billings tossed the paper on the end of the table and went back to his bowl of oatmeal.

Grant sat down opposite him, dressed in a flight suit, and carrying coffee and a plate of oversized Danish.

The general raised an eyebrow.

"Yes, I read it. Bastards!"

"What do you think will happen, Dallas?"

"You're the politician, General."

"I'm still interested in your thoughts."

Grant offered a scowl, took one bite of his offensive

319

and high-caloric breakfast, chewed, swallowed, and said, "First of all, the story may drive the aggressors to cover. We may never find out who they were, and that'll piss me off. Second, I'd guess that public pressure on Congress from the liberal populace might increase rapidly. In fact, I count on it. There's a chance for resolutions out of the Senate and House that would put us in suspension. Until the facts can be verified by four hundred and twenty-two lawyers. Third, the President and the SecDef will probably have to give in to it. Fourth, as soon as they do, we'll have more Tridents and Titans blowing up, and we'll sit here and watch them. They're all sons of bitches, General."

"Hell, Dallas, there's hope for you yet."

Grant squinted his eyes.

"Much as you profess to hate political manipulation, you understand it, or you're beginning to. You're going to need it for the balance of your career."

"Not so," Grant protested.

"There'll come a time when you have to leave the cockpit. Maybe I'll get you assigned as my administrative assistant when this program is killed. We can count noses or rolls of toilet paper together."

Grant's face displayed shocked horror. "You wouldn't!"

"You'll like Washington."

"I was at Andrews. I didn't like it."

"And you're maturing fast," Billings told him. "Another eight or ten years, and you'll be full grown."

The pilot took another bite.

"Finish that, skip the second one, because you don't need it, and come with me. We've got work to do."

*   *   *

Polly Enburton was in her office with Roberta Jamieson and two other staff members, preparing defensive responses for the arguments that were bound to arise when the appropriations bill went to the floor at one o'clock.

The intercom buzzed, irritating her.

"Yes."

"Polly, AP is on line one."

"Who is it, Doris?"

"Mel Ordway."

"Okay, I'd better take it." She picked up the receiver and punched the button. "Hello, Mel."

"Congresswoman, I've been trying to reach you."

"I was out of town until this morning."

"You're on the intelligence and armed service committees, so you've known about this air war for some time. You're also known as a levelheaded woman. What's your reaction?"

"Mel, anything I know is classified. I will not comment for the record."

"Background, then?"

"Even off-the-record, Mel, a statement from me is not appropriate."

There was a long pause. "I think I understand, Congresswoman Enburton. All right. I respect the position you're taking. Is Robbi there? I'll get some more from her."

"No." Enburton replaced the telephone in its cradle, and looked at Jamieson—who looked away from her, a red flush creeping up her throat.

"Debra, would you and Phillip please leave us alone for a minute?"

The two staff aides gave each other puzzled looks, got up, and left the private office. Debra closed the door softly behind them.

"Why, Roberta?"

"Why what, Polly?"

"Why did you go to Ordway?"

"Ordway?"

"You know I'm not naive," Enburton said. "Don't play with me as if I am."

"Well, first of all," Jamieson blurted, "he came to me, and it was just background, and I didn't know what he . . ."

"I think, Roberta, that you'll be much happier in civil or corporate law. Perhaps your father can arrange a position for you."

"Polly!" Jamieson's eyes clouded, as if she were about to start crying.

"It will be best if you just clean out your desk and leave, Roberta."

Silence.

"There will not be a recommendation, and there will not be a position for you with any House or Senate member."

Jamieson looked stricken.

"That will be all, Roberta."

Dmitri Vidorov and Pyotr Nemorosky walked over to the operations building together. Inside, the red air force general stopped by his office for mail, then they went down the hall to the small conference room. Billings, Restwick, and Grant were waiting for them.

"Good morning, gentlemen," Billings said. "Have a seat. We've got a lot on our agenda. Some of it's good, and a lot of it isn't."

Vidorov sat down in the chair next to Grant, who

gave him a big grin.

"Number one," the general said, "the President has received a letter from the Soviet President expressing his appreciation for Black Panther Squadron's assistance at Tyuratam. Colonel Vidorov is to be awarded a medal upon his return to the Soviet Union."

"Congratulations, Dmitri," Grant told him.

"Undeserved, I am sure," Vidorov said.

"Not to be outdone," Billings continued, "the President has started the paperwork to give Colonel Grant another Distinguished Flying Cross. That's rare in peacetime, and I'll add my appreciation to the President's."

Grant said, "You could have told me that in private at breakfast, General."

Vidorov patted Grant on the shoulder.

"And that takes care of the good stuff."

Vidorov watched as Nemorosky began to scan his messages and open his mail.

"Next item. The President, the SecDef, the Joint Chiefs, hell, everybody who outranks me and therefore counts, is hopping mad over this news leak. Investigations have been started everywhere, but between you and me, I doubt that they'll ever locate the leak, much less discipline the one responsible. They never do."

"Are we moving ahead, as if nothing has happened?" Restwick asked. "As prime contractor, my company is getting edgy. I've been getting calls on all four of my lines. And damn it, I'm getting a little tense, myself. Do I still have a job, General?"

"I can't tell you shit, Jerry. I just don't know. My orders have not changed yet, and I'm going to act as if they're not going to change in the immediate future. I will tell you this. General Hansen, everybody around

323

the SecDef's office, and, I assume, the President, is going to stall for as long as possible. Unless I get an order to the contrary, we'll proceed to the next mission."

"No timetable at all, General?" Restwick asked.

"None."

Vidorov continued to glance at his superior as he went through his messages. Nemorosky's face paled. He folded the last page he had read and placed the whole bundle of mail in his lap.

"Number three. Grant, how are Tim Forrester and Kerry Rand coming along?"

The ordnance research and development group over at Edwards proper had been working long days and many nights since the episode at Tyuratam.

"Given the length of the launch tubes in the weapons pod," Grant said, "they've been able to lengthen the electronics section of the missile by three-and-a-half inches. That's not a hell of a lot of room to work with, but it might be enough for more powerful transmitters. We're not doing anything with the laser designation system since we can't see the hostiles up there, anyway. We're hoping to achieve at least another four or five miles of range on the infrared seekers. Plus, we're going to try to lower the tolerance. If we can get a missile within ten miles of the target, we think we can track on just the hot metal of the nozzle, even if the engines have been shut down. On the negative side of that, General, is the fact that we won't have an operational missile for another two or three weeks."

"Questions, anyone? Okay, Jerry, how about the infrared cameras?"

Restwick sat up in his chair. "We've decided to put another acrylic window in the nose and move the existing video cameras to one side. It's tight, but we've been able to sneak in a Forward-Looking Infrared camera. Like the video camera, we don't get a lot of movable tracking arc with the FLIR, but at least we have some capability. We've worked out the interface with the computer, the screen display, and the weapons systems. As of yesterday, XSO-6 has been fitted. XSO-5 will be completed by late this afternoon. Dallas and Dmitri have scheduled night flights for the first tests."

"Good, good. We going to have the other two finished by the ninth?"

"Damned right," Restwick said.

"That brings up the next item. The French President has requested that the White House assign two of the sub-orbitals to cover a *Rapier* launch on the late afternoon of September eight. What do you think about it?" Billings's tone was neutral, but Vidorov had heard rumors circulating that the general was unhappy with the French for some reason.

Grant groaned. "I suppose we could send Billy Shepard and who, Dmitri, Valerie Zbibari?"

Vidorov nodded.

"They could leave here on the seventh with the C-141 and a couple ground crews in support, but I doubt that we'd have them back in time for the Vandenberg launch. That is, we can get them back, but they'll be fatigued. Dmitri and I can handle Vandenberg on our own, though."

"The French have not been cooperative, I believe?" Vidorov asked.

"You could say that," Billings said.

"To use the American expression, then, I would say, 'fuck the French.'"

Restwick fixed the alibi. "I think I'm going to have all of the birds grounded for maintenance on September eighth, General."

"That's the message I'll have to send, then," the American general grinned, then frowned. "Number six, Alexander Murychenko. Pyotr, I guess the proper way is to have you make the report."

Nemorosky nodded his head absentmindedly, then shook it. He sat up in his chair and said, "The Federal Bureau of Investigation examination is not yet complete, but they have provided General Billings and myself with progress reports. From abrasions on Alexander's neck and a bump on the back of his head, they seem to believe that his death did not result from a fall from the balcony of the house. The assumption is that his neck was broken, and then his body was dropped from the deck."

Vidorov shuddered. An accident was one thing, but murder? Alexander, no matter what his other faults might prove to be, did not deserve it.

"The house was purchased for slightly less than a million U.S. dollars over two years ago with a cashier's check, and it was in the name of Gerhard Strichmann. Besides the driver's license, Alexander had obtained a Social Security card and a passport in the Strichmann name. That was learned from the agencies involved. None of those papers were found in the house, and it is believed that the killer took them, attempting to conceal a link between the Strichmann name and Murychenko. Perhaps one day, a false relative of Strichmann will appear with a fabricated will, attempting to claim the house. The FBI believes that Alexander was maintaining a separate identity into which he could step when his involvement with the program here came to an end."

"Do they know the source of all this money," General Nemorosky?" Vidorov asked.

"No. Under the seat of his car was a freehand drawing of the Hellwinder missile, along with a duplicate of one of the new circuit boards we are using in the missile. It is obvious what he was doing."

Nemorosky looked quite ill, Vidorov thought. He would be under great pressure from Antonovko and Brezhenki for allowing a defection, even if it were a future defection.

"I'm sorry about all of this, Pyotr," Billings said. "Have you passed the information on to your people?"

"Only the news of his death, Lane. I was going to wait until the final report of the Federal Bureau of Investigation before mentioning the other."

"*Was?*" Billings asked.

Nemorosky held up his folded paper. "Colonel Vidorov and I have been recalled to Moscow. Two others have been named to replace us."

Vidorov's head sagged, and he forced himself to hold it upright. It should have been wonderful news, news that reunited him with Nadia.

But he knew that would not be.

Generals Brezhenki and Antonovko considered him a failure, and so he was.

Grant felt badly for Vidorov and was going to suggest a drink together as the meeting broke up.

"Grant. Stay." Billings had not bothered to lever himself out of his chair.

He shrugged and said, "Sure thing, General."

When the room had cleared, Billings said, "Polly

327

Enburton called me."

"She did?"

"She found the source of the leak, and she took care of it. There won't be any publicity about it."

Puzzled that he was included in the revelation, Grant said, "That's wonderful."

"Got any ideas about who it is?"

Grant could not figure out what his role was here. Then, from the disgusted look on Billings's face, he knew what his guess should be. "Jamieson?"

"Goddamned right, first time out of the chute."

"Shit. Why?"

"Damned if I know. I thought you might have a clue or two for me."

"General, all I did was have dinner with the lady and then not sleep with her."

"I don't know what her motivation was," Billings said, "but woman scorned is always a possibility."

"No."

"You certain of that?"

Grant sighed. "I guess not."

"Hell, this morning, I was ready to believe you were catching on to the game, Grant. I was wrong."

Grant left the conference room feeling as if he'd lost two or three feet of stature. He hurried to catch up with Vidorov, who gave him a wry smile.

"Come on, Dmitri, let's find a bottle. We've both got something to cry about, and I'd like to do it together."

Twenty

On the morning of the eighth of September, in narrow votes, both the Senate and the House passed similar resolutions calling for a suspension of activity in the USAF Research and Development Command's Experimental Sub-Orbital Program. Both suggested full disclosure of the facts in a hearing before the Senate Armed Services Committee.

When asked, the President said that, although he saw no reason to suspend the program, he did not have a problem with disclosure. Neither did the Secretary of Defense, who then diverted media people to the Joint Chiefs of Staff.

The Chairman of the Joint Chiefs was also open to full disclosure, but he referred additional questions to the Chief of Naval Operations, who had, the way things developed, become the chairman of the ad hoc committee investigating the sub-orbital conflict.

The CNO was in conference.

He was on the telephone with General Lane Billings.

"First of all, Lane, I've got a positive response on

your request of yesterday afternoon."

"I appreciate that."

"Don't thank me. The President took care of it. Now, let me tell you about these damned resolutions."

Billings listened carefully as Zeiman read each of the resolutions to him over the phone. There had been television reports, but Billings had not yet seen written versions.

"Pretty general, Bart."

"Yes, but clear enough."

"Shit. I've got two pressing problems here. One, Rosie's swamped with broadcast and print reporters. I've had to call in fifty air policemen from Edwards to get them out of our hangars and buildings and back outside the fence. There's seven TV vans sitting on the other side of our main gate."

Zeiman laughed. "Hell, Lane, what'd you join the Air Force for, to avoid war? You should see the Riverfront Entrance. My switchboard's overloaded. My aide is having second thoughts about a Navy career. What's your other problem?"

"Tomorrow's launch at Vandenberg."

"Yeah. NASA's running that, right?"

"Correct. It's a CRO satellite. I believe it's a joint effort by a number of research universities. It's a one-of-a-kind satellite, Bart, and costly as hell. I don't want to leave it unprotected. Do we ask NASA to hold off?"

"No, we don't. We won't delay, and we won't leave it unprotected."

"I hate to mention this, Bart, but I'm going to have to have something on paper. This is a real good time to cover my ass."

"You'll get your paper, Lane. Within the hour, you'll

330

have instructions from Mark Hansen to comply with the wishes of Congress and suspend flight tests in the XSO Program."

"That helps," Billings said.

"You'll also receive your orders from General Alan Messerman at Headquarters, Aerospace Defense Command. Those will give you the authority to fly a protective mission for the launch."

Billings whistled. "That's playing a dangerous game, isn't it, Bart?"

"You don't like it?"

"Hell, yes, I do. Goddamned politicians want to have exact data, but they don't write very accurate resolutions. Yes, I like it. My operational command is unaffected by the resolution?"

"That's the way we read it."

"As soon as I get my birds off in the morning, I'm going to dig a deep foxhole. This is going to be a big, big fan, and a hell of a lot of shit."

"Look at it this way, Lane. If Grant doesn't run into anything up there, nobody's the wiser."

"I don't know about that. I think the media's going to camp out at the main gate, and they'll see the takeoff. What if he jumps on an aggressor?"

"Tell him to shoot carefully. We'd like to have pieces of a pilot who can still talk."

"Pyotr," Billings said, "I think there's a rather large communications gap between your general staff and your Politburo."

Grant worked diligently on a wedge of apple pie that was still warm. The dollop of vanilla ice cream on top of it was melting fast. It was eight-thirty, and the dining room had cleared of everyone but the kitchen personnel and those at the big round table where Billings presided.

The two generals had requested the company of Grant, Shepard, Vidorov, Smertevo, and Zbibari for dinner.

"What is it that you are saying?" Nemorosky asked.

"I think it relates to the difference in our military philosophies," Billings said. "American planning staffs issue pretty generalized orders, and subordinate commands are given a fair amount of latitude on how they achieve the objectives. The on-site commander, be it regimental or platoon, makes his own decisions within stated parameters. We allow for individual initiative."

"I have read that at several military institutes," Nemorosky grinned ruefully.

"And the Soviet structure is much more rigid. Your training programs instruct commanders at various levels to perform in expected ways. The philosophy expects that a central command will know exactly what is going to happen in the field because the field commander *must* do exactly what he was trained to do."

"This is true," the Soviet said.

"But you and I know that conditions in the field are not always what we think they are. An American staff command halfway expects to have things go wrong, and it relies on the competence of its local commanders to put things right. The Soviet system, well . . . you know what I'm getting at."

"We do not have to agree, Lane. Yes, sometimes the

Stavka becomes slightly addled when a mission does not develop as foreseen. We are more apt to change field commanders, if the first commander has not achieved his goals."

"In the example before us," Billings said, "it was a case of the Soviet President not knowing what his generals were doing. Or of the generals not informing the President. The communication chain broke down, and General Brezhenki, or maybe it was General Antonovko, made a decision that was unexpected by higher authority."

Nemorosky watched Billings intently.

"What I did, through my chain of command, was ask the President to speak to your President. He told the President that we were extremely satisfied with the performance of General Nemorosky and Colonel Vidorov, and hinted that we would not approve the replacements suggested for them. It turns out that the President didn't know anything about your recall, and he was quite unhappy, especially since he had just authorized an award of heroism for the Colonel. General Brezhenki has been directed to rescind your recall orders."

Grant thought that the look on Nemorosky's face was a trifle confused. He did not know whether to be relieved or fearful. Vidorov's face, though more stoic, showed the same reaction.

"I think we are grateful," Nemorosky said.

"I know the way it works," the American commander said. "Brezhenki and Antonovko are going to think you went behind their backs. But hell, Pyotr, you can blame it on me. And then, we're going to bull our way through this Congressional snafu. It may be two or three years before you go back, and they'll have forgotten."

"I trust you are correct."

"Don't look so damned glum, Dmitri," Grant said. "Nadia would rather have you come back to her in Moscow in a couple years, instead of having to visit you at Kamchatka Air Base."

Vidorov smiled, but uneasily.

Billings cleared his throat. "Next. Grant, you people ready to go in the morning?"

"Eager."

"Who's going?"

"Billy and I, Dmitri and Anatoly." In fact, there had damned near been a fist fight between Anatoly Smertevo and Valerie Zbibari over who was selected. They were both excellent pilots, and Vidorov had settled the matter in an American way, with the toss of a quarter.

"The sub-orbitals?"

"The birds are in top shape, General. Restwick's people have done a fine job. Let's give them a medal."

"They're civilians."

"Who cares?" Grant said.

"Got your strategy pinned down?"

"As well as we're going to get it. We're relying heavily on the FLIR, but it looks good to me."

"Dmitri, what do you think?" Billings asked.

"There is an excellent chance for success," Vidorov told him.

"The Joint Chiefs would like to have you down at least one of the hostiles in big enough pieces that we can trace the ownership."

"Screw the Joint Chiefs," Grant said. "My goal is to

334

get us down in four complete pieces."

"There you go again, being diplomatic." Billings laughed, but Grant was taking such comments more personally, and it stung.

"Okay, hit the sack. No carousing tonight."

The five pilots walked back to the residence hall together and split up to go to their own rooms. In his first floor room, Grant found a Michelob in his refrigerator, decided to allow himself the one, and settled into his easy chair. He unlaced his shoes and tossed them under the bed.

Picking up the phone, he dialed the familiar number.

"Hello?"

"Hi, love."

"You're getting to be almost a regular on the phone, you know that?"

"This is my Hawaii watch."

"Your what?"

"I have to keep checking in to find out if you're still an L.A. resident."

"There's been a change," Tricia said.

"Oh?"

"Some of Dan's money people have backed out. It's taking longer than expected to raise the capital, but we have about half of it."

"How much is that?" Grant asked. "How much does something like this take?"

"It's a small project, and the budget is only twenty-two million."

"Hey, Tricia, nobody's going to miss a measly million or two. You grab that, we'll buy us an airplane and go to Tahiti. Live like Fletcher Christian."

"I don't want to live like Fletcher Christian. He had

outdoor toilets."

"But he had all those topless babes wandering around."

"And I'm not especially interested in other topless babes."

"Well, then, in the meantime, do you have a schedule?"

"Dan's in New York, chasing investors, then he's going back to Honolulu. I'm sticking around Tinsel Town for awhile, to start casting."

"Thank the Lord. And Dan Moretti."

"Hey, boy. You're starting to sound earnest."

"I am always earnest," Grant claimed.

"Are you coming to town tomorrow night?"

Was he? Grant had an uneasy feeling about the ninth of September. It was difficult to plan beyond takeoff. "I'll have to call you tomorrow."

"Uh-huh," she said, sounding skeptical.

"Problem?"

"We've been talking for three minutes, and you haven't mentioned even one of the stories that have been in the paper or on TV."

"I don't like to bring my work home with me."

"Dallas, did you really shoot down another airplane in Russia?"

He had explained the differences before, but she still thought of the sub-orbitals as oversized Cessnas. "He kind of got in my way."

Long, long pause. "I've never been particularly school-girlish, have I?"

"No," he admitted.

"I like you because you're you, not because you're a hotshot test pilot."

"You really like me?"

"Shut up. You've never told me anything, in a serious way, about what you do, and while I know it's dangerous, I just don't dwell on it."

"And?"

"And it's still something of a barrier between us, Dallas. I don't want to get attached to a dead man."

"Ah, hell, Tricia . . ."

"And I don't like reading in the papers that you're getting shot at. Damn it, Dan saw it first, called me, and wanted to know if you'd be available to play a fighter pilot role."

"Me? In the movies?"

"I told him no."

"Well, don't jump to . . ."

"The best thing that's happened is this Congressional inquiry," she said. "At least I know you're on the ground for awhile."

Grant did not have an answer for that. At least, not one that he wanted to give her.

Twenty-One

The launch was scheduled for eight o'clock in the morning, California time. That was eleven o'clock at night at Sun Land, and Yakamata had scheduled the takeoff time for his squadron for eight-forty-five. With climb-out through the lower layers of the atmosphere, and four five-minute, engines-off glides, that would place them in position a few minutes before the Titan IV was due to be launched.

The distance from Sun Land to Southern California was just over 8500 kilometers at surface level, passing to the west of Anchorage, Alaska. The round-trip, with orbit time at the target site, taxed the range of Nesei Aerospace's sub-orbitals. The four unpowered glides that Yakamata had calculated into the first leg of the flight would cover 1660 kilometers and save them twenty minutes of fuel. The return leg required six glides in order to give them thirty minutes over the site and twenty minutes of reserve fuel.

The NAI sub-orbitals had a 3.5-hour duration at cruise speed, compared to the 3.75 hours of the Soviet-

338

American machines, as reported by Kyoto's informant. Yakamata did not know what caused the difference— weight, changes in air frame or rocket engine design, something. Still, with prudent use of the engines, he could go almost anywhere in the world. When Kyoto went public with the sub-orbitals, some time in the near future, Yakamata was going to attempt an around-the-world flight, following the Equator. He had estimated he could do it in slightly more than eleven hours, with one load of fuel.

The record-setter would establish Nesei Aerospace—through the front company Dissonex International—as a prominent designer. Yakamata's reputation as an aviator would not suffer, either.

Kyoto was at the airfield to see them off, as he always was. Yakamata knew that as soon as they were of sight, the man would return to his office to work until he learned of their return.

The rest of the airfield was deserted, the workers returned to their apartments and dormitories, and the six sub-orbitals were fully fueled and lined up outside the hangar. Yakamata stood by his unmarked craft, known on the radio as Red Dagger One, and bowed slightly in Kyoto's direction. His leader bowed back, and Yakamata turned and scrambled up into the cockpit. Daggers Two through Six checked in on the radio with their readiness reports, and Yakamata gave the signal to start engines.

The man tending the start-cart parked next to him turned on the auxiliary power and the high-pressure airflow. Yakamata depressed the turbojet cranking button, and when he had twenty percent RPM, ignited the turbojet. It whined into life and the RPM counter continued to climb. He signaled the crew chief, and the auxiliary power unit was disconnected. The wheel chocks were pulled away, and the ground crewmen ran for the safety of the hangar.

Yakamata released the brakes and led the way toward the end of the runway, the five other craft pulling in behind him, one by one. He turned on his exterior lights—anti-collision strobe, landing lights, and running lights. As soon as he turned onto the runway, the runway lights came on. He did not hesitate, but thrust the throttle lever fully forward. The heavily laden sub-orbital took a while to come up to speed. As soon as the readout indicated 460 kilometers-per-hour, Yakamata rotated, the nose coming up ten degrees. The wheel rumble ceased, and he immediately retracted the landing gear. Air speed picked up instantly.

In his rearview monitor, he saw Matsushima's red and green wingtip lights rise from the runway. That was his signal to turn off all of his own lights, and he did so. Steadily checking the small screen, he counted the five sub-orbitals as each lifted off, then extinguished its lights.

Red Dagger One had achieved 950 kilometers-per-hour and 600 meters of altitude by the time it crossed the northern coast of Hokkaido Island. Yakamata turned to a heading of thirty-five degrees in order to avoid Soviet air space around Sakhalin Island. The Sea of Okhotsk was dark and cold and ominous below him.

Twenty minutes later, Red Dagger Flight was assembled in one formation, successfully converted to rocket engines, and climbing through 16,000 meters of altitude.

340

Yakamata leveled them off at seventy kilometers. Half an hour later, halfway through the first leg of the flight, with the pre-dawn city lights of Anchorage off his left wing, he reshaped them into attack formation.

Slowing the rest of the flight and starting a climb, Yakamata allowed Daggers Three and Four to pull ahead by 400 kilometers. He kept himself and Dagger Two in the middle of the formation while Daggers Five and Six dropped back by 400 kilometers. The first element flew at seventy kilometers of altitude, the second at eighty kilometers, and the last at ninety kilometers. Each element would climb at a rate of 300 meters-per-minute, in preparation for the third glide period where they would again lose altitude.

In stepped pairs, Dagger Flight streaked toward California. Each pair was separated by a distance greater than the radar range of the Western suborbitals.

Dagger Flight was prepared for three fatal thrusts. Yakamata thought that the last two of them would be totally unexpected.

Grant had his Black Panthers aloft by 0730 hours. As they spiraled upward on rocket engines, he keyed his mike on Tac-2. "Panther three, you sure you don't want to trade positions?"

Shepard came right back to him. "Hell no, boss man! I got the straw I wanted. I get in there first, and there won't be shit left for the rest of you guys."

"Last chance, Billy."

"Gone by," he said. "I want one of those little flies painted on my bird."

341

Using orange epoxy paint, Gloomy had hand-painted a four-inch-long silhouette of a sub-orbital below the left hand side of the canopy on Grant's craft. The outline deviated very little from that of their own sub-orbitals since neither Gloomy, nor anyone else, had actually seen a hostile machine.

As they passed through 150,000 feet, Grant ordered, "Everyone on FLIR."

He keyed in the command to display the computer-enhanced image from the Forward-Looking Infrared camera on his screen. With the other sub-orbitals behind him, the lens did not pick up their heat sources.

"I see you," Shepard said. He was a hundred yards back, on Grant's left wing, visible by virtue of his running lights. The Soviets were stepped back on Grant's right.

"Activate the ECM panels."

After warming up for two minutes, the green LEDs started popping on, showing him he had active chaff, flares, radar and radio jamming, and threat warning.

"Let's drop the weapons pods."

He found the switch and activated it.

"Arm the Hellwinders."

Grant rotated the collar securing the switch lever, then flipped the lever to arm the missiles. Four lights indicated four weapons ready. He selected the first missile and set it for its heat-seeker guidance system.

"Everybody clear?"

"Panther two is prepared."

"Panther three, yo."

"Panther four is ready," Smertevo told him.

"Remember we're going to try and do this primarily on infrared. Don't anybody go playing with the radar,

342

except as planned. Billy, you stay off active."

He got three assents in reply.

"Let's do a radio check," Grant said.

On Tac-1, they each contacted Rosie and received "loud and clear," replies. On Tac-2, they had intercraft communications on the standard radios. Tac-3 was to be used for intercraft communications on the low-power radios.

"Go to Tac-three now."

Vidorov, Smertevo, and Shepard each announced their arrival on the short-range band.

As they reached 300,000 feet, Grant said, "Okay, Billy, here's your stop. Read it back to me."

"I orbit five-zero miles south of Vandenberg, and I jump with both boots on the first son of a bitch that gets in the way of my Titan."

"And watch your back," Grant added.

"Ta ta, chappies." Shepard peeled off, dousing his running lights, and disappearing against the black sky.

Grant continued climbing, but turned onto a heading of ninety degrees. Five minutes later, almost two hundred miles east of Los Angeles, and at 325,000 feet, he pressed the mike button. "Panthers two and four, your bus stops here."

"Good luck, Dallas," Vidorov said.

"And to you and Anatoly."

The Soviets would orbit there, out of radar range of Shepard's coordinates, but ready to strike the moment they were alerted.

Grant continued climbing to the northeast for another fifty miles until he reached 360,000 feet, then turned into a tight circle. Every time he came around to the southwest heading the infrared lens at full zoom picked up the tiny hot dots of Vidorov and Smertevo. If he depressed the lens as far as it would go, and put his nose down a little, he picked up the trails of commercial and private aircraft in the coastal air corridors. A few staionary heat sources might be identified as power plants. The freeways were ribbons of orange.

His mouth was dry, and the oxygen flow through the mask tasted like rubber. The cockpit was warm, and Grant turned the heat down a few degrees. He did not want to be comfortable. A slight chill kept him more alert.

Settling in to wait, Grant keyed in the frequency for the Vandenberg launch controller on one of his auxiliary channels.

T-minus twelve and counting.

Lane Billings was nervous. With the success of yesterday's French launch, he was half afraid that the aggressors had been frightened off by the loss of one of their own over Tyuratam. The one thing he did not want was to never know who they were. And with the way things were moving in Congress, this might be their last shot.

He sipped from his heavy coffee mug and paced the operations room.

The communications officer waved at him from his console, and Billings crossed the room toward him. "What have you got, Captain?"

"The CommNet is set up, General."

"Good. Run it down for me."

"The Command Net includes us, Admiral Zeiman's communications center in the Pentagon, General

344

Messerman's communications center in Colorado Springs, and General Antonovko's site at Tyuratam. It's all scrambled."

Billings had sent a colonel and two armed airmen to Tyuratam with a matching scrambler on loan since Antonovko insisted on being included in the communications, but refused to fly to California.

"All right. And none of them can talk to Grant?"

"No sir. They will be able to hear Panther Flight on their Tac-one and Tac-two frequencies when we kick in the relay, but they can't talk to them. We can also relay the Vandenberg controller."

Billings did not want Grant or Vidorov receiving a half-dozen conflicting orders from do-gooders in Washington or the Soviet Union. He knew who was in command. That was the man who would get his ass reamed if anything went wrong. Billings, Lane, BG, USAF, 0-998164.

"Tac-one and Tac-two are also scrambled," the captain added.

"Thank you, Captain Mavis."

Billings stepped over several temporary cables snaking over the floor and crossed the room to where Nemorosky leaned over one of the two radar consoles. Other than those for the instrument landing system, Rosie did not have radar. These consoles were connected by datalink to an E-3 Sentry Airborne Warning and Control aircraft that Billings had commandeered for the morning. There was nothing showing on either of the radar screens.

"Tiger Eye in place?" Billings asked.

Nemorosky straightened up. "Yes, Lane. It's at forty thousand feet, some eighty miles off the coast. They

345

have their radars scanning upward, but they see nothing."

"We did too well with our job, Pyotr. We can't even see our own craft."

"Be happy that we did, Lane."

Billings refilled his mug, then went to the table in the middle of the room and sat down. An Air Force colonel named Danubal, on loan from Edwards, sat on the opposite side of the table, a pedestal microphone in front of him. He had his own communications network connecting him with Army, Navy, and Air Force search and rescue units at locations stretching from Nellis Air Base in Nevada to Davis-Monthan in Tucson to Travis in Northern California.

"How we doing, Ned?"

"Fine, General. I've got over two hundred and twenty Chinooks, Sea Stallions, Seasprites, and Hueys on tap. If we see anything go down, I'll have a chopper on-site within ten minutes."

"Good. It's a hell of a big area to cover," Billings said. "Captain Mavis, let's put it on the speakers."

After the communications officer activated the overhead speakers, Billings pulled one of the microphones—labeled "COMD NET" with a black marker on masking tape—close and depressed the talk-bar. "This is General Billings. I have General Nemorosky with me. Who else do we have on the net?"

"Admiral Zeiman here."

"Colonel Conrad Weitz sitting in for General Messerman, sir."

"This is General Karl Antonovko."

"Good morning, gentlemen, and good evening, General Antonovko. At the moment, Vandenberg's

346

showing a go for the launch. We're eight minutes away. In a moment, I will put Vandenberg on the net for you. We have radar coverage in place, but I don't know that it's going to show us a great deal. We will be able to hear Panther Flight, but I don't expect them to say very much. I am in contact with Colonel Grant, and if something develops this morning, and you have a suggestion, please let me know."

Billings reached out and brought another microphone close to hand. It was labeled "Tac-1." He continued his briefing, outlining the position that Grant and his pilots had taken. "Any questions, gentlemen?"

"Zeiman. You put Panther three up as bait, Lane?"

"That's right, Bart."

"Voluntary?"

"Absolutely. The man knows the risks."

There were no more questions, and Billings pointed at the speakers in the ceiling. "Let's listen in on Vandenberg, Captain Mavis."

The controller's voice was a monotone. ". . . minus four and counting."

"Jasmine."

The codeword came in Meoshi Yakamata's intersuborbital frequency, and he and his wingman immediately went into a wide circle. The first element of the flight was in place, begining their orbit. They would be 160 kilometers west of the American Coast, waiting for the right moment.

It was soon to come. Yakamata had been listening to the Vandenberg launch controller for the last half

347

hour. Everything was on schedule, and his calculations had been accurate. Yakamata took pride in being accurate.

He was above the Pacific Ocean, which was very blue. Off to his left was the American mainland, perhaps fifty miles away. The Sierra Nevada range was snowcapped, and there was a lot of brownish haze along the shoreline toward the south. Most of the landmarks were blurred by particulates suspended in the lower atmosphere.

"We have ignition!"

Yakamata took the risk of going active with his radar for three sweeps of the antenna. Except for his wingman, there was nothing to be seen. He was out of range of both the first and third elements of his flight. He saw no opposing forces near his altitude. Below were commercial and perhaps military flights.

He shut it down and waited.

"One zero zero thousand."

Red Dagger Two would be preparing to strike. When the rocket achieved 180,000 feet, he would dive on it, go active with his radar to locate the missile precisely, and then line up so the Samurai's heat-seeker could lock onto its target. Red Dagger Three would cover for him and provide a secondary pass at the Titan if it was necessary.

As soon as Matsushima made his move, he would issue the code word, and the second element—Yakamata's—as well as the third element would move forward into their new positions.

"One five zero thousand."

Yakamata had armed his missiles earlier, but he double-checked their readiness on the armaments

348

panel. He scanned all of the instruments. Altitude eighty kilometers—264, 000 feet. Velocity Mach 4.3. Temperatures and pressures all within acceptable ranges.

"One seven seven thousand," intoned the launch controller.

"Orchid," Matsushima's voice yelled.

He was early, too eager.

Yakamata increased power while still in his turn, then pulled out of it on a heading of 150 degrees. He blinked his running lights once and looked out the right side of the canopy.

His wingman, Red Dagger Four, flashed his exterior lights in return. He was about a kilometer away, and he began to close as soon as he had located his leader.

Yakamata relished the surprise he was bringing to the American continent.

Billy Shepard could almost feel the adrenaline pumping through his system. His eyesight was sharper than ever. The stars, the readouts on the panel, everything was crystal clear and larger than life.

He should have been tense, but he felt as relaxed as he had ever been.

He eased out of his turn and headed west, directly toward the three heat signals showing on his screen. The closest was the Titan, beginning to move toward him as it fell into its course to the southeast. The other two had shown up about two minutes before, circling to his west. They were almost ninety miles away, tiny dots at the extreme limits of his FLIR. He would not have been so sure of them if they had not been over the ocean and so clearly distinct from the blurred heat sources along the coast. He estimated that they were about 70,000 feet below him, and he had been steadily losing altitude since first spotting them.

From their movements, Shepard was certain they were unaware of his presence. If they had infrared available, they were not using it.

They came out of their circle pattern, closing quickly on the coast and the Titan, one blip almost ten miles behind the first.

Slamming his throttles to their forward stops, Shepard pressed the Tac-2 button. "I've got two bogies at two-two-five thousand, closing the Titan at Mach five plus. I'm engaging the fuckers."

The readout read Mach 5.2.

The blips on the screen enlarged rapidly as he closed the distance. Fifty miles away.

The Titan kept climbing, but it was now taking a more direct southeasterly course and would pass under him.

The J-band radar threat warning sounded. One or both of the hostiles had gone active, but the only thing they would see was the Titan.

The images on the screen, enhanced by the computer, took on definite delta shapes.

Shepard calculated quickly. Because of the differences in altitude, the hostiles were going to be in position on the rocket before he achieved interception.

He switched in radar to let the assholes see him. The second, trailing bogey diverted from the Titan almost immediately and homed on Shepard.

He studied the first one, wishing it away from the Titan.

At thirty miles, he cut back to FLIR, and the infrared images were quite clearly sub-orbitals.

"Panther one, they look like us. Same size, same shape."

Shepard punched the targeting key and a set of crosshairs appeared on the screen. He used his arrow keys to center the crosshairs on the leading hostile, then locked it in. Even if he took evasive action, the computer would keep the FLIR locked on the target. When he was close enough, the computer would hand off the target to the Hellwinder's guidance system.

He went back to radar once again.

The threat warning increased its pitch.

The lead target lost his confidence and broke off his run for the Titan.

Shepard was elated.

Twenty-five miles. He triggered the commit button with his forefinger.

The threat warning alarm suddenly escalated.

He took one last look at the radar screen set at the 220-mile range, saw two more blips approaching from the west, then killed the radar, and went back to FLIR. The threat warning tone died away as the hostile craft lost his radiation signal.

"Panthers, I've got two more bogies at one-nine-zero miles and closing. I'm engaging Hostile one."

Twenty-two miles. In his headset, Shepard heard the Hellwinder signal a lock-on. A second later, the computer released the missile.

He immediately pulled the nose up, hunting for the second aggressor on his infrared screen.

The ECM indicator reported that the hostiles had shut down their radar.

It did not matter. He still found the second asshole on IR.

It was above him. Where he might get a visual of XSO-3 against the sea.

Goddamn. Just a pussy hair too damned late.

Yakamata turned on his radar in time to see the sweep light up four blips. The rocket was moving to the southeast. One blip instantly disappeared, its radar shut down. Another blip also went black, then reformed into a thousand tiny dots. The last blip, probably Red Dagger Three moving eastward, then disappeared from the screen.

Only the Titan IV continued on its way, unmolested, and Yakamata cursed into his face mask.

A minute later, Red Dagger Three went to active radar again. He was circling back, looking for the enemy craft.

Yakamata was ninety miles from the coordinates when his Electronic Counter-Measures unit suddenly placed two new active radars on the screen. They were diving on Red Dagger Three.

He switched the screen from radar to visual, but of course, could see nothing but blackness.

Touching the radio button, Yakamata said, "They are there, Red Dagger Four. Stay with me."

It was difficult to keep the glee out of his voice.

Technical Sergeant Benny Valdez manned the starboard radar console aboard the E-3 Sentry. He had been staring at nothing for thirty-five minutes, then the

Titan for the last several minutes. When the intermittent radars starting lighting the scope, it came as a
surprise.

He shot upright in his chair, his eyes glued to the
screen, and tried to figure out who in the hell was who.
Then the blips winked out, except for a pattern that
looked like a Christmas tree.

He checked the readouts and spoke into his headset,
"Charlie Jack, this is Tiger Eye."

"Charlie Jack, go Tiger."

"Tiger. We've got a disaster coming down. I read it as
debris at about two-zero-zero thousand, longitude
one-one-eight degrees four minutes, latitude three-two
degrees, one-eight minutes. It's going to spread all over
hell and maybe La Jolla, too, Charlie Jack."

Billings remained silent as he watched Ned Danubal
run his finger down his listing of code names. He found
the one he wanted, and Billings read it upside-down as
the San Diego Naval Base.

"Manta Ray, this is Charlie Jack."

"I got you, Charlie Jack."

Danubal read off the coordinates. "Take a look-see,
will you?"

"Charlie Jack, Manta Ray. I copied Tiger Eye, and
we're scrambling now, and on the way."

Antonovko's voice came over the command net.
"Do we know who it is, General Billings?"

Billings depressed his talk-bar. "No, General. It's
coming down off the coast, just west of San Diego."

*   *   *

353

Major Billy Shepard came out of his turn slowly, looking for the heat signature of the hostile.

The sub-orbital was not responding well. He figured the rudder thrusters were responding at about twenty percent of normal. Not good. He wished he could see backward, see what was left of his rudders.

Almost as soon as his first target had erupted in a cherry-red and orange, oxygen-fed explosion, the other enemy sub-orbiter had launched two missiles at him. Shepard had been almost hypnotized by the two deadly heat trails on the screen, coming directly at him.

He had killed the engines, jinked left, lost one of them, then rolled and snapped the nose down. The second missile almost missed him.

Almost.

He had felt the impact shudder the air frame, and he had waited almost impatiently for the explosion that would incinerate him.

When it did not come, he was nearly as disappointed as he was relieved.

The J-band alert squawked.

He kept the nose down, losing altitude, and unable to sight the infrared camera on his antagonist. The sub-orbital, with the rockets shut down, was very quiet.

Vidorov and Smertevo had gone to active radar to try and draw Hostile two away from Shepard.

He could see the one who had fired the two missiles at Shepard moving in a twenty-mile-wide circle. To the west, two more hostiles had displayed on the screen for a moment. He could no longer see them, but the computer was calculating a possible track, based on the last known data for heading and velocity.

On Tac-3, Vidorov said, "Anatoly, you will take the priority one target."

The computer automatically assigned priorities to targets.

"I will, Colonel."

"Go off radar."

"Done," Smertevo acknowledged.

Vidorov returned to his own FLIR. Hostile two was clearly visible, and Hostiles three and four were just beginning to flicker on the screen.

Grant's voice came up on Tac-2. "State your location and status, Billy."

Shepard's response on the radio was lower in volume. "Going through one-eight-zero, Dallas. I'm dead-stick, and I've got her back to Mach 3.2."

"Are you damaged?"

"Fucker got lucky. I think I've lost chunks from both my rudders, but I don't know how much. Thrusters are slowly going off-line."

"Can you make it back to Rosie?"

"Negative. I don't think I'm going to have much control once I get into the atmosphere."

"See if you can start your engines, Billy. Then try to hold at one-zero-zero thousand, until one of us can get a look at you."

"Shit, why not?"

Vidorov went to Tac-2 to reach Grant, who was out of range of the low-power frequency. "Panther One."

"Got me, Dmitri."

He reported, "We are at five-zero miles inbound on Hostile two. Hostiles three and four are approximately nine-zero miles and closing."

"Okay. I'm coming."

"Hold a moment, Dallas."

Vidorov went to active radar. Smertevo was five miles ahead of him, diving hard on his target, the enemy pilot completely unaware of him. The radar did not pick up the next two targets.

Then suddenly, there were two more of them, radiating radar energy.

Jumping back to the FLIR, Vidorov keyed Tac-2. "Dallas! There are two more, Hostiles five and six, my bearing two-four degrees, two-one-zero miles."

"Son of a bitch!"

The people back at Rosie could monitor them on Tac-2, and would know about Shepard. Vidorov hoped they were sending rescue helicopters.

Vidorov was happy that none of them was yapping in his ear, telling him what to do. In the *Rodina*, he would have had two or three commanders making conflicting suggestions, each of them expecting to be obeyed. General Billings left the decisions to the pilots.

He trailed after Anatoly Smertevo, above him. Infrequently through the windscreen, he caught a glimpse of the sub-orbiter when it passed over a cloud formation far below. He watched Hostiles three and four on the screen. They were sixty miles away, apparently flicking on radar at random moments, tracking on their comrade's active energy emissions. The J-band warning chattered from time to time, for only a few seconds in each instance.

Smertevo launched a Hellwinder.

In seconds Hostile two blew apart and the intense heat flooded the infrared camera. Vidorov's screen was blinded for several seconds.

Looking up through the canopy, he saw a dozen streaks of burning shrapnel arcing away from where the detonation had taken place.

Against the red-orange flares, he saw Smertevo in a tight right turn.

"I have succeeded, Colonel."

Vidorov looked again at his screen as the camera recovered its vision.

There was Smertevo.

There were the two Hostiles, thirty miles away from Vidorov—twenty miles from Anatoly.

Four hot streaks appeared on the screen—new images, moving at Mach 8 or better.

Vidorov tried to keep his voice calm. "Anatoly, shut down your engines."

Smertevo's response time was either too slow, or the position of his super-heated rocket nozzles too apparent to the heat-seeking sensors of the missiles.

XSO-4 erupted in a blinding ball, and once again, Vidorov's screen was overloaded.

"Charlie Jack, this is Tiger Eye. I've got another cloud of debris for you."

Danubal wrote down the coordinates, then started to grab his microphone.

"Charlie Jack, another cloud."

"Shit!" Billings said. He closed his eyes and pictured relative positions from the radio conversations he had been monitoring.

Smertevo?

Danubal hit the talk-bar hard enough to break it. "Manta Ray, you copy that?"

"Roger, Charlie Jack. I'm sending more choppers and I've launched two choppers from the cruiser *Bainbridge.*"

Billings said, "See if he can send some escorts to meet Shepard."

Danubal relayed the message to San Diego. "I'll have Panther three squawk an IFF for them when they get close enough."

"Roger that, Charlie Jack. I'm scrambling a couple Tomcats."

Grant saw the two fireballs. They were small, over two hundred miles away. He slammed his throttles forward.

"Dmitri?"

"Yes, Dallas. Hostile two and Anatoly."

"Shit!"

"I am engaging."

They were too far away for the FLIR. Grant switched the screen to radar. Hostile three was emitting. He could not see Vidorov or the fourth aggressor. He did not see the fifth or sixth sub-orbitals either.

Mach 5.2

Target at 170 miles.

The radar screen blanked out as Hostile three cut his radar. In the upper right corner of the screen, the computer displayed the estimated bearing of the last blip.

Grant counted seconds.

Target ninety miles. He went back to FLIR.

Three small images, but he had to watch for several

seconds before he could determine identities, based on the direction of travel.

Hostile three had missed on his pass at Vidorov. He was in a left turn now.

Vidorov headed straight at Hostile four.

Grant involuntarily strained at the throttles trying to shove them past their stops.

A Hellwinder blossomed away from Vidorov's sub-orbital.

Seventy miles. Grant lined up on the circling target.

Hostile four bloomed on the screen, still far enough away that it did not overwhelm the camera.

The J-band alert screamed as Hostile three went active. He pulled out of his turn, rolling back toward Vidorov. The threat receiver went dead. He probably had Vidorov visually, against the sea.

Fifty miles.

"Dmitri, he's on your ass."

XSO-6 disappeared from the screen as Vidorov killed the engines.

Two missiles launched from the aggressor.

Vidorov must have looped back toward the hostile to hide his nozzles from the missiles, for they dove toward the sea, then blinked out.

Forty miles. Grant checked the armaments panel. It showed heat-seeking guidance on Hellwinder one.

A new signal appeared on his screen, from the vicinity of where Vidorov's sub-orbital had disappeared. Though he was dead-stick and probably on his back, Vidorov had launched a Hellwinder.

Hostile three shut down and vanished from the screen.

Twenty miles.

The screen showed him two new targets. They were eighty-five miles to the west, coming hard.

Grant estimated he was ten miles from Vidorov. Off to his left he started to pick up the bare outline of a sub orbital. At close ranges, the FLIR would display the images of objects emanating less heat. In this case, i was the skin of a sub-orbital that had been warmed by its passage through the thin atmosphere.

That was one of them, but who?

Then to his right, another image appeared, looping back toward him.

"Dmitri?"

Vidorov flashed his anti-collision strobe.

He was on the left.

Grant rolled hard to the right.

The Hellwinder chattered a lock-on, then lost it.

The target came out of the loop, rolling upright. He could not be aware of Grant coming at him.

The target's engines ignited.

The Hellwinder chattered.

Lock-on.

Grant squeezed the commit button, and the computer released the missile immediately.

Hostile three shut down again, shoved his nose down, and dove for the ocean.

The Hellwinder streaked past his tail, then winked out as the propellent was exhausted.

"Dallas."

Grant went into a tight left turn and found Vidorov on the screen with his rockets in action again. The next pair of aggressors had closed to forty miles.

The threat warning sounded off. The hostiles were looking for them.

"I've got the right, Dmitri."

"And I the left."

Hostiles five and six never saw them. As soon as Grant and Vidorov launched their Hellwinders, they shut down radar and engines, but it was too late.

"Two more orange blossom specials," Grant said as the sky lit up ahead of him.

He dove away to the right, to avoid the debris.

"I am right behind you, Dallas."

Grant could not see him on the screen, but Vidorov's infrared would be tracking him.

"What the fuck's going on up there?" Billings's bass voice carried a tone of frustration.

Grant keyed Tac-1. "Five hostiles down. Panther one and Panther two are going looking for another one."

"I want his fucking ears," Billy Shepard said.

Twenty-Two

Meoshi Yakamata's hands shook uncontrollably.

He was still inverted, the sea filling three of his horizons. It took a moment to refocus his eyes on the instrument panel.

Indicated air speed Mach 2.6.

Altitude thirty-one kilometers.

Still over 100,000 feet, above the ceiling of American interceptors, but he was dangerously visible to sub-orbitals above him.

He eased the stick to the right and rolled out. It was a shaky maneuver.

What was on his right? San Francisco. The Golden Gate Bridge.

He took two deep breaths. The oxygen was dry and rubbery in his mouth.

So close. He had thought he was going to die.

He forced himself to concentrate. Ignition procedure. He had to get power on, get away from here. Afraid he would miss a simple toggle, he called up the checklist on the screen and carefully followed it.

The rocket engines ignited smoothly, and Yakamata pushed the throttles full forward and pulled the nose up. He needed altitude in order to perform the six glides necessary to reach Sun Land.

No. The fuel indicator read forty-six percent. Calculating roughly, he decided that seven glides would be required.

He had to get away from the coast. Yakamata turned into a gradual left bank.

Climbing. Forty kilometers.

He desperately wanted to use the radar, to see what was around him in the darkening skies, knowing they were there somewhere, but that would be suicide.

The Soviet-American machines had been better equipped. It had to be. Infrared probably. They had eyes when Red Dagger Flight was blind.

Five of the best were dead. Five sub-orbitals were lost to the sea.

Kyoto would be furious. Yet, the fault was that of his designers, not of Yakamata and his pilots. The engineers had not prepared the sub-orbitals well.

He kept scanning the darkness above and around him, but there was nothing. He would make it.

A black circle surrounded by white fire coming right into his video screen. He would never know how he had avoided it. Instinct. Reflexes.

At seventy kilometers of altitude, he felt much better. He was once again hidden in the heavens.

He studied his hand on the stick. It was solid and certain.

This was but a setback. There were two more sub-orbitals near completion. The Soviet-Americans had lost a machine, and they were down to three machines available. It was an even match, or would be, when Kyoto's shortsighted engineers gave him infrared cameras.

He had only to convince Kyoto and to devise a suitable explanation for the events off the Southern California coast. Surely, his five pilots and their craft had gone to the bottom of the sea, in minute pieces. There would be no evidence pointing in the direction of Sun Land. That would be Kyoto's worry, and Yakamata would have to persuade him.

By the time he reached eighty kilometers, Yakamata's confidence had returned.

His shoulders were squared away, his hands and feet steady on the controls.

There was just an annoying tic in his right cheek, a minute jumping of the flesh that rubbed against his face mask.

At 45,000 feet, Shepard met up with the Tomcats from San Diego.

He had squawked his IFF at the direction of somebody he had never talked to before as he began his descent.

The F-14's could barely keep up with him, of course, at his minimum rocket throttle settings. They took up a tight-radius circle inside his wider circle.

The new voice came in on Tac-1. "Panther three, this is Charlie Jack."

"Go, Charlie Jack."

"Delta one wants to talk to you on two-four-three-point-zero."

"Roger, Charlie Jack. Panther three's going over."

Shepard dialed in the emergency channel, 243.0, and said, "Somebody named Delta One looking for a date?"

"That's me, Panther. You want to slow that thing down some more?"

"I'd have to shut down my engines, Delta, and this old boy's not ready to do that just yet."

"You kidding? No, I suppose not. Okay, I'm going to intercept and look your ass over. Somebody told me you lost it."

The F-14 cut out of his circle in a tight bank and aimed ahead of Shepard, preparing to intercept at a ninety-degree angle.

"Don't get too close, Delta. I don't think I'm up to much buffeting."

"Wilco."

Shepard held the stick and rudder pedals as steady as he could. The muscles in his calves felt like they were bunching up. He expected a charley horse at any moment.

The Tomcat shot out in front of him, turning into his track, and climbing above him. As XSO-4 went under, the pilot examined it.

"That's an airplane?" Delta One asked him.

"Hell, no. You got an airplane. I got a fine piece of high tech. Tell me what's left of it."

"I'm assuming you started out with two stabilizers, Panther. The starboard is gone. On the port side, you've got the substructure and the skin on the inside. The movable surface is gone, too."

"Shit."

"Tell me how it feels."

"I don't have any directional thrusters left," Shepard

365

said. "The more dense the atmosphere gets, the more skittish the control is. My fucking leg muscles are so tight, I'm not going to walk for a week."

"You want to try for San Diego?"

"I can still turn on ailerons and elevators, but I'm not going to have any fine control near the ground. What do you think, Delta?"

"I think you're going to lose the rest of that stabilizer, and pretty damned soon at this speed. It's wobbling bad. You'd better bleed off speed and prepare to eject when we get to a decent altitude."

"I'm not ejecting."

"Why the hell not?"

"No ejection seat. No parachute."

"Both good points, Panther."

Shepard made his decision. "Okay, Delta. I'm going over to turbojet now and get sub-sonic. Call me a chopper with a guy who can swim, will you?"

"We got choppers all over the place. Where do you want to go in?"

"Let's try for Long Beach. I know a girl there."

As he descended through 30,000 feet, Shepard shut down his armaments panel, retracted the weapons pod, opened the generator and jet intake panels, and successfully started the turbojet. He killed the rockets, and the velocity indicator went down through the numbers rapidly.

The sub-orbital shook violently as he dropped through the sonic barrier. He thought he had lost it for a minute.

"The skin just peeled off that stab, Panther."

"Go ahead, Delta. Make me feel good."

The two Tomcats moved in and took up positions off

each of his wings.

He opened the emergency valves and shot compressed air through the hydrogen tanks. The liquid vaporized as it hit the atmosphere, and a 400-yard-long vapor trail appeared in the sky behind him.

"What the hell was that, Panther?"

"Hydrogen. Stand aside, my brothers. Here comes the oxygen."

Shepard dumped his oxygen tanks, getting another vapor trail.

The sub-orbital felt a little better to him when the weight of the fuel was gone, and Shepard felt less like he was riding a bomb.

At 20,000 feet and 500 miles per hour, XSO-4 skidded sideways. The rudder pedals did not do a damned thing for him.

He finally got it under control by banking into the skid, then leveling out. He came out of the skid facing the coast, about twenty miles away.

"Nice job, Panther."

Shepard did not answer. He watched his angle of attack, rate of climb, and turn-and-bank indicators. Quick glances at the velocity.

Quick glance out the canopy. There were helicopters and ships everywhere. Search patterns.

Back to the panel. Coming up on 10,000 feet. Speed holding at 500.

Back outside. The smog-drenched shoreline looked damned good to him. He wondered if he really was anywhere near Long Beach.

At 2,000 feet and 400 miles per hour, the sea looked like concrete. Far ahead, he could see helicopters converging on him.

"How far's the coast, Delta?"

"Eight miles. No sweat, Panther. You're not going to hit it."

Shepard pulled the throttle back and killed the jet engine. "The time is now, Delta. Thanks for the company."

"Deploy flaps, Panther."

"Would, if I had them."

"Hell, you guys ain't prepared for anything, are you?"

The F-14s pulled ahead, then turned away from him, as the sub-orbital slowed to 300 miles per hour.

With his left hand, he started ripping at tubing, unhooking himself from G-suit couplings, oxygen, and communications lines.

Shepard began to worry about getting the canopy open after he was in the water. There was no way to jettison it.

The left wing dipped, and he righted it with a light tug on the stick.

Speed 270. He should be down, but he wanted to keep it aloft as long as possible, stall it, and drop.

At 250, the right wing went down, and he had to dip the nose for air speed as he leveled it. He did not want to hit wrong, on a wing tip, and kick it into a ground loop. Was there such a thing as a water loop?

The water did not look any softer to him now than it did earlier.

There was a helicopter directly in front of him. Big call letters on the side. TV station. If he had had a cannon, he would have shot it down.

He dipped the nose just as the chopper climbed, and he shot underneath it.

Pull the nose back.

The tail end hit the top of a wave.

And the son of a bitch bounced twice, then acted just like the hydroplane it was. It skimmed the surface on the rocket engine nacelles, quickly losing speed.

The velocity indicator quit on him, but when he judged he was under fifty miles per hour, Shepard opened the canopy. A flood of air and salt water spray engulfed him.

And felt damned good.

He let go of everything. There was no more control. The sub-orbital began to slew sideways.

He popped the buckles on his harness.

The left wing tip caught a wave, and the right side bucked up, throwing him against the side of the cockpit. His helmet slammed into the windscreen frame. Shepard grabbed the frame with both hands.

The craft was moving too slowly to be thrown completely over. It banged down and came to a stop.

Shepard stood up, unbuckled his helmet, and dropped it inside the cockpit.

He looked around. The sea had only a slight chop to it and was comfortingly blue-green. Ahead on his left, the coastline was four or five miles away. Several white yachts and two Coast Guard cutters were bearing down on him, but were still several miles away.

The goddamned helicopters were everywhere. About seven of them were racing toward him.

The sub-orbital was sinking fast, the fuel tanks taking water through the open dump valves. The top surface of the wings were awash.

A blue JetRanger came in above him, its hoist line already lowered. It took three tries before he captured

369

the line. Shepard slipped his arms into the horse collar, and they lifted him right out of the cockpit.

Damn. He was not even going to get wet.

The rotor wash swirled his hair into his eyes as he was lifted to the cabin door. Arms reached out and dragged him inside. Some guy helped him out of the collar, and he sagged onto the seat. He realized he was pretty damned tired. His legs felt as weak as a baby's.

"What's your name, Major?"

Shepard looked up into startlingly blue eyes framed with a ton of yellow-gold hair. The dream licked her lips, and he knew there was a heaven.

"Billy Shepard."

"Do you have a story to tell me, Major Shepard?"

"Fuckin' A."

"Hold it," she said. "We've got to start over."

Shepard looked past her at the guy in the seat facing him. He had a video camera resting on his shoulder. The camera was labeled "Channel 4."

"Now, let's start at the beginning, and please, Major, watch the language."

Shepard grinned at her. "Okay. I was born in Canton, Ohio. . . ."

Grant and Vidorov had turned on their anti-collision and running lights, so they could see each other, and spread apart by about fifty miles. They were at 350,000 feet, searching with radar, infrared, and true video in sequence.

The hostiles had approached the rocket launch from the west, so they had started their search in that direction. When they were 1700 miles off the coast,

Billings called Grant.

"Panther One, this is Charlie Jack."

"Panther. Go Charlie Jack."

"What's your position?"

Grant told him.

"No contact?"

"Not yet. There will be," Grant promised. "What's the word on Billy?"

"Down safe, as far as we know."

Grant felt immensely relieved. "What do you mean, as far as you know?"

"He's been captured by the enemy."

"What! What enemy?"

"A goddamned TV crew. He'll spill his guts."

Grant held the mike open and laughed. "Not unless it's a female reporter."

"Blonde and blue-eyed. They're live on Channel Four right now."

"I wish I could see it," Grant said.

"No, you don't. I'm going to kill the son of a bitch when I get my hands on him. Give me a plan, Grant."

"We're going to keep looking for the bastard as long as we can stay aloft."

"Where?" Billings wanted to know.

"It's got to be west. Maybe they came out of China, Southeast Asia, the Philippines."

"Try this, Grant. A Navy Sea Knight was on the scene, looking for debris, when a damned fuselage hit the sea a quarter mile from them. They jumped on it and got a cable around it."

"The whole fuselage?" Vidorov asked.

"No. Aft section with part of a wing root. It's on board the *Bainbridge,* now."

"Don't hold out on us, General," Grant said.

"The jet engine was manufactured by Kawasaki."

"No lie?"

"No lie. It may not mean anything, Grant."

"Panther one out."

Grant keyed the computer and called up a chart of the northern Pacific. As he studied it, he called Vidorov on Tac-3. "Let's turn right and head north while we figure this thing out, Dmitri."

"Turning now. If they came from Japan, Dallas, they would take the Alaska route."

"My thought exactly. But they don't have the range for a round trip, if they're built anything like our own."

"Which they are, from what I saw on the FLIR," Vidorov said.

"But they can coast it, part of the way."

"Yes. That is possible."

Using the computer and the chart on the screen, Grant calculated a flight plan from Tokyo to Southern California, along with a return that followed the same route.

"Roughly, Dmitri, the route would leave them short of fuel by maybe fifteen or twenty minutes. They could easily make up that, and more, by gliding."

"It means something more than that, now, Dallas. It means that our escapee does not have fuel for evasive maneuvers. He must go straight to the nest."

"What about your own fuel status?" Grant asked.

It was the same as his own. They had about two hours of rocket engine time remaining.

"I have calculated an intercept course, Dallas."

"Tell me."

"I am assuming that the hostile uses a cruise speed

372

similar to our own, about Mach 4.2, and that he will lose speed each time he utilizes a glide mode. If we maintain Mach 4.5, to conserve some fuel, we should intercept his course. And I believe we need not worry about using radar."

"That means we're going one-way, Dmitri. We won't get home."

"Not today, perhaps."

Grant called Rosie. There was a momentary lapse in the transmissions, as the radio signals passed through the Defense Satellite Communications System. He gave Billings their flight plan.

"All right. Approved."

"You're not checking up the line, General?"

"Hell, no. This place is a madhouse. The media is everywhere, and we're under siege."

Meoshi Yakamata was in complete control by the time Anchorage passed on his right. He was in another long glide from ninety kilometers down to seventy kilometers, and the silence of the sub-orbital was almost complete. There was a minute hum generated by the electronics. Whenever he made a correction in his flight path with the directional thrusters, he could feel a slight vibration resulting from the hiss of moving gas.

He was an hour away from Sun Land, and though his fuel margin was slim, he would not again have to climb to higher altitudes. In three minutes, he would go back on power.

Four times now, he had activated the radar and found no pursuers. He was home-free.

"Red Dagger Flight, come in."

Yakamata was so accustomed to the quiet, that the voice of Maki Kyoto in his ears made him jump.

"This is Red Dagger One."

"So. It is you who has survived."

How did the man know? So soon?

He responded simply. "Yes."

"The international television is alive with your exploits, Red Dagger One."

"I do not understand," Yakamata said.

"You are not to return here," Kyoto ordered.

"What! But I must!"

"No."

"There is nowhere else to go!" the colonel insisted.

"There is the Sea of Okhotsk. You will use it."

"But . . . but I must be picked up."

"Perhaps there will be a fishing boat."

The radio remained silent, though he tried several times to re-establish contact.

He was to be abandoned, after all he had done for Nesei Aerospace. Thrown out, like a sinful child. Yakamata's lungs hurt as he considered that reward.

Kyoto expected him to cheerfully accept suicide, rather than lead anyone to Sun Land. Kyoto looked up to the heavens, where America's satellites were probably looking for him, though unsuccessfully.

Wait.

He had already missed his engine starting point. He was at fifty-five kilometers. Quickly, he went through the checklist and started the engines.

The speed picked up from Mach 3.3 to Mach 4.1 as he climbed back to seventy kilometers. He watched the fuel remaining percentage with a critical eye.

374

He would not give up so easily.

He could land at Hakodate Air Base. What would they, the Japanese Air Defense Forces, then say to Mr. Kyoto?

Yes.

He was a hero in the eyes of his Japanese homeland, a master pilot, a man who had faithfully served. He would put the sub-orbital down at Hakodate and let the chief executive officer of Nesei Aerospace Industries explain it to the world.

Yes.

He switched his screen from video to radar, to get a fix on his position.

And then, fifteen minutes from Hokkaido Island, his threat warning receiver yelped.

Grant locked the target position into the computer the minute it appeared on the screen. Two seconds later, the blip disappeared.

"Did you get him, Dmitri?"

"Yes. My bearing three-three-eight. Distance two-zero-five of your miles. I believe his heading is about two-one-five degrees. It has to be him, at that altitude."

"I've got the same readings. Let's punch it."

Grant advanced his throttles to the stops and put the nose down four degrees. The velocity quickly moved up to Mach 5.2. Vidorov's running lights stayed right beside him, slightly above him on the right.

"We have an angle on him, Dmitri. We probably can't catch him, so let's cut him off."

"He could turn away from us."

"Not if his fuel's getting short."

"True. Let us go to two-eight-zero degrees."

"You go that way, and I'll go two-seven-five. One o[f] us will pick him up."

"Done," Vidorov agreed.

Nine minutes later, Grant tried his FLIR and picke[d] up a target at 130,000 feet, almost 90,000 feet belo[w] him.

"Got him on FLIR, Dmitri. My bearing zero-zero-five, distance eight-two miles."

"Altering course."

"He's slowing way down," Grant reported. "Hell, [I] think he's on the turbojet."

The distance was forty-two miles.

"I've got him now, Dallas. He is sub-sonic."

"Where's he going?"

"Perhaps he was headed for Hakodate Air Base?" Vidorov suggested.

"And then decided he couldn't make it? Maybe. You know of any landing fields on the north end of the island?"

"No. I believe he is going to land wherever he can."

Grant pulled his throttles all of the way back. If he was not careful, he would overshoot his target.

"I am twelve miles behind you, Dallas, and slowing."

He checked the fuel readout. In a few minutes, he would have to start thinking about a critical shortage.

Altitude 90,000 feet. The sub-orbital was beginning to feel the bite of denser air.

He eased the stick over and banked slightly to the left, lining up on the hostile.

Twenty-six miles to target.

He looked up through the windscreen. Hokkaido Island was coming up quickly. He increased the angle of his dive and killed the rocket engines.

He passed through 60,000 feet.

"Did you flame out?" Vidorov asked.

"Shut it down. Got to lose speed. I'm going to turbojet."

"Not and also use your weapons," Dmitri Vidorov reminded him.

The weapons pod was in front of the intake.

"I'll dead stick it."

Grant dropped the pod, and that helped to slow him. He deployed the speed brakes.

His speed dropped to Mach 1.8 as the altimeter read 46,000.

"I have shut down engines also," the Soviet pilot informed him. "Start coming out of your dive, Dallas. The wings will not take the loading if you pull too many G's."

He was right. Grant pulled the nose up a trifle. At ten thousand feet and Mach 1.1, his target was nine miles ahead of him. The hot spot of the turbojet exhaust vanished from the screen. The other pilot had shut down his jet, attempting to extinguish a target for a heat-seeking missile.

Grant armed Hellwinders three and four, switching the guidance system to laser designator.

He looked up and saw the hostile as it crossed the coastline.

"I've got him visual, Dmitri."

The computer told him that distance to target was 6.2 miles.

"Panther one, what the hell you doing?" Billings asked him on Tac-1.

"Hot pursuit, General. Penetrating foreign air space.

You've got two seconds to notify the Japanese."

The target had slowed to 400 miles per hour, almost wallowing, and lining up on . . . a runway dead ahead.

Grant keyed the laser designator. Using the arrow keys he jiggled around until he saw the red dot appear on the left wing of the hostile craft. He tapped it to the right, centering it on the fuselage, and locked it into the computer.

The earphones hummed as the missiles accepted the computer's instructions.

He squeezed the commit button.

The computer launched both Hellwinders instantly.

They streaked out ahead of him, their vapor trails white against the black asphalt of the runway.

Grant banked left, retracted the weapons pod, and pulled in his speed brakes.

Buildings. Hangars. Fenced compound.

As he rolled upright, passing over the hangars, the hostile sub-orbital blew up right beside him. It had nearly touched down when it was engulfed in a ball of red and yellow flame. Streams of white-hot fire and shrapnel erupted from the ball, and pieces of titanium, steel, and carbon skin hit the runway, skidding and bouncing.

"Dmitri, put your missiles in the last three hangars!"

"I have but two missiles."

"They'll penetrate all three. Maybe they'll hit something."

Grant pulled his nose up, began a 270-degree turn to the left, and started into his turbojet ignition procedure. He paused to look aback as Vidorov shot over the airfield.

A miniature mushroom cloud still hung over the

runway. A few hundred people were running through parking lots.

Vidorov was a hundred feet off the ground when he launched his Hellwinders.

The first ripped through the roof of the third hangar from the end, and the second slashed through the second hangar. It must have gone through the walls because it was the first hangar that exploded.

Not a big explosion, but enough to start a good fire.

Two minutes later, Vidorov was alongside him, and they were both on turbojets, making 650 miles per hour, and climbing to 10,000 feet.

Grant pressed the Tac-1 button. "Charlie Jack, Panther one."

"Go ahead, Panther one."

"Mission complete. Departing foreign air space."

"Good job, Panther Flight. We'll let the State Department take it from here."

After Billings signed off, Vidorov came on, "I hate to mention this, Dallas."

"Oh, go ahead."

"I have but twelve minutes of JP-4 left. Perhaps that much."

"I thought about landing at Hakodate, but I suspect they'd want to detain us for a week or two. What's your oxy and hydrogen status?"

"I estimate fifteen minutes."

"You like Guam when we made our visit?"

"No."

"We might make it."

"Panther one, this is Panther three."

"Billy? Where in the hell are you?"

"A bunch of Shore Patrol guys brought me down to

San Diego. I think I'm under arrest, but nobody's saying."

"The brig might be better than facing Billings, for awhile," Grant said.

"Yeah, but there's something I wanted to tell you, Dallas. Don't worry about a damned thing. Those babies float for a full ninety seconds."

Twenty-Three

In the pilots' ready room at Anderson Air Force Base, which Grant and his crews had taken over for two days, he and Vidorov drank a last cup of coffee and waited with the pilots of the C-141.

Outside, under the early heat of Guam's morning sun, Gloomy and Drandorov directed their men with typical American obscenity and, Grant supposed, with similar Russian idiom. The hydrogen tankers had pulled away and were already inching up the ramp back into the C-141. The oxygen tankers were backed up near XSO-5 and XSO-6.

Heat waves shimmered on the asphalt.

Grant gave up the window and went back to sit beside Vidorov on the couch. Two well-read newspapers were spread out on the coffee table, and Grant had been through most of the articles twice. He and his partner had been kept away from the media, but Billings and Nemorosky had done a credible and understated job of explaining the attack on an American space vehicle and the gallant efforts to repel it. They could do no less after Billy Shepard had provided Channel 4 with all of the juicy details. And it was Billy who had fully, publicly, and emotionally eulogized Major Anatoly Smertevo of the Red Air Force.

The President had lamented the necessity of activating a combat unit of the Aerospace Command, but had also firmly stated his resolve to take similar action whenever it was required. Further, he applauded the cooperative efforts of the Soviet-American squadron. The comments from an ebullient Soviet President and a seemingly reluctant General Grigori Brezhenki also supported the combat mission.

Spokesmen from the State Department, while pressuring the Japanese government for intensive investigation, appeared relieved that the adversary was an industry, rather than a nation.

And in Congress, honed verbal arrows were flying in all directions, most of them missing their targets. The incensed senators and congressmen called for complete embargoes of Japanese goods, for diplomatic ostracism, for the assembly of an international tribunal. None of which would happen, Grant was certain. Polly Enburton and a number of her colleagues were leading a wave of support for the XSO Program. Donald Sunwallow stood in opposition.

The Japanese Air Defense Forces had taken over the property of some outfit called Nesei Aerospace Industries. The company's chief executive officer and nine members of the board were under house arrest, pending the outcome of the government's investigation. Japanese newspapers and television were decrying yet another scandal.

Vidorov dropped the paper he had been reading on the table. "It is amazing, Dallas."

"What is?"

"How your country ever accomplishes anything."

"Tell you the truth, Dmitri, it frustrates me from time to time, but also, I wouldn't have it any other way. There's nothing like a little dissension to keep the juices flowing and the mind working."

"I suppose."

Grant phrased his questions carefully. "Don't you like living with compromise? Instead of ultimatum?"

The Soviet pilot mulled it over. "It is enticing, perhaps. But I am an officer in the Soviet Air Force. I do what must be done."

"Maybe it will change?"

"Perhaps. In time. Do you not also follow your orders?"

Grant laughed. "From time to time. But I'm working on a new resolution, Dmitri."

"What is that?"

"To stay far away from good-looking congressional aides."

Sergeant Gloom stuck his head in the door. "Five minutes, Colonel."

"Hey, Gloomy, did you bring some extra seats along?"

"Yeah, Colonel, I did."

"You want to ride with me?"

"Damned right!"

"Put a seat in XSO-6 for Drandorov, too."

Gloom shut the door and trotted back toward the sub-orbitals as Grant and Vidorov stood and finished zippering their pressure suits. Grant had not brought his emergency AWOL bag along for the first time, and his flight suit was getting ripe.

They walked out to the flight line and performed their ground inspections. Two small vapor clouds on the left wing of XSO-5 suggested small leaks in tanks or fittings. Nothing to worry about, Grant thought.

Gloomy and Drandorov fought their respective ways into pressure suits, then climbed into the aft cockpits.

Vidorov said to him, "Two hours and we'll be home, Dallas."

"Ah, ah, Colonel. You're beginning to think of Rosie as home."

"But only for the next two or three years, your God and your Congress willing."

Grant laughed.

Vidorov scampered up the ladder and settled into XSO-6, and Grant climbed his own ladder.

Grant was looking forward to a long, long weekend. He swung one leg over the coaming, then hesitated.

"Damn it!"

He worked his leg back out of the cockpit, and started down the ladder.

"What's the matter, Dallas?" Vidorov called.

"I've got to make a phone call."